THE NORTH LIGHT

Also by Hideo Yokoyama

Six Four
Seventeen
Prefecture D

HIDEO YOKOYAMA

THE NORTH LIGHT

Translated from the Japanese by Louise Heal Kawai

riverrun

First published in the Japanese language as *North Light*
by SHINCHOSHA Publishing Co., Ltd in Tokyo in 2019

First published in Great Britain in 2023 by

riverrun

An imprint of
Quercus Editions Ltd
Carmelite House
50 Victoria Embankment
London EC4Y 0DZ

An Hachette UK company

A CIP catalogue record for this book is available
from the British Library

Hardback ISBN 978 1 52941 113 3
Trade Paperback ISBN 978 1 52941 114 0
Ebook ISBN 978 1 52941 115 7

10 9 8 7 6 5 4 3 2 1

Typeset by CC Book Production
Printed and bound in Great Britain by Clays Ltd, Elcograf S.p.A.

Papers used by riverrun are from well-managed forests and other responsible sources.

CHARACTERS IN THE NORTH LIGHT

Minoru Aose	architect
Yukari Aose/Murakami	Aose's ex-wife, interior designer
Hinako	Aose and Yukari's daughter
Akihiko Okajima	Aose's boss, President of Okajima Design Company
Yaeko Okajima	Okajima's wife
Isso	Okajima's son
Yutaka Ishimaki	all-round architect and barrier free specialist at Okajima Design Company
Ringo Takeuchi	young architect at Okajima Design Company, low-cost/eco design specialist
Mayumi Tsumura	accountant at Okajima Design Company
Yuma	Mayumi's son
Takao Nishikawa	freelance renderer / perspective draughtsman
Touta Yoshino	Aose's client, owner of the Y Residence

Karie Yoshino	Touta's wife, joint owner of the Y Residence
Haruko Fujimiya	Japanese painter (deceased), the subject of the "Memoire" memorial competition
Bruno Taut	German Architect (deceased)
Erica Wittich	Taut's common-law wife (deceased)
Takumi Nose	President of Nose Architects, ex-colleague of Aose's and rival for Yukari's affections
Hatoyama	architect at Nose Architects, expert in museum design
Takahiro Ikezono	newspaper reporter from J— Newspaper in Takasaki, Gunma
Kasahara	reporter from A— Newspaper in Atami
Mitsuru Shigeta	reporter from Toyo Shimbun newspaper
Kusao Yamashita	elderly man, used to work at the National Research Institute of Industrial Arts in Sendai
Ozawa	Yamashita's son
Koji Yanagiya	the artist Haruko Fujimiya's nephew
Various politicians, Yakuza type, etc	

THE NORTH LIGHT

I

In Osaka it had been raining since early morning.

Minoru Aose pulled on his clothes as quickly and quietly as he could. By the sound of it, his clients were up and about already. The previous night he had successfully reached an agreement with this young couple for him to build their new home. Afterwards they'd celebrated with a lavish dinner and copious amounts of high-end saké. It had been too late for him to make the train back to Tokyo, so he'd spent the night on a futon on the living room floor of their rental apartment. Now he needed to hurry — barely time to splash water on his face. He politely refused the offer of breakfast and made a beeline for the front door, bowing deeply all the way. He retrieved his folding umbrella from his briefcase and stepped out into the rain.

He really was pressed for time. If he hurried, he could walk to Yodogawa station in about ten minutes. And from there he could make his way to the JR line at Umeda and on to Shin-Osaka to catch the shinkansen bullet train home. If he managed to catch the 9.30 he'd arrive at Tokyo station around midday, and though slightly late, he could still make his meeting with Hinako.

It was Sunday, and the shinkansen platform was crammed with families and young couples. Judging by the number of groups in formal dress, it must have been an auspicious day for a wedding. About half the people wore heavy winter coats, and the rest were in light spring jackets, giving a rather mixed impression of the season. The sky was adding to the confusion. The rain was neither cold winter downpour nor spring shower but that disheartening drizzle typical of early March.

Aose had just been hired to design a forty-million-yen home, yet he felt no sense of exhilaration. The clients' request had been straightforward:

'Aose-san, we'd like the same one you built in Shinano Oiwake.'

But it would be impossible to build the exact same house – for a start the location was not at all similar, and their family wasn't the same size. On top of which, he preferred not to repeat himself; he enjoyed being creative and original. And then there were times that Aose wasn't even sure that he liked that particular house. Some mornings he awoke believing he'd created something extraordinary, but by nightfall he wished he'd had nothing to do with it at all.

Aose looked up to see the sleek aerodynamic form of the series 700 shinkansen glide into the station. Once on board, he stood in the area between cars and got out his mobile phone. Hoping that Hinako wouldn't have left yet, he dialled her number. It rang several times before she picked up.

'I'll be a bit late,' he told her.

''kay.'

She hung up.

He sighed and put the phone back in his breast pocket. These monthly parental visitation meetings with his daughter were always difficult, with him struggling to get through a range of topics with no warm-up time. It was like trying to cook food on full heat, when what it really needed was a slow simmer.

His phone rang. He pulled it out and saw the call was from his office in Tokorozawa, Saitama prefecture. He answered, and his ear was immediately assaulted by the enthusiastic tones of his boss, Akihiko Okajima.

'Hey there. Got a minute?'

Aose leaned back against the door.

2

'Sure. What are you doing in on a Sunday?'

'You're one to talk. You still in Osaka?'

'On my way back. What's up?'

'How did it go? Does it look promising?'

'Already got the go-ahead.'

'You've got to be kidding. They haven't even seen a rough draught yet.'

'They agreed on the spot. We've already drunk a toast to it.'

'Seriously? But anyway, it's good news. Well done.'

Every time he received praise from his boss, Aose would secretly cringe. They were both forty-five years old, both Class-1 registered architects. They'd been classmates in the same department of architecture. But one of them had graduated; the other had dropped out and taken a different route. Now it was universally accepted that one was the boss and the other his employee.

'What's the plan?'

'They've got the land already. Their budget is forty million. Came into some money, apparently.'

'Generous parents, perhaps? So, what are they asking for? Are they going to be picky?'

People generally didn't approach a small firm like theirs that specialized in original and unique houses if they weren't already somewhat picky; it was when that pickiness crossed a certain line that it could turn into a headache for the firm.

'No, they're not picky. They're only asking for one thing.'

'What's that?'

'To cut a long story short, they want a copy of Shinan Oiwake.'

'The Y Residence from the top 200?'

'Yeah.'

Aose tried to sound casual about it.

At the beginning of the year a major publisher had put out a full-colour coffee-table book titled *Top 200 Homes of the Heisei Era*. The book featured some of the best designs of the past fourteen years, and somewhere near the end was the house in Shinano-Oiwake, identified only by the initial 'Y'.

'I see. Pretty influential, that book.'

Okajima's tone was an awkward mix of banter and envy.

'Just last week that couple from Urawa said they'd seen *Top 200 Homes* too,' he added. 'Which reminds me, the wife sent me an email. Seems she went up to Shinano to take a look at the house.'

The couple had asked where the house was, and Okajima had drawn them a simple map, but Aose was surprised to hear that they'd actually gone up there.

'She says it looked like there was no one living there.'

'No one living . . .?'

'But there is, right?'

Okajima sounded so serious that Aose couldn't help laughing.

'Of course there's someone. Well, unless they've put it up for sale.'

Okajima laughed too.

'They were probably just out. Anyway, the Urawa woman said she liked it even more now she's seen the real thing. Looks like we've got ourselves another client.'

'Well, let's not get ahead of ourselves. At least not before she's seen the inside.'

'Anyway, things are looking up. The influence of the famous Y Residence has spread to Urawa and Osaka.'

The influence of the famous Y Residence . . . It felt as if a label had been attached to the awkward, nagging feeling he'd had in his chest since this morning.

'Look, Okajima, are you going to be okay with this? The travel expenses are going to be ridiculous if I'm supervising the whole thing properly. It'll eat into the profits.'

'Don't worry. Everyone will be talking about it. It'll be good for the company. And I'll tell you what – I'm not going to finish in the minor leagues.'

As soon as Aose heard this favourite expression of Okajima's he made to hang up the phone, but Okajima stopped him.

'I need a good renderer as soon as possible. Do you happen to know any?'

That was the real purpose of Okajima's call. Renderers, or perspective draughtsmen, were indispensable to a project. The quality of their drawings made all the difference when making a presentation to a potential client.

'Isn't Kato-san available?'

'Unfortunately, he won't take on anything outside of Tokyo.'

'How about Otsuka from Omiya?'

'No, not him. I'll never win with his drawings.'

Win?

'Is this for a competition?'

'There'll be one before long. You know, a police box or a public toilet or some piddling little project like that. So I need to get myself a good perspective draughtsman.'

The way he said the phrase 'There'll be one before long' caught Aose's attention. From time to time, Okajima would casually mention 'prefectural people' or 'conservative representatives'. Aose suspected that his boss may have been given a confidential heads-up about something in the works. From his cheerful tone and the fact that he was in the office on a Sunday, he was clearly feeling positive about something.

'I might be able to get Nishikawa-san,' said Aose.

'Huh? Who's that?'

'Takao Nishikawa. He used to draw for me when I was at the Akasaka office.'

'Yes, yes, I know him! That guy's drawings are amazing. Feels like you're seeing stuff you could never imagine for yourself. Could you give me his number? I'll ask him directly.'

'He switched firms. When I get home, I'll look for the postcard he sent.'

'Do you have his mobile number?'

'Sorry, no. Too long ago. Back before we had mobiles.'

He must have sounded too laid back, because Okajima told

him to hurry and get the number to him by the end of the day. By the time he hung up, Okajima had taken on the tone of a typical employer. This was actually a bit of a relief to Aose. His boss was probably trying to snap up some dull community building project or other commissioned by the prefecture or the city, but it was always good to hear his boss in ambitious mode.

There was a loud pop and the windows began to rattle. The Osaka-bound train was passing.

Aose started back towards his seat, but there was still something nagging at him. *No one living there . . .?* He turned around and went back to the standing area, scrolling through the list of contacts in his phone until he found Yoshino, Touta. He felt a slight pain behind his eye. Four months had passed since he handed over the keys to the Y Residence. He scrolled on further to the home number of the house, and his tired eyes became blurry for a moment. His thumb accidentally pressed the call button and as it connected he realized his mistake and tried to hang up. But then he decided to let it ring after all. He did have a reason to call. He could ask if they'd mind showing the couple from Urawa around the house.

The answer machine picked up. Which meant, of course, that the house's landline was connected and the family was just out. He couldn't help feeling relieved. He thought about the day he had handed over the keys, ending his relationship with the Yoshino family. The interview and photos for the *Top 200 Homes* book had already been finished, so there was no need to visit again for that. Aose's company had a rule that after the handover was complete, unless the client approached them with a question, the architects were to refrain from making any contact. There were plenty of clients who found it a nuisance to have the architect drop round after they'd moved in, either because it communicated a sense of dissatisfaction or disappointment with their own work, or a feeling of ownership towards the property. Some clients preferred to keep in close contact with the construction company that had actually built the house; others chose to leave the upkeep of the property or any renovation projects to a cheaper contractor. It was up to the client whether they wanted to befriend the architect and enter into a longer-lasting relationship.

Yoshino had not contacted Aose. He'd never called or sent a postcard to let Aose know his feelings about living in the house, nor for that matter had he expressed any dissatisfaction.

And yet . . . at the beginning it had been very different. When he'd come to commission the design, in some ways Yoshino had felt like more than a friend.

'We'll leave everything up to you, Aose-san. Please build a home you would want to live in.'

And in that moment his brain had lit up.

It wasn't about being featured in some design book that made the house special. It was the feeling that Aose had experienced when he accepted the job. And now it was as if the job had never happened. Yoshino's long silence since the completion of the project was a cloud in Aose's mind. It had drained him of so much of his passion, turned him bitter.

A sudden sound made him glance up. Raindrops were striking the outer window of the train door and streaming in horizontal lines across the glass. Beyond, the leaden sky and endless lines of roofs glistened in the rain.

It looked like there was no one living there.

Aose stuck his phone into his breast pocket. Besides the family simply 'being out', no other explanation came to mind.

Aose dreamed about a mother bird calling to its young.

He'd seen some flurries of snowflakes around Sekigahara but remembered nothing after that. It wasn't until they'd left Shin-Yokohama that Aose became conscious again. Soft sun had broken through the clouds and the upper windows of high-rise apartments sparkled.

He changed at Tokyo station for the Chuo line and got off at Yotsuya. Then he headed along Shinjuku-dori towards the Imperial Palace, adeptly dodging around strolling pedestrians. He lifted his wrist to check his watch, simultaneously making sure his breath and shirt sleeves didn't smell of alcohol. When he was alone, he usually limited himself to a single can of beer. He often wondered if Hinako had noticed the change in him from his heavy-drinking days.

Picking up his pace, Aose turned into a backstreet. Before anything else, he planned to ask Hinako about her end-of-term exam results. Then he would move on to finding out what tune she was practising on the *electone* electronic keyboard. And then he was going to try to get the details of those odd phone calls. She said that the calls had stopped, but he still wanted to know who had been making them. He cut through a neighbourhood of tightly packed apartment buildings and turned at a crossroads equipped with curved mirrors for better driving visibility. By the time he spotted the blue signboard for Café Horn, he was a little out of breath. The cowbell on the door jangled as he entered the mint-green Tyrolean-themed interior. There was no need to look around for Hinako; she was tucked away at the back of the café at their usual two-person table. The owner and his wife, who already knew the situation, were watching over her. Aose nodded to them and then with an appropriately contrite expression made his way over to Hinako.

'Have you been waiting a long time?'

'Yeah. I got sick of waiting for you. I was about to go home.'

This was her usual style of banter. She pretended to sulk, but her eyes were smiling. This must be how thirteen-year-old girls were, but every time they met he was taken aback by the changes in his daughter.

'Hey, listen, Daddy, I really messed up in my exams. I might have to retake first year.'

The look of amusement in her eyes was still there.

'That's bad,' said Aose.

'Really bad!'

'Maths again?'

'Yeah, maths sucks! There's no way I'm telling you my score.'

'But English was okay, right?'

'Not so great. That's why I'm in trouble.'

'Yeah, that really sounds like trouble.'

'What am I going to do?'

'You'll get through this. I know you can do it if you try, Hinako.'

'I'm scared. The teacher might say I have to stay back a year.'

The dialogue was slightly off. Maybe telling her she could do it was where he'd gone off script?

'Do you want something to eat?'

'I already ate. But you go ahead, Daddy.'

'I already ate too. On the train.'

'Oh, okay then.'

Hinako gave her father a quizzical look. It was the look of someone who had learned to ignore the lies adults tell. She'd

9

really begun to resemble Yukari. The more expressive her face, the fewer words she actually used.

He ordered a café au lait. On the table in front of Hinako were a cup of cocoa and a mobile phone wrapped in a pink handkerchief. She carried it in case of emergency.

'When you called me before you were on the train?'

'Right! I was on my way back from a job in Osaka.'

'You went to Osaka?'

She was trying to show interest, but Aose could tell by her expression that Osaka didn't really mean anything to her.

'Just on the outskirts, really. Oh yes, I know – close to Universal Studios Japan. That theme park with *Jaws* and *Jurassic Park* and stuff.'

'Did you go there?'

Seeing his daughter's face light up, he panicked a little.

'No, no. I was just close to there, that's all.'

'I see. Yeah, so it was for work then?'

The café au lait arrived. As he listened to the owner's footsteps walking away, he managed to muster a small amount of courage.

'Shall we go?'

'Where?'

'To Universal Studios.'

Hinako's expression clouded.

In the past, Aose used to take his daughter shopping or to the pool. She'd even managed to pester him long enough to take her to Disneyland and Sanrio Puroland. But for the past two years she hadn't wanted to go anywhere. Maybe it just meant she was growing up. Or perhaps it was Yukari who didn't approve?

'I'll ask your mother if it's okay.'

'But isn't it really far?'

'We'll be there and back in no time by Shinkansen.'

'Will we stay the night?'

'Yes, why not? It'll be fun to stay in a hotel.'

'Maybe, then.'

'Really? Great. Just let me know when you decide. We can go in spring break or the summer holidays.'

Hinako nodded slightly, then shifted her gaze as if to say, 'That's enough of that topic.'

Aose's vision faded and was replaced with a memory of the back view of his little girl, her nursery school bag swinging back and fro as she waddled along. She had such trouble with her *sa*, *shi*, *su*, *se*, *so* sounds . . . In fact, her beloved budgerigars' pronunciation had been better than hers. It was around that time that Aose and Yukari got divorced. His first parental visit after that, Hinako had been sitting in her high-sided booster chair, restlessly kicking her legs. Even now, she was still so small, so skinny, that Aose couldn't help talking to her like a little kid. But the muted lighting of the café revealed breasts that were beginning to grow. And she was getting taller. In fact, her whole silhouette was beginning to look like Yukari's. But it wasn't only her appearance. Aose could see each aspect of her personality, each emotion, develop and blossom one by one. After eight years of monthly meetings, she really did seem to have it all worked out – how to deal with the father who has a different surname. When she calls him 'Daddy' without a hint of embarrassment it isn't that she's still his little girl. It's as if she understands that this is what he wants to hear more than anything else in the world.

Aose had begun to suspect that Hinako knew the reason her parents had split up. He wouldn't be surprised if Yukari had decided, now that her daughter had become a junior high school student, well on her way to adulthood, that now was the time to tell her. He'd been wondering about it since last year. What had Yukari told her?

'Oh, by the way, what happened about those phone calls?'

He phrased it as if the question had only just occurred to him. He really was lacking in the fatherly chat department.

'Phone calls?'

'Don't you remember? We talked about it the time before last. Did you get any more calls after that?'

It had been a rare occasion for Hinako to ask his advice on something. The last time they'd spoken she'd told him that the strange calls that had been coming to the house had suddenly stopped. She'd said, 'So that's the end of it.' The phrase 'end of it' had sent chills down his neck. He couldn't help asking, was it a boy calling? Hinako shook her head. Then was it a friend? This time she didn't shake her head. So who was it? For a moment, Hinako looked lost, but then, with 'Whatever, it's fine now,' she'd put an end to the conversation, flashing her father a dazzling smile.

'They didn't call again.'

Hinako's voice was flat. Clearly this was not her favourite topic of conversation. On the other hand, she didn't seem all that bothered that it had been brought up again.

'Never again?'

'Not even once.'

'How long were you getting these calls?'

'Um . . . they started about a year ago.'

'That long ago?'

'But they hardly ever called, really.'

Hardly ever? So this wasn't a regular occurrence.

'They weren't anonymous calls, were they?'

'No, no. Nothing like that.'

'Hmm . . . I see . . .'

Who on earth was this caller? It was on the tip of his tongue to ask, but he was afraid that Hinako might shut him out again. Anyway, he had guessed who it was.

'So, what was that club your friend asked you to join again? Patchwork, or quilting, was it?'

'Right, but mostly I just come straight home after school.'

'Why?'

'Everyone's busy with *juku* cram school.'

It was back in the third grade of primary school that Hinako had been treated by her classmates as if she were invisible. She had no idea why.

'Are you getting on with your friends?'

'Yes, I'm doing fine.'

Aose nodded. He laced his fingers together on the table.

'You can tell me all about it if you want.'

'I already said, I'm doing fine. But Daddy—'

Just as Hinako spoke, the mobile phone in front of her began to ring. It played the theme song from the *Sazae-san* anime, which was the ring tone she used for calls from her mother, Yukari. Whenever she heard the tune, Hinako always looked relieved but at the same time a little irritated.

'Ah, yes. He's here. I'm fine.'

Hinako watched her father mischievously as she talked on the phone.

'Yeah, yeah. OK. See you.'

She hung up and grinned and then leaned forward as if confiding in her father.

'She called to ask how you were.'

Aose smiled. At moments like this Hinako reminded him of his late father. Whenever he was in a good mood from drinking, he would tell the biggest whoppers. He loved to make his family laugh. They'd always say, 'Rubbish! We don't believe you,' and fall about laughing. This made him happier than anything, and he'd laugh along with them.

'What was that just now?'

'Huh?'

'You were about to say something.'

'Oh, that's right. I was going to ask you about work. Your job is building houses, right, Daddy?'

Aose was taken aback. This was the first time Hinako had ever asked him about his work.

'Yes, kind of, but I don't actually do the building. I'm not a carpenter.'

'I know. You design them, make the plans. That kind of thing.'

It must have been a homework assignment or something. Or maybe she'd read about it in one of those magazines that listed different occupations that junior high school students liked to flick through and her interest had been sparked. Or more likely, Hinako being Hinako, she'd prepared a topic of conversation to keep things going. But it didn't matter to Aose what the reason might be, an interest in her father's job could easily be turned into an interest in her father himself.

'In the design company where I work, there are four people with first-class qualifications in architecture. People call us architects or designers.'

'Oh, architects!'

'That's right. Put simply, we're people who design houses. We think about their shape, figure out how the rooms should be arranged. And then we draw a plan or a blueprint. And we build a model of it. Then we consult with someone who knows about construction and installation to work out the details.'

'Construction and what?'

'Installation. Even if the design looks really cool, the house might be difficult to live in, or easily damaged. That'd be a big problem.'

'Yes, I get it.'

'After that it's the turn of the carpenter. Our company uses a very good contractor and they build excellent houses for us. And then our clients' dream home is finally ready for them.'

'So that's what you were doing today? Building a house in Osaka?'

'Right. I met some people who want to have a house built, listened to their specifications – what kind of house they'd like. That's the most important part of the job. If you build it for them and then they say they don't like it, it's too late.'

He was suddenly reminded of the Y Residence. But it was no competition for the sight of his beloved daughter nodding her head in response to his words.

'One question.'

'What?'

'Does your company have any TV commercials?'

'No, no. We're just a tiny architects' office.'

'So then those people who want to build a house in Osaka or in other places, how do they know about your company? From the internet?'

'Yes, it's true that recently more and more people are finding us from an internet search. But mostly it's by word of mouth.'

'Huh? Word of mouth? . . . So not the internet?'

She didn't get the concept right away.

'For example, say we build a house for someone, and then their friend comes over to visit . . .'

'Uh-huh'

'And the friend really likes the house, then, when they want to build their own place, they come to our company.'

'Oh, I see now.'

'Or sometimes, like in the case of the people today in Osaka, they see photos of a house we built in a book or a magazine and they get in touch.'

Hinako looked impressed.

'You mean a house that you designed was in a book?'

'Ah, yes. A little while back.'

'That's so cool!'

'It's not that cool. It was just one of many houses in the book.'

'I'd like to see the book.'

'Hmm. I'm not sure where I put it . . .'

'Please? I want to see it.'

Aose remained poker-faced, but inwardly he was thrilled at the interest Hinako was showing in him. It seemed to him another example of what Okajima had called 'the influence of the famous Y Residence'.

'I'll have a look for it.'

'If you find it, bring it next time. Promise?'

'Promise. I'll dig through my stuff.'

For a moment he was at a loss for words.

'I'll do my best . . . but why are you interested in that house?'

'Mummy says she doesn't really like the apartment.'

He knew. He knew exactly how Yukari felt about her home.

'Does she want to move house?'

'She hasn't exactly said so . . . Actually, she says our place is really convenient for her job. And it's close to my school.'

'That's true.'

'But sometimes she yells out, kind of like a joke, "I want to live at ground level. Feel the earth beneath my feet!"'

Her impersonation of her mother was so good, Aose forgot to laugh.

The café's mint-green wallpaper suddenly seemed to take on a life of its own. He pictured Yukari, one foot on a stepladder, giving considered directions on the colour of the walls. Theirs had been a marriage of architect husband and interior decorator wife, and yet somehow, they had completely failed to build a house of their own.

'So don't forget you promised, Dad.'

Hinako got up from the table. The phone in her hand was playing the theme tune from *Sazae-san* again. She was going directly to her keyboard class. He quickly asked the prepared question 'What tune are you learning now?' but her reply meant nothing to him. She picked up a bulging bag and slung it over her shoulder. Aose guessed it was full of sheet music.

He walked her out of the café. She set off with a spring in her step, but as she got further away her footsteps seemed to get slower. Maybe her winter coat was too heavy. Beneath the hem her skinny white legs looked cold. She reached up to put earphones in and dropped something. As she stooped down to pick it up, her long, straight black hair was blown up by the breeze, revealing one young, rosy cheek.

In his head he urged her to hurry and grow up. These days he found himself looking for new signs of maturity every time he met her. Because if he wasn't able to be with his daughter any more, to scold her or to hug her, if she couldn't stay young for ever, then he'd rather she just grew up and got it over with.

Hinako turned when she reached the crossroads and waved to her father. Aose waved back. He wondered all of a sudden what his ringtone was. If she'd chosen the cheerful and friendly *Sazae-san* for her mother, what kind of tune did she find appropriate for her father?

3

One by one, sparrows came fluttering down on to the rain-soaked pavement.

Aose was reluctant to follow the same route Hinako had taken, so he headed in the opposite direction, towards Akasaka Mitsuke subway station. He just couldn't bring himself to head for work right away. No matter how much he normally kept his guilt level under control, time spent with his daughter would always shake him up. His daughter, but no longer his family. It was impossible to build that proper, slow-simmer relationship with her. The food he tried to cook would inevitably turn out a burnt mess. He sighed at the artificial nature of these father–daughter visits. Were there really any fathers and daughters out there who managed to keep a smile on their face for two to three hours?

When Hinako was still little, he'd always been able to turn the conversation around by reassuring her that he was, and always would be, her daddy. The main purpose of the visits used to be for him to be a large, comforting presence, there for his daughter, in the hope that it would somehow make up to her for the loss of a father. But now they were at a different stage. He no longer had to play the comforting father figure. And he wasn't confused – he was completely clear about his own feelings: having a daughter on the edge of puberty terrified him. And his sin wasn't that he was wishing for her to hurry up and reach adulthood. He was guilty of just trying to get through this stage of her life by staying neutral and trying not to make waves.

How far was Hinako just playing the role of daughter for him? Whenever they met, she would chat about Yukari. She was trying to minimize the reality of the divorce. Sometimes he'd look into Hinako's eyes and see hope in there – hope that if she continued to be brave and upbeat and get on well with both her father and mother, then one day a miracle might happen.

But there were other times when the look in those eyes would put him on his guard. They seemed to be asking him a question.

Hey, Daddy, why did you and Mummy split up?

He was sure Yukari would have concealed what an abyss lay between them. She had probably invented a story that consisted of no quarrels or feuds in order to keep Hinako from feeling ashamed of her family background. In their insecure hearts, clouded with anxiety, they had both tried to tell a tale of a mother and a father doing their best to follow their separate paths, living a positive life for each other's sakes. Yukari had done her best to keep her beautiful child from pricking her finger on the poisoned spindle and had no intention of letting that poison affect her in the future – for that, Aose had to thank his ex-wife. He had nothing to blame her for, and yet . . .

He couldn't help feeling that Hinako didn't believe the story. One day she was going to want to know the truth. There would come a day when, regardless of her parents' wishes, she would need to know. Because one day she was going to fall in love with somebody. If she was going to envision spending her future life with them, then she would have to come to terms with the reality that her own parents gave up their future together.

The sparrows hopped from side to side, preparing to take off and avoid the approaching feet of the crowds.

He should prepare himself, stop drowning in an ocean of atonement and regret. He should prepare a small drop of truth in his heart for Hinako's future. That was his task as a separated father.

What truth would Yukari tell?

The old feeling came over him of tumbling down a steep slope. He couldn't forget the days they'd spent climbing a much gentler hill together. They'd been married for ten years. What had gone wrong? What had been their mistake? He could list everything that had happened between them, but it required an interpretation of each of these things to get to the truth. And the older he got, the less he understood. He'd given up trying to understand.

He was sure Yukari understood. As the two of them spent so much time together, shared a space, she must have known all the forks and the bumps in their road. He wanted to ask her when it was that she had given up on him. What was it that she ultimately found impossible to forgive?

Aose looked up. In front of him, he could see the tower of the Hotel New Otani.

I want to live at ground level. Feel the earth beneath my feet.

His mind was replaying Yukari's words even though he had never actually heard her say them.

It was typical of Yukari not to say right away what she was thinking. She preferred to store it up until one day it all exploded out of her. She'd drop hints but, if asked what was up, she'd decline to answer, and then she'd finally let it all out right when they were about to sleep. She'd pull his hands towards her, wriggle her hips in annoyance and cry out something like, 'I miss eating chargrilled saury sooo much!'

It would make Aose laugh and he would tell her how much he missed eating it too. The two of them would go to sleep, their mouths watering with thoughts of the cooked fish they would treat themselves to the next day. It was a happy time for the two of them, right on the eve of Japan's huge period of economic growth, commonly referred to as the 'bubble economy', and looking back now, he could smile at how they could yearn for such simple things, how innocent their greed and frustration.

Back then Aose had been working for an architecture firm in the upscale Tokyo district of Akasaka where forty or so architects competed with each other for recognition from their big-name boss. The economy had been on the upswing for a while, but by the time the bubble economy was at its peak Aose was constantly on the go. It was only in the early years that he could say he'd been happy; the office with its massive volume of work projects began after a while to feel as deadly as a battlefield. The young architects would continually push the boundaries of their energy, stamina and potential in a building that had become a city that never slept.

Eventually people began to fall away. And others were lured away by competing firms. In order to counteract this, salaries were increased and bonuses began to be paid at an unprecedented rate. Aose worked on his shopfloor plans like a creature possessed — it was all about the steel and the glass and the concrete with him. Boutiques, hair salons, restaurants, showrooms, wedding palaces, it felt as if he was constructing life-size models. Appearance was everything. He was trying to be someone in an oppressive, terrifying world where only beautiful people and things could survive.

Yukari had also been working her way up, in the field of interior design. She belonged to an association of young designers who incorporated the flags and coats of arms of western countries into their designs using the traditional Japanese ombre dyeing technique. Their work was very well received and her group became part of a new wave of design in Japan. Her own creations were frequently featured in magazines, and the orders were pouring in.

In no time at all, they were a dual-income couple on high salaries, returning home to their little two-room apartment only to sleep. Aose remembers the moment something seemed to explode in his mind. *Yes! Let's do it!* They spent a huge sum of money to move to an apartment in fashionable Roppongi, he chose a brand-new imported Citroën from a catalogue, and whenever he had a little time after work they would slip into a top-class restaurant just in time for the last order of the day. He'd hang out in trendy bars and pubs and pour alcohol into his exhausted body.

Look, when things settle down, let's have a kid and build our own house. One night he'd suddenly come out with this to Yukari. It was the most excited he'd been since the day he proposed. He'd been dying to say it and couldn't keep it back any longer. A promising young architect and interior designer coming together to build their dream house. It would be a way of ensuring that the brief hours they managed to spend together were the best they could be.

But it never happened. This was because the home that Yukari longed for was a traditional house constructed from wood. Whereas Aose was envisioning a western-style house with naked exterior walls of unfinished concrete that would change appearance as they reflected the moving sun. This image of what he wanted to build was too vivid and specific. Yukari was not receptive to the idea of what he termed his 'sundial house', a house that marked the passage of time, and suggested that he build it for a client instead. She told him she could put up with a concrete apartment as a temporary option but that humans and concrete were not meant to exist together indefinitely.

These words brought Aose back to his senses. It wasn't Yukari's professional sensibilities that made her want the wooden house, it was the combination of material and spiritual aspects of her upbringing that had given her the undeniable belief that a real house had to be made of wood.

As an architect, he understood. People's obsession with their homes was never a matter of simple preference or taste. It was rather a manifestation of their personal values and their hidden desires. It was not a view of the future but rooted firmly in the past. A person's history whispers in their ear what is important and what isn't, what is permissible and what can never be. Yukari had a clear response. The place she'd lived in Hamamatsu when she was a child had been a traditional old farmhouse with a gabled roof – 'just a really big house,' she used to say. From the time Aose met her, Yukari would talk fondly of her childhood. She'd tell him how beautiful the first star at night would look from the little platform up on the roof they had for drying clothes; about the amazing ant colony that lived under the front porch; how the first time she got in trouble with her father he made her sit on the cold, earthen floor of the *genkan* porch. She'd talk about her memories with such joy and nostalgia there was no doubting that this was something she cared about deeply.

The plans for their dream home were left up in the air.

Aose never mentioned it again. He felt that all of his skills as an architect had been rejected. However, he could have lived with that kind of resentment. It was Yukari's guileless confidence that made him feel deflated. He felt that his own roots had been disrespected. He pictured Yukari warm and comfortable in the embrace of her hometown, looking down on him for having no hometown of his own.

This all happened before Hinako was born. If he were asked to explain the reasons for their divorce, he could cite the number of times he was in financial trouble after the burst of the economic bubble. But was that the real reason? No, it was much more than the money he'd lost. Now that he lived alone without his wife and daughter, could he really deny that it had nothing to do with the way he had been raised?

Aose suddenly stopped walking. It was always here, this place, where his feet seemed to be unable to continue. He looked up at the towering Hotel New Otani. He loved this angle. The curving surface of the walls reminded him of the arch of a massive dam. He can still see it – hundreds of metres above the ground at the top of the dam, leaning over to fix a concrete panel into the dam wall, the proud figure of his father.

4

The Seibu Shinjuku line wasn't crowded today. Aose stared out
of the window. He'd never spoken to Hinako about his migratory upbringing, although he'd opened up to Yukari about it
before they'd got married. A difference in upbringing can have
both beneficial and harmful effects on a relationship, so Aose had
told the most convenient version of his story. Kawamata, Takane
Dai-ichi, Sameura, Houheikyou, Touri, Yagisawa, Shimokubo,
Nagawado, Yahagi, Shintone, Zao, Kusaki, Kiryu . . . and there
were even more dams he couldn't recall the names of. From when
he was a baby carried on his mother's back, he had moved house
twenty-eight times. Through the nine years of primary and junior high school he had changed schools seven times. The family
would be put up in a series of prefab workers' lodgings that consisted of just a couple of tiny rooms. Aose had heard that when he
was a baby he had slept with his parents and two sisters in a single
three-tatami-mat room.

But they hadn't been poor. The construction of new dams was
an ostentatious public works project that had symbolized Japan's
period of economic growth. The form work for the concrete
used to be assembled and the concrete poured on site. Being a
specialist form-setter by trade, his father was in great demand,
due to both the precision required and the dangerous heights
involved.

Aose's mother worked as a cook. They always had an eighteen-
inch TV in their tiny home, although it didn't work well, and his

parents would buy them books, coloured pencils and expensive paint sets if he and his sisters asked. However, the dishes, plates and cups in the house were all made of cheap plastic. Aose's mother wouldn't buy glass or ceramic tableware for fear it would break as they moved from one place to another.

Due to the nature of his father's job, whatever accommodation they were in, the route home from school would inevitably consist of an interminable uphill climb. On the way, he would notice the difference between the neater, prettier homes here and there along the route and the many shabbier houses. He heard the reason from his older sisters. There were families who had accepted reparation money from the government and built brand-new homes on higher land, and those who refused to leave their houses along the roadside. The young Aose would dream of being able to rush home to one of those brand-new houses. To go directly to the kitchen, to pick up his own glass, to mix melon-flavoured powder with water and drink the whole thing down.

It had been very rare for Aose to be invited to a classmate's house. Whichever school he was at, the 'dam kids' were considered a nuisance by everyone; they might as well have been called 'damn kids'. Now when he thought about it, the instant acquisition of land by those who were affected by the dam construction had led to disparity and in-fighting in these mountain villages, and it had had an effect on the children too. The dam kids were taunted, alienated, even had stones thrown at them. He didn't remember ever being too bothered by it – he'd soon be moving on to the next school anyway. As 'migration' was all he'd ever known, he had no concept of settling down somewhere. His dream sequence always ended after he ran into the kitchen and finished his glass of juice.

Aose closed his eyes.

He remembered the features of the land at all the different places. He thought back to the birds or the flowers or the trees that were native to those specific regions. And yet he had never thought of going back to pay a visit to any of them. Each one of them was finished with, over, as if his memories had been abruptly cut off midway. The different locations failed to intersect with each other but lay separate and unconnected in the shadows of his mind. If your hometown is the place you think of when you come to a crossroads in your life, or when you find yourself in crisis, then Aose had none. All he had was the light.

There were times when he longed to return to that soft light. For some reason, all of the workers' prefab lodgings he had lived in had the same large windows on the north side. He had loved to read or draw in the light that came in through those windows. It was a soft, north light that neither burst in nor drenched them with its rays. That light from the north would almost apologetically enfold the room in gentle arms. It was different from the sharp brightness of the east window or the cheery sunniness of the south. The light from the north was quiet and serene, as if it had reached a state of enlightenment.

The train slowed down.

Please build a home you would want to live in.

Aose opened his eyes and stood up.

He had built a wooden house up in Shinano-Oiwake. With a view of Mount Asama, its windows welcomed in all the north light his heart could desire.

5

The sun was already setting.

Aose exited the west ticket gate of Tokorozawa station and entered the shopping street known as Prope Street. It was always crowded on weekends and holidays. He walked with his shoulders hunched to avoid bumping into people, and passed through the mall between Marui's A and B buildings to get to Showa Street. The office of Okajima Design Company faced this street, on the second floor of a small building.

The door was unlocked, but Okajima was nowhere to be seen. Instead, the bearded face of Yutaka Ishimaki was there behind his computer. He was using computer-aided design (CAD) to touch up a floorplan.

'No family time today, then?' Aose asked.

The thirty-eight-year-old father of four gave a pointed sigh and spun his chair around.

'It sucks, but the owner is in a rush.'

Owner, proprietor, client. Architects used different words for their customers depending on which company they'd done their training at.

'Any particular reason?'

'His mother is turning eighty-eight and she's in a care home. He wants to get it finished while she's still living so he can move her in.'

'That's sweet. Can she still walk?'

'Been in a wheelchair for years.'

'It's just up your alley.'

'I guess.'

Ishimaki was a very competent all-rounder, but his speciality was designing barrier-free homes. He took pride in ensuring that all his designs met Level 4 or higher of the criteria related to senior-friendly design. Since the collapse of the bubble economy, the considerations of environment and welfare had become essential elements in the world of architecture and design. Ishimaki was an indispensable member of the team. He used to work in the design section of a major construction company, but with the prospect of being laid off looming he had gone out on his own. Unfortunately, that hadn't worked out, and in the end he had to give up his struggle to gain a slice of the ever-shrinking pie. For a while he had been reduced to working for his wife's family business, a fertilizer factory, but a thread-thin connection had finally led him to Okajima Design.

His story was a common one. Aose was also one of Japan's bubble economy's 'fallen warriors'. He'd lost his job at the Akasaka office and, following his divorce, had resigned himself to picking up temp work at one architecture firm after another. His income dropped to a third of what it had been in the past, but as long as he was able to pay child support for Hinako he didn't care about the rest. He wasn't in any position to pick and choose his work, so he simply made himself useful and drew what he was told to draw. At one point he had worked for a shady housing company that sold cheap homes by giving seven different facades to seven houses sharing the exact same foundation. Every day he seemed to be drowning in such cheap tricks. And then he would spend his nights drowning in alcohol, because when he was drunk he lost the ability to complain. Then, just three years ago, he'd got a call from Okajima, who'd probably heard the rumours of his diminished circumstances. *Don't sell yourself short. Come and work for me . . .*

'The problem isn't really the barrier-free stuff.'

Ishimaki put his forefinger and thumb together to symbolize money.

'The owner's only giving me ¥120,000 per square metre to work with.'

'Including everything?'

'Yep. Not only the lighting but the external water supply, drainage and septic tank. It's ridiculous.'

'Yeah. Unreasonable.'

Getting nothing but this brief acknowledgement from Aose, Ishimaki turned his gaze back to his computer screen and began to stroke his beard, as was his habit when anxious.

'Maybe I'll talk to Takeuchi about it,' he mused.

'That'll make him very happy,' said Aose.

Ringo Takeuchi was the youngest architect at the firm. He'd graduated in architecture from university just four years earlier. He still had something of the student about him even now, and was the most enthusiastic member of the company when it came to research. In particular, he had a passion for the production of low-cost housing, and lately he'd broadened his interests to the development of eco-friendly homes.

'Where's the boss, by the way?' said Aose.

'Do you need him for something?'

'He was here earlier, wasn't he?'

'Yes. You missed him by about thirty minutes. He said something about dropping in somewhere on his way home.'

'What the—,' thought Aose, but he let it go. Probably it had something to do with that public design competition Okajima had been talking about.

'Hey, I heard from the boss that the Osaka trip went well.'

'Yes, nothing in writing yet, but I think we'll have a contract signed by the end of the month.'

'They want a replica of the Y Residence?'

'Yeah, pretty much.'

'Did you see the email from that Urawa owner about the Y Residence?'

'That's why I came in today – to read it.'

Aose took the seat by the window and turned on computer #1. With the addition of Mayumi Tsumura, in charge of accounting, the office had a total of five employees, but the nature of their work meant that the office had nine computers, occupying a total of six desks.

The email that Setsuko Yoda of Urawa had written to Aose was buried among a whole bunch of work emails.

Aose-sensei, I apologize for bothering you while you're busy . . .

He skipped past the greetings to the main body of the message.

I took the map you kindly sent and went straight up to Shinano to check out the house. What a beautiful exterior! It has the look of a holiday villa. The complexity of its shape meant that seeing the real thing, I discovered many more features than were obvious from the photos in the book. And I love that it's built on a small hill. My husband loved it as much as I did and we got so excited that we decided, rude though it was, we really had to ask to see the interior. We rang the bell, but unfortunately nobody seemed to be home. In fact, it looked as if the house wasn't occupied, that no one was living there at all. Perhaps the family who owns it has decided only to use it as a holiday home on weekends? We would really love to have a chance to see how the light plays inside the house, so I wondered if I might ask you to have a word with the owners on our behalf?

Best wishes

Aose frowned. A second home? Yoshino-san had never mentioned he wanted it as a holiday home. The Yoshino family were supposed to have moved out of their rental house in Tabata, northern Tokyo, and the very same day started their new life in Shinano-Oiwake.

Aose shut down the computer and leaned back heavily in his chair.

He could see both of the Yoshinos' faces. It was just around this time last year that they'd come to the office and told him that

30

they'd fallen in love with a two-storey house he'd built in Ageo. They were both about forty, short in stature, and initially had been extremely nervous. Aose's reception of the couple had been less than enthusiastic. The house in Ageo they were referring to had been built on an awkwardly shaped piece of land in the corner of a housing estate. Aose had tried all sorts of things to make it work, but the client had done nothing but complain. In the end their relationship had soured and the resulting house was somewhat lacklustre.

But Touta Yoshino had been impressed by the beautiful form and strong presence of the building, despite its small size. His wife, Karie, had sung the praises of the dormer windows that compensated for the lack of light, and the short flow lines in the kitchen. Her love for the house had been so strong it was almost like an infatuation with the architect himself. But at the same time, the couple's attitude to Aose wasn't one of blind worship. As Aose had talked to them, he had taken a liking to this calm, well-balanced pair. They told him they had two junior high school age daughters and a son who was in the first year of primary school – the same pattern as Aose's own family growing up. It made him feel some kind of a bond with them. He'd had to leave for a moment to take a call, then, when he returned, the couple was sitting up straighter as if to make an announcement. Then after they had signalled to each other with a deep nod, Touta Yoshino began to speak.

'We have 265 square metres of land in Shinano-Oiwake in Nagano prefecture and a budget of thirty million yen for construction. We'll leave everything up to you, Aose-san. Please build a home you would want to live in.'

Yoshino's words had an instant effect on Aose. It was as if a switch had been flipped. *A home he would want to live in . . .*

He instantly saw a wooden house – well, not an actual house. It was the trees he saw – the woods, the forests. Morning mist and birds twittering. The breeze that brushed his cheeks. All of these pleasant feelings, memories from all of his five senses, flashed through his mind. Together they formed the hazy image of his dream wooden house. He was completely taken aback. There was no sign of any concrete walls, no building where sunlight and shadows mingled to mark the passing of time. The western-style house that had been his long-term project did not put in an appearance in his imaginings. Several days later, it was the same. His precious house that marked the passage of time stood abandoned, covered in a thick layer of dust. It made no move to appeal to him.

Aose decided on the wooden house. He believed his intuition was a pure impulse that had nothing to with surrendering, or giving up, and certainly had nothing to do with digging up the past. He had long since drawn a line under his connection to Yukari. For a start, it hadn't occurred to him to build a traditional Japanese house like the one his ex-wife had grown up in, so he was able to immerse himself in these musings without any awkward feelings. Nor was there any pressure to conform to traditional aesthetics or conventional building techniques. He was completely free to consider what kind of home he would want to live in.

He would travel up to Shinano and stand on the future site of the Y Residence, checking the specifications and allowing his imagination to take flight. Whenever he got inspiration, he would work on the plans through the night. He drew dozens and dozens of rough sketches. He barely drank at all. Moreover, he was completely absorbed in his work to even notice. He felt bad towards his boss, Okajima, who had so kindly rescued him and taken him on, but he had to admit that this was the first time he had really put his heart into his work. The bursting of the economic bubble had severely dented his confidence and his pride. It was much more than a simple after-effect – it had affected his whole philosophy on life. He had stopped pushing himself, his mind doing no more than processing requests that came in to the office. In order to avoid any kind of conflict or discord, he had been compromising his own views and approach. He felt he was trying to keep up the facade of being a first-class architect but his actual state of mind was the same as when he'd been a sell-out architect for hire, drawing up plans that pandered to the client's tastes.

He'd caught a glimpse of himself through Touta Yoshino's eyes, fading and dried up. But then came a request that was pure magic. He'd been exhorted to build a house that he himself would want to live in. And with that, his creative juices were flowing again. His passion for architecture came bursting forth.

He would build a house that faced north. When the idea popped into his head, Aose slowly clenched his fists. He'd found it. He was sure of it. The plot of land in Shinano was blessed with the most beautiful living environment, open spaces on all sides, at the top of a hill facing Mount Asama. In a place like that, Aose could open up those north side windows as much as he wanted – something that was always forbidden in the city. He would use north windows for the main light source and the other sides merely for supplementary lighting. His heart skipped a beat. He pondered how he would like to meet an architect who had never had to deal with insufficient light. In Japan, the south and east are the holy grail to those who design houses. Aose discarded that doctrine entirely. Turn the heavens upside down and build a wooden house that breathes with north light. He wasn't doing it because the location limited the available light from the south and the east. On the contrary, he could have made as much of the south and east sides as he wanted. It was the ultimate inverse plan. He would design a home that was truly worthy of being called one. Aose drew as if possessed. Ground plans, elevation plans, cross-sections – he drafted, rejected them and redrafted. The shape of the house was based entirely on the concept of natural illumination. It was a partially two-storey structure, with its highest eaves on the north side. The north wall was also the longest, and the walls on the east and west boldly narrowed away from it to make the south side the shortest. In other words, viewed from above, the house was in the shape of a trapezoid. He made a 1:25 model and examined the way the light would hit the interior, calculating the angle it would hit for every season and all times of day. From these calculations he determined the interior structure and the size and position of the windows. And then, to compensate for any lack of light – or rather to make this a true 'North Light House' – he meticulously designed what he called 'chimneys of light'.

Construction took four months to complete. Every five days or so he visited the site to supervise the work and give further directions for every detail. To be sure that the house would be able to withstand heavy snowfall, he used a couple of varieties of hardwood oak. For the *genkan*, and in the interior to separate the different spaces, he used the softer Japanese cypress. The subtle scent of the wood beautifully matched the soft natural light. He did everything to the utmost of his ability. For him, the house elicited a deep nod of satisfaction. And he believed that the Yoshinos had felt the same way.

On the day that the Y Residence officially became the Yoshino Residence, the couple looked up at their new home with an expression of deep emotion on their faces. They were amazed when they entered the house and found themselves in a space filled with clear autumn light. Smiles spread across their faces, and Touta Yoshino's expression in particular was halfway between tears and laughter. He apologized for himself, explaining that he was deeply moved. There had been no doubt in Aose's mind that his clients were extremely satisfied with their home . . .

'No, I get that!'

Ishimaki's voice reached Aose's ears. He was in the midst of a long phone conversation with Takeuchi.

'If I wanted to cut costs by using lower-quality materials, I could do it myself. I don't want to do that, so that's why I'm asking you—'

Aose turned his gaze to the window.

Four months had passed. Aose had been careful to adhere to the company rules of not contacting the client. He had expected a call from Yoshino in the first few days, thinking his client would want to let him know how the family was settling into their new home. When half a month had passed, he began to get anxious. It didn't matter how fine the interior and exterior of a house, it was impossible to know its true quality until it was actually occupied by human beings. He began to feel afraid of hearing their judgement. Many times, he'd been on the point of picking up the phone, but then he would imagine the smiles fading from the Yoshinos' faces and lose his nerve. He threw himself instead into the other work that had been piling up over the previous few months. There would never be another opportunity to design a house with total freedom. He was forced to return to the usual daily grind of trying to accommodate his clients' more self-indulgent requests.

It was nothing but an illusion created by nostalgia. It was just a house. He got into the habit of telling himself that every time his head became filled with thoughts of the Y Residence. Just a run-of-the-mill wooden house with no special merits that would prompt its owners to pick up the phone or send a postcard. At the same time, totally without those sorts of faults or problems that would precipitate a visit to the company to lodge a complaint. If he stopped telling himself this, then he would have to believe that out of his own self-importance he had somehow managed to force upon the Yoshino family a bizarre, topsy-turvy house that had north and south completely backwards. In his dark moments, he imagined the owners of the house had tons of these complaints, but because they had given him free rein they were loath to speak out now; they'd had enough of the utter self-indulgence shown by the designer and were now lamenting that this was nothing like they'd expected. His flights of negative emotion were endless, while positive thoughts barely got off the ground. Whatever the case, it was clear that the Yoshinos did not want a relationship with their architect. They did not regard Aose as a friend. He felt disgusted at himself for working up such a passion for this project. When the *Top 200 Homes of the Heisei Era* book arrived, he threw it into his desk drawer without even opening it, sealing away all his self-importance.

. . . it looked as if the house wasn't occupied, that no one was living there at all.

If that was true, what did it mean?

'Aose-san?'

Ishimaki had finished his phone call and was speaking to him.

'What?'

'Want to get some dinner?'

Aose glanced at the wall clock.

'Bit early, isn't it? It's only five thirty.'

'It looks like I'm going to be here all night.'

'I'm fine. Why don't you go?'

For a moment Ishimaki looked suspicious, but then he grinned.

'Think I'll get some tonkotsu ramen. Better not let the wife know.'

Aose turned his back on the chubby figure of Ishimaki rubbing his ample belly. It was probably just because he was in a bad mood that Ishimaki's behaviour was getting on his nerves. They were fellow fallen warriors, but Ishimaki had somehow managed to hold his family of six together.

'But I'm a bit envious of you.'

Taken by surprise, Aose turned back around. He'd thought Ishimaki had already left, but he was still there, standing at the open door.

'Why?'

'The Y Residence. It keeps getting attention. And everyone really rates it. I keep thinking that's how a legend is born.'

36

'It's not exactly a masterpiece.'

'You know, it really took me by surprise. I always had you pegged as a realist.'

Realist?

'I don't have the imagination or the guts to design something so outside the box,' Ishimaki went on. 'I guess I know how to make buildings, but I don't know how to make art.'

Aose sent Ishimaki on his way with a vague response. He waited until the sound of his footsteps had faded away then pulled out his mobile. He dialled the Y Residence's landline, telling himself that if Yoshino answered then he would be embarrassed.

The answer machine picked up.

So? That just meant that they were out for the day – no, half a day, he told himself. He tried Touta Yoshino's mobile and was greeted with the familiar announcement: *Either the phone you are trying to reach is turned off, or there is no signal.*

Then he tried the house in Tabata.

The number you are calling is currently out of use.

Aose was thrown. The Yoshino family had moved out of their rental home. Well, obviously – because they had moved to Shinano-Oiwake. There was no other way of looking at it. What kind of idiot would leave his newly built family home and go and live somewhere else?

Aose let out a deep breath, slapped his knees with both hands and stood up. Tucking his phone back into his pocket, he pulled his bag towards him. However, he couldn't shake off the nagging feeling that something was wrong. He stared at the computer screen for a moment and, clicking his tongue, pulled his phone out again. He dialled the Shinano-Oiwake house once more.

'This is Aose from Okajima Design . . .'

This time he left a message on the machine.

'I'm sorry I haven't been in touch for a while. There is something I'd like to ask you, so would you mind giving me a call back? It doesn't matter how late.'

6

Outside, it was beginning to get dark.

It was a short walk to the company car park. A breeze had got up – one of those winds of early spring that whistled between the tall buildings.

Aose looked up. This place, Tokorozawa, Saitama prefecture, north-west of Tokyo, was a mixed-up, higgledy-piggledy, dis-ordered city. Sometimes it felt like utter chaos. Each area seemed to be confused about its identity – as if it couldn't make up its mind whether it was a commercial or a residential district. Here and there, giant apartment blocks stuck their heads into the sky. Down at their feet, traditional narrow-fronted shops surrounded them like a scene from *Gulliver's Travels.* Tobacconists, shoe shops, ironmongers, second-hand bookshops, decorations for Children's Day in May, office supply shops . . . Then, within the same view there was a crêpe shop with a terrace, a signboard opposing the construction of high-rise apartment blocks, a chic, glass-fronted hairstylist, the torii gate to the rustic-looking Inari shrine and a dilapidated little roadside statue.

Aose was fascinated by all these disparate elements, but he had never felt like a true resident of this city. He had no special attach-ment to it. Maybe it was due to his long, aimless search for a place to live. Because he was working for Okajima Design he had decided he'd better live nearby, but he'd wandered round and round the streets, seeing nothing that inspired him. Then he'd spotted the name Hoshinomiya-cho and decided he liked the sound of the area. He found an estate agent there, but he'd ended up taking a room in an old apartment building in Nishi-Tokorozawa, just one station over. The experience had forced him to admit something to himself: although he'd been an architect for years, somewhere along the way he had lost sight of the kind of place he wanted to live in.

Aose snorted.

Now that he'd left a message on the Yoshinos' answer machine, the nauseous feeling in his stomach had subsided. He felt as if he'd shaken off a kind of sickness that had been plaguing him for a long time. All he had to do was wait for Touta Yoshino to call him back and hear whatever he had to say. Then the four months of doubt and speculation would be at an end.

He turned at the corner of the street and got into his Citroën, the only material thing he had left from the old days in Akasaka. It had got old and was definitely too big for one person to drive alone. He often thought about selling it, but each time his heart would rebel. He had an overwhelming sense that if he got rid of it, it would be like all his memories of that episode of his life driving off into the sunset.

Aose's apartment was only a few minutes away by car. He stopped off at a convenience store and bought a pack of sushi rolls and a can of beer. As he waited for the apartment building's elevator he was joined by an elderly woman pushing a rolling walking frame. They exchanged a brief greeting. The woman had a carrier bag from the same convenience store hanging from the handles of her walking frame. She got off at the tenth floor and Aose continued up to the twelfth. His bag was heavy because at the last minute he'd pulled out his copy of *Top 200 Homes* from his desk drawer and stuffed it in.

All that was visible in the dark apartment was the blinking red light of the answerphone. Although he already knew the message would be from Yukari, his mind was prepared to hear the voice of Touta Yoshino.

'Thanks for today. Hinako was really happy. She's looking forward to seeing you on the first Sunday of next month.'

He let out a long breath, trying to work out whether there was any emotion behind the rapid-fire platitudes. He did occasionally have phone conversations with his ex-wife. Back when Hinako was being bullied, they would talk every day. However, the rules were clear: never meet in person, and never talk about our personal lives on the phone. The only time they heard each other's voices was as parents, when they needed to communicate about their daughter.

Someday Hinako would need to learn the truth.

That situation met the conditions for communication. It was definitely a matter that he had to discuss with Yukari in preparation for that 'someday'. Aose would convey his thoughts and listen in turn to Yukari's. It seemed so simple, but Aose wondered if he was brave enough to start the discussion. If he put one word wrong it would no longer be a conversation for Hinako's benefit but would revert to being all about Aose and Yukari.

Aose pulled the ring top on his beer can, took a sip, then walked over to the sofa by the window and opened the pack of sushi rolls. Beyond the sash window he could see a night view of the city.

After the embers of all talk of building their own home had finally died out, conversations between the couple had somehow failed to connect. Well, it would be fair to say that for the duration of the bubble economy their whole lives were in a state of disconnect so, on the surface, nothing seemed to have changed. It was not clear to Aose which of these disconnects in particular symbolized to Yukari a marriage in crisis.

One day, after seeing a doctor for anaemia, Yukari had vowed to cut back on her work. And she followed up. She made sure he was home in the mornings and evenings. She was in unusually high spirits. They laughed a lot, just like when they were newly-weds. Instead of basic communication, she made an effort to make the conversation at mealtimes fun. She talked about how she wanted children.

'Right then, I'm going to hold my nose and eat as much liver as I can!'

The light that Hinako brought into their lives was immeasurable. Yukari's exclamations of joy also lit up every corner of their home. It didn't matter how tired Aose was when he came home, he always looked in on his daughter, curled up asleep in a fluffy ball, and his wife asleep next to her, worn out after the exhausting struggles of the day, and he would always think that this moment, right here right now with his family, was all that was important.

Still, he would continue to avoid all discussion of building a house. Yukari would sometimes mention it, but he'd brush it off, saying they would get around to it. Aose genuinely didn't know when he would get around to it, but the seasons passed, and eventually the economy tanked. Work disappeared like trees being bulldozed. Even works in progress fizzled out. Clients vanished, and all kinds of projects and plans were abandoned and shredded.

The office began to fire people. The boss would make eye contact, give them a sorrowful nod of the head, and that was it. The architects working in the private sector were in instant jeopardy, and the only people likely to be kept on were those specializing in public work projects, which were expected to continue to trickle in.

Takumi Nose was one of the victims, even though his talent was well established. Nose had once been extremely fond of Yukari and had even taken her on several dates. Because of him, Aose had proposed to Yukari two months earlier than he had intended to. Nose was fired right before Aose's eyes. It made him feel faint just thinking about it, but he knew it was only a matter of time before his turn came. He wrote his letter of resignation before the boss had a chance to give him the nod. The boss shook his hand, apologized and promised to hire Aose back someday.

Aose really had been naïve. He'd shaken his boss's hand warmly, believing he still had a bright future – after all, he had both qualifications and a great work CV.

'You quit? Of your own free will?'

Yukari had been aghast.

But in the end, there hadn't been anything he could do. No matter where he looked, or who he asked, he couldn't find a firm to hire him. Many of his colleagues found themselves in the same boat. Over the next six months to a year, Aose's phone would ring late at night. One of his ex-colleagues was now a salesman working on commission, another a waiter at a chain restaurant; yet another was cleaning buildings. The calls he fielded were filled with the laments of these men who had resorted to taking anything they could get to make ends meet. Right before hanging up, they'd always ask, 'How about you? Are you still holding out for a job in architecture?'

Aose was obsessed with the Yellow Pages directory. Red pen in hand, he'd circle architecture or design companies in the Tokyo metropolitan area and call, day in, day out.

'I'm a highly experienced shop designer. Now is the perfect time for you to hire new talent.'

He expanded his target areas to Osaka and Nagoya. When he realized he wasn't getting anywhere over the phone, he would turn up without an appointment.

His savings were dwindling fast, but still, he wouldn't give up. He just knew if he could show them his designs and photographs, he could convince them. And surely the economy would pick up sooner or later? But he just kept being turned away at the door. It was frustrating and he would become enraged. He took to yelling a parting shot: 'Screw you! I wouldn't be caught dead working in a third-rate company like this anyway!'

Those nights, he would drink to escape, and the amount of alcohol he'd consume steadily increased.

Yukari would do her best to encourage him.

'Hey, why don't we move back to our old place? I know it was tiny, but we had a lot of fun there, didn't we, even without a car?'

But he had no inclination either to move out or to sell his car. He just got irritated.

'I'm not obsessed with a fancy lifestyle either!' he yelled at her. 'It's not all about material possessions with me – don't insult me. But don't you get it? I'm just trying to make the best use of my skills. Why would you say something like that when I'm just doing my best to find a job? That really pisses me off!'

It was the first time he'd ever raised his voice. He slammed his fist into the wall. Yukari looked frightened, but at the same time there was a hint of sharpness in her eyes. She began to call around to her contacts, trying to find extra work for herself, which seemed to Aose her way of trying to rile him. That provoked another argument, but it was in vain anyway, as the market for interior design was in a similar decline. And so the family finances failed to improve. The arguments became incessant, but he would never raise his voice in front of Hinako. That was the final rule that the couple agreed together.

Hinako was a total mummy's girl. Whenever Yukari looked miserable, Hinako would cry.

He'd tried the job centre one time only. The place was filled with grey-looking men. It reminded him of footage he'd seen on TV of people in Russia or somewhere lining up for rations. He joined the queue, and immediately the line began to grow behind him. His stomach seemed to rise up into his throat, and his mouth began to gasp for breath. There was bile in his throat. He didn't make it as far as the counter, turned and walked out. He cursed himself for his weakness, but only for a moment. The look of surprise on the faces of all the men around him gave him such a sense of superiority that there was a spring in his step all the way home.

From that day onwards, he never saw Yukari smile. He saw her cry, he heard her yell, he learned the fear that a lack of money could provoke – he learned it to the depths of his soul. But by that time, he was knocking back cups of saké while it was still daylight.

'Minoru? Here.'

Her voice was calm that morning. On the dining table, the divorce papers, every field still blank. They didn't even have Yukari's signature. She didn't mean it. He knew she had no intention of breaking up with him. It was her last desperate attempt to get him back on his feet. Aose knew all this, but his heart froze. All he could see were the words 'Application for Divorce'. Words of retaliation rose in his throat. He could picture the empty, endlessly vacant world that he would find himself in if he let those words out. '*Don't say it, don't say it!*' his brain told him. And yet he said it. Why did he ever say it?

'Good thing we never built that house.'

His chopsticks stopped moving. He shut the plastic pack with its remaining sushi roll, replacing the elastic band around it to keep it closed. He hated that sound. Then he reached over to his bag and pulled out the *Top 200 Homes* book. The cover photo was a house designed by an unknown architect featuring a partially underground stone garden. It was cutting edge. Aose felt mildly envious as he gulped down the last of his can of beer.

Your job is building houses, right, Daddy?

By the time he was Hinako's age – no, probably even before that – Aose had dreamed of becoming an architect. He'd found a tattered book in the school library with pictures of representative styles of architecture from around the world. He never got tired of looking at them, and he often used to sneak the book home with him. The photos inspired him to draw his own sketches of buildings. In his renderings, even the dull barracks where his family lived were transformed into a great palace, big enough to keep an elephant or a giraffe. His sisters would tease him about them, while his mother would laugh and tell him how much she'd love to live in a place like that.

44

As he moved up to junior high, his passion for architecture only grew stronger. He would never forget his surprise when he found a photo of Fallingwater in a bookstore in town. Designed for the Kaufmann family by Frank Lloyd Wright, one of the greatest architects of the twentieth century, the mansion straddles a waterfall on a hillside of dazzling greenery. 'Fusion and harmony with nature'. He remembers the caption on the photo. However, to the young Minoru Aose, it looked as if the house and its human inhabitants were conquering the power of nature. It was such a rush.

His reaction also showed clear aspects of his father's influence. Dam construction was also a suppression of nature's forces: flood control; power supply; the securing of water resources. Back in those days, when the whole of Japan desperately needed a better infrastructure, Aose's father, as a specialist form-setter, was on the front lines of this project, challenging Mother Nature head on. He was a hero to his young son, and Aose was always begging to ride on his shoulders. Sitting on the sturdy frame of his father, gazing at the soon-to-be-completed dam, the young boy also felt like a hero.

'A dam is like the hand of a god. It collects every single drop of rain or snow that falls on the mountains, and quenches everyone's thirst.'

Aose took the entrance exam for the architecture department of a technical high school. His father seemed to think it was a training school for carpenters, because on the day his son was accepted to the school, he drank saké to celebrate, saying, 'Great job! I'll buy you a good saw.'

Aose found he couldn't join in with his mother's and sisters' laughter. For the first time in his life, he'd felt pity for his father, who knew nothing of the world beyond manual labour. He was a man who spent his whole life either on the job site or in those cramped living quarters. Aose was ready to fly the coop. Becoming an architect had ceased to be a dream and had become an attainable goal. He couldn't wait to start learning.

He immersed himself in the study of drafting and surveying. Soon after entering his final year, he won a prize in a national competition for high school students. It was a proposal for a low-rise apartment complex that incorporated the tranquil scenery of a suburban setting. It was an idea that had come to him as he pondered how to make the tiny sardine-can workers' accommodation more liveable. His work had already caught the eye of one of the teachers, himself a licensed architect. This teacher would always praise Aose's draughts but also his designs. He taught Aose that you couldn't become an architect without a love of drawing. Aose felt gratitude towards the parents who had bought him unlimited art supplies when he was a child, as well as the children of the various mountain villages for always refusing to play with him.

Aose flipped the pages of *Top 200 Homes*. He'd never really looked at it properly before. The photos managed to say far more than the captions or explanatory notes. Self-confidence; defying challenges; honour and reputation; pushing limits – each one of the works expressed the heart of its creator. He took a deep breath and turned to the Y Residence. His eye was caught immediately by the sloping sky-blue roof. And then he didn't need to look further; right away, everything came back to life for him. The three oval-shaped skylights that he'd nicknamed 'chimneys of light' equally spaced across the length of the roof. He'd painstakingly designed them to combine the functions of skylights and dormer windows. By incorporating highly permeable polycarbonate material and carefully adjusting the screw-shaped reflector, it meant that while the north light would enter directly into the room by the windows, light from other sources was reflected off the curved surface inside the chimneys and distributed across the ceiling and walls.

He closed his eyes and shut the book.

'Someday I'm going to build my own house.' As a young, spotty-faced kid, he had already decided this. The desire had been alive in him, but Yoshino had said the magic words that had let him put them into reality. He knew now that the choices of a north-facing house and a wooden house had been inevitable. He hadn't grown up seeing only the good and heroic side of dam construction. He also remembered the rich, green forests before they were blasted out of the earth. His father would apologetically show him homes, fields and little stone bridges that were about to be swallowed up by a huge man-made lake. Everything that Aose had seen in his migratory years was indelibly there in his memory. The landscape of a hometown that he had always believed hadn't existed for him was packaged and rolled up in the north light and had transcended time. After losing his wife and child he'd also lost sight of his own heart and had been wandering in the dark for years. Yoshino's request had been light to his soul; he'd been able to unroll with great trepidation the package that contained his past world, and finally he'd realized that there was no longer any need to envy or reject Yukari's world.

Aose glanced at the wall clock. It was just before seven thirty. His home phone sat in the darkness on a side table by the wall; his mobile sat ready and waiting on the table in front of him.

What's happened to you?

As he said the words out loud, suddenly a picture of the youngest Yoshino child's face popped into his mind and he got a sense of foreboding. The youngest was a boy who had just started primary school. Despite barely having met him, Aose felt as if he knew this boy, simply because he too had two older sisters. On the day of the ground-breaking ceremony for the house, he had called out to the boy as he was fidgeting, half hidden behind his mother, Karie.

'Are you excited about your new home?'

There was no reply, just a pair of eyes that stared up at him. This was a child who had already learned to be suspicious of adults. Aose didn't recall the boy hanging around his father. Perhaps he didn't get on with him very well . . .

It turned eight, then nine, but neither phone rang. Aose didn't move from the sofa. He crushed the beer can slightly and thought about heading back to the convenience store. He turned on the TV, briefly surfed the channels before turning it off again.

Was Karie out too? And what about the kids? The two daughters and the son? They should be there at this time. No, no, the wife wouldn't be the one to call Aose back. Yoshino must be working late and hadn't listened to his voicemails yet.

You didn't abandon it, did you?

Suddenly Aose felt faint.

Was it so awful that you had to move out? If that was the case, you should have said something to me earlier.

The moment it turned ten o'clock, Aose found himself staring at the screen of his mobile. He pulled up the number of the Y Residence. He didn't intend to call. If the answerphone was still turned on, that would leave a third record of a call from him. There was nothing urgent and his behaviour would seem really bizarre to them.

The phone rang. It was the landline. The Y Residence's number was still displayed on his mobile screen, so it made him jump out of his seat in horror, as if he had been caught in the commission of some bad deed. His heart began to race, and words of apology for doing whatever it was he could have done flashed through his head.

'This is Aose.'

'Oh, you're there.'

It took him a moment to register that it was the voice of his boss, Okajima.

'Why are you calling me at home?'

His sharp question was met by an equally sharp retort.

'Because you told me you'd be able to find the number when you got home!'

'Ah, sorry, hold on a minute . . .'

Aose put the phone on hold and ran into the next room to grab the shoulder bag that he kept his mail in. He tipped a bunch of postcards on to the floor and scrabbled around until he found the one he was looking for, from Takao Nishikawa. He confirmed that the message contained his new address, home phone and mobile number and took the phone off hold.

Okajima listened to the information and hung up without bothering to thank Aose.

Aose sighed and got to his feet. He threw away the empty beer can and the leftover sushi roll. There was nothing left to do but watch the clock. His mind was running in circles. Was Yoshino home yet? Would he call back? Or was there really no one living in that house up in Shinano-Oiwake?

The silence was eerie and the night view pretty unimpressive – not like Tokyo at all. Around midnight the number of lights diminished drastically. All of a sudden Aose imagined the face of the old woman at the elevator. She stared out of the window, unable to sleep. He had the feeling she was looking at the same night view as he was.

At precisely midnight, Aose hit the call button on his mobile. Even before the other party spoke, the unmistakable sound of loud karaoke music assaulted his eardrums.

'Oh, what's up?'

This time, Okajima's voice was cheerful.

'Thanks for the number,' he continued. 'I called him right away and he agreed to help. He even thanked me for the opportunity.'

'Okajima?' interrupted Aose. 'Can I go on a business trip tomorrow?'

'Where to?'

'Shinano-Oiwake. I want to check something out.'

7

The next morning the weather was clear and sunny.

It was a beautiful day for a drive, but Aose wasn't feeling it. Worse, he had a companion. His boss sat beside him in the passenger seat of the Citroën. During their late-night phone call, Okajima had suggested coming along. Aose had tried to put him off, saying that it was too trivial a matter for the boss to concern himself with, but he'd insisted, saying it wasn't that he was concerned or anything, it was just that he wanted to take another look at the house, at the Y Residence.

The engine seemed in good shape. Okajima asked what route Aose planned to take. He replied that he planned to get on to the Metropolitan Intercity expressway from Iruma interchange, then transfer to the Kan-Etsu expressway and the Joshin-Etsu expressway. There was no need to worry about snow; Aose had called the Karuizawa town office first thing in the morning to confirm that road conditions were good.

'Don't get annoyed if I fall asleep. I drank a little too much last night.'

Okajima tilted his seat back a little. He didn't seem inclined to talk about the public design competition, and Aose didn't feel inclined to ask. Despite being colleagues in the same office, they rarely discussed their work in detail. It was a habit that Aose had acquired during his Akasaka days. In an office packed with forty or so architects, the everyday discussion and exchange of ideas just didn't happen – they tended rather to regard each other with suspicion.

At the first traffic light, Aose decided to double-check.

'It's a long drive. Are you absolutely sure you want to go?'

'Why are you bringing that up now?'

'Well, you seem really busy these days.'

'I told you, I really want to see the amazing Y Residence again.'

He was probably hoping to get inspiration for his competition, Aose thought. He'd seen the Y Residence once when it was completed and the design had stuck with him. But even if that were true, Okajima would never admit it. The inner world of men like Okajima, not yet well known in their field, was complex. Many of them even hesitated to call themselves architects. Some seethed with distorted pride – the intense belief that they were different from all the others, unique. And holding a fierce belief that, without being exclusive and egotistical, you can't design anything. But on the other hand, aware that if you can't recognize the worth and the beauty in someone else's creations, then you no longer have the right to call yourself an architect or even a builder.

Okajima had changed. Aose really felt it.

When he was a student, Okajima had been quite obnoxious. Idle, cocky and the type to sleep around. He opened his first office with money from his parents, and after marriage was lucky that his wife was an insurance salesperson making a good salary. He spent most of his time sitting at a desk with a pipe in his mouth, flipping through architectural magazines. Aose heard from another graduate of their architecture department that Okajima often featured in the newsletter of the local chamber of commerce and industry as an 'up-and-coming architect'. Despite having no actual experience or achievements, he would paint himself as a big shot, brazenly talking about things such as his 'grand design for a vibrant city'.

But in recent years, Okajima had become a completely

different person. To put it bluntly, he had come down to earth. He'd lost a lot of his pretentiousness, he'd earned the trust of many through steady, reliable working habits and he now had an impressive list of contacts. Most surprising to Aose was how he had lost his condescending manner and no longer talked down to people. Although still moody at times, he had become the kind of person anyone could have a normal conversation with. There was one likely explanation: he had suffered just as much as everyone else with the bursting of the economic bubble. Perhaps it was the passing of his parents one after the other, or maybe the fact that he finally had a son of his own. In any case, the old Okajima would never have openly expressed a desire to go and visit something that Aose had created. Whatever his secret ambitions might be, he had become more humble, at least with regard to architecture.

'How's Isso doing?'

Aose kept his eyes on the road as he asked, but he could sense Okajima's face breaking into a smile.

'He's almost too well. Did I show you the photos of our trip to Nagatoro?'

'Not yet. How old is he now?'

'Eleven. He's in sixth grade.'

'Whoa. Already? Other people's children always seem to grow up so quickly.'

'Hinako's in the first year of junior high, right?'

Aose realized that he'd got on to a topic he didn't really want to continue.

'As long as the end-of-year exams don't go too badly, she'll be a second year soon.'

'They live in Yotsuya, don't they?'

'Yes, how did you know?'

'Eh? You told me once before. In a low-rise apartment building.'

'It's not a fancy place or anything.'

'Do you have much contact with Yukari-san?'

Okajima vaguely knew Yukari, so he sometimes brought up the topic. There was a very organized type from their university days who always planned an annual reunion of the architecture department. Although Aose had dropped out of the course partway, he was still invited, and as plus-ones were welcome, he had taken Yukari several times, hoping that she could do some useful networking. Okajima would often get talking to her, telling her how he and Aose had been the best of friends. He'd make her laugh by telling her a pack of lies. But those days were long gone. The reunion parties had petered out, along with the economy, and a few years later the organized type ended up committing suicide.

'You saw her again this month?'

Okajima had already returned to the topic of Hinako.

'Yesterday.'

'Oh, it was yesterday? How did it go?'

'Well, she seemed to be doing okay, at least.'

'Don't say that. If she's doing okay, that's great.'

'She's a girl. Things can be difficult . . .'

He spoke lightly, but putting it into words made him feel as if he were revealing a huge secret.

'Sure it does. Boys are difficult too. But it's all part of the joy of parenting.'

'Hinako wants to see the Y Residence.'

'Wow, that's great. Are you going to show her?'

'Photos, probably.'

'Why don't you bring her to see the real thing? It's your masterpiece!'

'Not sure it's a masterpiece . . .'

'It's not?'

'Well, I suppose so.'

'Of course it is. You put so much into it.'

'Yeah, well . . .'

53

'You built a house that expressed yourself. You must be pleased with it.'

'Yeah. Kind of.'

'What's going on with you? Why are you acting weird?'

'Well, the problem is, I'm not sure the Yoshinos were satisfied with it.'

'They were just out. Don't worry about it.'

'I'm not worried.'

'Okay, okay, I get it. But there is one thing . . .'

Okajima let his voice taper off.

'What one thing?'

'Huh?'

'Tell me. Now you're the one acting weird.'

Okajima clicked his tongue.

'Well, I'm generalizing, but they do say that an artistic design is not always the most practical for living.'

So the truth was out – Okajima was also feeling anxious about the Yoshinos. It was probably true that he wanted to see the Y Residence again, but he'd also come with his business head on.

'Wake me up when we get there.'

Aose glanced at his boss, who had skilfully managed to avoid any further conversation, and then put his foot on the accelerator.

8

It was almost noon when they exited the Usui Karuizawa inter-change on the Joshin-Etsu expressway. As they drove along the Wamitoge Pass, the view ahead was dominated by the famous towering rocks, the twin peaks of Medake and Odake; symbols of this pass, they were strange to behold. Their brownish surfaces were painfully steep, and they had the effect of adding a layer of unease to the otherwise tranquil landscape.

Aose felt the Citroën's lack of power as he tackled the sinuous mountain pass. Although he'd driven this route many times while supervising the construction project, today it didn't feel familiar. He had never felt back then that the distance from Tokorozawa to Shinano-Oiwake was far.

Aose had the car radio on, and the lunchtime news was report-ing that in some small town a boy had been killed by his step-father. In the passenger seat, Okajima reeked of alcohol. He opened one eye as they passed through a toll booth but otherwise was sound asleep.

They do say that an artistic design is not always the most practical for living.

It looked as if no one was living there.

What kind of architect would imagine that nobody was living in the house he designed? He laughed at the ridiculousness of the idea. Outside the car, a pleasant landscape flowed by where noth-ing bad could ever happen. The road was clear, and there was far less snow piled up on the hard shoulder than he'd been led to believe. When they stopped at a traffic light, Aose could hear a bird singing.

Tsu–tsu–pi, tsu–pi, tsu–pi . . .

He couldn't see it, but it was probably a coal tit. The great tit had a similar call, but the tempo was faster and it sounded more like 'teacher, teacher, teacher'.

As he moved off again, he lowered the driver's side window slightly. The chilled air caressed his cheek. He could hear more birdsong coming from a forest of silver birch trees. A winter bird, the Eurasian siskin. They stayed up there in the countryside until late spring, but their migration season was fast approaching. The call was higher pitched than usual, more urgent sounding, as if the bird was anxious to get on its way.

Aose felt his mind being hijacked by memories of birds and their songs. It was different from nostalgia. It overlapped with Aose's own family's pattern of migration. On his way to and from school, the chorus of birdsong overhead had been like rain falling, sometimes a comforting mist, sometimes pelting him with its malicious chant, 'Dam Kids, Dam Kids!' As he approached the temporary accommodation, the voices would fade away into the distance. As they neared completion, the giant dams that now loomed above the mountains had already swallowed up the woods and forests that had been sanctuaries for all kinds of wild birds.

Aose had once rescued a long-tailed rose finch with an injured wing. It was a lovely bird about fifteen centimetres long, with a white head and a long tail. On his way home from school, he'd found it huddled among the fallen leaves. He couldn't leave it to die so he'd scooped it up gently in his hands and, its heart beating fast from the warmth, had rushed back to the prefab lodgings with it. He'd painted its wounds with a red merbromin solution, and then cut holes in a cardboard box, lining it with straw to make a bed for the bird. Anticipating his family's objections, he'd announced loudly that he was going to care for it because it had been about to die. His mother had said, 'No way!' and when Aose had resisted, she had explained why it wasn't appropriate to keep wild birds. His older sisters had agreed with her. At that time, they were a family of five sleeping in a single bedroom, six tatami mats in size, and a bird was not a welcome addition. Aose's father had been drinking saké and pretending not to hear the conversation. When his mother had knelt down and asked him to please say something, he'd just mumbled, 'Hmmm, guess you're right.' Aose had tried his best to win his father over to his side. He'd promised to take good care of the bird, that he would leave it outside during the daytime. He'd ended by hugging his father tightly and begging him to buy him a birdcage.

A few days later, on his day off, Aose's father had gone to the local town and come back with a birdcage dangling from his hand. Aose had been astonished to see, sitting on the perch inside the cage, a bird with pitch-black feathers. It was a mynah bird.

'Minoru, this bird is much better than that other one,' his father had told him. 'You can teach it to talk.'

Then he'd lowered his voice.

'Migratory birds need to migrate or they will die. They're just like us.'

Aose's father probably just hadn't wanted his son to resent him. Doubtless he'd felt sorry for him, constantly changing schools and never having the chance to make friends. Anyway, this had inspired him to make this impulsive purchase. His mother and sisters were very upset, but Aose's father, looking pleased with himself, had pressed the birdcage to Aose's chest. 'First, give it a name,' he'd said.

Aose had burst into tears. Was it because he hadn't been ready to say goodbye to his rose finch? Was it his father's lack of tact in thinking he could simply replace it? Or was it that his young mind, still not familiar with the concept of grief, had panicked when he heard the phrase, 'They're just like us.'

Despite this, Aose soon became completely smitten with the

mynah bird, whom he named Kyutaro. In fact, his previous passion for the rose finch, which he had vowed to protect even if it meant running away from home, seemed to have flown the coop. He had just a vague memory of a young construction worker by the name of Toshio-san visiting them at their home and promising to mend the damage to its feathers . . .

Looking back, Aose winced at how fickle he had been with his affections, but Kyutaro held a fascination that captured the heart of a young, friendless boy. It learned to say, 'Goodnight', the very first day it joined the family, and by the next it had mastered 'Good morning', 'Hello', 'Welcome back' and 'Minoru'. Kyutaro seemed to be more intelligent than a regular mynah bird. In no time, it had surprised not only Aose's family but also all their neighbours by learning their names and matching them to faces. It mastered a hundred to two hundred words and could even sing the chorus of a popular song. Needless to say, Kyutaro was closest to Aose.

'Minoru-kun, welcome back! How was school?'

If you asked Kyutaro to introduce itself, it would say, 'I'm Kyutaro Aose. I live in the dam complex. Nice to meet you.' It was usually cheerful and mischievous but would occasionally be out of sorts and refuse to look at Aose. It was incredibly human in its moods. Aose's mother and sisters soon forgot they had objected to keeping Kyutaro, and when, two years later, the bird died, the only person who didn't weep for it was Aose's father.

Several years later, long after the family had recovered from the loss of their beloved pet, Aose's father bought another mynah bird. At the time, they were living in workers' lodgings at the Miho dam construction site in Kanagawa prefecture. It was right after Aose's elder sister had got married to a man from Yamanashi. His father was the type who hated sitting down to meals or going out without the whole family together, so perhaps he was attempting to fill the void left by his elder daughter's marriage.

The new mynah bird, which his father named Kuro, didn't

have the abilities or the charisma of Kyutaro. Additionally, Aose was in his final year of high school by now, and was busy preparing for university entrance exams.

'Hey! Minoru Aose-kun!'

The bird would call from its cage by the window and, although it was a distraction from his studies, it was rarely a welcome one.

Kuro would eventually be the cause of his father's death.

After work was finished on the Miho dam, Aose's parents migrated to the construction site of the Kiryu River dam in Gunma prefecture. Aose didn't go with them. The younger of his two sisters had taken a job at a restaurant in Kawasaki city, and he moved in with her. His exams were close and he needed a good library to study in. It would have been impossible to commute all the way from Gunma. Aose asked his father to take Kuro with him.

Aose passed the exam for the architecture department at his first-choice university and moved into a cheap flat in Tokyo. His father's sudden death came two years later. Kuro had managed to open the door of its cage and had flown away. While searching for the bird in a nearby wooded area, Aose's father had fallen off a cliff. His mother called her son, sobbing, but Aose had been unable to really take it in. He was stunned.

It seemed that his father had spent three full days searching for Kuro. Each day he had got up before dawn and gone into the woods, and every evening after work he had walked those mountain paths with a flashlight in his hand.

'Minoru will be heartbroken,' he would say. It didn't matter how many times Aose's mother assured him that their son would be fine with it, Aose's father didn't listen. On the evening of the third day, right before he left home, he had said, 'I just can't face Minoru.' Those had been the last words he ever spoke.

The funeral was hurriedly arranged, and the official forty-nine days mourning period passed in the blink of an eye. One day, Aose was walking along the path that led to the Kiryu River dam. The sun had just set and the whole area was enveloped in darkness. It was impossible to make out the path any longer, let alone the surroundings. Imagining his father stumbling along the path, calling Kuro's name into the pitch-black night, Aose's tears wouldn't stop. He had grown up in the care of his father. He had watched those muscular shoulders as he worked, and been protected by those great strong arms. It was his father who had taught him the names of all the flowers and trees and birds. No son had ever been cherished more. Why hadn't he gone with his dad to Gunma prefecture? He could have studied for his exams in the prefab lodgings. He should have spent longer with him, at least until he started university. He was sure that was what his dad had really hoped for. To have migrated with the whole flock intact . . .

The steering wheel vibrated more strongly. Aose glanced at Okajima in the seat next to him, then looked back out at the road, blinking several times in the sunlight. The road stretched straight ahead.

Six months later, Aose had dropped out of university. It wasn't for financial reasons. After his father's death he had taken a part-time job at an architect's firm in Akasaka. He was only supposed to be an errand boy, but his boss had spotted him reading a biography of Le Corbusier during his breaks and this had turned out to be his lucky break. The boss was a self-taught, hard-working type, one who never stopped talking, and he happened to love Le Corbusier. He took Aose under his wing and in his spare time taught him the principles of architecture. He seemed particularly impressed by all the questions that Aose would ask, and took quite a shine to the young man. Aose would be invited to accompany his boss on his tours of the firm's various construction sites. This proved such an excellent practical learning experience that university lectures began to feel like a waste of time. Aose was fascinated by the technique of 'pilotis', reminiscent of Le Corbusier's methods. The design style, in which the first floor of a building is raised up on pillars, leaving the ground level open to the air, was very forward-looking for its time.

Aose started to drift away from campus, and his credits were soon in jeopardy, but by that time he could no longer suppress his eagerness to get started on his working journey. On receiving assurance of a probationary period from the architecture firm, he officially withdrew from the university. He thought how his father would be pleased by that. Even at the lowest rank in the company, he was free to take whatever drawing board was available and work hard on his designs. He was eager to absorb whatever he could, aspiring to become a master of steel, glass and concrete – which his boss referred to as the 'three sacred elements'.

Kee, kee, kee.

That sound like metal scraping stone was the distinctive cry of the Daurian redstart, and it caused Aose to ease off on the accelerator pedal. He was surprised to hear its call at this time of year at such a high altitude. Normally, the redstart was to be found in suburban parks and back gardens until the early spring. Smaller than a sparrow, this was the first wild bird that had taken Yukari's fancy.

'Hey, does a strawberry finch look a bit like a redstart?'

Shortly after they were married, she had suddenly asked Aose if they could keep a strawberry finch. When he'd hesitated, admitting that he wouldn't be able to stand it when the bird died, Yukari had snorted, 'Whose fault is it that I'm a bird otaku now – a total geek?'

This was a typical lead-in to her recollection of the time they'd visited Shinjuku Gyoen Park shortly after they'd begun dating. Aose had correctly guessed five or six different bird calls and Yukari would say that it was the moment she'd decided she was going to marry this man.

Yukari soon became busy in her job and no longer had any spare time to think about keeping a bird. Then Hinako was born, and when their daughter was about two, Yukari had gone ahead and bought a pair of budgerigars without consulting Aose. Although there was friction between them over the topic of building their own home, they weren't actually quarrelling about it at that point. Their relationship was very good, and the glue between them was Hinako, who was growing cuter by the day. Or was it only Aose who thought things were fine . . . By this point, Yukari was no longer talking about building a house. It must have been Aose who made her stop. Now Aose understood Yukari's feelings – her desire to harness the power of the love birds. She might have changed her mind from strawberry finch to budgerigars when she remembered Aose's stories of Kyutaro and Kuro, deliberately choosing a variety that could talk. Yukari being Yukari, she may have been trying to use her imagination to put herself in Aose's shoes and understand some of the workings of his mind, slowly created over years by his history of migration.

The lively Pippi, and somewhat skittish Pico became great playmates for the young Hinako. Pippi could remember simple words, and whenever the bird called her Hina-chan the little girl would jump up and down in delight and rub her cheek against the bird's yellow-green feathers. When Aose moved out after the divorce was finalized, he didn't even think about taking the budgerigars. Yukari pleaded with him to take them. It would be too hard on Hinako to hear Pippi say 'Daddy' every morning and evening. He was on the point of replying that maybe Hinako could keep Pico, who didn't talk, but the irony of separating a pair of love birds caused the words to stick in his throat.

Within a month of moving into his new apartment, Aose released the birds into a local park. What Yukari had feared would happen to Hinako had happened to him. Pippi never forgot how to say 'Mummy' and 'Hina-chan'. He could tolerate 'Mummy', but every time he heard 'Hina-chan', all the feelings that he thought he had under control came bubbling up again.

He'd be sitting in a quiet room, fearing the moment that Pippi might decide to speak again. He couldn't bring himself to give the birds away to someone else, because all the memories and secrets they held belonged to his family.

Released from their cage, the tame pair of love birds fluttered their wings weakly and soon found a perch in a nearby ginkgo tree. They remained there, huddled together, motionless. He felt a fierce pang of guilt. Not only had he torn these two birds away from Hinako, as if uprooting something from her life, he had now sacrificed their little lives to a winter they would not survive. He approached the ginkgo tree and called out, 'Pippi! Pico!' in turn, but the birds didn't stir. They stayed on their perch until it turned dark. And they never returned to the apartment; in fact, by the next morning, they were gone.

He wasn't sure how Yukari had managed to contrive it, but Hinako never once mentioned the names of Pippi or Pico in front of Aose. She must have cried her eyes out when he first took the birds, but in the eight years since she had never brought them up once.

'Are you trying that old trick?'

The voice came from the passenger seat.

'That's what taxi drivers do to wake up their drunk passengers.'

Okajima was referring to the cold air blowing on him from the open window. The car was on Route 18 now and, according to the dashboard thermometer, the outside temperature was 2°C.

'It probably works just as well for a hangover,' Aose said, grinning and rolling the window back up.

'Are we there yet?' said Okajima, stretching.

'Almost.'

'What shall we do for lunch?'

'Let's get something after we've seen it.'

'Yes, on the way back, of course,' Okajima agreed. 'Seeing as we're here, why don't we get some soba at Kagimoto-ya?'

'Sounds good.' Kagimoto-ya was a famous old soba shop in front of Naka-Karuizawa station. Back when the Y Residence was under construction, Yoshino-san had invited Aose there, and he'd been back many times since.

'You seem to know the area well,' he remarked to Okajima.

Okajima nodded proudly.

'When I was a student, I came up here a lot, researching country homes. The Y Residence is just by one of those stone monuments, isn't it?'

'Yes, there's a slight right turn.'

'I remember now. By that Sherlock Holmes statue?'

'Just up ahead.'

Aose stared ahead as he spoke. They were already in Shinano-Oiwake. If he didn't pay attention, he would miss the route marker standing at the corner of the Hokkoku Kaido and Nakasendo routes.

'Oops, there it is – Holmes.'

'Ha! Should I call you Watson?'

Aose laughed as he slowed down and turned the wheel. The surroundings still had the feel of an old-fashioned tourist town. Passing the statue of Sherlock Holmes on the right, Aose drove a short distance further, then turned on to a road leading north. Now they were in an area crowded with resort or recreational facilities owned by various companies and universities. The engine revved as they began to climb, and the buildings thinned out until both sides of the road were covered with woodland. The top of Mount Asama peeked out above the trees, and then it came into sight. Aose felt his neck and shoulders tense up. It was the first time he had seen the Y Residence in four months. There was the trapezoidal blue roof open to the sky and the three 'chimneys of light' protruding from it. Okajima leaned forward from his seat.

'Those three chimneys are certainly eye-catching. They make it look more like a luxury liner than a house.'

'You think so?'

'They raved about it in *Top 200 Homes*. They say you've created an original structure that sends light in four directions and still somehow manages to prevent snow from accumulating.'

'Well, I had to. They get quite a bit of snow around here. The cross-section of each chimney is teardrop-shaped with the narrow end of the tear to the north.'

'It's a design that would make a roofer weep.'

'He really did cry. It cost a lot of money too.'

'They say it fills the whole place with north light,' said Okajima. 'Hailed it as an invention on a par with the sawtooth roof.'

'That's what I hear.'

'That's a lot of bay windows.'

'They were necessary.'

'Let's see . . . "The combination of the diagonal walls and bay windows with their abundant direct light is a truly brilliant touch."'

'Is that another quote from *Top 200 Homes*?' asked Aose.

'Yep. You must have read it, surely?'

'I glanced at it.'

'Those wooden decks like a kind of open veranda?'

'It was modelled after a traditional *engawa*. It goes almost all around the house.'

'And the white part – is that stucco?'

'The parts that won't get rained on.'

'You used pine bark to decorate the lower exterior walls?'

'To decorate? No. It's for thermal protection.'

'Hmm. It's somehow Japanese style yet not traditional at all. Nor is it western style, or even a mixture of the two. It has an intriguing kind of global feel.'

He could tell that his boss was impressed. There was no sign of amusement, nor a wink in Okajima's eyes.

They were rapidly approaching the house. There were no other buildings in the vicinity, nor had any landscaping work been done around the exterior, so the house itself was revealed in all its glory. Was the Yoshino family there or not? Aose felt his heart begin to pump faster. Okajima stuck his head out of the car window.

'It really is rather eccentric. I mean, it makes me want to own one, and yet . . .'

Aose stepped hard on the brakes, silencing Okajima.

His eyes and his ears were on the alert, searching for signs of life in the Y Residence or anywhere around it.

9

The gravel crunched under their feet. Standing in front of the house, Aose felt a cold sweat break out on his forehead. There was no car in the parking space, and the ruts left by the wheels were dry. The living room curtains were closed, and it seemed the same went for all the rooms on the ground and upper floors.

'Looks like the Urawa woman was right.'

Okajima's tone was so nonchalant that Aose turned and gave him an evil look.

'You mean that no one's living here?'

'I mean that they're using it as a holiday home.'

But this just riled Aose more.

'Then they would have said so when they asked me to design it!'

The nameplate on the gate was blank, but an architect didn't need to check that to know whether a house was occupied or not.

'What's going on?'

Okajima looked perturbed. He rang the doorbell but, getting no reply, started to walk around the west side of the house.

Aose followed. An image flashed through his mind of the Yoshinos, a memory from the day they had officially taken possession of the house. They had bowed deeply to him as he'd handed them the keys.

Aose and Okajima made a full circuit of the house and returned to the front door. Curtains and blinds were all drawn on the north, west and east windows, so it was impossible to see inside.

The exterior had no visible clothes line or laundry pole; there were no bicycles under the eaves. The electric meter was running, but ever so slowly, and certainly there was not enough power being consumed to run a household. There probably wasn't even a refrigerator plugged in.

'They've moved out!' blurted Okajima.

But Aose had a different take.

'I'd say they never moved in in the first place.'

He knew that Touta Yoshino had been making preparations to move in. At the time of the official handover, Aose knew that he had completed all the paperwork for the utilities — electric, gas, and water — and that a propane gas cylinder had been delivered to the back of the property. Okajima's assessment of the situation would normally have been accurate — the family had moved in but then moved out again. However, the house still looked brand new.

Aose pulled out his phone and called a number. A moment later, they heard the sound of a phone ringing inside the house, then the same answer machine as the previous day picked up. Aose hung up and called Touta Yoshino's mobile. This had the same result as the previous day — it didn't even connect to an answering service.

'Where was the client from originally?' Okajima asked.

'Tokyo. But that number is already disconnected.'

Aose stuck his phone back in his pocket. His fears had become reality — the Yoshino family wasn't living in this house.

'Aose?' Okajima's tone was high-pitched. 'Come and check this out.'

He was pointing at the front-door lock. Aose came closer to look. It was covered in scratches — and not only the lock itself. The wood all around was damaged with heavy marks, the work of something like a screwdriver. A burglar. Instinctively, Okajima tried the door handle, and with a click the door swung open. At once there was fear in his expression.

'Should we call the police?' he said.

'Let's look inside.'

Because it's my house. That lingering sense of ownership pushed Aose to make an on-the-spot decision.

'No, that's a really bad idea,' said Okajima. 'We've no idea what we might find in there.'

The expression on his face said he was expecting to find the whole family slaughtered in their beds.

'We won't know until we look,' Aose retorted.

'Wait! Just a minute. What line of work is the client in?'

'Well, he isn't involved in illegal moneylending, if that's what you mean.'

'Give me a serious answer.'

'He's an imported-goods wholesaler.'

'Let's give his company a call.'

'I don't have the number.'

'You don't know—'

'How about you? Do you ask all your customers for their business cards?'

Building your own home was a deeply private matter. Clients never invited their architect to meet them at work.

'How about the company name? I'll look up the number.'

'Leave it, would you?'

Aose spoke sharply, pushed Okajima away and opened the door. The aroma of Japanese cypress caressed his nose. Even before the door was fully open, he could see the *genkan* with its pool of pale light and the mosaic tiled area for taking off shoes. There were pieces of paper scattered underfoot – usage notices for electricity and water, evidently dropped from the mailbox on the door. It seemed that the interior box that was supposed to catch the mail had been dismantled and dumped on top of the shoe cupboard.

'That doesn't look good.'

Okajima bent to look at the hallway floor. Visible through a thin layer of dust were shoeprints heading down the corridor into the house. They looked like the pattern on the sole of athletics shoes. And there was not just one set of prints; there were enough to belong to two or three people.

'Look, I think we'd better call the police.'

'There's no proof it's burglars.'

'Burglars would be the best possibility at this point. It could be kidnappers, or even bomb-makers.'

'Surely it makes sense to call the police *after* we've checked it out?'

Aose opened the shoe cupboard. It was empty. Not a single pair of shoes in it.

'Hey, Aose—'

'It could be the clients' shoeprints,' said Aose.

'I seriously doubt it.'

Ignoring Okajima's frightened tone, Aose bent down and took off his own shoes.

'Are you crazy?' said Okajima. 'They could still be inside.'

Aose stepped up on to the wooden floorboards of the hallway. It was true that the whole situation was a bit creepy, but right now his anger outweighed every other emotion. This house that he had lovingly designed and built had been left vacant, and now a bunch of strangers had invaded it with their muddy shoes still on.

Aose turned on the hallway light, and immediately the recessed downlights cast a warm glow over everything. The shoeprints became more clearly visible, heading straight towards the living room.

A jaybird cawed loudly just outside the house. Okajima gave a little shriek and covered his head.

'Was that a bird?'

'Don't worry. Crows or ravens are the evil omens.'

Aose continued walking towards the living room. He could feel soil and dust on the soles of his feet along with the smooth feel of the wood flooring.

'Don't tread on the footprints,' whispered Okajima from close behind him. 'And be careful. They might still be in here somewhere.'

Aose ignored his boss and opened the living room door, but then for the first time he hesitated. Okajima stopped too, cowering right behind him. The carpeted living room was bare. There were no chairs, no sofa, no tables or TV set. Besides the light fixtures and curtains that had come with the house, there were no ornaments or decorations of any kind. There was just one object sitting there in the middle of the room, directly on the carpet, with its red voicemail light blinking. A telephone.

'Do you think the burglars took everything?' whispered Okajima.

'Is that what it looks like?'

It seemed the burglars' footprints had stopped when they reached the living room carpet. They'd headed instead to the adjacent dining room. Aose believed that there had never been anything in here to steal in the first place. He turned on the light and examined the carpet surface more closely. If this house had ever been occupied, the legs of the sofa or tables or other furniture would have left indentations in the pile of the carpet. But there was no trace of anything. There was no longer any doubt in Aose's mind – the Yoshino family had never moved into this house. They hadn't brought in so much as a television set, so it was safe to say that they had never had plans to use the house as a holiday home either.

Aose looked up at the three massive tubes jutting down from the high, open ceiling. As calculated, the north light made the off-white diatomite walls look much whiter. All this space he'd painstakingly created was now somehow unpalatable to his clients? It was baffling to him and, frankly, illogical. He couldn't think of a single reason why a client would fail to move into their long-awaited, brand-new house and leave it sitting unoccupied for four whole months. Perhaps he shouldn't be looking for a reason but instead some kind of unavoidable circumstance?

71

He shook his head and turned towards the dining area. There was a large circular table and five dining chairs – furniture that Aose had given his clients as a gift for their new home. Apparently, the intruders had not even touched them. Admittedly, the table was supported by a thick log that was permanently fixed to the floor. Aose had employed an expert craftsman to create it for him in the image of the low wooden tables his family used back in their prefab lodging days. He felt that the fun of sitting around the table for dinner with his family was in part due to its circular shape – everyone was sitting either next to or opposite someone else. The image of the Yoshino family, also a family of five, sitting around this table in a lively atmosphere had stimulated Aose's desire to design the house. 'A home you would want to live in' did not mean, of course, the home you would live in alone. A house and a family are inseparable. And yet this house had yet to hear the sound of a happy family.

Aose felt a sudden tightness in his chest.

'Okajima?'

'What?'

'Do you think this place is impractical to live in?'

'What are you talking about? Let's just get this over with.'

Okajima was already in the kitchen. The cupboard doors hung open, but there were no dishes in sight. There was no refrigerator, no sponges or washing-up detergent on the sink. And yet the water and gas were connected. The island drawer was half open and someone had pulled out a pile of manuals for the hot water, the dishwasher and other utilities. Mixed in among them was a key with a tag that read 'back door'. Even though such a key was apparently unnecessary for burglars to gain entry, Aose decided it wasn't a good idea to leave it lying around, so he snatched it up and shoved it into his trouser pocket.

The utility space was empty, without so much as a washing machine. In the bathroom and the toilet there was nothing – not even a bar of soap. All the cupboards in the bathroom were closed, as if there'd been nothing worth ransacking.

They continued along the corridor, which was built in a semi-circle and looped back towards the front door. By now Aose could recognize the different shoeprints and he could tell that there had been two intruders. Only one of the trails led upstairs. He could imagine the conversation between the two: 'I'll check upstairs, just in case.' He said something similar to Okajima and headed up. The spiral staircase was an ingenious way of allowing more light distribution to the corners of the room, as was the construction of alcoves and intricate recesses – all to create dramatic lighting effects. In that sense, the Y Residence could also be called a 'house that marks the passage of time'.

He looked around the three children's rooms. They were empty shells. Not even a study desk. Every room had its own loft, but only one room had a perfect rectangular shape, due to the trapezoidal house structure. He'd been concerned that there might have been a fight over it, but it had turned out to be a moot point after all.

He stared for a moment or two at the master bedroom door, then pushed it open. The curtains were drawn and it was dim inside the room. As the intruders must also have concluded by this point, Aose didn't expect to find anything inside. And that was why when his eyes fell on the old, well-used chair in the centre of the room he didn't immediately register it as out of place. Apart from the telephone downstairs, this was the sole object in the house that must have been brought in by the Yoshinos. It was a simple wooden chair with armrests, placed so it faced the window. It was a period piece, its back and seat made of slatted wood which had warped slightly. However, there was nothing poorly constructed about it. It was a good-quality chair, that much Aose could tell.

'Hey! What's going on?' Okajima called from below.

'Nothing!' Aose called back, then entered the walk-in

wardrobe. All of the drawers had been pulled out, exposing the unfinished wood inside, and there were muddy footprints on the floor here too.

Aose let out a long breath. He no longer cared about the burglars.

He went over to the window and did what he had been longing to do from the moment he'd entered this room. The window was oversized for a Japanese house, reaching from around chest height right up to the eaves. A north-facing window. He pulled on the cords and the curtain opened. Light entered the room; not rays, nor a flood, but a delicate veil of light that gently enveloped the entire space.

During construction of the house, Aose would stand in that spot, marvelling at the magnificent panorama. There was nothing as impressive as that view of Mount Asama up close. Its silvery-white peak with gently rolling clouds was close to divine. But the true star of this room, one that was superior even to the view, was the north light itself. Right now, in that very moment, the window was not so much a picture frame to accentuate the painting beyond but a gateway of light.

Aose's father used to say the sun should be treated as a treasured guest and welcomed into a house. Hearing that Yoshino's wife, Karie, had a talent for painting had sparked an idea in Aose's mind about dormant light. While Aose was visiting the family at their rental apartment in Tabata, his eye had been caught by a small oil painting on the living room wall. Karie had blushed when he complimented her on the beautifully depicted still-life of hydrangeas in a vase. Her husband had explained, teasingly, that she had been leader of the art club in high school, and that she still enjoyed painting whenever the children were out of the way. Aose was aware that the creation of skylights or high windows to allow north light to fall had been a popular practice in artist's studios for a long while. That was because it created the best natural-light environment for painting and sculpture.

'I'd like to design the master bedroom in the style of an artist's atelier, and then you could use it for your hobby when the children fly the nest someday.'

Aose's proposal had delighted not only Karie but also Touta Yoshino, who said he would love it if she would do that, but at the same time, he had also uttered the magic words: 'I want an architect by the name of Minoru Aose to build a house he would like to live in. Please don't worry about us.'

'Don't worry about me either,' Aose had replied. 'I've always wanted to build that house – a home that is open to the light, that really welcomes it in . . .'

Had that been no more than a daydream?

Reality was before his eyes. The Yoshino family had disappeared without trace, leaving behind no clue.

No, not quite . . .

Aose turned to look at the chair behind him. A single chair, facing the window. Why had this object been placed in that position? Well, to sit. It wasn't difficult to imagine Touta Yoshino sitting in that chair. Carrying it upstairs, placing it in the middle of the room, sitting, and then, of course, looking out of the window at the view—

He walked over to the chair. It really was quite old. He wondered if he could sit on it, whether it might break under his weight. Very carefully, he lowered himself on to the seat. The mountain and the clouds disappeared from view, and the window became a bright blue sky in a giant picture frame. Aose felt dizzy. It was a peculiar sensation – that blueness. It was no longer a view, or a space. It was just blue. He'd lost his sense of perspective; he had the feeling of being sucked in. The sensation wasn't unpleasant. It was like a sense of nostalgia – something he had seen sometime, somewhere. Or perhaps like looking down at the earth from outer space, beautiful, liberating; his heart felt free.

The chair itself amazed him by how comfortable it was. His whole back felt right at home. Unlike most wooden chairs, it didn't feel hard and there was no pressure on his spine or tailbone. He leaned back and realized after a few moments that what he had originally thought to be warping of the slats in the back and seat was in fact deliberate flexion, a kind of spring or even elasticity. The chair had been built to bend to a person's weight. Aose discovered this secret by feeling around with his fingertips and discovering that the seat and the main body of the chair weren't connected by nails or screws; they were fastened together with copper wire. The armrests, too, were ingenious. They sloped slightly forwards, allowing the sitter to rest their elbows and allow their arms to hang loosely downwards.

It was a comfortable yet somehow unassuming chair, allowing a person to forget its existence and float in that enchanting blue sky.

When he closed his eyes, there was still blue sky. He could see the carp streamers that swam in the air in celebration of Children's Day. At the Shimokubo dam lodgings, his mother and father had sewn together rice sacks to make them. The Girls' Day dolls had also been handmade by his mother. He and his sisters rarely asked his parents to buy anything for them. He was always surrounded by simple things, with warmth and texture, for example, the scent of plum blossoms. He used to walk to school down a slope that was lined with plum trees. His sisters would take it in turns to hold his hand.

At Nakawado dam he had walked along to the rhythm of a ropeway. *Click clack, click clack*. It was a cable for transporting timber; the logs crawled up the mountain alongside him. The local school was a tiny one, with primary and junior high school combined, and no more than about ten pupils per school year. One time a rock slide blocked the route to school and everyone had to study at home for almost six months. When the family moved to Zao dam, Aose had tasted pears for the first time. They were so delicious that he wrote an essay about them for school. He dug up mountain lilies and evening primrose and planted them under the window of their prefab. Winter was hard – he had to walk about two kilometres every day through snow that was sometimes waist deep. The water supply in their accommodation used to freeze up, and he'd go down to the stream with his father, break the ice and fill buckets with hands numb from cold. On the way home, the buckets were so heavy that he thought his arms would fall off. His father would pat him on the head and say, 'Great job, Minoru! You're so strong I think you're going to turn into Ultra Man.' They stored the water in barrels in the prefab. Aose used to drink the water that stunk of wooden barrels, and long for spring to arrive. Kyutaro the mynah bird used to hate the barrel water. 'Stinky, stinky. Give me juice,' it would whine, which would crack everyone up.

Okajima was calling him again.

The light had been a rare and valued guest at the Yahagi dam, where the workers' lodgings were at the foot of a V-shaped valley. There, the sun would rise at 10 a.m. and set at 3 p.m. In the morning, the mountainsides would be tinged red with the morning sun, but after midday they were already blue-black. Flocks of crows would turn the sky to a seething black blizzard. Aose would spend the long, sunless afternoon playing cards with his sisters. The mere five hours of north light they got each day was precious to them.

'Hey! Where are you? Answer me, at least.'

Okajima appeared, moving rather more cautiously than his chiding tone would have suggested.

'What are you doing, lounging around here?'

'I'm not lounging – what are you talking about?' Aose retorted, getting to his feet.

Okajima peered nervously into the walk-in wardrobe.

'Anything in here?'

'Nothing. Just this.'

Okajima turned his gaze on the chair.

'You didn't put this in here for them?'

77

'Not me.'

'So, the client brought it here?'

'Unless it was the burglars.'

'That's not funny.'

But the frown quickly disappeared from Okajima's forehead.

'Hey, that chair! It couldn't be—'

As he spoke, he crouched down to get a closer look. Then he reached out and touched it.

'What's up?' said Aose.

Okajima looked up at him.

'This is one of Taut's chairs!'

'Taut? You mean Bruno Taut?'

Okajima threw him a scornful look.

'Do you know any other Taut?'

Bruno Taut was a German architect who had fled his home country in the 1930s to escape Nazi persecution, and he'd come to Japan. He was famous for having 'rediscovered' the beauty of the design of the Katsura Imperial Villa and had been an important figure in the promotion of Japanese traditional design as well as artefacts and crafts. That was the extent of Aose's knowledge, as, when he was a student, he'd devoted himself almost exclusively to the study of Le Corbusier and Josiah Conder. To him, Taut was just one of the names listed in the chronology of modern architectural history. The main reason for the shallowness of the impression left by Taut was that the German had had few opportunities to demonstrate his architectural skill in Japan. Conder, on the other hand, during his stay in Japan had designed such renowned buildings as the Rokumeikan, Nicolai Hall and the Iwasaki Residence.

Nevertheless, the key phrase 'Taut's chair' had rung a bell in Aose's mind. He had heard a story somewhere before . . .

'Is it the sort of thing you could get in an antiques shop?' he asked.

Okajima dismissed the idea.

'Of course not. Every piece by him is carefully managed.'

'So you're saying that this chair is a fake?'

'Well, that would make sense, but from what I can see this looks like the real thing.'

Okajima was totally serious. He sat himself down in the chair.

'Have you seen the real thing?' said Aose.

'I've sat in one.'

A tinge of pride entered his voice.

'It was at a house in Atami – the sort-of-famous Hyuga Villa. Some company owns it now, and until a few years ago they used it as a recreation centre. When Taut was in Japan, a businessman asked him to renovate the residence, and Taut apparently designed all the furnishings himself. I went there right after I graduated from university and a set of these chairs was in the hall, I think – yeah, and they were really comfortable, too, just like this.'

Aose began to recall the story. He'd read in a newspaper somewhere that chairs designed by Bruno Taut had been discovered after being lost for decades. He'd skimmed the story without much interest.

Now, he prodded the chair back with the tip of a finger.

'If this is the real thing, then how did it get here?'

'Hmm . . .' Okajima became thoughtful. 'If the client brought it here, then he might have some connection with Taut.'

Aose nodded vaguely. Just like the question of why the Yoshino family was not here, this seemed to be another unfathomable mystery.

'So, what should we do now?' said Okajima, getting to his feet. The anxious expression had returned to his face.

'As we planned – go for lunch.'

Okajima looked shocked.

'Aren't we going to contact the police?'

'Nothing's been stolen.'

'What are you on about? It's a genuine case of house-breaking.'

'If you're going to get technical about it, we've done the same thing.'

'Listen seriously for a moment. The front door lock was broken!'

'We can just call a locksmith and get it fixed.'

'You—'

'I just hate getting mixed up in anything.'

Aose spoke firmly. He had started to feel sorry for this poor house without an occupant. It would be so much worse if the police came and tramped through it; then it would acquire something of a shady reputation.

Okajima was silent for a moment, apart from the long, very pointed sigh he expelled. Then he began to speak again.

'Apart from the burglars, shouldn't we be telling the police about the missing owner?'

'You saw the footprints, didn't you? It was just some thieves sneaking around. There was no sign of a struggle with the householder. The Yoshinos never moved in. If there's any need to look into it, I'll do it myself.'

'How are you going to do that?'

'I suggest we discuss it at the soba restaurant.'

'Don't get snippy, Aose.'

'You're the one who's acting all out of character. Not yourself. All of a sudden, you're behaving like some kind of responsible middle-class citizen.'

Okajima's mouth twitched.

'I'm just trying to be the voice of reason here.'

'Oh, so there's a different level of reason depending on whether you graduate from uni or drop out?'

'Hey, stop inventing complexes where they don't exist.'

'Then it must be the difference in responsibility between the boss and the employee. Let's go. Seriously, let's get out of here.'

'You want to leave this chair sitting here? Until the locksmith gets here, this gives anyone free rein to come in and steal it.'

'You suggest we take it with us? Then we really would be burglars.'

'But it could be Taut's chair!'

'It may well be, but to a common thief it's nothing but a worthless piece of junk.'

In the end, they compromised by shutting it in the walk-in wardrobe.

'Don't bump it, just in case . . .'

Okajima treated the chair with meticulous care.

Aose went out of the master bedroom before Okajima, but when his boss didn't follow him, he went back in to look for him. Okajima was standing in front of the large picture window, staring out. It was a long while before he even stirred.

'Well, I suppose it's a blessing that they didn't set it on fire,' he muttered as they descended the stairs.

It sounded as if he was referring to more than Taut's chair.

10

It was long past lunchtime, and there were hardly any customers in Kagimoto-ya. Aose and Okajima ordered the speciality, hand-made soba noodles with seasonal tempura, and as a matter of courtesy for a while made sure that nothing but the sound of slurping was heard.

Before going to lunch, they had contacted a locksmith, who said he'd be at the Y Residence by the evening. There was no deliberate intent to deceive, but the man had assumed Aose was the homeowner, and they didn't tell him otherwise. The two men also checked the papers scattered on the *genkan* floor and discovered that the utility bills had been paid regularly. The base rate for electric, gas and water had all been paid by direct debit.

'It means they still plan to live there sometime,' Okajima said, shovelling soba noodles into his mouth. 'And they haven't disconnected the phone line either.'

Aose nodded silently. His stomach felt bloated and he'd lost the will to argue.

'Still,' Okajima continued, 'I'm a little worried that we can't get in touch with the client.'

'Uh-huh.'

'First of all, you should go and get a copy of their residence certificate from the town hall. Check if they have officially moved out of Tokyo yet.'

'Good idea.'

'These days, they won't give it out to just anyone at the

Residents' Affairs division, though. You'll have to go to the Building Guidance division. Do you have any connections there?'

'There might be someone.'

'Right, well, you need to sweet-talk them into going and asking at the Residents' Affairs division. If the family hasn't moved into the Y Residence, then their residents' registration would still be at Tokyo's Kita-ku ward office. Do you know anyone there?'

'I'll check my business cards later.'

'Oh, I just thought, if Matsui is still around, I can get him to do it. Why don't you leave this one to me?' said Okajima.

'Really? That'd be great.'

'And if the authorities won't give us a copy, we'll just have to try the kids' schools. If we hit schools both in Tabata and here, we should be able to find them.'

They'd thought all this up in the car on the way to lunch. But their first port of call was going to be the rental house in Tabata. The phone line may have been disconnected, but that didn't necessarily mean that the family had moved out.

'And, just in case, I'll ask for a copy of the registration certificate for the Y Residence too,' Okajima said. 'I can't imagine the ownership has changed, but I think it's worth checking.'

'Okay, thanks.'

'Hey, are you sure you don't know where he works?'

'I already said so.'

'Okay, okay,' said Okajima before continuing, 'People who work for listed companies will tell you where they work even if you don't ask. Let's see, he's a wholesaler of imported goods? Not one of the biggest ones, then. Trouble is, there are a lot of companies like that in Tokyo—'

'Well, er . . .' Aose interrupted. 'I think he might have quit.'

'What?'

'He was saying something about going out on his own one of these days.'

'Freelance? When?'

'He told me one time that he wanted to go into online business. He was looking into it.'

'You should have told me that before.'

'He was just looking into it. The impression I got was that he wanted to do it somewhere down the line. That's all.'

Okajima brushed that off.

'You mean there's a chance he's already quit and started a mail-order imported-goods business?'

'Possibly.'

'Online shopping, eh? Well, if you're looking for one of those, it might be harder than finding a company.'

'I'm sure it would be.'

'Imported goods is too broad a category. What kind of goods did he deal in?'

'I didn't ask. He said he worked for a company that imported miscellaneous goods. A kind of jack of all trades.'

Okajima rolled his eyes.

'Well, I suppose what we do know is that he's got money, for sure. Enough to go freelance, and to purchase a house outright without a loan. He must be independently wealthy.'

Aose shrugged.

'Nah, I don't think so. The Tabata place was a forty-year-old rented house, and the way they lived was anything but luxurious.'

'So? It's possible to save up. How old is he?'

'He's five years younger than us.'

'Forty? That's pretty young. So, like that couple in Osaka, he must have inherited money from his parents.

'He never mentioned an inheritance.'

'Perhaps the money ran out,' suggested Okajima. 'He started his own company and failed.'

'You mean he's hiding under a cloud of debt?'

'It's possible. Good job we got our fees while he still had funds. Our company's safe.'

'Safe? This is a house that appeared in *Top 200 Homes*. With that big competition coming up, you really don't want any funny rumours flying around.'

Aose had managed to hit on Okajima's true motivation. His boss turned away and laughed, then looked back at Aose.

'The bigger question is, why Shinano-Oiwake?'

'Huh?'

'I mean, why did they want to move out here, from Tokyo to the middle of nowhere? It must be inconvenient both to live and work out here. And tough to raise kids too, I would think.'

Aose had asked Yoshino the same question, albeit casually. Yoshino had replied that he could manage, the company had flexible working conditions, and that once he went freelance he'd be able to work entirely from home. He added that he wanted his children to be raised in a rural environment, pointing out that the primary school was close by and that it would be easy for the girls to commute to junior high school by bicycle. He hadn't been worried about anything.

There had however been something a little gloomy about Yoshino's expression as he spoke about his family's future plans. One of his children, probably the youngest, must have been having problems at his current school — most likely he was being bullied. Aose had come up with this suspicion because of his own daughter's similar problems. There was a time that he had seriously considered that the only way to solve the problem might be to have Hinako change schools.

'I think their priority was to bring their children up in a better environment,' Aose explained to Okajima.

'Their children? Were they being bullied or something?'

'Well, they never said anything specifically, but that was the impression I got.'

'Yeah, the city can be tough on sensitive kids. So you reckon the parents had always wanted to give country life a try, and they decided to go for it?'

85

'I don't think it's that unusual nowadays.'

'Yeah, it's kind of trendy now,' said Okajima, nodding in approval. Then he seemed to drift off into a daze. 'Imported goods and Taut chairs . . . Seem to be related, yet they aren't.'

'Right?'

'I'm really curious how Taut might be connected to all this. Aren't you? You know, I can give you some books on him to read. I have a whole cardboard box full.'

'Yeah, I'd be interested.'

'And you know, if you decide to go to Atami to investigate all this, give me a call. I'll show you around.'

'Ah yes, I'll be needing your help.'

'And if you're going to approach it from the Taut angle, after Atami, you should try Takasaki and Sendai,' Okajima added rapidly. 'You've heard of Senshin-tei, haven't you?'

He put his hand in his breast pocket. His phone was vibrating.

'Ah, hello. Thank you so much for calling. I'm so sorry – I was planning to give you a call this evening when I got home.'

Aose grimaced and indicated with his head that Okajima should take the call outside, but his boss was already out of his seat.

'Oh, really? Hakamada-sensei is there too? I'm honoured.'

Aose's eyes followed the rotund figure of his boss as he disappeared out of the restaurant. The name Hakamada sounded familiar. Okajima had called him *sensei*, so there was no doubt about it. It was a certain influential conservative member of the prefectural assembly.

Aose slurped his buckwheat noodles. His mild disgust at his boss, however, was subsumed by the much stronger current of anger in his chest.

Yoshino.

He realized his fists were clenched. The fierce emotions that he should have been feeling after his break-up with Yukari but which he had been unable to locate (or even been sure if they were really there) had now found a place to erupt.

I can't leave it like this. I have to settle it. I'll find Touta Yoshino and question him as to why he trampled on the dignity of that house. And then, depending on how things turn out—

'Hello there. It's been a while. Welcome back.'

Aose looked up.

An old man, evidently the restaurant owner, was standing on the other side of Aose's table. He had a friendly smile on his face. Aose remembered him from the last time he'd visited, so he took the plunge and asked a question.

'You remember the short man who used to drop in here with me? Did he ever come by after that?'

The old man looked happy. He nodded.

'Yes, I believe he came once.'

He'd been here!

'When was that?'

'Let's see . . . It was last December. No, it was still November.'

Late November? It was 3 November when he'd handed over the house to Yoshino.

'Was he alone, or with his wife and children?'

'Just the two of them. Him and his wife – the tall woman.'

Aose kept a straight face as he thanked the owner.

You could have asked a hundred people. Only a really young child would describe Karie Yoshino as tall.

Twilight turned to night.

The streets of Tokorozawa came into view, lit by the Citroën's headlights. Aose had dropped Okajima off in S— city, Assembly-man Hakamada's constituency, but Aose barely registered the fact. His mind had not left Shinano-Oiwake.

After leaving the soba restaurant, the two men had paid a visit to the town hall. The head of the Building Guidance division had remembered Aose and had put them in touch with the Residents' Affairs division. The result was that there was no evidence the Yoshino family ever officially moved to Shinano-Oiwake. They also paid a visit to Property Registration, but there was no official name change of the Yoshino home, nor had any mortgage been taken out on the property. Their hypothesis that Yoshino had failed in his online business and fled his creditors had been quickly discounted.

Aose adjusted his grip on the steering wheel.

A search for a missing client. His mind swirled with confusion at such an irregular occurrence. Just last night it had been no more than a suspicion in the back of his mind, but not any longer. Now that they had searched the Y Residence, found its owner missing and seen the official documents, his imaginary puzzle had become a real mystery. The Yoshino family had not made it to the Y Residence either on paper or in the flesh. How had this happened? Were they adrift somewhere?

Him and his wife – the tall woman . . .

How to interpret what the soba restaurant owner had told them? Karie Yoshino was no more than about 150cm tall. It was safe to assume that the woman who had been with Touta Yoshino last November was someone completely different. And yet, Aose had been to that restaurant with both the Yoshinos. How had the owner mistaken the tall woman for Yoshino's wife? Had he just happened to be in the kitchen when the three of them ate there? Or perhaps he had seen Karie but had believed her to be Aose's partner?

Somebody honked behind him and he realized the traffic light had turned green. He was already on Showa Street, close to the company's rented parking space.

This is what Aose knew: Touta Yoshino's long-awaited house was finally completed, but he never actually moved into it, never changing his official address. Instead he had turned up at a soba restaurant in nearby Karuizawa with a woman who wasn't his wife.

What if Yoshino and the tall woman were having an affair?

But hold on, that wasn't necessarily the case. When the restaurant owner told him that Yoshino had been in, Aose had asked if he was alone, or with his wife and family? That might have been why he'd replied that he was with his wife. Someone in the service industry would probably think that a middle-aged man and woman coming to eat together were husband and wife. It would be the most natural assumption.

But now that the suspicion had snuck into his head, it was hard to get rid of. Perhaps Yoshino and the other woman had a kind of intimacy between them that would make them seem like a couple by anyone's standards. Perhaps Touta Yoshino had a dark secret that meant he needed to keep his family away from the Y Residence.

Aose got out of his car and began walking towards the company building. He regretted that he hadn't talked to the soba restaurant owner in more detail. The same went for the answer machine at the house. He wished he'd replayed its messages. There might have been some kind of clue among them.

'*Okaerinasai* – welcome back! You were up there late!'

The company accountant, Mayumi Tsumura, was in the office with the lights half dimmed.

'Wasn't the boss supposed to be with you?' she added.

'I dropped him off on the way back. But shouldn't you have picked up Yuma-kun by now?'

The thirty-two-year-old divorced mother usually left the office at six on the dot to pick up her three-year-old son from the unlicensed nursery she used.

'I got my mum to watch him. She's always over the moon when I ask her.'

Aose smiled at her casual, cheerful way of talking. Mayumi had once told him that she used to be a *yankii* – a teenage rebel – but the only remainder of that look was something in the angle of her eyebrows. She had graduated from a commercial high school which she'd attended online, and Aose wasn't sure how she'd ended up at this company, but he knew that she'd been working for Okajima ever since he'd decided to get serious about running his own business.

'How about Ishimaki and Takeuchi?'

'Takeuchi-san's staying overnight in Higashi Murayama, and Ishimaki-san's going straight home after today's site survey. It's his wife's birthday.'

Ishimaki must have asked Mayumi to prepare a presentation board for a client, as she was busy cutting out and pasting pictures of lighting fixtures on to a newspaper-sized floorplan of a house. Each room was sketched with coloured pencils and a suggested lighting and furnishing plan had been added using images cut from catalogues. Mayumi was proud of the fact that her layouts were far and away more popular with clients than computerized versions. Mayumi's talent for room coordination, which she'd learned on the job from assisting the architects, was quite astonishing. She also had an impressive ability to read blue-prints, so whenever the relatively inexperienced Takeuchi drew an inaccurate line she would be quick to pull him up on it.

'What do you call that? A fault line?'

'Is that job urgent?' Aose asked her now.

Mayumi stopped working and turned to look at him. There was a resigned expression on her face.

'Not really. So, I was wondering . . .'

'Wondering what?'

'How did it go up there? Did you meet Yoshino-san?'

Aose felt a stab of pain in his stomach. It seemed that Okajima hadn't pretended to Mayumi that their trip to Shinano-Oiwake was for a site inspection. Of course. Everyone in the office must have known that the after-care service of the Y Residence wasn't going well, but nobody mentioned it in front of Aose out of concern for his feelings. Okajima had probably said that he was going to take a look because he was worried about the house, and it irritated Aose that Mayumi was now poking her nose into the matter. At times like this he thought of Ishimaki, who always liked to joke around:

I bet the boss and Mayu-chan are hooking up. My masculine intuition tells me . . .

'No, we didn't see them today,' Aose said. 'I'm not sure what's going on, but it looks like they haven't moved in yet.'

'You're kidding! Not moved in?'

The tone of her voice was jarring.

'I'll go to Tabata tomorrow. Try to reach them there.'

'You mean at their old house?'

'Well, they haven't moved into the Y Residence yet, so they must be there.'

'Have you tried calling?'

'Can't get through. So I'm going to visit them in person.'

'Can't get through. So—'

Aose hurriedly cut her off.

91

'Sometimes people just change their phone number in preparation for moving.'

It was the same speech that Okajima had used on their return journey from the Y Residence. Just like Aose himself, Mayumi did not seem at all convinced.

'Could you print this out for me?'

Aose took a digital camera from his bag and held it out to Mayumi, who still looked as if she had something to say. He'd taken a photo of the 'Taut chair' at the Y Residence. Just as he'd finished his call to the locksmith and was about to close the front door, Okajima had grabbed him by the arm.

'We've got to get a picture of that chair!'

'Tomorrow'll be fine,' Aose told Mayumi.

He'd been planning to print it out himself, but he felt awkward sneaking around the office.

The phone in front of him rang.

'I'll get it,' he said.

It was the young president of Kaneko Engineering. They were constructing an apartment building in Yorii that Aose had designed.

'Is Aose-sensei back?'

'What's up?'

'Oh, Aose-sensei! I tried to call you about an hour ago.'

Aose glanced at Mayumi. She seemed to have figured out who was calling, because she looked guilty that she'd forgotten to tell him.

'Is there a problem?'

'Yes, it's about those ALC panels you ordered for the exterior walls. I'm afraid they're not going to be delivered in time. Is there any chance we can switch to a similar one from another company?'

'How much of a delay are we talking?'

'They say ten days to two weeks.'

That would seriously delay the construction schedule.

'OK. Go ahead and use a different brand.'

'Thank you! You've really saved us. I knew you were someone I could talk to.'

The young president cheerfully reeled off the names of companies that made similar ALC panels. Aose chose a couple that were close in price, added that the president could call him on his mobile if he needed anything else in a hurry, and hung up.

Mayumi was still sitting there, her hands together in a gesture of apology.

'It's fine. Don't worry.'

He sounded rather grumpy.

I knew you were someone I could talk to.

An architect who wasn't picky. He could smell the insult behind the young president's delighted voice.

'Well, I'll be getting going,' he said, and headed for the door. However, he heard Mayumi's footsteps behind him.

'Aose-sensei! I think that house is a masterpiece!'

He half turned to listen.

'I might be out of line, and I've only seen the photos, but I think it's amazing.'

He wanted to say thank you, but it seemed the Yoshino family had stolen the words from his mouth. Mayumi was getting flustered.

'I mean it. No one would be able to replicate it. Even the boss was totally jealous. He said how he would love, just once, to have the chance to design a house like that.'

Aose forced a smile and left the office.

He would love, just once, to have the chance to design a house like that.

If Okajima had really said that to Mayumi . . . Perhaps it was about time they all stopped sniggering at Ishimaki's masculine intuition.

93

12

Aose ate out, then returned to his apartment to find his answer-phone light blinking. Hoping it might be Yoshino, he kicked his shoes off and hurried to listen. However, he was disappointed to hear the voice of the renderer, Takao Nishikawa. He sat on the sofa, composed himself, then called him back. After several rings Nishikawa picked up.

'Hey, Ao-chan! How've you been? Still alive then? It must be ten years already. Not since we used to go drinking at Candy. Remember that barmaid, Kana-chan? She ended up marrying that pretentious guy with the Armani suits.'

'How are things with you?' said Aose.

'Oh, you know – just an endless cycle of draw and eat, eat and draw.'

Ever since design school, Nishikawa had concentrated exclusively on architectural perspective. Architectural drawings using the perspective technique were also known as renderings, hence the job title 'renderer'.

'So Okajima contacted you?'

'Yes, that's why I was calling you. I wanted to say thanks for sending it my way. Sounds like a great job. Seriously, thank you.'

Aose was at a loss for words. This didn't sound like the Nishi-kawa he knew.

'No, no, please don't thank me. I was worried that I might be putting you under pressure when you were busy.'

'Not at all, I was hurting a bit for work. It's not often that

I'm not going to finish in the minor leagues.

He'd thought that Okajima was referring to his business ambitions, but perhaps he had underestimated him. Still, at the age of forty-five, it wasn't as if Okajima was trying his luck in the architecture game. Working for a major company on a number of commercial buildings, becoming an independent architect, competing for and winning public design projects, eventually being invited to enter an international design competition where he'd be awarded first prize for a building that would go down in history, bringing him both fame and wealth. It was probably embarrassing to think how long it had been since he'd had such a dream of making it in the world of architecture. It wasn't only Okajima, but Aose too, and every other hard-working unknown architect who had once had that dream.

So then, what was it?

Enchantment? Just like Aose, Okajima was bewitched by the tale of the lonely painter who'd died an unnatural death. 'Mémoire to Haruko Fujimiya', the grand gallery where she will live on for ever . . . Dead, yet existing for eternity. Was it the beauty of that concept that had inspired Okajima?

Aose came back inside. The chill of the wind had caused his body temperature to drop, although there was a slight feverishness on his forehead. He went into the next room and pulled a handful of magazines from the bookshelf. They were PR magazines that always featured showpiece works by no-name design firms and local construction firms, lavishing praise on them in exchange for advertising fees. Aose sat cross-legged on the floor and opened one of the magazines. It was an issue specializing in houses constructed on small, irregularly shaped lots. He had placed a sticky note on the page that featured the house he had designed in Ageo that the Yoshinos had claimed to have fallen in love with. He'd never asked them, but he assumed they had seen the house in this magazine and then gone to take a look at it.

We have 265 square metres of land in Shinano-Oiwake, and a budget of thirty million yen for construction. We'll leave everything up to you, Aose-san. Please build a home you would want to live in.

The whole day long, Aose had been searching for the sleight of hand behind those magic words.

He thought of the face of each of the Yoshino family members in turn. It's said that when a married couple have been together a long time, they begin to resemble each other. That was the case with Touta and Karie. Of course, both junior high school age daughters and the first grade boy had features from each of their parents. They had seemed a genuinely happy family, and when Aose met them they were all wrapped up in a real sense of joy and excitement at owning their first home. There was just one slightly odd thing – the way the children stared at Aose almost with suspicion in their eyes. Well, all except the youngest, the boy . . .

So had they all been wearing masks after all? Was the truth that each family member was at a different place in their head, but they were playing a part for him or for each other, pushing reality to the back of their mind? And had the boy been the only one telling the truth? He'd seemed to be shouting, 'I don't like this!' The thought sent chills down Aose's spine.

Initially, Aose had suspected that the boy was being bullied at school. Then he wondered if it might simply have been that he was in a bad mood. Maybe he was just a spoilt brat. But now Aose began to look for other causes. Perhaps the tall woman who had been with Yoshino had torn the family apart. Having no other information, that's where Aose's thoughts began to drift.

He took a swig of beer and put the can down on top of the open magazine. Droplets of condensation ran off on to the narrow little house in Ageo, and the picture began to blur. That had been the beginning – the chance encounter between this house and the Yoshinos, which had been the catalyst for such magic.

Aose stared at his hand. Was there something different about it?

Had something changed inside him before and after building the Y Residence?

Something must have changed. He'd dragged himself out of the hole he had been in, out of the pits of self-pity and self-sabotage. He'd faced the future, a new life, in which he created the house he would want to live in. His heart had been lightened, and he'd found himself able to move out of the past and into the future. He'd poured every bit of his experience, knowledge, sensibility and soul into the project. He'd stood in front of that completed house, filled his lungs with air and let loose all his emotions into the open sky. He'd wanted to show his father, and he'd wanted so badly for Yukari to know that this was Minoru Aose's creation – a house where light and wood blended perfectly together. On that day, in that moment, Aose was an architect. With both feet firmly on the ground, he stood proudly and announced to the world, 'Here I am!'

But eventually the spell had been broken. Time had passed without word from the Yoshinos, and his confidence had been gradually whittled away like thin layers of fruit peel. There was nothing special about the house. He had become a prisoner of his own words and thoughts, had somehow summoned his own demons, and they were nibbling at his soul until he crept into his hole. He'd gone back to being a sell-out architect for hire, silent, holding his breath. Once again, he was pandering to the client's tastes, being taken for a ride by presidents of engineering compan-ies. He'd reverted to being an insensitive hired hand of an architect who felt no pain. Except . . .

Except that he'd built it, that house. He'd realized his ideals in tangible form.

It was impossible for nothing to have changed. Somewhere in this body, this blood, this spirit, there must be proof that some-thing had changed.

Aose let his fists fall on his knees – once, twice, three times.

Thump, thump, thump.

Nothing happened. No response. When he stopped striking his knee, his spacious apartment was filled with nothing but silence.

13

For the next few days, Aose was caught up in paperwork and client meetings, so it was the weekend before he could get out to Tabata to check on the Yoshinos. The address was technically in Tabata, but it was quicker to get off at Komagome station. He took the east exit, walked along Azalea Shopping Street for a short distance, then passed through the Tabata Ginza Shopping Street. This area had a real flavour of old post-war Japan. For many years, all kinds of small speciality shops had been packed together along the narrow, winding streets, competing to sell their products. Vendors touted their wares with utter confidence, enveloped in the tantalizing aroma of yakitori charcoal-grilled chicken and other prepared food. The place was full of life. The sheer numbers of people gave the illusion that you'd somehow found yourself in the middle of a street festival.

Every time Aose walked through this neighbourhood it reminded him of being back in the old workers' lodgings. People packed together in close proximity to one another, the intimacy of shared conversations. The only real difference was the sense of time perpetually flowing here in Tabata; not so much back in the prefabs. Once the construction of each dam was finished, time and human connections were abruptly severed and a whole community vanished. It was as if, along with the rest of the local landscape, his home village was continually swallowed up by the water.

As his *dango* – sweet rice dumplings – were being wrapped,

Aose gazed absent-mindedly at the faces of the elderly people walking by. He wondered what it would have been like to have been born and raised in this part of the city. What would life have been like if he had been able to stay near to the things he wanted to be near to, but at the same time be unable to escape the things he wanted to escape? What if these had happened to be the cards he was dealt in life?

Aose took his change and moved on. This part of town was also undergoing a gradual transformation. Turn at the end of the shopping street, and the old residential areas were looking a bit worse for wear. The whitewashed walls of large and small apartment buildings became more prominent. During the bubble economy many people had given up their home and the land it was built on because they couldn't afford to pay inheritance taxes. In one of the rivalries between old and new, two old rental houses stood side by side, to their north a posh-looking apartment building and to the south a cleared lot that was being used as a car park.

The Yoshino nameplate had been removed from the door.

Aose let out a deep sigh. In the back of his mind, he had been preparing to laugh at his own paranoia. Okajima had checked with the ward office and let him know that no notification of moving had been issued, so Aose had held out hope. But the nameplate was gone. And if they weren't in Shinano-Oiwake, and they weren't here either, then the whole family had vanished into thin air.

He rang the doorbell, but there was no response. The sliding front door was locked and, just as with the Y Residence, all of the curtains were tightly closed. There was nothing for it but to try the rental house next door. The French windows facing the street were open. An elderly, bearded man lay on a thin futon. He was swearing at a middle-aged woman who appeared to be some kind of home help. Aose stuck his head in through the windows and waited for the man to notice him.

'Excuse me, are your neighbours away at the moment?' he called.

'No idea,' replied the man, clearly annoyed by the question. 'Don't even know them. I'm more concerned that this old cow is telling me I'm filthy and I need a bath. Me – filthy? Ha! What a joke! Tell that to your husband instead!'

All Aose was able to get out of him was the landlord's address. The landlord's name was Noguchi, and if Aose turned right at the next crossroads, he would see a house with a red roof and a garden. It turned out to be easy to find. On the road directly in front of the house, a rather overweight and unkempt fifty-something-year-old man was hosing down a red BMW.

Aose offered the man his business card and the packet of sweet dumplings. If the Yoshinos had been home, he would have sat down and shared them over a cup of tea. He explained the situation briefly; that he had been worried that the family hadn't moved into their new house.

Noguchi didn't seem in the least surprised.

'Ah yes, come to think of it, Yoshino-san told me he was moving to Nagano prefecture.'

'He definitely said that?'

Aose couldn't help himself.

'Did he mention any specific place? Like Shinano-Oiwake, or Karuizawa, or somewhere?'

'No, just Nagano.'

'Just Nagano . . . Can you remember when he told you that?'

'Shortly before he moved out.'

'And when was that?'

'Last year. I think it was about mid-November. Well, when I say "moved out", he was on his own so there really wasn't much stuff to shift.'

Alone?! Aose couldn't believe what he was hearing.

'But what about his family?'

'He was divorced. Quite a while back, apparently.'

Divorced? A while back? Aose's head was spinning.

'When was that divorce? Do you know?'

'Hmm. When was it? My mother was taking care of the rentals, but she's been in hospital a while now . . . Let me see . . . All I recall her saying is that the wife took the kids and went back to her hometown.'

'Moved back in with her parents? Then maybe it's just a temporary separation, rather than a divorce?'

'Yes, I suppose it could have been.'

The middle-aged man in front of Aose had the look of a young child about him. Had he lived his whole life with his parents, until his hair had started to thin?

'How did it come about?'

'How did what—'

'The wife moving back in with her parents. Why was that?'

In his mind, Aose was picturing the tall woman.

'I don't know. My mother said she had no idea either.'

'Do you have any idea where the wife's parents live?'

'No, none at all.'

It appeared that Noguchi could tell him nothing useful at all.

'So, the wife left a while back, taking the children with her. Was Yoshino-san living in that house all alone after that?'

'As far as I know.'

As far as he knew?

'When you say quite a while back, how long are you talking?'

'I'm sorry, I don't know. I didn't have anything to do with the rentals.'

'Would it be possible to ask your mother?'

'Ah, not really. She was hospitalized because her mind was starting to go. She used to get frustrated and throw things at my wife. In the end she had a big fall over the doorstep.'

'I see.'

'And besides, it was really none of our business if Yoshino-san got divorced. As long as he paid the rent on time, we didn't go prying. It's not like the old days. Everyone is concerned with privacy and suchlike nowadays.'

Aose nodded, hiding his distaste.

He was having trouble getting his head around it. Divorce or separation; either way, the Yoshino family had split up. And by 'quite a while ago', it sounded as if Noguchi meant six months, a year, maybe even longer. If so, the story had taken an odd turn. When Yoshino had come to Aose to ask him to design their house, he was already—

The phone in his pocket began to vibrate, causing Aose to jump. He quickly thanked Noguchi, then turned his back.

'This is Kaneko from Kaneko Engineering. I do apologize for calling you on your mobile, but I took you up on your offer to call you anytime.'

Courtesies were quickly dispensed with and the young president spoke plainly.

'I'm sorry, there's been another mistake. The sash window frames are not grey, as specified. They sent me black instead. It was an error on the part of the manufacturer, and they told me they'd take care of it. As you know, the construction schedule is pretty tight. I'm leaning towards going with what they sent for now and then they'll owe us a favour. How would that be?'

Aose listened in silence, his eyes closed.

'Sensei? Aose-sensei? Can you hear me?'

'Do it in grey, as specified.'

'What?'

'As specified.'

It wasn't anger. He was being protective. He was going to stand firmly behind his decisions, for what he believed in. Just as he was going to protect the Y Residence, in its precarious state up there on the Shinano-Oiwake plateau.

14

Beyond the roofs of the nearby houses, Aose could see what looked like a primary-school building. He sped up his pace, but at the same time his mind faltered. His initial surprise had now turned to incredulity. The Yoshinos were separated? Could it be true?

It wasn't until he saw the padlock on the school gate that he remembered today was Saturday. But then he realized how bizarre it was that he was trying to find out where the Yoshino boy had transferred to. He was only in the first year of primary school. If his parents had split up a while ago then he would only have been in preschool at the time.

Aose turned on his heel and began to walk back the way he came, but of course he wasn't thinking straight. There were two daughters in junior high too. However long 'quite a while back' may have been, at least the younger one could have been at this school before the family split up. If he could find out which school she transferred to, then he would have an idea of the location of Karie Yoshino's parents.

He looked over the sliding gate into the school grounds. There wasn't a soul around. In the four-storey school building there was one ground-floor room that could have been a staffroom, but it was dark inside. His gaze moved to the padlock on the gate before him. It looked rusty. He reached out and touched it, and as he did so he heard a woman's voice immediately behind him.

'Can I help you?'

The tone was harsh.

Taken by surprise, he turned to see a middle-aged woman dismounting a bicycle. She looked suspiciously at Aose from behind her glasses. Even if she hadn't addressed him first, Aose would have placed a bet that she was a teacher.

'No . . .'

Aose faltered. The teacher's obvious wariness had reminded him of several recent incidents of violent assailants breaking into school grounds. His hesitation seemed to make her all the more suspicious and, with a pointed scowl, she squared up to him.

'If there's something you need, you can just tell me.'

Hastily, Aose searched his pocket for his business card case. Normally, a card that introduced him as Architect, First Class was enough to gain anyone's trust, but today he wasn't here to inspect a piece of land. The teacher glanced down at the card and then back up at his face, her expression stony.

'You aren't a parent or a guardian, are you?'

Aose was mildly shocked by the level of certainty in her tone.

'No, I'm not. Actually—'

The desire was strong in him to prove to her that he wasn't a suspicious character. He began to explain his situation as politely and meticulously as possible. How he had built a house in Nagano for a family called Yoshino, but they had never moved in. How he had visited their home in Tabata only to find they had already moved out . . .

'So I was thinking that if I could find out which school the children had transferred to, I'd be able to locate their parents.'

The woman didn't even nod in acknowledgement.

'You don't happen to recall any girls by the name of Yoshino, do you?' Aose went on. 'There may have been a time when both sisters attended this school. Anyway, they must have transferred to another school midway.'

'That's a very strange story.' The teacher's voice was more

severe than ever. 'Why having built them a house, are you now trying to find this Yoshino family?'

'Well, it's—'

'Is it the money?'

'What?'

'Did they not pay you for the house you built?'

Of course, when you hear a story about a family vanishing, you assume it's about debt.

'No, it's not that. There's no trouble between us.'

'Then why do you need to look for them?'

'Because I'm worried about them.'

The words came out naturally. The woman seemed to waver for just a moment.

'I'm worried about where they went,' Aose continued. 'I'm looking for clues to find out what happened to them. Is there any possibility you could help me by looking into it?'

Doubtless, she was regretting her momentary lapse. The look in her eyes sharpened.

'If you are so close to this family, then surely you should be able to find out where they are without our help.'

'I'm not close to them, exactly. It's more of a designer–client relationship.'

'Then perhaps you would be better off talking to the police?'

'Yes, I'd already thought of that, but then I was afraid that if there was nothing wrong I would just be causing trouble for Yoshino-san.'

'Well, then—'

For a moment the teacher was at a loss for words, but then she pulled herself together.

'You're also causing us trouble. It's just not reasonable for me to believe what you're saying. If I trusted people that easily, then I wouldn't be able to protect our students. Just recently there was a case of a strange man asking around the parents, trying to get hold of a list of the students at the school. He used a fairly plausible story that there had been a printing error and he needed to collect up all the incorrect lists. There was also a case of a man in a car who stopped and asked a third-grade girl for her phone number. And another girl was almost dragged into a car by another man. Anyway, things are very dangerous for children these days.'

Aose let out a despondent sigh.

'Have you been a teacher at this school long?'

'Yes, a long time. Why?'

'Do you recall any female pupils by the name of Yoshino?'

'As I've said—!'

'Could you maybe just have a word with the head teacher or the office staff?'

'I can't give out any information to people who are not parents or guardians,' she said crisply. The business card, which she had been clutching between her thumb and forefinger, she now thrust back at Aose.

Aose experienced a rush of blood to his head.

'As you have already said, this may become a matter for the police. If an officer were to turn up at the school, would you agree to talk to him?'

It was futile. The only thing that mattered to her now was to chase away this man standing in front of her school.

'I can't promise anything,' she said. 'These days, there are even bad people who pose as police officers.'

15

Aose didn't return the way he'd come, instead taking a narrow alleyway on to Shinobasu-dori Street. He remembered there was a coffee shop on Dozaishita-no-dori he had gone to once with Touta Yoshino. Just as he'd remembered, the café was on the corner of the crossroads. There were quite a few customers inside. Aose was shown to a table and ordered a coffee. It was possible that Yoshino had been a regular here, and Aose wanted to find out if that was the case. However, he didn't feel like asking straight away. If he started questioning people at random like some sort of fake detective, then he was going to be treated with suspicion. He had learned that from his earlier experience with the schoolteacher.

You aren't a parent or a guardian, are you?

It meant that he didn't look like someone's father. He looked like a man who was out of place in an educational environment. Perhaps it was the black leather coat – or perhaps his whole image. There were many in his profession like that – something a bit different about them compared to the average working man, characters who tried to cultivate the image of a lone-wolf type. Determined at all costs to be individual, they exhibited an obsessive level of self-consciousness. Or maybe the teacher had just seen through Aose, the father whose affections and responsibilities for his child were limited to monthly visits. Perhaps the rest of the time he appeared free and without restraints or responsibilities. Maybe that was what the teacher saw in him.

The coffee-shop owner brought him his coffee, but Aose didn't glance up. He wasn't a Sherlock Holmes or even a Dr Watson, he told himself. In fact, what would a real detective do? He would probably still be prowling around that rental house. Maybe he would be knocking on doors, visiting every house in the street, searching for kids who had gone to school with the Yoshino children. He'd be researching removal companies, finding out where the contents of the house had been moved to.

First of all, he had to calm down. Think calmly and try to get a handle on the situation. What did what he'd heard from the soba restaurant owner and the landlord have in common?

Aose took a sip of coffee, placed the cup back on its saucer and folded his arms. Quite a while back, Karie Yoshino had taken the kids and gone back to her parents' place. After that, Touta Yoshino had lived alone in the house they'd been renting. The handover of the Y Residence had been on the third of November last year. In the middle of the same month, Yoshino had moved out of the rented house, telling the landlord he was moving to Nagano. However, he didn't move into the Y Residence, instead showing up later that month with a 'tall woman' at a soba noodle restaurant in front of Naka-karuizawa station.

His brain refused to acknowledge it. The only possible explanation was that it was some sort of maliciously constructed piece of fiction. He had a vivid memory of the day he handed over the keys. The Yoshinos had been overjoyed at the completion of their house. And yet, at that time, they were no longer a couple. How could anyone believe such a story?

The one thing that was undeniably fact, not fiction, was that the family hadn't moved into the Y Residence. And at this very moment, their whereabouts were unknown.

Aose closed his eyes. One of his eyelids was twitching.

The couple had lived apart for quite a while. And this situation had continued up until the handover of the Y Residence. How about if he went back to when they first came to him to ask him to build them a house? That had been in March of last year. Could that have been *before* the 'quite a while back', or would it have been *after*?

It had to have been before. At that time the couple were still getting along well, well enough to be talking about building their own home. In other words, it was after they'd commissioned the house that the couple had fallen out. Aose had drawn up the plans, proceeded with the construction, and then eight months later had handed it over. At what point during those eight months had the Yoshinos split up?

He had no idea. The couple had behaved in exactly the same way throughout the whole process. Although he wouldn't have described them as very intimate, they had both shared a lot with him, while also avoiding other topics. He would have characterized their relationship as a close friendship. He'd looked at their faces and wondered why his own relationship with Yukari couldn't be like theirs. But those eyes of his must have been blind. No! He may not have noticed any sign of marital dispute, but he would surely have detected a change if they had separated or divorced. But there had been no signs of a rupture. He had never even sensed any discord. The couple had been looking forward to the completion of their new home; even now he was totally convinced of it.

So then, it must have been after the divorce. Quite some time ago, the couple must have suffered some kind of crisis. But then they had got back together, and the crisis had made their family bond stronger, leading to the decision to build a new home together.

It made sense. However, it was at odds with the landlord's story. He had claimed that Yoshino was alone when he moved out of the rental house. And if the couple had resolved their differences, why, after four long months, had they still not moved into the Y Residence? Perhaps they had reconciled, the house had been completed, and then the tall woman had barged back into their lives and everything had gone back to the way it had been?

It was a hard sell. Before or after, neither version made for a satisfactory storyline.

He decided he should be sceptical of the landlord's observations. Yes, they had split up, but the reason wasn't a disagreement or a breakdown in marital relations. Something must have happened, entirely unforeseen, that meant the family couldn't live together any more. It could be that Yoshino had run up a large debt, and to protect his wife and children from the debt collectors he had sent them back to her parents for a while. Or he might even have got one of those divorces that are only on paper so that the collectors couldn't come after his wife. All that would be consistent with the landlord's story.

On the other hand, how could Yoshino possibly have got into such dire straits in just eight months? There's been no sign whatsoever that Yoshino was strapped for cash when he had commissioned Aose to design him a house. He'd provided thirty million yen in funds without taking out a loan. And he'd had 265 square metres of land in Shinano-Oiwake.

Was that what had happened? He had seemed to have owned a lot for a forty-year-old salaryman. Aose had assumed that he'd inherited land and money from his parents, but perhaps he had been naive to think that. A wholesaler of miscellaneous imported goods, jack of all trades – now that Aose thought about it, it sounded suspicious. A dodgy business with a murky backstory?

'I just don't know,' he thought. 'I can't get my head around it.'

All of a sudden, an angry voice popped into his mind. That old man with the beard in the rental house next door. He had looked like an obstinate old man irritated with his home help, and Aose had dismissed his attitude as being due to that, but now that he thought it over, he found the old man's menacing air and foul language a little too theatrical. 'I don't even know them.' Had that actually meant 'I don't want to get involved'? Had he raised his voice in the same way before in order to avoid getting mixed up in something?

Maybe there'd been some trouble regarding Yoshino's business and some unsavoury characters had turned up at the rental house. Aose thought of the broken door lock and muddy footprints at the Y Residence. Maybe that hadn't been the work of burglars after all. What had been the purpose of the break-in?

Aose felt a stab of pain between his eyebrows and opened his eyes. He could hear customers' laughter. His coffee had gone cold and he felt the urge to smoke a cigarette – a habit he had long since given up. It was hopeless – this wasn't a case for an amateur like him. He needed to get a real detective to investigate. But no. That was unacceptable. These were his clients. It would be an unacceptable breach of trust to ask a stranger to help him delve into their private lives.

Or . . . was Yoshino even still his client in a situation like this? Whichever way you looked at it, the Yoshinos had made a fool of Aose. He'd made gestures of friendship towards them and been rejected. For no reason that he could understand, they had cast their spell on him and got him to build them a house.

He just didn't get it. He had visited that rental house many times and drunk tea with the Yoshinos in their sitting room. He'd spread the drawings out on the table and the couple had leaned in to get a better look. 'We're looking forward to it. So excited about it!' There had been a spark in their eyes as they exchanged smiles. Nothing had been odd about any of it. The sitting room had always been clean and tidy, and free of any fancy furnishings or gaudy ornaments.

Aose was suddenly spooked.

The family had three children, the youngest of whom was in the first year of primary school. And yet the sitting room had been as neat and tidy as a showroom. There had been no clothes or toys, books or school supplies, or any of the other clutter that's impossible to hide if you have young children. A woman who liked things tidy – that had been Aose's impression of Karie Yoshino.

It was true he had never seen the children when he visited the house. He'd always had the vague impression that they must be in some room at the back or upstairs, but he'd never set eyes on them. He'd never even heard them. He tried to recall the shoes he'd seen in the entrance. Had there been any umbrellas or bicycles or coats hung up to dry? He couldn't remember, but he was absolutely sure that he had never seen the children themselves.

He shuddered. He'd come out in goose pimples all over.

It was because they didn't live there! They'd never lived there – not since the first day Aose had visited that rental house. Because the Yoshinos were already separated. Despite being separated, Touta and Karie Yoshino had showed up at Aose's office together. Finally, the realization dawned on Aose. The landlord's account, which he had initially found hard to believe, now appeared in his mind underlined and in bold. And that made him think of something else. Every time he had called the rental house, it was Touta Yoshino who had answered the phone. Karie had never picked up, not once. Yoshino must have contacted her each time to tell her that Aose was coming over for a meeting and she must have arranged to be there, cheerfully serving tea and sweet cakes while Touta sat there calm and collected, smoking his home-made pipe. It was odd. Now that Aose looked back, he couldn't believe the atmosphere of total harmony in that sitting room.

Aose gathered together all the different threads of his thoughts.

To summarize, although they still got along with each other, it was looking extremely likely that Touta and Karie Yoshino were separated. Circumstances had prevented the family from all living together in that rental house. And that was the crux of the matter. It was hard to imagine that these circumstances had nothing to do with the disappearance of the Yoshino family. He thought again about the old man, and stood up.

As he paid his bill, he asked the café owner about Yoshino, giving his name and a brief physical description, and mentioning that they had come here together once before. The owner told him that Yoshino would come in sometimes and read the *Nikkei* newspaper. That was the sum total of information that Aose could get, but he nodded, his detective's instincts sharpened and ready to be put to use.

16

Ten minutes later he was back at the rental houses.

The French windows of the next-door house were still open and, to Aose's surprise, the old man was happily chatting with the same home help as before. He no longer had a beard, and his appearance had been greatly tidied up. Evidently, despite all his earlier protestations, he had taken a bath after all.

'I apologize for earlier,' began Aose.

Immediately a look of panic crossed the old man's face.

'I already told you I don't know anything,' he snapped.

Ignoring the man's indignation, Aose approached anyway.

'I'm not going to take up much of your time,' he assured him. 'I just need to have a quick word with you.'

'I've already said—'

'Did you ever see any kids next door?'

'Kids?'

'About a year back. Did you see them?'

'I don't know. Don't remember.'

He was feigning ignorance.

The home help looked like she had no idea what was going on and quickly got to her feet to leave. By the way the old man watched her go, Aose guessed that he was a little more faint-hearted than he was trying to appear. He could use that to his advantage.

'Can I ask you another question? Did anyone else besides me come around here asking about Yoshino-san?'

118

He had hit a nerve. There was a change in the old man's expression.

'Ah, yes . . . Is he an acquaintance of yours?'

'No, he's not.'

Aose emphasized that as strongly as he could, at the same time offering the man his business card. He waited a moment for the man to compose himself before continuing.

'I'm a friend of Yoshino-san's. I have no connection at all to the man who came around asking about him, but I'm wondering if that person knew where Yoshino-san had moved to.'

'I don't think he did. He also said he was looking for the man next door.'

Unfortunately, it looked like Aose's hunch had been right. There was somebody after Touta Yoshino.

'When was it he came? Around the end of the year?'

'No, it was definitely this year.'

'Just one man?'

'Yeah.'

'What did he say he wanted?'

'He was looking for the man next door. Was he still living there? Where had he moved to? That kind of thing. He was all worked up about it. But I can't pretend to know what I don't know. We didn't have any kind of relationship.'

'What kind of a guy was he?'

'Shady-looking.'

'Shady-looking? You mean he was yakuza?'

'I wouldn't go that far, but he looked pretty scary. All red in the face and big – like one of those rugby players. Oh, and yes, I remember now, he had a cast on his hand – on three of his fingers.'

A cast on his fingers . . .

'About how old?'

'Must have been around fifty. But one look at him and you could tell he wasn't in an honest line of work.'

'You mean he was a debt collector or something?'

'I couldn't say. I mean, you don't look to me like a debt collector either.'

Aose chuckled. He wondered if he ought to report the incident to the police.

'Look, I don't know any more than that,' the man continued. 'Please leave me alone now.'

'Just one more thing,' Aose said hurriedly. 'Do you know what Yoshino-san's line of work was?'

'Importer of furniture, I think.'

Aose was taken by surprise. Furniture?

'Did Yoshino-san tell you that?'

'No. The old woman who used to be the landlady. She told me he'd given her a discount on a table and some chairs.'

Furniture was a different category from miscellaneous goods.

Not for the first time, Aose felt he had run up against something about Touta Yoshino that didn't add up. He'd called himself a jack of all trades, but he'd never said anything about furniture. What's more, he hadn't noticed any furniture in the Yoshinos' home that looked imported. And when Aose had asked him how he would like to furnish the Y Residence he had responded that he would leave the whole thing up to the architect.

There was a single exception: the Taut chair in the master bedroom of the Y Residence. Now that was most certainly something you would call a piece of furniture.

The Citroën's engine began to sound like it had some sort of chronic breathing disorder. Aose was driving north on Route 17, taking care with the way he worked the accelerator. He'd already reached Takasaki city in Gunma prefecture, heading for the Senshin-tei house in the corner of the Shorinzan Daruma-ji temple, famous for its Daruma dolls. This small house was where the architect Bruno Taut had made his home for two years, after fleeing Germany with his companion, Erica Wittich. Aose had spent the previous night on the internet, learning more about Taut. He'd discovered that there was an exhibition room at the temple dedicated to him and that in it was a chair that he had designed.

Although he hadn't been invited, Okajima had expressed his regret that he couldn't join Aose on today's outing. He'd asked how the visit to the Tabata rental house had gone, and what Aose had intended to be a brief response had somehow turned into a long conversation. Okajima had been very surprised to hear of the developments, but he was currently preoccupied with his endeavours to become one of the selected contractors for the memorial competition and quickly deduced the reason why the Yoshino couple was separated and yet not at loggerheads.

'Must have been the school. They probably wanted to move to the parents' school district.'

'Why do you say that?' said Aose.

'Didn't you tell me the youngest boy was getting bullied? They must have wanted him to go to a different school.'

'But what about his older sisters?'

'They must have been living there at the rental house. You probably just didn't see them because they got home late from after-school-club activities and stuff. Or else, once the couple stopped getting along at all, maybe all three kids changed schools. Or perhaps the parents got back together again but the three children wanted to stay at their original school so the dad moved out by himself. How about that?'

When Aose asked Okajima what he thought about the red-faced man, he suggested that he might have been the husband of the tall woman from the soba restaurant. Aose thought that this was one possible interpretation, but it annoyed him that Okajima had the tendency to think aloud and always go with whatever popped into his mind first. In the end he had to stop him and tell him to get on with his own work. Then Aose had left the office.

The car's satnav had been quiet for a while.

Aose's thoughts remained with Yoshino's work troubles and the red-faced man. Yesterday, after leaving the elderly tenant, he'd gone back to the landlord's house once more. As he'd hoped, the bright red BMW was gone, along with its owner, but he was able to have a chat with the landlord's wife, who was sweeping the porch. It turned out that the red-faced man had also paid a visit to their house when he'd come by a few months back. It had been the wife who had answered the door and she'd been a little frightened of how angry he'd been. She said that he had a slight regional accent, but she couldn't place from exactly where. She reported with some indignation that she'd asked him his name but he'd refused to tell her.

Aose also asked about the table and chairs, but she didn't know that they'd been purchased from Yoshino. They were apparently Scandinavian-made and brand new, so Aose was sure they weren't related to Bruno Taut. Mentioning the furniture triggered complaints about her mother-in-law.

'That woman has never told me anything. Then, after she got

dementia, she started accusing me of being after her savings and the rent money from the houses.'

So had it all been for the sake of the children's schools?

He didn't want to be won over completely by Okajima's optimism. He would really like to believe that it was the correct explanation, but he knew it probably wasn't. There was still no call from Yoshino. Were there circumstances that prevented him from calling? From way back, had he and Karie had problems that they had to keep secret from other people, and eventually had these problems forced them into a situation where they were going to have to separate? Was it at this juncture that they had come to Aose to ask him to build them a house?

But of course that was the biggest riddle of all.

Had they been planning to hole up there? By moving to the mountains of Nagano, had they been planning to escape something or someone in Tokyo? Perhaps they had expected things to turn around for them. By the time the house was finished, perhaps their problems would have been solved and the family of five would be able to embark on a new life together.

Aose was getting more confused. The more he thought about it, the less he understood.

Build a home you would want to live in.

Those words didn't correspond with any of the imagined scenarios. Had it been more of a prayer than a spell? Why would you bet a whole family's future on the vision of a nameless architect?

The satnav indicated a slight left turn.

Aose repeated it under his breath and turned the steering wheel. Less than three minutes later, he crossed over the Usuigawa River and came to the Daruma-ji temple gate.

He got out of the car and was enveloped in a deep silence. He looked up at the stone steps, shaded on both sides by groves of cedar trees. There were a significant number of steps stretching up into the sky which, from this angle, looked extremely small. The scene was like a classic perspective drawing. A hollow stone structure, possibly a bell tower, straddled the steps way up at the top.

According to the map of the temple grounds, there was a path that turned off about three quarters of the way up the 'great stone steps'. A short distance ahead was the Senshin-tei house. Besides the guide map, there was a signboard with the words 'Taut's Path of Contemplation'. This area around the pavilion was said to be Taut's favourite place to take a stroll.

Find a temple employee and ask him about the possible connections between Taut's chair and Yoshino. That had been his plan, but Aose found himself distracted by the curious connection between the great architect and this historic temple.

Aose began to climb the steps. Tranquillity – that was the word that came to mind. After about a hundred steps, when he was just starting to curse his aching legs, he finally spotted the entrance to the path. A little way along, the thick grove of trees temporarily opened up to give a sweeping view of gently sloping mountain ridges – probably Mount Akagi and Mount Haruna. He stopped in his tracks, amazed that a mere hundred steps or so could offer such an amazing panorama.

The path gently ascended further and when Aose raised his eyes to check ahead he saw the black-tiled roof of a house peeking through the trees. He felt a mild shock. Could that be Senshin-tei? The building before him was barely more than a shack – too small and humble to deserve the moniker of house.

However, as he approached, that initial impression of shabbiness changed to one of simple beauty, from meagreness to modesty. It was an old but distinctive residence in the style of a traditional Japanese house. The doors and *shoji* screens were open, as if someone had gone in to clean, and Aose could see what appeared to be two rooms. The *engawa* porch was L-shaped, connected to the two sides of a six-tatami room. That room also had a *tokonoma* alcove. In the centre of the back room was a hole dug in the floor to make an *irori* sunken hearth.

It was soothing to the eyes. In a word, the feeling it brought to him was nostalgia. He'd experienced something similar when he'd sat in Taut's chair at the Y Residence. It was as if the touch of the chair had reawakened something and he was back designing the Y Residence. He revisited the moment that he came up with the concept of a wooden deck with rounded edges and felt a sense of serenity return to him.

He began to walk around the perimeter of the house.

One of the leading architects of the twentieth century had once lived in this house. Of course, it was natural that this unique history should evoke some kind of emotion in the visitor, but even without knowing any of that, Senshin-tei would have been impressive. Moreover, it was a home that had lost its occupant. Houses where lives had been extinguished shared a common kind of pathos. Aose thought of the abandoned homes along the construction routes of the dams and how the Y Residence might end up suffering the same fate. If Aose observed Senshin-tei with a mind that saw darkness in everything, the gloomy space consisting of only two tiny rooms, surrounded by those antiquated exterior walls, could be seen as a mysterious puzzle box containing the whole mystery of the Yoshino family.

However, personal feelings could not be allowed to interfere. This sanctuary unmistakably belonged to Taut. Nearby was a stone monument with Taut's words engraved on it. They were in German, but Aose had looked them up and knew what it said.

'I love Japanese culture.'

It was a strange set of circumstances that had brought the German-born architect to this location and inspired him to leave these words behind. Seventy years previously, on the eve of the Second World War, the rise of the Nazi Party under Hitler's leadership and the oppression of thought . . . Taut, one of the leading lights of German architecture, and a frequent critic of militarization, had been blacklisted, suffering loss of reputation and prestige. Forced into a corner, he had taken advantage of an invitation from the International Architecture Association of Japan and fled the country along with his romantic partner, Erica Wittich. If he had delayed his escape by even a few days, he would no doubt have been arrested.

'Excuse me.'

Aose turned to see a tall, skinny man of around thirty-five standing a short distance behind him. The man was dressed in a blazer and carrying a heavy-looking black bag over his shoulder. Encouraged by the inquiring look on Aose's face, he smiled and approached.

'Where have you come from today?'

He didn't look like a priest, but his tone of voice made him sound like one.

'From Tokorozawa,' Aose replied.

'I'm glad to see that there are Taut fans in other prefectures too.'

With an even bigger smile, the man produced a wallet of business cards from the side pocket of his bag.

Takahiro Ikezono, Culture Section, J— Newspaper.

It turned out that Ikezono was a reporter with a local newspaper who had been following the work of Bruno Taut for a while.

'We're putting together a special feature on Taut, so I'm collecting comments from some of his fans.'

Ikezono opened a large notepad.

'Would you mind giving me your name and your age?'

Aose was at a loss for words. He'd been interviewed in the trade press several times, but this was completely different.

'Sorry. I'm not exactly a fan—' Aose began, but he was cut off.

'Then why are you here?'

'I just wanted to look into something, so I thought I'd drop by.'

Aose realized that he'd been careless with his response when Ikezono's eyes immediately lit up.

'Looking into something? Is it about Taut?'

'Um, well . . .'

'I might be able to help you with that. If you'd like me to.'

Aose thought it was a good opportunity. This local journalist seemed to know a lot about Taut, and if asked about the provenance and authenticity of the 'Taut chair' in the Y Residence, he might be able to give Aose the answer right there and then. That said, Aose couldn't mention the disappearance of the Yoshino family. It could be damaging for the family if the newspaper reporter heard those details.

'If you like, I can introduce you to the priest here,' offered Ikezono. 'He knows way more about Taut than I do. I'm meeting my photographer here in a little bit, and then we're going to pay a visit to the priest.'

There was no reason to refuse. The very reason Aose had come here was to talk to someone at the temple.

'Can you tell me your name?' asked the reporter.

'Aose.'

'What do you do for a living?'

Already resigned to the knowledge that there was no escape, Aose handed the reporter his business card.

'Wow! You're an architect.'

'Not a famous one.'

'Well, well, that's great luck for me.'

Clearly delighted, the reporter seemed to relax a little.

'So tell me, what is a practising architect doing researching Bruno Taut?'

'Well, it's about a chair,' Aose admitted. Any hesitation would have seemed strange, and he'd already drawn a line in his head between what he was willing and unwilling to tell this reporter.

'A chair?'

His response had taken Ikezono off guard. Aose supposed it was because his research wasn't architecture-related after all.

'You're studying Taut's chairs?'

'No, not exactly. An acquaintance of mine left me a chair from his house and it looked a lot like a chair designed by Taut that I'd seen in a book or a magazine somewhere.'

'You wanted to check its provenance?'

'Yes, well, something like that. I was just wondering where it came from.'

Ikezono grunted.

'It may not be that easy, you know. There are a vast number of items of furniture and craft designed by Bruno Taut all over Japan. And that includes a lot of chairs. Okay, what kind of chair is it? Do you have a photo?'

When he replied that he did, Ikezono invited him to sit down for a chat. They sat down side by side on the edge of Senshin-tei's *engawa*.

Aose got out the photos that Mayumi had printed out for him. There were two, one from the front and one from the side. Ikezono studied them.

'That is a very Taut-like chair.'

'Is it a genuine Taut?'

'Hmm. I can't really say from a photo alone . . . But, you know, a chair isn't a unique one-off like a painting or other work of art. You can't really call it an original or a forgery. Taut designed chairs, and prototypes were produced at the Industrial Research Institute. Then they were marketed by craftsmen in the towns and villages around Takasaki. Much later they discovered drawings and blueprints of Taut's chairs at the home of the institute manager at the time. In other words, Taut's designs weren't strictly controlled and, anyway, they were always intended to be sold as commercial products. So, to put it bluntly, it's no surprise at all to find that someone has made a reproduction of one of Taut's chairs. Do you see?'

As he waited for Aose's reaction, Ikezono let out a deep breath. Then, in a quieter voice, he said, 'But there is a way of checking if it's an original.'

'What's that?'

'Did you look at the back of the chair? If there is a "Taut-Inoue" stamp, then that means it's an original, made right here in Takasaki under the guidance of Taut himself.'

'Taut-Inoue?'

'Back in those days, there was a man called Fusaichiro Inoue, who looked after Taut. Inoue had a shop called Miratiss in Ginza, and Taut designed furniture and craft items for him to sell. The goods were sold under the names of both Taut and Inoue and are all stamped with a particular seal.'

'I see. I didn't realize that. I'll have a look later,' said Aose, concealing his disappointment. The story of the seal was interesting, but even if he could confirm that the chair in the Y Residence was a genuine one made back in Taut's time, it would be difficult to trace the buyer if they'd been sold in a shop for the general public.

'Ikezono-san, regardless of authenticity, have you ever seen a chair similar to the one in this photo? I think it's quite unusual. For example, the back plate here is slightly warped, and it's not connected to the seat by any kind of nail or screw. That seems like a very distinctive design.'

Ikezono looked at the photos again.

'Yes, I think I have seen something like this before. But I can't be sure if it was the exact same design.'

'My colleague says he's seen something like it at a recreation facility he visited in Atami.'

'Ah yes, the Hyuga Villa.'

The Hyuga Villa was the only Taut-designed building still in existence in Japan. To be precise, Taut had designed the basement of an existing house – the place that Okajima had called 'the sort-of famous residence', as, without Taut's work, the Hyuga Villa would not have left its mark on future generations. The owner had changed and it was currently known as 'the former Hyuga Villa'. Aose was perplexed to find that even such rudimentary knowledge had somehow slipped from his memory. When he'd re-read a book on architectural history, he'd found he didn't remember hearing about the Hyuga Villa in either high school or university. The degree of the teachers' and professors' attachment to the famous architect may have varied, and there may have been some bias or deficiencies in his education due to him dropping out of university, but he couldn't help but wonder at himself for somehow having passed over Taut in the years he spent studying to become an architect.

'Have you ever been there?' Ikezono asked him.

'No, I haven't. I have to confess that before now I wasn't particularly interested in Taut.'

'Really? I find that a little surprising. Anyway, your colleague says he saw a chair like this one at the Hyuga Villa?'

'Yes. He says he sat in it.'

Ikezono folded his arms and cocked his head to one side.

'I've only been to the Hyuga residence once myself, but, hmm . . . I wonder about this particular design . . .'

'It wasn't there?'

'There are a lot of random pieces of furniture and hand-crafted objects scattered around the basement level that Taut designed . . . But, you know, if it really was at the Hyuga Villa, then it would be more likely to be a one-of-a-kind item. He didn't just design buildings. He also specialized in furniture and furnishings.'

Taut had designed furniture exclusively for the Hyuga Villa. Okajima had said the same thing.

'I would say it's an exclusive piece, but from a dining set,' said Ikezono. 'From the shape.'

Aose nodded. It meant that the chair had most probably originally been part of a set with a table and a few chairs. Somehow or other, at some point, one of the chairs had been removed from the set and brought to the Y Residence. He supposed it was possible.

'There's a man who was a student of Taut's at the time. He's still alive, and I think he might be able to tell you where that chair came from. Either that, or you could go to the Hyuga Villa and check for yourself.'

I'd like to go there, Aose thought. If there was a chair there that looked exactly like the one in the Y Residence, he would have established its origin once and for all. And perhaps while he was there, he might be able to ask someone how one of the chairs could have been removed from the house. And on top of that, even if it was rather late into his career, he would very much like to see Taut's work with his own eyes.

'If you like, you could go with me. The Hyuga Villa was used as a corporate recreation centre for years, but it's been closed for some time now. There have been talks of selling it off, and the local Atami community has been debating what to do about preserving it. Right now, the University of T— is conducting a survey of the building to ascertain its historical and artistic value. I'm planning to visit the site soon for an interview so, if you'd like, I could give you a call when I'm heading that way.'

Aose readily accepted. Because of the conservation issue, if he went there now simply as an architect, no doubt he wouldn't be able to gain access to the building.

'Ikezono-san, I heard there's also a chair designed by Taut in an exhibition hall here at the temple.'

'Yes, there is. It's a completely different style of chair, but I'd be happy to show you.'

With a quick glance at his watch, Ikezono got to his feet.

'I wonder what's happened to the photographer?' he muttered, stretching his neck to look down the path. 'He said he wanted to get detailed photos of the interior of Seishin-tei so I had it unlocked specially . . . Aose-san, are you all right for time? You'll be able to meet with the priest after this, won't you?'

Aose nodded vaguely.

If the chair in the exhibition room was a completely different type, it would mean that there was no connection between this temple and Touta Yoshino. And yet, he had no sense of having wasted his time. Feeling the breeze on his cheek, it was as if his mind's focus had shifted. The sky stretched wide above him. In the distance, an egret took off from the rice paddies and drew a white line across the blue mountains of Joshu. His own existence seemed insignificant. He was separated from all earthly evils by that long flight of steps he had ascended on his arrival at the temple. Even the flow of time spent here in this space dedicated to the memory of Bruno Taut was somehow purer.

Was this a house to cleanse your spirit? That was the literal meaning of the Japanese characters for 'Senshin-tei'.

'Was Senshin-tei built especially for Taut?'

He hadn't meant to ask; the question had just come bursting out.

Ikezono shook his head and sat back down on the porch.

Apparently the house had originally been built for the president of a university of agriculture, and when Fusaichiro Inoue had heard that it was vacant he had asked the priest of Daruma-ji at the time if Taut might live there.

'The plan initially was to have him stay for about a hundred days,' Ikezono explained, 'but he ended up living here for two years and two months. He spent a total of three and a half years in Japan, so a large proportion of it was here in Takasaki. In the end, he left Japan to take up the post of chief adviser to the Turkish government's Architectural Engineering department. His farewell party was held right here in this temple.'

'He must have really liked it here.'

'Well, he was exiled from his home country. He must have had a lot on his mind, but, yes, from all the diaries and other stuff Taut left behind, it's pretty clear that he enjoyed living here.'

Aose wondered for a moment if those had been Taut's true feelings. It was all well and good to talk about Taut, but what had he really been thinking every time he climbed that long stone staircase?

'How do you see it from the point of view of an architect?' Ikezono asked him.

'See what?'

'Senshin-tei. I'd like to hear your impressions.'

'Hmm. Yes, its simplicity is very pleasing. Its space is limited but it has this surrounding *engawa*, a *tokonoma*, an *irori* – all the essentials of a traditional Japanese home. And yet . . .'

'And yet?'

'The size of the house must have been very hard on the couple. I think it must have felt horribly cramped.'

Aose imagined how Taut must have lamented their fate. A master architect forced to flee his homeland in his early-twilight years, ending up in this remote house in the Japanese country-side.

'I see,' said Ikezono. 'But Taut didn't seem too bothered about it. He complained a bit, but he was generally complimentary about Senshin-tei. It sounds as if Erica was bothered by all the insects, though.'

'She wasn't his official, or rather, his legal wife, was she – Erica?'

'No, she wasn't, but practically everyone believed she was Mrs Taut. They got to know each other in Brandenburg when Taut was working as a foreman in a gunpowder factory in order to avoid military service. They had been together ever since, up until Taut's death in Turkey.'

Ikezono had given a gentle response to Aose's rather sharp question.

Taut was blessed with love. Was that what Ikezono was trying to say?

'Ikezono-san?'

'Yes?'

'Apart from the Hyuga Villa, Taut had very little architectural work here in Japan, didn't he?'

'That's right. He even wrote himself that he was taking a "vacation from architecture".'

'Did it have an effect on Japanese–German relations? After all, the two countries ended up forming a military alliance.'

Ikezono frowned and gave a quick nod.

'It would have been an insult to Hitler if Taut had been allowed to display his artistic skills with too much flair. That's what the government of the time probably thought. They granted him asylum in Japan, but they never offered him any kind of public office. I think they just wanted him to stay quiet.'

'Leaving him in a state of limbo.'

'Yes, that's certainly true. But—'

Ikezono turned slightly to face Aose.

'—it may actually have been a blessing in disguise for Japan.'

'What do you mean by that?'

'I think it may be the wrong expression to use, but because, as an architect, Taut's hands were tied, he was able to focus his attention on the art movement.'

Ikezono explained that Taut's goal had been to raise the regional traditions of arts and crafts to a national level. To promote craftsmanship and make it something that specialist artisans made, rather than folk craft made by ordinary people in their spare time.

'That's why, as well as making large items of furniture, he also spent time creating all kinds of traditional smaller objects such as bamboo baskets, umbrella handles, buttons and buckles. It's impossible to measure Taut's influence on and contribution to the development of modern Japanese craftwork. At the same time, he visited many different regions of Japan, discovering examples of Japan's architectural beauty, and helped to make them better known in the west. Some of his favourites were the Katsura Imperial Villa, the Ise Jingu shrine, and the houses of Shirakawa-go with their steep, thatched rooves. He kept a detailed journal of his travels, and wrote books, including *Nippon, Seen Through European Eyes* and *Houses and People of Japan*. He couldn't have achieved any of this if he'd been concentrating the whole time on architecture. I'm very grateful that Taut decided to take his "vacation from architecture" here in Japan.'

Ikezono was a little choked up.

'I could never completely return the favour that Taut did for Japan, but I do think it's Japan's turn to rediscover Taut. There are a number of Taut experts across the country. Here in Takasaki, Atami and up in Sendai in particular, movements have taken root to memorialize his work, but he really isn't well known among Japanese people. The greatness of the man and the scope of his achievements are largely forgotten, or were never known in the first place. It's largely due to the fact that he didn't leave behind any buildings that attracted attention. But he was so much more than a brilliant architect: he was a remarkable thinker and also a highly skilled artist. Personally, I consider him to have been an outstanding journalist too. Both his diary and his books were all high-level reportage. I'm struck by how his insights into Japanese culture were more profound than those of Japanese people themselves. Rediscovering Bruno Taut is also a way of looking at our own culture in a new light.'

Ikezono had apparently come to the end of his speech.

'I'm sure Taut would be delighted to know how enamoured you are—'

Ikezono broke in.

'No, I'd like to ask you a question. How have you managed to evade Taut up until now?'

'Sorry!' came a loud voice from behind them, and a young man with a camera bag came running up the path.

'You're late,' said Ikezono, getting up.

The two of them began to discuss the photo shoot.

How have you managed to evade Taut . . .

Aose continued to sit there on the *engawa*, not quite understanding what this meant but feeling somehow that Ikezono had hit the nail on the head.

18

He drove absent-mindedly along the Kan-Etsu expressway, heading home.

Once he had come down the mountain, the Senshin-tei house had seemed as far away as a foreign country but at the same time as close as the vibrations he was feeling through the wheel of the Citroën. Time and space were paralysed, and it was all down to the death mask of Bruno Taut he had seen at the temple. He wouldn't say the mask was at the back of his mind, so much as burnt into his brain.

After being interviewed, he had been led by Ikezono to a building in the temple grounds known as the Zuiun Pavilion. The priest was just coming out and the three men had stood outside and chatted. The priest had a gentle smile and the aura of a man of great wisdom. Ikezono had introduced Aose as an architect and he had shown the priest the photos of the chair. The response had been that it was a fine piece of workmanship but, unfortunately, he didn't recognize it.

Aose had also tried bringing up Yoshino's name – the owner of the chair was a man by the name of Touta Yoshino – that he didn't know where he had moved to but that the chair was the only clue to finding out. It was a lame story. The priest had immediately replied that he hadn't heard the name before. Ikezono's curiosity had been piqued by the odd story and, after the priest had left, he had questioned Aose about his relationship with the missing Yoshino. Aose had somehow managed to bluff his way through by explaining that it wasn't really the owner of the chair that interested him but finding out whether the chair was a Bruno Taut design or not. As for the vanished family, Aose had learned that as long as he kept that part to himself, the reporter wouldn't jump on the story.

The 'Taut Exhibition Room' was located in the Zuiun Pavilion. It was a small room with a number of glass cases containing photographs, handwritten scraps of paper, letters and artefacts from Taut's time living in the Seishin-tei house. The chair that Aose was anxious to see was there too, but as Ikezono had said, although it was similar in terms of its simplicity of design, it was an entirely different item of furniture.

The death mask was discreetly placed in its own glass case. Aose had spent the most time in front of that case, unable to tear his eyes away. Taut's nose was remarkably long, his head tilted to one side, giving the impression of someone deep in thought. Before his death, Taut had indicated that he would like his bones to be interred here on Mount Shorin. That wish was never granted, but after Taut's death in Turkey Erica had come all the way to Japan to deliver the death mask. As Aose listened to Ikezono's explanation, he had been deeply moved.

Was that a true story?

Taut's period of exile in Japan had come to an end. For Taut, Senshin-tei had been a temporary place of refuge from Nazi Germany. He could not have known when, but he knew that one day he was going to have to leave. Migration: staying at a place was not the same as living somewhere. Or had he been living here, Taut . . .

He must have felt indebted to the local people. He would have been greatly touched and grateful for the warm welcome he received during the most difficult period of his life. But to want to return to a foreign land after your death was no trivial matter. And yet that had not apparently just been the wish of a man in a state of emotional turmoil. The fact that Taut had truly wished to return was borne out by Erica's arrival with the death mask.

Ah, was it because Erica had been here with him that he considered his time here as living rather than staying? In a remote house in a foreign country with no atelier, terrace or study, but where they were free to truly have a life together. Was that why Taut would have wanted Senshin-tei to be his final resting place, his home—?

There was no such place in Aose's heart. That fancy two-bedroom apartment in Roppongi floated in his mind, along with Yukari's words.

Hey, why don't we move back to our old place? I know it was tiny, but we had a lot of fun there, didn't we—

The photographer needed Ikezono, so Aose had left the exhibition room when the reporter had. On his way out of the temple, he had noticed that they were selling keyrings with a mini Daruma doll attached. There was a mechanism that made the doll's eyes pop in and out. Apparently, this was meant to be a pun on the word 'eye-popping'. He had bought two, but he knew that if he met Hinako he would only be able to give her one.

Finally, he exited the expressway. Instantly, the volume of traffic increased and Aose's solitude became absorbed by the twilit streets of the city.

19

'No, there wasn't just one chair. Didn't I say that? It was a set – a dining table with three or four chairs.'

'Which was it, three or four?'

'I'm not sure. Don't really remember, but a usual dining set comes with more than three chairs, doesn't it?'

'Yeah, normally at least four.'

'Yes, well, it looks suspiciously like that chair at the Y Residence was lifted straight out of the Hyuga Villa,' Okajima concluded. 'When they shut it down as a recreation centre there must have been some confusion for a while.'

'If there were only three chairs when you saw them, it may have already been taken by the time you visited the place.'

'And then it got passed around until it ended up in Shinano-Oiwake? That's certainly an interesting theory. But not helpful unless it leads to finding our client.'

Aose had got home and had just been thinking of making a phone call to Okajima when his boss beat him to it. The casual, thoughtless tone he'd taken that morning was no more, and an unusually warm and amicable voice now greeted Aose. Did it mean that he regretted how he'd spoken to Aose before?

Aose shut the refrigerator door. He held the phone under his chin as he tugged the ring-pull off a can of beer.

'You drinking?'

'Just one.'

Okajima laughed.

'I don't care how many you have.'

'Are you forgetting you're the one who warned me about it?'

'Anyone would have done the same thing. Do you remember how much you used to drink when you started at the firm?'

Aose snorted and sat on the sofa.

'So you're going to the Hyuga Villa with this reporter guy?' Okajima went on.

'Only if he gets in touch with me. But first I want to find out if the chair in question has this Taut-Inoue stamp on it.'

'Taut-Inoue stamp?'

'You've not heard of it? I was told it was the way of knowing whether something's a genuine Taut. The journalist told me that if it has that seal it means it's authentic but that it was made to be sold at the furniture store Miratiss. But then it wouldn't be a custom-made chair for the Hyuga Villa.'

'Miratiss, huh? I knew there was a specialist shop, but I'd never heard about this seal.'

'Even you have gaps in your knowledge, eh?'

'No limit to excellence. Well, you certainly managed to grab this otaku reporter at the right moment, didn't you?'

'I was the one who was grabbed.'

'Don't get me wrong, I don't care either way.'

There was a bite to the comment.

'So when is it you're going to the Hyuga Villa?'

'Like I say, when I'm asked.'

'Be very cautious. It's okay to go and get information, but if you're not careful you could stir up a hornets' nest. You know what reporters are like.'

'Don't you need to get off the phone?'

'Eh?'

'I thought you were busy trying to get officially selected.'

There was a slight pause before Okajima responded.

'Nishikawa-san told you?'

'He was thrilled.'

'Well, that's good to know.'

'That's going to be a really big job. A memorial, eh?'

'I'm not counting my chickens. Have to be selected first.'

'Right.'

Despite the breech of the dam wall, Okajima's thoughts on the topic did not come flooding out. It appeared there were two options in his head: to tell everything, or not to speak of it at all. Apparently, he'd decided on the second option and a lot was to be kept from Aose.

'Okajima? Can I ask you something?'

'Could you wait a bit?'

'Where do you want to die?'

'What the hell? What's that all about?'

'If you were dying, where would you want to return to?'

'Are you drunk?'

'I'm only halfway through that one can.'

'Home, of course. Like anybody else.'

'I'm asking about you in particular.'

'Home. Die right there on the tatami, be put in the grave. Family visits during the Obon festival. There. Satisfied?'

'Which home?'

'Hey! Half a can of what, exactly? Home is home! My dad built this house, and I was brought up in it. I've done a lot of work on it, and my whole family lives here now.'

'Including your wife.'

'Ah, I see what you mean. You're right. Wherever your family is, that's home. What exactly are you trying to say?'

'I was just wondering . . .'

Aose should have stopped there, but he didn't.

'I wondered whether you'd want to die at Mayumi's apartment.'

There was a long pause.

'Just joking.'

There was still nothing from Okajima.

'I'm sorry. Forget it. My head's a bit messed up since seeing that death mask at the temple today.'

'Ah . . .'

Finally, Okajima found his voice again.

'Taut's? Yes, that's a powerful object. I heard that his wife came all the way to deliver it to the temple.'

'Yes. But Erica wasn't his wife,' Aose pointed out.

'Oh, that's right. When Taut fled Germany he left his wife and children behind. Did you have a problem with that part? You know, he didn't abandon them. I think he probably decided at the last minute it was better to leave them in their home country.'

'Then what was Erica? The pilot of his ship? Secretary slash mistress?'

'His fellow-traveller.'

'Ha! That sounds like an *enka* song!' said Aose mockingly.

'Travel companions in the era of Naziism. Kindred souls, and comrades in arms at the same time.'

'Is that what kindled their passion, then?'

'I used to wonder the same thing. Erica was such a mystery to me that I looked her up at the library.'

'And your conclusion?'

'Couldn't find anything. But I could imagine. They were concentric plum blossoms.'

'What the heck is that?'

'It's a kind of Chinese flowering plum tree. Two flowers bloom from the same core.'

'I see. One flesh. Two hearts beating as one.'

'Sounds cheesy when you put it like that. Concentricity. Two bodies that share the same core. Two shapes that share the same centre. People like that do exist. It's tiresome to explain in words, but it's like your heart synchronizes with another's, as if an electric current is passing between you.'

'Really?'

'As you seem to have got the wrong end of the stick

completely, I'll explain it to you. It's like me and Mayumi. I've known her since she was little, ever since her father's construction company failed and she became a delinquent. I always know exactly what she's thinking, and she knows what I'm thinking too. That's how I saw the concentricity between Taut and Erica. It's a whole other dimension, a whole different thing to sensual love.'

Different from sensual love. That was what Okajima wanted to emphasize.

'Got it.'

'Are you sure you've got it?'

Okajima's voice was dripping with sarcasm. There was the sound of a long intake of breath.

'And what about you?'

Predictable. Aose had expected the conversation to come around to him.

'Do you want to die there, in that rented room? Where do you want to go to die? You must have given it some thought, seeing as you're asking others about it.'

'Well, yes, I've been thinking about it.'

'So, where will you go home to die? The apartment you lived in before your divorce? One of those dam workers' prefabs you lived in as a kid?'

'There's no physical location that comes to mind.'

'Then will you let me guess?'

'Guess?'

'The Y Residence.'

It felt to Aose as if he'd slapped someone only to receive a knockout punch in return.

'That's somebody's house,' he protested.

'It's your house.'

'Don't be stupid.'

'We're the same. We both want to go back to the house we created, the one that we put our soul into. That's the house we think of right before we put on that death mask. You think it. I think it. That's what I'm talking about.'

And with that the call abruptly cut off. The conversation that he'd thought would go on for ever was now swallowed up by emptiness. Aose stared at the receiver in his hand. He could hear the ticking of the wall clock. The beat of the second hand, which was normally too quiet to reach his ears, was coming across loud and clear. His heart felt uneasy and he found he couldn't stay still. He couldn't understand why Okajima's words had had such a profound effect on him. Suddenly he was seized by an urge and his fingers frantically tapped out a ten-digit number on the keypad. His heartbeat increased as the ringtone sounded in his ears.

'Hello? This is Murakami speaking.'

Her maiden name . . . He could hear the caution in Yukari's voice.

'It's me. Aose.'

'Oh. Hello . . .'

After the vague response, silence. Then the sound of a door closing, cutting out the sound of the TV.

'What's the matter?'

What's the matter with Hinako? Usually, the phrase sounded sharper. She hadn't been expecting a call from her ex-husband, or she had noticed something wrong in the tone of his voice as soon as she picked up the phone. Noticing it was already dark outside, Aose turned to look at the clock. It was around 8 p.m.

'Sorry to call so late. Where's Hinako?'

'She's watching TV.'

'Have you had dinner yet?'

'What's the matter?'

The same phrase repeated, this time urging him to hurry up and state his business. Aose had the sense that, from the other end of the phone, Yukari could see straight into his head.

'It's about Hinako. I wanted to ask you something about her. Well, it's not something that has to be dealt with right away, but

144

it's something I felt we needed to discuss. She's thirteen now — not a child any more. Well, she is a child, but she's on the cusp of adulthood. I thought that before she starts asking questions about the divorce, we should decide how we plan to talk to her about it.'

He was babbling. He hadn't even planned this speech, it was just coming out. Yukari was silent. Did she not understand what he was trying to say?

'I get the feeling that she wants to know why we divorced,' he continued. 'I got that impression the last few times we met.'

'Did she say something to you?'

'She hasn't said anything, but I can tell. She wants to know. So I thought we should be ready to answer her questions. But I also thought, even if she doesn't ask directly, we might prepare how to talk to her when the time's right. Anyway, I don't want Hinako growing up confused about things. Eventually, she's going to fall in love, and if the foundation she starts with is unsteady, then it's going to be difficult for her to build an adult relationship.'

Yukari let out a small breath.

'I know, but— Prepare, did you say?'

'Yes, that's what I'm saying.'

'Prepare how to explain to Hinako?'

'Yes.'

'It's not necessarily the same.'

'What do you mean?'

'I mean that the reason you think we got divorced and why I think we got divorced are not necessarily the same, and I don't think it's right for us to attempt to sync our answers.'

For a moment, Aose's thoughts went somewhere else.

'I'm sorry,' Yukari continued, 'I know exactly what you mean. And I understand your concern about Hinako. But I'm dealing with it in my own way. Hinako and I are already talking about the issues together.'

'The issues?'

'I've talked about it. In my own way.'

What did you say? It was on the tip of his tongue to ask.

'We're together every day. It's just the two of us. How many times do you think she's asked me, and how many times have I answered? That's how it's been.'

'So Hinako— What kind of—'

'Don't worry, I haven't said a single negative thing. I couldn't do that to her. But you have to understand, we can't make up a story together to tell her. I just can't do that.'

'Okay.'

Aose stared into space.

'I understand that,' he said. 'But don't misunderstand me. I didn't call you with the intention of making some kind of arrangement. I just wasn't sure whether or not it was okay for me to keep the truth from Hinako, so I called to get your thoughts.'

Yukari was silent for a moment, then she began again in a more relaxed tone of voice.

'You know, she tells me it's pretty common these days for parents to get divorced.'

'Hinako says that?'

'Yeah. She says there are several kids in her class with divorced parents. She says they talk about which one of them has it the worst. And then they laugh about it and say none of them really has it that tough. That's how she tries to catch me off guard.'

'Catch you off guard? She's trying to make you feel better about it, I suppose.'

'I mean, I think she's trying to make it easier for me to talk about the divorce. Trying to tell me that it's no big deal to her. At those times, it's too painful for me to look her straight in the eye. You're right – Hinako wants to know the truth. She's so afraid to hear it, but she still wants to know. It's as if she's digging at her wounds, trying to make them deeper. And that's why I never tell her the truth. I don't want to tell her anything that would make her feel any worse. And I want you to do the same.'

Aose nodded.

'You know, I've never apologized to Hinako . . . I've never even apologized to you.'

'Stop it,' said Yukari with a laugh. 'There's no need to apologize. It was both of our faults. I'm forever apologizing to Hinako in my heart. But if I ever put it into words, it would make her cry.'

'Yes. Yes, you're right.'

'You know, I'm always telling her, "You are you."'

'You are— what?'

'You are you. Mummy and Daddy both love you very much, and you'll always be their little girl. But you should walk your own path too. Walk towards the thing that makes your heart soar.'

Aose felt a deep sense of relief.

I see. I see. That is what you told her.

'By the way, I've started taking English conversation classes. And I'm competing with Hinako to see who can improve more quickly. We joke that one day we'll be New Yorkers.'

'Wow, that's great. A job in New York?'

'It's just a dream. What about you? How's work going?'

'I'm getting by.'

'Really? Have you built any houses that really spoke to you lately?'

'I might have.'

'You're doing great. Hang in there.'

She was trying to cheer him up because she could sense he was feeling vulnerable. Yukari had always been like that with everybody.

Aose gave a little cough.

'Actually, there's one more thing I wanted to talk to you about regarding Hinako.'

'What?'

'She told me back at the beginning of the year that those phone

147

calls she'd been getting had suddenly stopped. She said it meant that was the end of it. There was something kind of odd about the way she said it that concerned me. Do you have any thoughts about it?'

Yukari didn't reply.

'Hello?'

'Not really.'

Yukari's voice was strained.

'I don't think the calls were from a boy,' Aose continued. 'I think something probably happened with a friend or something.'

'I'll ask her about it later. Is that okay?'

Aose suspected that Yukari already knew more about it than she was letting on. Was it something that she couldn't talk to him about? He frowned slightly, but then it hit him. 'Oh,' he said faintly. It was barely audible. What if the calls hadn't been for Hinako at all? What if they had been for Yukari? Could that be it? It must be. Hinako had been sending her father a sign. She had sensed the presence of another man in her mother's life and she had been unnerved by it . . .

The call ended. Aose hadn't quite caught Yukari's last words as she hung up. Had they been 'Bye then', or was it 'See you'?

Aose lay down on the sofa. It had been eight years since the divorce. It would be strange if there was nothing at all going on in her life. It wasn't as if men would ignore her. Even Aose had some history. During the time he was a heavy drinker, shortly after joining Okajima's firm, he had had a regular partner with whom he spent the night.

Good thing we never built that house . . .

He closed his eyes and saw a death mask. The face was both Taut's and Aose's father's. The scene was still, like the moment of death depicted in an old western painting. Aose shuddered. There was an intense agitation in his chest, caused no doubt by the sudden consciousness that death would come to him before long. Nothing ever seemed to be resolved before it came to an end.

Like the phone call with Okajima, and the phone call with Yukari, both disconnected abruptly and sunk into darkness. Would he and Yukari connect again? There was no way of knowing whether this would be the last time or not, or whether they would stay sunk in the darkness. How many more times would he meet Hinako? What would he be able to tell her, and what would remain unsaid before he was gone for ever?

Aose's father's ashes had been scattered in a designated part of Gunma prefecture, up in the mountains, in accordance with his wishes. As soon as they were tipped out, the wind had caught them, and although the ground was slightly whitened with the ash most of them had flown up into the air and set off on their journey through the sky.

'What a fool – well, I guess he just does his own thing,' said Aose's mother, laughing. She would pass away two years later. Her ashes waited for two hours for the wind to pick up, then went dancing their way after her husband.

Aose pictured many faces and heard many voices. The closest face was Yukari's. The closest voice was hers too.

He realized he would sleep well that night. He knew the reason why: because Hinako had told him that the man's phone calls had stopped. *That was the end of it*, she'd said.

20

Time passed and the Yoshino family's whereabouts remained a mystery.

It was in early April, just as the cherry blossoms were falling, that Aose went back up to Shinano-Oiwake. With the start of the new financial year, the company had a lot of site supervision work. Ishimaki and Takeuchi were off sick one after the other with colds or the flu, so nights were the only time Aose had free to dedicate to the search for the Yoshinos.

The question that really needed to be answered was whether the chair in question had a Taut-Inoue stamp or not.

Engulfed in the vast darkness, he realized that the Y Residence would have been completely inaccessible if it hadn't been a house he'd designed himself. Aose had come up to Shinano-Oiwake without telling Okajima. Perhaps a decision was about to be made on the firm's selection for the competition, or perhaps he was re-evaluating his relationship with Aose after that phone call, but he had barely mentioned the matter since, except to ask from time to time, 'How about the Yoshinos?'

Aose let himself into the house using the spare key to the back door, which he had taken with him last time. Inside, it was cold. He switched on as few lights as possible and made his way upstairs. A scene from a horror movie flashed through his mind in which the chair had disappeared into thin air, but it was still there in the master bedroom wardrobe where he and Okajima had left it. He pulled it out, turned it on its side, upside down, running his flashlight over every millimetre of it, but there was no trace of a seal stamped anywhere on it. This meant that the chair had not been made to be sold at Miratiss; in fact, it was more likely that it had been specially made to furnish the former Hyuga Villa in Atami. Of course, there still remained the possibility that the chair was a knock-off made by some unknown imitator of Taut's work, but a second examination reinforced his impression that in both its style and its painstaking construction it was not a chair of humble or inferior origin.

He went back downstairs and to the front door. Then he traced the intruders' footprints from their start at the front door through the house. Unlike the previous time, he now knew of the existence of the red-faced man. With this in mind, and with fresh eyes, he hoped he might discover something new. Were the intruders just thieves, or did they break into the house for an entirely different purpose? It was impossible to know. It would all look the same to him whether they were searching for money or precious objects or anything else, and he couldn't tell if it was an amateur or a professional job. He headed for the living room, where, in the middle of the carpet, the red light on the telephone answering machine was blinking. He felt guilty about it, but he decided to listen to the messages. Telling himself it was for the sake of the Yoshino family, he went ahead and pressed play. There was a total of five messages, the first four of them from Aose himself, asking Yoshino-san to give him a call back. The last one was blank, but there was a faint sound in the background like somebody breathing or the sound of wind that lasted for a few seconds. The call had come in at 10.55 p.m. on 8 April – five days previously – but there was no caller ID. Aose checked the phone's call history. Every six to eight days there was a call with a blocked caller ID. The last of these was on 8 April. This meant that usually the caller would hang up right away, but on 8 April they hadn't.

Aose replayed that last message. He listened carefully – was that breathing? Or was it the wind? It sent a shiver up his spine. He could sense Yoshino's presence. Was it Touta Yoshino in a lonely place or in some distant land, standing with his phone to his ear, calling his house to see if anyone had come here looking for his wife and children?

And if that was the case, who was the person that Yoshino would expect to have come to the house? Was it the red-faced man? A police officer? Or maybe even the tall woman? No . . .

Aose had forgotten all about the tall woman . . . If it was Yoshino who kept calling the Y Residence, then he was alive, at least. That was important. He wanted to believe that the Yoshino family was safe, and the theory of them doing a moonlight flit, going into hiding of their own free will, fitted in with that line of thought. But occasionally Aose would lose faith and worry that something had gone horribly wrong, and it was connected to the red-faced man. Whether he and the Yoshinos had crossed paths yet, he didn't know, but certainly they were pieces in the same board game.

There were ways to find the Yoshinos. He knew from watching news reports that it was possible to locate someone based on the weak signals emitted by their mobile phone. Only the police were able to use that technique. Pretty much once a day, he thought about going to the police, but he couldn't summon up the courage. It was partly because of his concern for Okajima, wanting to spare him bad publicity.

Aose's gaze fell back to the phone. Perhaps Yoshino would call again tonight, and Aose might even be able to hear his voice. The last call had been on the eighth and today was the thirteenth. Going by the call pattern, it was quite possible. He checked his watch. It was 9.47 p.m. Perfect.

Aose decided to wait, but he felt very uncomfortable about being in someone's house without permission. He walked around turning off the lights until only the red, blinking light of the answerphone remained. He sat down cross-legged on the floor and pulled the phone over to him, turning off the answerphone, but on reflection, he turned it back on again. When the phone rang and started recording, then he would pick up the receiver. That was his plan.

Now it was a quiet battle against time. Aose let out several long breaths. He was at the Y Residence, a place he was not supposed to be. He had sneaked in, walked around, and now he was waiting for a phone call that may or may not come. It was all down to fate. The darkness and silence robbed him of all sense of mind and body. The bead-sized red light on the answerphone began to resemble a bird's eye. It was the eye of a black-necked grebe, similar to a duck's, but slightly smaller. The eye was bright red, making him think of blood. A long time ago he'd seen one in a swamp somewhere, but he had no recollection of where and which swamp it was. He knew the species of bird, so he must have been with his father. And young . . . yes, he must have been very young . . .

The room became faintly bright. It was the moon. It must have started to rise in the eastern sky. Aose pictured how beautiful the Y Residence must look, viewed from the outside by moonlight.

That was it – he had built a house he wanted to see.

The phone rang. Aose jumped. His eyes popped wide open and his pulse began to race.

It rang a second time, then a third. Finally, on the fifth ring, the answerphone picked up. '*Sorry we're not home right now. If you would like us to call back, please leave a message after the tone.*'

The caller ID display lit up: *Blocked number.*

Aose got ready. His hand reached for the receiver. '*Not yet,*' he thought.

Beep!

No one spoke for one second, two seconds . . . Aose couldn't wait any longer. He snatched up the receiver and put it to his ear.

'It's Yoshino-san, isn't it?' he said.

There was no reply, but there was a faint sound. Was it the

wind? Yes, it was the sound of the wind. Whoever it was was calling from outdoors.

'This is Aose. Are you all safe? Where are you? Please tell me. Where are—'

The call cut off.

For a while, Aose couldn't move. He felt as if his soul had been torn from his body. It must have been Yoshino. It had to have been him. He knew now that Aose was at the Y Residence. He knew that Aose was looking for him. But he had said nothing. He hadn't asked for Aose's help. The flimsy thread that connected the two men had been snapped, and it was Yoshino who had snapped it. He could be crying right now. Wanting to appeal to Aose for help but unable to, perhaps Yoshino was crying.

Creee, cree-cree.

Aose looked up at the ceiling. He had heard the sound of wood creaking. The new house was muttering, making micro-adjustments to settle itself into the most comfortable position. But then it seemed to him that the sound might not be coming from the house after all but the Taut chair. As if to say, 'Hey, I'm the only signpost in your search for the Yoshinos.'

21

Aose waited anxiously to hear from the newspaper reporter. Ikezono had promised to invite Aose the next time he visited the
former Hyuga Villa. If it turned out that the chair in the Y Residence had been made exclusively for the villa, a connection
between that villa and Yoshino, or even between Taut and
Yoshino, might emerge. Would that turn out to be a clue to the
disappearance of the family? It was in the back of Aose's mind,
but he didn't try to expand his imaginings any further than that.

He was struggling to draw some plans for his clients in Osaka.
The order for a house just like the Y Residence had turned out to
be more problematic than he'd imagined. There just wasn't any
way to build exactly the same house in a different location. But
worse, he'd discovered that he didn't want to build a clone of the
Y Residence at all. The feeling of resistance grew stronger in his
mind day by day, and he spent the evenings standing in front of
the draughting board staring at it, arms folded.

By the third week of April there was still no word from Ikezono. Had he forgotten his promise, or maybe it had been a
spur-of-the-moment suggestion that he hadn't meant seriously?
Aose took out the journalist's business card and considered calling him, but he was aware that showing too much enthusiasm for
investigating the chair was going to look suspicious. He'd already
aroused too much curiosity in Ikezono by his behaviour at the
temple.

How have you managed to evade Taut . . .?

Aose was still haunted by the question the reporter had asked him while they sat on the porch of the Seishin-tei house. For Ikezono, who was fascinated by Bruno Taut, the existence of a man who had studied architecture, subsequently became an architect, and yet had no interest in the man or his work must have been incomprehensible. The phrase had seemed less an expression of irony and more akin to indignation. Aose had flinched, thinking that Ikezono had been right on target with his comment, but now, on reflection, there was no way Ikezono could have been trying to guess Aose's inner thoughts. Besides, they had never met before – the man knew nothing at all about him. There was no way it had been intended as a personal comment.

Nonetheless, the phrase 'managed to evade' lingered in his mind. He had begun to believe that it hadn't been at all by chance that he had overlooked one of the great masters of architecture with an association with Japan. There must have been some reason. Even now, when he was driving or trying to sleep at night, the death mask he'd seen at Daruma-ji temple would flash through his mind. He finally gave up one night and opened the cardboard box that Okajima had sent him. In it were almost a dozen books on Taut, as well as the architect's own writings and the diary he had kept during his stay in Japan.

It was immediately apparent that Taut couldn't be put into any one box. He was a leading architect of the German post-First World War Expressionist movement, a Utopian who proposed alpine architecture, one of the designers of the famous Weissenhof housing estate, a wizard with colour, an unparalleled painter and writer . . . His architectural principles, with their complex interplay of ideas and philosophy, were both brilliant and elusive, and Aose realized it would take him a long time to fully grasp them all. He had the very sobering feeling that at this point there wasn't much to be gained by studying Taut, and that it would simply serve to further underline the difference between his own abilities and those of the master. It would be like comparing a builder to an architect.

Aose's memories of nerve-wracking years spent trying to build relationships with clients and his childhood years of migrating from one temporary workers' lodgings to another were all gradually fading. What he longed for was a brand-new house built on high ground. Although he didn't realize it at the time, as a boy he had fallen in love with the idea of a house as a symbol of settling down. Living creatures instinctively seek shelter. Only when they have something firm and immoveable do they then have the freedom to go somewhere else.

Aose's migratory upbringing was his architectural origin. But he knew he was deluding himself. He wasn't embracing any architectural philosophy or ideals; he just wanted to build himself a house to live in. Taut's mysterious presence was making him feel like this. Experience only trumped talent and ideology up to a certain point. Beyond that, his meagre experience was nothing in the face of the ideals and principles that had been formed by a great talent.

That was why Aose had bypassed Taut. Afraid of getting burnt, he had never lit any fires. By the time he set out to enter the world of architecture, he had already understood that great secret.

He did, however, recognize that he had had some contact with the master architect. As Aose read through the books on Taut, he came across a number of photographs of his work that gave him a sense of déja vu. He'd seen a picture of Taut's Glashaus, or Glass Pavilion, in a library book back when he was a junior high school pupil. It had been constructed by the thirty-four-year-old Taut for the 1914 Deutscher Werkbund Exhibition in Cologne, organized by the German Association of Craftsmen. The structure was a dome of latticed concrete and glass. Its shape was a rhombic polyhedron, reminiscent of a giant crystal. Even now, a century later, the design was original and innovative, and yet somehow the striking design had completely passed by the fourteen-year-old Aose. He wondered how he had felt when he first saw that photo. Had he thought it was beautiful? He had no recollection of the moment. Had he admired it, or had he been indifferent? Certainly, it had not left a deep impression on him. He couldn't recall having any flashbacks to the Glashaus during his Akasaka years. Although he had made full use every day of those three sacred elements of steel, glass and concrete, he'd had no connection with Taut at all.

He was also surprised to discover that he had forgotten all about Taut's Falkenberg Garden City housing project. It was a progressive housing complex, incorporating the surrounding landscape. There were commentaries on the work, such as 'Taut has enticed urban housing into the suburbs.' Aose knew he must have seen references to these projects when he was at his technical high school. Back when he'd participated in that design competition and come up with that prize-winning project, the 'attractive low-rise apartment complex', he must have looked through reams of material beforehand. It was inconceivable that he'd missed Taut's Falkenberg Garden City, which was on exactly the same theme as the apartment complex he'd designed and was one of Taut's best-known works. But he couldn't remember. All he remembered was his burning-hot desire to smash to tiny pieces the long, narrow, sardine-can image in his own head of workers' housing complexes.

Taut would have lamented Aose's entry into the world of architecture without having had any proper exposure to his work. That the young Aose hadn't put up a picture of the Falkenberg Garden City on that fifty-square-centimetre area of wall above Kyutaro's birdcage that was his to decorate as he pleased. Taut, who had appreciated the traditional Japanese beauty of the Katsura Imperial Villa and the Shirakawa-go thatched-roof houses, had reverted to being a nameless designer because of his deep love for Japan. Placing a chair in the Y Residence, having

Aose look upon his death mask, inviting him to come over and sit down next to him. Dizzying fantasies in Aose's head of a sense of familiarity between Taut and himself. He spent night after night on the sofa or in bed reading books on the famous architect.

Of the greatest interest to him were the three volumes of Taut's diary. They were a detailed account of the places he visited, the people he met, his feelings and the minutiae of his daily life during his stay in Japan. As Ikezono had stressed at the Senshin-tei house, the sharpness and depth of his insights into Japanese culture were nothing short of brilliant. His perspective moved freely between micro and macro, and when his writings turned to architectural and cultural theory his enthusiasm overflowed. However, Aose's main interests lay somewhere else. He was trying to read between the lines and the descriptions of Taut's feelings, who had been forced in the later years of his life to flee his home country. With each turn of the page, Aose found himself searching for Erica's name. How had Taut lived as a world-renowned architect and how had he lived his personal life? How had he spent his time, and in what kind of space had he spent it? Had it all been about Taut's own inner psychological world? Or had it been a time and space that could not exist without Erica?

The Erica in the diary was portrayed in a very matter-of-fact way. Although they were as close as husband and wife and had risked life and death in order to escape from Germany, Taut did not show even a glimmer of emotion. 'Erica both nurses and polices me,' he wrote. Such a thought-provoking expression. Aose could only imagine the depth of respect and trust for Erica behind it. The pronoun 'we' appeared throughout the diary, but without any reference to the concentric plum blossom level of relationship that Okajima had so nonchalantly mentioned. It was only after a considerable amount of time spent reading the diaries that Aose finally realized that Taut had essentially answered his question. '*I am with Erica. We share the same time and space. What else is there to say?*'

Aose let out a sigh.

Were there no times of crisis in that tiny, temporary living space? Aose didn't feel despair over Yukari. He hadn't despaired of himself. He'd felt despair over the space. Aose despaired at the crumbling, the disintegration of the space that he had built up with Yukari. An elegant apartment in a high-class apartment building in Tokyo had metamorphosed into a steel container in an arctic location. Everything became glacial. The space became more claustrophobic than a tiny three-tatami room in workers' lodgings, more impenetrable than the ice on the midwinter river when he had gone to fetch water. The air was thinner than that of a classroom where nobody speaks to you.

Back then, if only he had agreed to go back to their little two-room place.

Back then, if only he had proposed building the Y Residence as their own home.

Aose closed Taut's diary.

If a house had the power to make people happy or unhappy, that would mean that architects had the power to play either God or the Devil. Taut's experience in the tiny Senshin-tei house may have been a lesson that it was in fact people who had the power to make other people happy or unhappy.

Taut was never permitted to return to Germany. With Erica by his side, he migrated from Japan to Turkey, where he finally passed away in the house he had built for himself in Istanbul. It would be another seven years before the Second World War ended. He never got to see a post-war Germany, nor did he ever again meet the family he had left behind.

22

When Aose arrived at work on Monday morning, the first thing he noticed was Takeuchi's excited expression. And next to him, Ishimaki's grinning face.

'What's going on?' he asked.

'Aha,' replied Takeuchi mysteriously. Then, 'Hey, boss, Aose's here!'

Okajima and Mayumi appeared from behind the dividing partition, mugs of something in hand. Both of their faces wore a wide smile.

'Can I tell him?' Takeuchi continued. 'It's okay to say it, right?'

He looked around the assembled staff members, and then, without waiting for confirmation, he raised his voice to a loud pitch.

'We're in! We've been selected!'

Aose looked at Okajima.

'Is it true?'

'Yeah, we just got the call: "S— city is planning to build a memorial to the artist Haruko Fujimiya. Okajima Design Company has been selected as one of the firms to compete for the contract."'

Aose extended his hand to his boss.

'You did it!'

'Oh no, I can't celebrate. When I think of all the companies who must be in tears because they didn't make the list.'

Despite the mischievous tone, Aose could hear the emotion and determination in Okajima's voice.

'We're in the competition! Let's do it!'

Takeuchi, who had no real experience of competitions, looked as if he might break out into a dance at any moment.

'Okay, I'm counting on all of you,' announced Okajima. 'This is our chance to move up from the minors to the majors. Let's come up with a design that astonishes the world and knocks those Tokyo companies into the kerb.'

Mayumi raised her hand, like a schoolkid.

'I'll help! I want to help too!'

'Yes, let's do this thing!' yelled Ishimaki, snapping his knuckles. 'None of us'll be going home at night for a while.'

He ground his fist into Takeuchi's belly. Screams of laughter filled the office.

Aose also felt his blood heating up. He had no experience of competing to design cultural buildings, even back in his time at the Akasaka firm. A reclusive painter who made a living selling postcards on a Paris street . . . Not a soul had ever set eyes on her incredible body of work, not until she had died, at the age of seventy. The story of Haruko Fujimiya appealed to his imagination. Her life and her paintings. What kind of vessel would be fitting as a memorial that encompassed both?

And yet, somehow he couldn't bring himself to join in, to yell, 'Let's do this!' What was Okajima really thinking? Did he even want Aose to be part of this project? They'd barely spoken since the phone call they'd had on the day of Aose's visit to Taut's home in Takasaki. He found himself unable to look genuinely happy.

'Aose, could you come with me a minute?'

It was as if Okajima could read his mind.

They left the office and headed for a coffee shop a little further down Showa Street. On the way, Okajima told Aose to go ahead and ducked into an empty car park, mobile in hand. He was probably going to thank either the prefectural assemblyman or some official of S— city for the nomination. Apparently, he didn't want Takeuchi or Ishimaki to overhear his call. Aose entered the café and took a table at the back. Not long afterwards, Okajima came in, beaming.

'Looks like it went well,' said Aose, to which Okajima frowned and nodded.

'It was a struggle,' he said. 'I'm worn out and the competition hasn't even begun yet.'

'Hey, you can't give up yet.'

'Of course I plan to win. Or die trying.'

The forcefully delivered line lacked only the words 'without your help, of course.'

'Do you have a concept in mind?'

'I'm working on it. First of all, I'm going to pay a visit to the bereaved family.'

'Talk to the family?'

'I want to get them to show me Haruko Fujimiya's paintings, and then I'm going to think about the design. After all, the artwork is going to be the star of the show. And you can't get a real feel for them without seeing them in person, right?'

'Right.'

'I want to see them before the other firms get there. I've asked some of the people at the city to put a word in for me with the family.'

'You're really on top of this.'

'I am. I'm going to do everything I can to win.'

Good luck. It was on the tip of Aose's tongue, but he couldn't quite bring himself to say it. It wasn't the right line from someone who should be working on the project himself.

'Hey, Aose—'

Just as Aose was preparing himself to hear the real reason for being called away from the office, in his inside pocket he felt his phone vibrate. *From Touta Yoshino,* he thought, as he always did these days, but when he took it out he didn't recognize the number on the display.

'Is that Aose-san? This is Ikezono, from J— newspaper. We met the other day at Daruma-ji temple.'

'Oh, I've been expecting you to call.'

He'd accidentally expressed his true thoughts.

Aose started to get up but, looking around, he saw that there were no other customers in the café, so he figured it would be all right to continue the call where he was.

Ikezono's voice was animated.

'Sorry to take so long to get around to calling, but I'm going to pay a visit to the former Hyuga Villa on 10 May with a reporter from down in that area, and I wondered if you'd be interested in joining us?'

'Yes, please. I'd love to.'

'Great. So where shall we meet up, Tokyo or Atami?'

Aose thought for a moment.

'Let's make it Atami.'

He knew that it would be awkward to take a train with Ikezono when he was forced to hide part of the story from him.

'Got it. I think my meeting will be in the morning, but I'll talk to the local reporter and get back to you. I'm looking forward to it. The Taut chair. I'm kind of excited about it too.'

As soon as Aose hung up, Okajima opened his mouth.

'That must have been the reporter you told me about.'

'As you probably heard, I'm off to the Hyuga Villa.'

'You haven't heard anything from Yoshino then?'

Okajima lowered his voice. He may have already been nominated for the competition, but he still wanted the business with the Y Residence to be sorted out before the competition was over.

'Don't worry, I won't let the press get wind of any of that,' Aose assured him.

'Please don't. I wouldn't want things to blow up right now.'

Having just referred to the situation as a ticking bomb, Okajima quickly tried to smooth things over.

'So where do you think he is, Yoshino-san?'

'I think he's done a runner.'

'To escape the red-faced man?'

'Most likely.'

'And the tall woman? Do you think she has any connection with the red-faced man? Think it's some sort of blackmail trick? A honey trap or even a badger game?'

From his tone, he seemed to have completely forgotten that he'd previously had them pegged as a couple.

'Could be. We have no idea who either of them is, so we can't rule out either theory – that they're a couple, or it's a blackmail scheme.'

'A couple . . .? Hmm. I think that something like a badger game is more likely to cause Yoshino to disappear like that.'

Aose felt very distant from Okajima. Their feelings on the topic of the Yoshino disappearance were very different.

'True, true,' he said, 'but about the existence of the tall woman – we only have the word of the soba restaurant owner to go on, and we can't even be sure that it was Yoshino she was with.'

'And what about the landlady? No luck there?'

'I got her son to talk to her, but he says that her mind's getting more confused by the day and she can't give us any answers. The removal company's a dead end too. I've called every firm in the city, and not one of them can tell us where Yoshino moved to. They won't even tell me if he hired them.'

'Suppose not.'

'So there's just the Taut chair. It's the only clue we have at the moment.'

'If it turns out to be authentic.'

'I'll know when I go to the Hyuga Villa. I'll find the chair you sat in, and if there isn't a full set, then there's a chance that it's one of them.'

'Right.'

They'd returned to the subject of Taut, but for some reason Okajima wasn't in the mood for sharing his extensive knowledge of the architect. He seemed to have other things on his mind.

Aose decided to broach the subject. He wanted to hear the bad news as soon as possible.

'So, what do you want to talk to me about?'

Okajima hung his head.

'It's about the Fujimiya memorial.'

He blinked a few times then looked up at Aose.

'I need your help.'

It was totally unexpected. Aose couldn't help looking puzzled.

'Listen to me.'

For some reason, Okajima's words were tinged with anger.

'It's frustrating, but I have to admit my own limitations. I'm not sure I can beat those Tokyo guys. But I think you might be able to win.'

'You overestimate me.'

Aose looked away, but Okajima responded by leaning across the table and coming almost nose to nose with him.

'I'm trying to make my office a major-league player.'

'I know. I get it.'

'That's why we need to get this memorial. It's a once-in-a-lifetime opportunity. I was desperate – I bust a gut to get selected. I want to win so badly.'

'I told you, I get it.'

'It's going to be a short battle. One design against the other.'

'Of course I'll collaborate on it.'

'No.'

'No?'

Okajima contorted his face.

'I want you to come up with a design on your own. And when it's done, we'll compare it to mine.'

Suddenly the significance of what Okajima was asking leapt out and struck Aose between the eyes.

'So we're not going to work together on this?'

'In the end we will.'

'But first you want to compete against my design?'

'That's right.'

'And if your proposal is much better than mine, then my design will be rejected?'

'Yes, that's a possibility.'

The situation was not completely unexpected, and yet it was so much worse than he had feared. First there would be the Okajima design. If it was judged that it couldn't win the competition, then the merits of the Aose design would be considered . . .

'But then it would always be credited as your work.'

Aose spoke with bitterness, but Okajima was undaunted. His eyes seemed to gleam with a startling blueness.

'Just one. I want to leave some kind of legacy.'

'Legacy? We're not old enough for that kind of talk yet.'

'It's all right for you. You've already left your legacy.'

Aose rolled his eyes.

'Don't use that place as an example. It's a pitiful excuse for a house, abandoned by its owner.'

'Admit it. That house will be the last place you think of before they put that death mask on you. I don't have anything like that.'

'I don't want to have this conversation.'

'You're the one who brought it up in the first place,' Okajima retorted.

'And I've already apologized. Now let's drop it.'

'But that's not all. It's not only about me.'

Okajima stared into space.

'I want to leave a legacy for Isso. I want to be able to tell my son that I created something great.'

In that instant, Aose saw a clear blue sky and a giant, majestic dam. And way up at the very top, the figure of his father.

'Aose, this time I need you to be my backstage crew.'

For a moment, Aose was speechless.

'Aose?'

Aose laid a reassuring hand on his boss's arm.

'I'll do it. I am an employee of Okajima Design Company, after all.'

23

The last Saturday of the month was bright and sunny.

Aose was at the Café Horn in Yotsuya. It was five minutes past two o'clock, but Hinako hadn't turned up. They'd been supposed to meet during the spring break, but it had to be postponed as they hadn't been able to find a date that worked for them both. They'd exchanged a few phone calls, and it had ended up being May before they met. April's meet had to be abandoned. Aose gave up on the plan to go to Universal Studios Japan or go for a drive somewhere, because by this point he was just anxious to see Hinako's face. Today's meeting had been set up in a hurry.

Aose had been wondering all morning whether the things he'd talked about with Yukari on the phone had had a knock-on effect on Hinako. Apart from when they'd had to deal with the bullying issue, it was the first time since the divorce that he'd had a long conversation with Yukari, and it was certainly the first time they'd ever touched upon their feelings for each other. It was unlikely that Yukari had said anything to Hinako after the conversation, but it was possible that she had been able to sense something out of the ordinary.

Aose glanced at the clock on the wall. Seventeen minutes past two. He could see out of the corner of his eye that the owner and his wife were looking a little concerned. Breathing a little heavily, he pulled out his phone and called Hinako's mobile. Worry that she might not show up had now become a fear that something might have happened to his daughter. That the recent horrific cases of men targeting young girls were no longer something that happened to other people.

The ringtone echoed in his ears two or three times, and then the shop door opened with a bang. Hinako entered, searching through her shoulder bag. She found her phone, which was playing the *Sazae-san* theme tune, turned it off then turned her flushed face to Aose.

'Sorry I'm late.'

'That was your mum calling, wasn't it? Shouldn't you answer?'

Hinako looked confused.

'No, it wasn't. It was you.'

Hinako pressed a button on her phone and held it up for her father to see.

'See, it says "Daddy".'

'But it was playing *Sazae-san* . . . Oh I see!'

Hinako giggled.

'You're registered in the group. Look.'

Hinako changed the display screen. It now read 'Groups: Family'. Underneath were the mobile numbers marked 'Daddy' and 'Mummy'.

'So that's why you get *Sazae-san* too,' she explained.

'I get it now.'

He was still staring at the word 'Family'.

'Did you know that when Mummy answers her phone she still says, "This is Aose"?'

'What?'

'So . . .?'

Hinako would try to bring up the subject of 'Mummy' from time to time. But this particular piece of information was no surprise to Aose. When they'd divorced, Yukari had officially declared that she would continue to use her married name at work for continuity's sake.

'Come on!'

Hinako's mouth twitched at Aose's lack of response, but the

bright smile soon returned to her face when she got on to her next topic.

'Hey, you haven't forgotten your promise, have you?'

'Eh?'

'A house that you designed. You said you'd show me.'

'Yeah, I brought loads of pictures.'

Aose bent down and reached into the large paper carrier bag at his feet.

'Cool. Show me.'

He pulled out a few magazines and placed them on the table. Hinako's pale hand reached out to grab them. Most of them were PR magazines with advertising tie-ins. He'd mainly picked ones that had come out during his time in the Akasaka office, guessing that the urban confectionery shops and beauty salons would be of most interest to his daughter.

'Awesome!'

Every time she turned to a page with a sticky note on it, she exclaimed in admiration.

'Wow, a cake shop! Did you design this one too, Daddy?'

'Yes, I did.'

'Do you even like cake?'

'Not much, but before designing their shop I tried some of the cakes they were going to sell there. I wanted to get an image of what they were about.'

'I see. It's all white. Like a house in a fairy tale.'

'Then that must have been how it tasted to me.'

'Now I want to try some.'

Hair salons, wedding palaces in the style of a western church, restaurants, boutiques, Hinako said, 'Wow,' at every picture, and expressed many of her thoughts. She seemed innocently happy, but at the same time she displayed a maturity in her comments that seemed carefully considered.

There was only one magazine left. Aose took out his copy of

Top 200 Homes of the Heisei Era. He placed it carefully on the edge of the table.

'Wow, it's like an encyclopaedia.'

Hinako picked it up and began turning the pages. Aose held his breath.

. . . sky-blue roof thrusting northwards . . . three distinctive-looking chimneys . . . white living room enveloped in soft north light . . . over-sized windows with a sweeping view of Mount Asama . . .

Hinako sat in silence taking in the photographs. It was as if she was all out of compliments.

Eventually a small breath escaped her lips.

'I like this.'

'Really?'

'It's the best. I like this one the best.'

'Me too,' said Aose. 'This is my favourite too.'

'Really?'

'Yeah. I like it so much that I think I became an architect just to build it. It's a house that someone else asked me to build, but I built a house that I wanted to live in.'

He realized he could say it. And realizing it made his heart feel strangely lighter.

'I've never told you this before, but ever since I was born, I was travelling all around with my parents. All over Japan – every-where, really. We lived in one place for a bit, then moved, then lived in another place. And so I've always wanted a house where I could live for ever.'

Hinako received her father's sudden revelation gently and gra-ciously. She didn't seem surprised, nor did her expression ever harden, although it was a little odd that she didn't ask any ques-tions in return. He talked about the dams, and about his father and his mother. He told amusing stories about life in workers' temporary lodgings. He described the mountains, forests and birds. It was all rambling and unfocused. He had no idea why it was all coming out now. Maybe he was attempting to tell the prologue of a long story that ended at the point where he had to part from his mother.

'Daddy, I'm sorry.'

Hinako joined her palms together in front of her face in a gesture of apology.

'I have to go.'

'Go where?'

'I explained to you on the phone. I have to go and buy a new school uniform.'

The uniform she'd had made at the start of junior high was too small for her. They'd purposely had it made large, but she'd grown ten centimetres in one year.

'I'm second from the back now when we line up. I hate it. What am I going to do if I get taller than Hana-chan too?'

Hinako blurted this out as she got up from her seat. Then, as if it was an afterthought, she bowed her head to her father.

'Sorry – I'll get something much looser this time.'

'No, don't do that. You'll look messy. Make sure you get something that fits.'

'Tell me more stories next time. I want to hear more about my grandad and grandma.'

'Ah, yes. We'll talk more next time.'

Aose started to get up too, but he was stopped by Hinako's exaggerated hand gesture.

'Stay, Daddy. You haven't even taken a sip of your coffee. Stay and drink it.'

'It's fine.'

'It's not fine at all. And to tell the truth, I don't really like it any more when you see me off outside. It's a bit embarrassing. I'm not a little kid any more.'

There was nothing for it but to force a smile and concede.

'Well, if you insist . . .'

He grabbed his cup in a deliberately comic way, which seemed to delight Hinako. She left the café in a cheerful mood.

Aose exhaled deeply. He felt different this time. Even though Hinako had left, he didn't feel the usual sense of distress and drain on his emotions. Something had begun to shift in the landscape that had remained static for eight years. It was because he'd talked about the past. And it was Hinako who had made him do it. She had dropped that simple phrase 'I like this one the best' into the bucket of water that was his emotions and now everything was overflowing.

'Oh, that one!'

The voice came from behind him. He turned to see the café owner, tray under his arm, staring at the open copy of *200 Top Homes*, which was still open at the Y Residence page.

'Pardon?'

At Aose's question, the owner seemed to gather himself and nodded.

'Yes, this is the book that Hina-chan was reading the other day.'

'Hinako? She was reading this book? In here?'

'Yes.'

'When was that?'

'I think it was the last time you were here. The day that you came a little late.'

She had a copy of *200 Top Homes*. There was a copy there in the house. Yukari must have bought it. And Hinako had been reading it that day, while she was waiting for her father to show up. And yet, when he arrived, she hadn't let on, and had instead asked Aose to bring pictures of his work the next time . . .

It only took the few moments for the owner to clear away Hinako's cocoa cup for Aose to realize he'd been had. He looked at her empty seat and thought about the plan that the prism of her thirteen-year-old mind had come up with. She'd asked her father about the work he did because she'd seen *Top 200 Homes*. She'd wanted to tell him that she liked the Y Residence best so she'd come up with the perfect scheme, getting him to bring those books and magazines. He took a sip of tepid coffee. There was no need to weigh up or analyse what had just happened, he could sit and enjoy the feeling.

As he got up to leave, there was a little jingling sound from his inside pocket. He grimaced when he realized it was the keyring that he had bought Hinako as a present from Daruma-ji temple and that he had forgotten to give it to her. Hinako had also forgotten something. She'd asked him if she could show her mother the photos of the Y Residence, but she'd left the *Top 200 Homes* book on the table. That would be because there was another copy of it at home . . .

He stepped out into the soft sunlight.

Have you built any houses that really spoke to you lately?

Yukari may have been talking about the Y Residence. She may have been hoping he'd say yes.

Aose set off at a brisk pace.

He'd unintentionally given Hinako the answer. He felt time moving for the first time since the fateful night that Yukari and he had clashed over their ideal home.

24

The office was a buzz of activity. The desks had been rearranged
and two long benches had been set up in the space created, along
with a designated 'competition table'. All the documents from
the city's construction department had been laid out on it and
Okajima and Ishimaki were busy making notes and beginning
the initial verification process.

'There are so many requirements,' Okajima was saying.

'I know,' said Ishimaki.

Ishimaki began to read out the specifications.

'It says the specifications are for a two-storey reinforced-
concrete building. There should be three exhibition rooms, each
of which is between one hundred and one hundred and fifty
square metres. Storage rooms with more than two hundred display cases. The entrance hall has to be spacious. There also has to
be an office, a tearoom and a gallery to display the work of local
artists.'

'It all means there's less freedom than we had hoped,' said Okajima. 'Not only with the exterior, but the interior too.'

'Yeah . . . So, the rough estimate?'

'They're going to announce it shortly, but from the way the
project manager's been talking, it looks like it's going to be
around 600,000 yen per square metre.'

'Hmm. If that's the case, we need a good balance. Spend money
where we can and cut corners where we need to.'

It was an advantage to have worked for a major company.

Ishimaki was quickly becoming an invaluable presence on the project team. The situation was ideal from Aose's point of view. Although Aose was essentially the office's number two, Ishimaki's experience allowed him to take a step back. It didn't seem too unnatural that he wasn't pushing himself forward.

One wall of the office had been covered with posters and newspaper clippings related to Haruko Fujimiya. Mayumi had taken on that task with relish. The posters had been procured from the memorial exhibition that had been held in Tokyo the previous year. There was a photo of the artist, taken when she was around sixty years old. At first glance she looked quiet and demure, but you could tell just from looking at her that she possessed a keen sense of insight and a steely determination. There were also photos of three of her works, the first a blown-up colour copy of the featured painting from the memorial exhibition poster: an old man sitting on the pavement smoking a burnt-down cigarette, barely more than a stub. There was also a shoe-shine boy with a hunting cap pulled down at an angle, and a middle-aged woman leaning out of an upstairs window to hang laundry. All everyday scenes, but in the artist's work they became defining moments because of Haruko Fujimiya's profound knowledge of these people's lives. She understood exactly why they were doing the thing they were doing at each captured moment.

Takeuchi and Mayumi were also busy. Squeezed in side by side at their desks, which had been pushed to the edge of the room, they were using computers #1 and #2 to gather materials. Takeuchi was in charge of 'Domestic' and Mayumi, 'Overseas'. Using the key words given to Okajima for the project – 'innovative', 'simple' and 'tranquil' – they were searching and printing out pictures of every art gallery, museum or memorial building they could find.

'Takeuchi-kun, how about this one?'

'Perfect. I'd say that was both simple and innovative. Mayumi-san, you have a really good sense for this.'

'You're kidding. Really, I'm giving you nothing here.'

It was becoming clear that Takeuchi had feelings for Mayumi, although Ishimaki and his self-proclaimed masculine intuition didn't seem to have noticed. Mayumi might be harbouring only sisterly feelings towards Takeuchi for now, but if what Okajima said was true – that he and Mayumi were no more than concentric plum blossoms – then perhaps Takeuchi might have a chance.

'Aose-san, what do you think of this?'

Aose bent down to look at Mayumi's computer screen. It showed a private museum in a small city in Switzerland. The roof was gable-shaped with a steep slope, the roof ending only just above the ground. There was something too familiar about the design.

'That's not bad,' he said anyway, not wanting to burst their bubble. 'Print it out.'

Would they really get the project done in time? The competition deadline was the end of July, only three months away. The preliminary design had to be completed by then. That included the floor plan, elevation drawings and cross-sectional views. They would also need time to prepare the explanatory notes to accompany the drawings. It didn't take much to work out there was precious little time to work on the key aspects of the design itself. If they were going to spend all this time leisurely researching other museums, then it was going to be impossible to compete with the more experienced companies.

'This one's lovely. I'd love to have the chance to visit.'

Mayumi was enraptured.

'And that lake is beautiful,' Takeuchi agreed.

'I might go there after the competition is over. I still have my passport.'

'Still have it?'

'Yes, I got one made to go on my honeymoon. And that's all I'm willing to say on the subject.'

Aose wanted to get on to computer #1 to check his emails, but it looked as if Takeuchi and Mayumi were going to be sitting there a while.

'Aose, can I have a word?'

Okajima was calling him over.

'The boss here is an old colleague of yours, I heard.'

Aose knew who Okajima was talking about before he even saw the name: Takumi Nose, who had been a colleague of Aose's at the Akasaka company. They'd been competitors in the workplace, and also in a rather immature way over Yukari too. Although Aose had heard rumours that Nose had set up his own firm, Nose Architects, he had no idea what sort of work he dealt in. What he did know was this was a strong character, who had refused to be defeated by the post-bubble economy. Nose Architects had also been selected to compete for the memorial project, which to Aose was an ironic twist of fate.

'What's he like?'

'Same age as us. Extremely talented, especially with public works projects. Don't know what he's doing these days though.'

'I know him.'

It was Ishimaki chiming in.

'He's got a big, flashy company, employs around thirty architects. Builds apparel and brand-name shops all over Tokyo. Recently did La Alonso in Kichijoji.'

'Oh yes, I've heard of that place,' said Okajima. 'Pretty cutting edge. Just wonder why such a hip company is interested in Fujimiya's memorial.'

'They've started muscling in on small-town museum projects. They managed to poach a guy who specializes in that area.'

'Is that Hatoyama – the guy with the moustache?'

'Yes, that's him.'

'Wow. That means the Sasamura office over in Okachimachi is as good as finished. Hatoyama was there for ever.'

'Yeah, Sasamura's loss was Nose's gain.'

Okajima took another look at his list.

'Okay then, after that we've got Yoshihisa Tokuda at @Alpha Studios.'

'Now he's a formidable opponent,' said Ishimaki.

'Well, he's a famous company president, but I don't know any of his work. Has he done anything well known?'

'I don't know of anything. But it's a huge company. Must be fifty or sixty architects working there. They're bound to have a museum specialist. And they've got money too. I heard that after the economy collapsed, they got it all out of some safe . . .'

There was no break in the conversation. Aose decided to leave the office, telling Mayumi he was going over to Yorii. It was partly a way to escape, but he genuinely wanted to check in on that apartment building that seemed to keep running into trouble.

That said, the minute he closed the office door behind him, his world changed. Now that the world of the competition belonged to Okajima, the breeze that caressed his cheeks belonged to Aose.

There weren't any birds in Tokorozawa, were there? The thought suddenly occurred to him, and he looked up at the sky as he walked to the car park. He'd had the same thought yesterday and he'd opened his apartment window to listen. All he could hear were cars and people's outdoor air-conditioner units. Today there were no birds, but when was the last time Aose had looked for birds in the sky?

He got into his Citroën and drove off. The radio was tuned to the local station.

'*Today the weather in Tokorozawa will be hot and sunny, but from tomorrow low pressure will move in . . .*'

Had Hinako forgotten about Pippi and Pico? At Café Horn he had talked to her about his childhood, including his memories of his pet birds, Kyutaro and Kuro. He had berated himself later for doing an impression of Kyutaro saying, 'Minoru Aose-kun,' but when he thought about it, Hinako had listened to his stories with such a rapt expression on her face she could have been the model of the perfect daughter. It was something he would have been constantly fretting about before, but now something had shifted in their relationship. He was becoming more confident that he could step out of the safe cocoon he had wrapped around them. Sometime, he planned to tell Hinako how he had released Pippi and Pico from their cage in the park. It was surely not a major sin for them to talk father to daughter about how the budgerigars had probably not survived, but wonder if, by some chance, they had? Surely the memory of Pippi saying 'Hina-chan' and Hinako snuggling the bird's soft feathers was not taboo just because her parents had divorced? He hoped they could revisit it together.

There was some kind of chat programme on the radio now.

'I just don't see what can be done about it. I think the people in the neighbourhood who are properly following the rubbish disposal rules must be furious about it. What do you think, Mitchan?'

How was the Yoshino family?

People don't die that easily. People are always dying easily. If both are true, then surely you can believe whichever one you prefer. When he'd picked up the phone at the Y Residence, there had been a faint sound like the wind. Had it been a breeze that brushed Yoshino's neck or shoulder as it moved on past? The scene was becoming so fixed in his mind it was as if he'd actually witnessed it.

I just want you to be safe. Don't worry about the Y Residence. There's no need to feel guilty for my sake.

Ever since Hinako had told him she liked it the best, the Y Residence had become a very special house to him. His belief in it could no longer be shaken. He'd emerged from the dark tunnel of shock and anger and self-loathing he'd been wandering in at the discovery of the abandoned house. Now he just wanted to be in touch. Just a single phone call would be enough. He wouldn't ask Yoshino anything about his work, just one question: Is your family okay?

'Thank you for all your emails and postcards. This neighbourhood issue

is getting such a lot of feedback from our listeners that we're going to cover it again next week.'

How would Yukari have reacted to all this? Certainly, Hinako would have told her mother everything that Aose had said about Y Residence. It's possible that Yukari might have been confused about some of it . . . And if she had bought a copy of *Top 200 Homes of the Heisei Era*, why had she? When Aose had heard the story about Hinako reading the book from the café owner, he'd assumed immediately that Yukari had bought it because his work was in it, but when he'd got home he realized how presumptuous he'd been. Two hundred homes would have two hundred different interiors. Plenty of interior designers like Yukari would have spotted this book in a bookshop and bought it. In fact, it was even possible that Yukari's own design was featured somewhere in the book. Even if she had bought it for the houses themselves, there were 199 other possible featured homes that might have caught her eye. The book even featured a house designed by a young architect from Nose Architects, who had just become his company's rival in the memorial competition.

'It's not just good for you, it also tastes great! Which is why more and more people are incorporating it into their daily . . .'

Nose would probably be amazed to hear that he was an imaginary enemy in the mind of an ex-colleague he hadn't seen in over ten years. When Hinako had expressed her anxiety about the phone calls, and Aose had suspected the shadow of another man in Yukari's life, the first thing that had come to mind was the face of Takumi Nose. Only him. Well, of course, he had no idea about Yukari's relationships since the divorce, so inevitably Nose had remained Aose's imaginary enemy, forever linked to Yukari in his mind. Whenever Aose heard about one of his successes, or saw his photograph somewhere, he always thought of his own present, and Yukari's future. He wondered if there was anyone right for her – anyone but Nose. Fine if it was someone that Aose didn't know. Hopefully it would be someone who made her heart dance, someone with whom she could spend contented days in the wooden house she had always dreamed of owning.

Yorii station came into view. It was on the JR Hachiko line but was also served by two private railway lines. The area he was heading to around the town hall had what was described as a 'sunny town' feel and was pleasantly free of too many people and too much bustle. Aose stopped at a convenience store and bought some refreshments for the workmen. The apartment building site was just around the corner.

As he pulled up in front, the young president of Kaneko Engineering, wearing a hard hat, rushed out to meet him.

'Thank you for coming all this way, sensei. I'm so sorry for all the trouble I've caused. I really should have checked more carefully. I couldn't believe it when the carpet turned out to be red.'

Aose had already received a phone call to tell him of the mix-up. The 'B' for blue that he had written in the specifications had been mistaken for an 'R' for red.

'I'm sorry too. I'll make sure I write more clearly next time.'

'No, no, the fault was mine. The blue will be here shortly. Forgive me.'

Aose had spoken light-heartedly, but the tension on the young man's face didn't relax. It appeared that Aose's refusal to change the designation for the sash windows had had an effect on the president. There had been a marked improvement in his attitude since then.

Aose cast his eyes over the almost completed apartment building. He felt a slight pain behind those eyes. The client had asked for a 'stylish apartment building that would appeal to young couples'. Aose had done his best on a shoestring budget, but in the end all that they had been able to produce was a two-storey building with a pretty formulaic design.

'What shade of red is it?' he asked the president, who blinked his beady eyes in surprise at the unexpected question.

'Pardon . . .?'

'The carpet. Is it an orangey-red, or a dark red, or what?'

'Oh . . . yes. It's quite a tasteful shade. More like a burgundy or the red of a Bordeaux than a true red.'

Aose grinned.

'I see. So, it really was a "B" after all.'

'Sorry?'

'Can I see it?'

'Er, yes. Come inside . . .'

Just before following the heavily-built president into the building, he glanced up once more at the exterior of the building.

Given that the carpet was now going to be red, what modifications would Taut have made to the exterior of the building? This rather off-the-wall thought inspired many further eccentric ideas and made the rest of Aose's afternoon rather pleasant.

25

'It'll take forty to fifty minutes?'

'The satnav says thirty-two.'

'Can you hear a weird noise?'

'If you're so worried, then you should have taken the Toyota.'

Aose and Okajima were on their way to S— city to survey the site of the Fujimiya *mémoire*.

S— city. In the Citroën's rear-view mirror, Aose could see Ishimaki's Nissan Prairie; in the passenger seat, Takeuchi was talking animatedly. Those two had some research to do at the town hall and the library before joining them at the site, so they'd taken two cars. Needless to say, Mayumi, stuck behind, holding the fort at the office, was in quite a huff.

Okajima was flicking through some papers. The previous day he had visited the home of Haruko Fujimiya's family members and taken a look at some of her original pieces. 'Brilliant, dark, and scary' was how Okajima had characterized them.

'I get brilliant and dark, but what do you mean by scary?' Aose said, keeping his eyes on the road ahead.

Okajima stopped turning pages and looked at him.

'To put it bluntly, they look alive. The eyes of her subjects say too much. It's eerie.'

Aose nodded. He'd had a similar impression to Okajima just by looking at the three blurry pictures taken from the pamphlet. The old man with the stub of a cigarette in his mouth carried his whole history in his eyes, and somehow at the same time was celebrating the life of the artist, Haruko Fujimiya. The shoeshine boy's eyes, half hidden by his hunting cap, revealed a cynical mind and simultaneously a pride in his skills that would surface when the polishing was finished. The gaze of the middle-aged woman hanging out the laundry was even more complex, her hands moving independently of her brain as she registered disgust at the flabbiness of her arms. The portrait even evoked the sense of a mini-drama as she ignored her husband, or perhaps her father, calling her from somewhere inside.

'Were they all portraits?'

'Mostly, the family says. The pictures I saw were all of blue-collar workers or children and other ordinary city-dwellers. They all looked as if they had a hard life. I saw a bricklayer, a garbage-truck driver, an old man standing in the street, swigging something from a bottle.'

'Not very Parisian then?'

'Paris is a big place. She lived in the 18th arrondissement, at the northern edge of the city, and the family said it was a poor and unsafe place, with a mish-mash of old factories that had gone out of business a long time ago. There were a couple of popular tourist attractions: the Moulin Rouge and the hill of Montmartre with the Sacré-Cœur, but places like the Eiffel Tower, the Arc de Triomphe and the Champs-Élysées are far away from there. I guess she had no connections with the 'City of Lights', which is why she was able to paint pictures like that.'

Okajima was astonishingly relaxed. Perhaps it was Aose's ready acceptance of a role behind the scenes that had made him more secure, or had he come up with some secret plan to win the contest? Either way, the talk of competing with Aose first in-house seemed to have been put on the back burner.

Was Okajima just the same as he'd always been? It would be disturbing to find out that his apparent mending of his ways had been no more than a strategy to appear a better man in society's eyes and that, at core, he hadn't changed a bit. Looking down on people, getting whatever he could out of them, making himself out to be a big shot, an important person. Reckless with both money and women. Had he blown smoke in Aose's eyes with his story of the concentric plum blossoms? Whatever Taut and Erica's relationship, if Aose were to guess at the true nature of the relationship between Okajima and Mayumi, he found himself more inclined towards Ishimaki's way of thinking than Okajima's explanation.

There was one thing, however, that Aose believed in. Okajima's love for his only son, Isso, was beyond question. When he'd confessed to Aose that he wanted to leave Isso a legacy, that he wanted his son to be proud of him, Aose hadn't needed logic to understand where Okajima was coming from. If there had been any change in Okajima's heart, it was due to the good influence of Isso, who had moved up to the sixth grade that spring.

'Look at this!'

While the car was waiting at a traffic light, Okajima thrust a snapshot under Aose's nose. Aose couldn't immediately tell what he was looking at.

'That's Haruko Fujimiya's apartment. Isn't it amazing?'

Aose's eyes widened.

It was a one-room apartment. If you didn't know what it was, you could easily have taken it for some kind of a dimly lit passageway or corridor. The space was barely wide enough for a single person to pass through. At one end there was a waist-high window in front of which was a silhouette that appeared to be an easel. The reason the room resembled a corridor was that the majority of the floor space consisted of canvases stacked up in heaps, some of them reaching as high as the ceiling.

'Is it normal to stack paintings on their side like that?'

Such a trivial comment had come out of his mouth because what he really wanted to express had been swallowed up by his surprise.

'I don't suppose there was any other way. There were over eight hundred paintings in total.'

Aose put his foot down. The green of the traffic light seemed to blur for a moment. Eight hundred paintings. He'd never actually visualized it before.

'How long did it take her to paint them?'

'It seems she moved to France before turning thirty, so about forty years.'

Aose sighed.

'Without showing the paintings to anyone?'

'Haruko Fujimiya was a true artist. She didn't care about money or other people's opinions.'

It sounded as if Okajima had been studying his lines, which made Aose laugh.

'Huh? What's so funny?'

'According to your logic, there are no true artists in the world of architecture.'

Okajima laughed too.

'Well, we can't hide our work in our room. And if the client doesn't pay us, then we can't build anything.'

'There is an argument to be made, though, that an artist who doesn't seek recognition might not deserve to be called an artist.'

'Are you talking about Haruko Fujimiya?' said Okajima, sounding a bit miffed.

'No, I'm talking more generally—'

'No.' Okajima cut him off. 'You can't say that about her. You can see it in her paintings. Haruko Fujimiya was a true artist.'

'You've completely fallen for her.'

'What do you mean, "fallen for"?'

Okajima laughed again, but then, almost as if he were talking to himself, said, 'It means you can't let a real work of art live in a box. It's only right to surround it with the beauty it deserves.'

Behind them, the Nissan Prairie put on its right-turn signal. Okajima waved bye-bye to it in the mirror like a small child.

Aose pretended not to notice. He was more than a little ashamed that he had doubted Okajima's transformation.

26

Hira-cho in S— city, the site planned for the memorial, was a flat area of shrubland set against a backdrop of gently sloping hills. They'd heard that the whole area was covered with nandina bushes, but from a distance it looked just like any wide, open field found in the countryside. It wasn't a bad location at all. To the south there was a large park featuring a natural lake with a cycle path around it. There were no shops or restaurants apart from a single souvenir shop. To the west of the site was the odd house here and there, and a little further away what appeared to be a brand-new housing estate under construction. Several bulldozers spewed black smoke as they levelled the land. The area was described as a suburb of S— city but was easily accessible in fifteen minutes by car or twenty by bus from the city centre.

'Aose, keep driving.'

'What's going on?'

'We're not the first visitors.'

The Citroën had begun to slow down as it approached the site of the memorial, but it now picked up speed again and passed on by. The reason was a Porsche, with number plates from the Shinagawa area of Tokyo, parked on the side of the road. Nearby stood two men, one tall with a neat little moustache, the other wearing yellow-rimmed glasses on his round face. They were clearly discussing the memorial site and comparing it to documents they were holding.

'That one with the moustache is Hatoyama.'

Aose pulled over a little further up the road, and Okajima twisted his body around in his seat to look.

'He's that museum fiend headhunted from the Sasamura office. I've heard he's been made the number three at Nose Architects.'

Okajima had been doing his homework.

Aose also turned to look. Hatoyama's inspection seemed to be winding down. The two men looked around at the wide-open space with a calm, self-assured air, then got out handkerchiefs and began to wipe dirt from their shoes. The very obviously city behaviour was jarring.

'No big deal,' said Okajima, turning back to face the front. 'I heard he shaved that little moustache off when he went on an inspection trip to Germany. That's the kind of man he is.'

Aose didn't reply. Personal attacks on the man were not going to help. Seeing his rivals in the contest must have got Okajima's blood up. If he was honest, Aose felt the same. He fiddled with the angle of the rear-view mirror. The two men hadn't left yet.

'Do you have a concept in mind?' Aose asked.

Okajima snorted.

'Not yet. I'll think about it after I've looked at a few other galleries.'

'Will that be enough to win?'

'Are you saying that I can't win?'

'Don't be so touchy. If it comes down to a simple comparison of museums, those who are used to building them will have the advantage.'

'The brief is for a *mémoire*.'

'All the same, expertise is needed for an exhibition hall.'

'So, what do you think I should do?'

Okajima looked deadly serious. Aose searched for the right words to respond. He knew it was important not to say anything rash.

'Are you saying I ought to give up the idea of building any kind of traditional art museum altogether?'

Having answered his own question, Okajima exhaled deeply.

'I think so,' Aose agreed. 'Best not to get boxed in by any existing or fixed concepts.'

'What about your plan?'

Okajima didn't even hesitate before asking. There was no playfulness at all in his tone.

'Nothing yet,' Aose said. 'I haven't felt inspired.'

Okajima clicked his tongue. Aose spun his head to look at his boss, but Okajima was staring in the rear-view mirror. Aose checked it too and saw that the two men from Nose Architects were looking in their direction. They exchanged a few words with each other then started to stroll at a leisurely pace towards the Citroën.

'They're coming over, boss.'

'Oh well. Guess we'll have to pay our respects.'

In an attempt to gain the upper hand, Okajima opened the passenger door.

Hatoyama approached with a weak smile on his face. The other man, with the yellow-rimmed glasses, made a show of peering into the car through his tinted lenses. Was he pricing an old-model Citroën or asserting his dominance after mocking its Tokorozawa number plates?

'I knew it.'

After his odd opening remark, Hatoyama took out the aluminium business card case that seemed to be a favourite of people in the industry. Undaunted, Okajima pulled out his own Lanvin brand-name case. Despite Okajima's constant gossiping about Hatoyama, the two men had never actually met before.

'Wow, the big boss himself. Looks like the local team's strong. Please go easy on us or we won't stand a chance.'

Having displayed through sarcasm how very comfortable he was in the situation, Hatoyama turned next to Aose. The four men were busy passing business cards around.

'Oh, hello, Aose-san! I believe you're already acquainted with our boss?'

Aose had anticipated this. Feigning ignorance, he looked down at the card he'd just received from Hatoyama.

'Oh, I see. You work for Nose-san.'

'Right.'

'Yes, we used to work together in Akasaka.'

'Oh yes . . . I recall you were featured in that book recently. Hey, Miyamoto, what was it called again?'

'*Top 200 Homes*?'

It was Okajima who'd answered, before the yellow-rimmed glasses man had been able to. Aose inwardly clicked his tongue.

'Ah yes, the *Top 200*. The boss showed your work to everyone, Aose-san, telling them they should try to design a ground-breaking house like that one. Said you're his old friend, and it doesn't matter how big or small the company, it's all about the design. Oh, please excuse me for going on about it, but our boss was just so fired up about it.'

Okajima's smile stiffened.

'Oh, by the way,' Hatoyama continued, 'how many staff do you have in your office?'

It was a sneaky follow-up punch. Okajima's eyes began to dart about in panic as he realized Hatoyama already knew the answer.

'There are currently five of us.'

'Five? You mean on this project team?'

'Five total in the office. It's a concentrated effort.'

'Five? Well, that's . . . that's the ultimate select few, isn't it?'

Aose felt he had to intervene.

'Nose seems to be doing well these days.'

'Yes, he's doing fine. And all the young guys in the office are in great spirits too. You know, he was a little down after splitting up with his long-term girlfriend, but recently he's been out with us, hitting the bars in Ginza for three nights in a row. Oh yes, the other night—'

There was no choice but to listen to the rest of his story.

Having decided his work was done in goading Okajima, Hato-yama didn't bother to address him again.

'Well, we'd better be going. I'll tell the boss that I ran into you. He'll be delighted. But if you're going to take part in the competition, then we're going to have our work cut out for us. Now we know we've got to shape up . . . Well, I have to say, I really got a lot out of visiting this site today.'

And with that, the meeting of industry professionals was over with barely anyone but Hatoyama having had the chance to speak.

Okajima remained silent until the Porsche had driven away. Long after the roar of its exhaust could no longer be heard he sat with his mouth shut, staring at the grass on the future construction site. The pre-campaign skirmish had ended for him in utter defeat. He'd been caught unprepared by Hatoyama and must have felt the pain of being anonymous. Aose stuck his hands in his pockets and waited for his boss to say something.

'We can win this,' Okajima eventually blurted out. 'We have the bereaved family on our side.'

Hurriedly, he opened his bag and pulled out the photograph he'd shown Aose earlier. There was a second one beneath it.

'It's the exterior wall of Haruko Fujimiya's apartment. They took a picture of it from the outside too.'

Aose winced. The exterior wall was brick with a layer of mortar over the top. It looked like a ruined building, ravaged by war and the elements. Most of the dingy grey mortar had peeled off and the exposed reddish-brown bricks had deteriorated so much they looked as if they could crumble to dust at any moment. There was a single window in the wall; a long, vertical window that looked like a gaping hole. Pitch black. Or rather pitch dark. Not a glimpse to be had of those eight hundred-plus paintings sitting on the other side. The rust that had feasted on the metal window frames had left dribbles of reddish brown that trickled from the window all the way down to the ground.

This was where she had lived, and this was where she had painted. It wasn't possible to tell from one single photo, but when you put the two together – the interior and the exterior – it was then that you understood the level of her determination, her commitment. You became witness to the harshness of her life as an artist.

'The family told me they wanted me to create the memorial,' said Okajima.

He stared into the distance.

'I suppose they may not have really meant it. I was the first to visit them, after all, and S— city is my hometown, but she did say it quite clearly, Haruko's sister: "I'd like you to build it. I really hope you end up doing it."'

The two photos in Okajima's hands were his evidence. They hadn't been copied or reprinted, and they hadn't been shown to anybody from another firm of architects. Okajima needed to believe that.

Aose shifted his gaze into the distance.

The gauge in his heart was wavering again. If they hadn't run into Hatoyama here today, would Okajima ever have shown him the second photograph?

27

That night Aose had a nightmare. It was 3 a.m. when he woke up, his breathing erratic and his body soaked in sweat.

The nightmare was about Bruno Taut.

The architect was in a rage about something. His face was bright red; well, no . . . more like reddish brown. His glasses were fogged up and steam billowed from his wide forehead. He was standing barefoot, gripping the tatami matting of the Senshin-tei house with all ten toes and bending forward at the waist as if to prevent his head from hitting the ceiling. His index finger was wagging furiously at someone as he berated them in a kind of bestial howl. Aose couldn't see who it was who had incurred such grandiose wrath. The recipient was a shadow on the other side of paper *shoji* doors. It wasn't Erica — she was standing outside the Senshin-tei staring at him, an unreadable expression on her face. It was the same expression as in the photo Aose had seen of her.

Was he speaking in German? Russian? English? Or even Japanese? It was impossible to hear what he was saying, intermingled as it was with his animal roars. All Aose could tell for sure was that Taut was angry. Rumbling like a volcano, blazing like lava, merciless, relentless, raging at the figure on the other side of the *shoji*.

It was terrifying. Even after Aose woke up and realized it was a dream, the echoes of it seemed to linger in all of his senses. It was as if Taut's rage were continuing in an adjoining world, a kind of eternal hell.

He lay in bed for a while, trying to interpret the dream, but found it too bizarre to easily link it to reality. That night he had turned off the light without reading any books about Taut. He'd passed on his usual bedtime ritual because he'd wanted to focus his mind on Haruko Fujimiya, in the hope that an image of her memorial might appear in the darkness. But Okajima had got in the way. Ever since the firm had been selected for the competition, he'd been more interested in what his boss said or did.

In any case, Aose wasn't in the mood to immerse himself in Taut's lofty architectural principles. In three days, he would be visiting the former Hyuga Villa. If he were forced to theorize why he was dreaming of Taut, he would have to guess that it was because of his upcoming trip.

Come on, you're not a kid going on a school trip.

Aose got out of bed and headed for the bathroom, peeling his soaking T-shirt away from his body as he went. It would have made sense if the dream had been about Yukari. Right before falling asleep, he'd been thinking about Nose, and how the less information we have about our imaginary enemies, the better. If you don't know anything, then you can't really be enemies. Whether he extolled the virtues of the Y Residence, or he broke up with his girlfriend, or he'd been having a wild time in Ginza, all this information was meaningless to Aose now . . . except in the context of Yukari.

He got in the shower and closed his eyes . . . a memory of an industry party celebrating the seventieth birthday of a leading figure in the world of architecture. Yukari, in an evening dress, cuts across in front of him. Nose is standing next to Aose . . .

That was the beginning of it all. They were both smitten. Because it happened at the exact same moment, there was no time for either of them to try any of the little tricks or subtleties to make themselves seem more attractive than the other. Looking back, Yukari must have been amused to have two men hit on her so obviously and persistently. Apparently, Nose used to call her on the phone every single night. Yukari told both of them that she was a little uncomfortable meeting either of them alone, so they would all go out together to industry parties. As a result, they ended up part of a group of young people who regularly socialized together. Despite their gentlemen's agreement, Nose always talked to Yukari twice as much as Aose did.

The other day, Nose-san said . . .

Whenever Aose heard these words from Yukari's lips, his blood seemed to rise. He felt as if he were being put at a disadvantage. Even the boss of their office used to tease Nose and Aose, calling them the twins. There was little difference in their appearance and, although they worked in different fields, Aose was sure there was nothing inferior about his ability or taste. However, in contrast to Aose, Nose had an extraordinarily cheerful and positive personality. Despite his youth, he was a skilled conversationalist. He could talk about architecture, industrial design, theatre, film, classical music, and was even knowledgeable about subcultures like manga and the occult. Whenever he spoke about these topics, it was almost as if he were singing. He was crazy about Yukari, and when he heard her hobby was knitting he bought lots of books on the subject and read them all. He found out she loved *mame-daifuku*, a sweet bean-curd delicacy, and travelled miles to bring her some back. Aose was definitely right to feel that the odds were against him. In truth, there was a period when Yukari's feelings were most definitely leaning towards Nose.

And so Aose told Yukari about his history of migration. He had no other cards to play. His upbringing, which he had always felt was his weakness, he now turned around to use as a weapon in his battle with Nose and a fantasy story to seduce Yukari. What else was the past for? For one woman, he transformed those years spent without access to theatre or film or classical music into the tale of a long journey spent living in the mountains and forests with birds and flowers. To tell the truth, the pivotal moment was a bit hazy in his mind – had he told Yukari all about it because she'd asked him about his family background, or had he just decided to tell her? He guessed that, as he had no clear memory of her asking, it must have been the latter. Anyway, just as Hinako had done, Yukari listened to the long, long story without once interrupting.

The tide turned. Not long after, they went on their first exclusive date. Yukari rediscovered the term 'ornithology'. She began to refer to Aose as a bird. She would say things like, 'Clearly you wouldn't understand, Aose-san, being an ornithological specimen and all . . .' or 'Is that the way a bird's mind works?' This was her way of communicating what she was too shy to express outright – that she wanted Aose to be someone special to her. The distance between the two rapidly closed. He understood it clearly now – Yukari had already had in her mind the seed of a dream of building that dream wooden house. Believing that her world and Aose's overlapped, she'd taken that leap into Aose's heart.

Nose didn't give up. When his phone calls were refused, he wrote letters. He always reserved two tickets for concerts and musicals. At group drinking parties, even if he had to squeeze his way in, he would make sure he was next to Yukari. With a big smile, he would cut into the swiss roll cake that he had queued for two hours to buy, knowing it was her favourite. It was the smile of a man who believed in his ability to pull off a last-minute victory.

Never let an opportunity pass you by. This was Nose's policy both in his public and private life. That's why Aose decided it was time to make sure Nose was offered no more opportunities. He decided it was time to make Yukari his wife. Although they were in the kind of relationship where they came and went freely between each other's apartments, Yukari's head was filled with her design work from morning to night, and Aose had no idea whether the concept of marriage had even entered her thoughts.

'Shall we get married?' he asked her as they stood side by side at the kitchen sink, washing dishes. He didn't look at her face. Yukari's hand froze.

'What?'

'I said, "Let's get married."'

'Are you proposing to me?'

'Yes, I am.'

'But I'm a mere human. Are you sure you want to marry me?'

Aose had never laughed so much in his life. Yukari slid down to the floor and sat there in tears. He had never witnessed a human being cry with so much joy . . .

Aose stepped out on to his balcony, a can of beer in his hand. There was no nightscape; the lights of the city were all out. The sky was a hastily wiped blackboard – barely a star and a thin cover of cloud meant there was no hint as to whether dawn was near.

'Congratulations!' Nose had said brightly.

He'd offered his hand to Aose. The grip was strong enough to wipe the smile from Aose's face. He couldn't remember the expression on Nose's face as he didn't look up at his rival, showing him the compassion of the samurai warrior. Or perhaps he had just blocked out the memory, in the same way as he didn't recall the exact story he had told Yukari about his migratory upbringing. It was out of guilt. Certainly, Nose must have looked confused, unable to comprehend how he could have lost. In a thousand nights' worth of nightmares, he could never have envisioned his rival in love metamorphosed into a bird with flapping wings, as Yukari had imagined.

I'm sure Nose-san will never be able to hear birds singing.

There was always that persistent feeling of guilt regarding Nose that wouldn't let him erase the man's existence completely from his life. He knew that Nose was a good man at heart and therefore couldn't dismiss him completely. He wondered what Nose had felt when he heard of Aose and Yukari's break-up. Had Yukari met him since the divorce?

199

He went back to bed, but he couldn't sleep. He could create a space that was even darker than the night sky, but it was still not a safe place for his mind to roost. The sensation of Taut's anger existing beside him had not disappeared; rather, it had returned with even more clarity and detail. Was he being punished for having evaded Taut in his studies? He had no choice but to believe that the shadow behind the paper of the *shoji* doors was Aose himself. Was this apartment to become his endless abyss? Was he doomed to repeat for eternity these sleepless nights? For the crime of turning into a bird? Or for the crime of letting slip away the happiness of a lifetime?

Good thing we never built that house . . .

Aose shut his eyes tight.

Taut's anger didn't subside. Aose appealed to Erica for help. Nobody had told him, but he knew from instinct that this was the only way to counteract his rage.

28

It was 10 May, not long since the Golden Week holidays, but Tokyo station was as crowded as ever. Here and there, groups of schoolchildren on excursions swarmed like insects. Aose boarded the 9.56 shinkansen train, wondering how long it had been since he'd gone to Atami. He'd reserved a seat, but the train was surprisingly empty. Here and there, the odd salaryman leg was visible, but their owners seemed to be in relaxed mode.

Aose took various books, brochures and other papers from his bag and spread them out on the tray table in front of him – floor plans and articles pertaining to the former Hyuga Villa designed by Bruno Taut . . . *Construction was completed in 1936. Rihei Hyuga, a Japanese businessman with a profound knowledge and appreciation of art and architecture, commissioned Taut to construct a villa for him. Or rather, as the residence had already been completed a few years earlier, he entrusted Taut with the reconstruction of the basement area. This was hardly a job befitting a world-renowned master architect, but it was understandable that the Japanese government at the time could not afford to show too much favour to Taut following his defection from Hitler's Germany. During his stay in Japan, Taut was commissioned with only two architectural projects, and the Hyuga Villa was the only one where he was entrusted with the whole design – albeit a reconstruction. Taut created a space that consisted of three rooms: a social room, a western-style drawing room and a Japanese-style room.*

As he flipped through the papers, Aose's eye was caught by the phrase 'Precautionary Instructions'. It listed the points to pay attention to when surveying or touring the property. Ikezono from J— newspaper had faxed it to him a few days earlier. 'No naked flames permitted; be careful not to bump, pull on or rub against any object.' Whether you liked it or not, all the words and phrases in the form of a list of prohibitions made you feel you were visiting an important site of cultural heritage. His heart began to beat faster. Every night he would read something Taut had written and contemplate the depth of his thought, so much so that he was being plagued by him in his sleep. Aose had begun to admire the architect and would go so far as to say that he felt a kinship with him. Although the trip was ostensibly to discover the origin of the chair in the Y Residence, he would be deceiving himself if he didn't admit he was looking forward to visiting the Hyuga Villa. What's more, he secretly hoped that seeing Taut's work would inspire him to come up with a concept for Haruko Fujimiya's memorial.

The train arrived in Atami on time. Aose got off and looked around for Ikezono, thinking he was probably on the same train, but it seemed he'd got the next one. He arrived at the ticket gate a short while later.

'It's good to see you again,' said Aose. 'Thank you for that interesting day at the temple.'

Ikezono wore the same good-natured expression as he had the day they'd met at Daruma-ji temple.

'As luck would have it, there was a perfect train for me to get here on time. Did you come by car, Aose-san?'

'I got one train before yours. I was afraid of being late.'

'So sorry! I should have made arrangements for us to come down together from Tokyo.'

Aose put on a fake smile, hoping that Ikezono wouldn't guess that he'd deliberately avoided that very thing.

'Right then, let's get going!' said Ikezono.

'Is it within walking distance?'

'Yes, only about five or six minutes.'

They crossed the street in front of the station and turned on to a side road. It was lined with souvenir shops and family homes. The road sloped gently uphill, but further on it became steeper. As they walked, Ikezono talked.

'I'll explain more later, but my reporter friend Kasahara called earlier to say that a team from T— University has been in the house for about half an hour. It's just a supplementary survey they're doing, so we shouldn't be disturbed.'

As they climbed, they were rewarded with a view over the open sea, the calm blue of Sagami Bay. Straight ahead, slightly hazy, was the island of Hatsushima.

'This way,' said Ikezono, indicating a flight of stone steps leading down off the road. 'I hope you can find out about your chair.'

'Eh? Oh yes.' Aose was already in tourist mindset and for a moment couldn't think how to respond.

'There it is.'

As they descended the steps, Ikezono pointed out the flagstone path and gateway to the Hyuga Villa. Flowering plum trees and shrubs surrounded the house, and its white walls and wide-open wooden gateway gave a sense of age even from a distance. The building was a two-storey wooden structure. Although it used to be the property of a wealthy businessman, it wasn't ostentatious. The light above the doorway was in the style of a traditional paper lantern. There was no personal nameplate, only the name of the company that currently owned the villa.

'Come right on in, Aose-san. I've already spoken to the owners.'

As Aose stepped through the wooden door into the residence, the temperature seemed to drop slightly. Five or six pairs of shoes were neatly arranged on the concrete floor of the *genkan*. The strip of polished wood on to which visitors stepped was made of a sturdy piece of timber and, after removing his shoes and stepping up, Aose could appreciate the quality of the wooden floorboards under his feet.

But the architectural features they were here to see were in the underground section. Strictly speaking, it was what was known as a semi-basement. The original construction of the Hyuga Villa was rather unusual. It was built on levelled ground cut into the side of a mountain. The garden area was on an artificial base made of reinforced concrete on a slope facing the sea. The open space under the artificial base which protruded seawards Taut had used to build an addition to the residence. A semi-basement with unique architectural specifications: open to the sea, closed to the mountainside. The ceilings, floors, walls and concrete structure forming this semi-subterranean area had already been there, so Taut's design might be more accurately described as a 'reconstruction of the underground space' rather than an extension. In other words, he'd created a space rather than an architectural structure. That was the way Aose had interpreted it from his reading.

'Let's go down.'

'Sure.'

Immediately to their left was the staircase to the lower level, constructed over seventy years earlier. Aose followed the rather nervous-looking Ikezono. It was a steep staircase of about twenty steps. The delicate-looking treads must have been carefully preserved, as they supported the weight of an adult man without creaking.

As they descended the stairs Aose noted the first element of Taut's design concept – a bamboo handrail. It soon became clear that it wasn't just a random idea. In the hallway at the foot of the stairs there were walls lined completely with thin twigs of bamboo, and there were decorative structures resembling bamboo fences connecting the space between the hall and the next room. And beyond, bamboo continued to be the theme. From the hall, a staircase shaped like a quarter section of a round cake led into what was known as the 'social room', its handrail also made of bamboo. Four thin trunks of young bamboo had been bent and joined together to create the curved edge of the 'cake'.

Lines of naked light bulbs hung from horizontal bamboo poles suspended from the ceiling, and the cord of each bulb was decorated with chainlike strands of braided bamboo wood. Such attention to detail, Aose thought.

'Taut was fascinated by bamboo as a material,' said Ikezono, in the manner of a tour guide. 'Did I mention it was up in Takasaki where he first got into traditional bamboo crafts? He even devised bamboo desk lamps and standard lamps. You can tell that he loved to investigate the properties and possibilities of bamboo as representative of Japanese beauty.'

That would be the first thing to strike anyone who stepped into this underground space: the ingenious repetition of the same material.

Perhaps because Aose was silent, Ikezono told him to take his time looking around and walked off towards the men standing in the Japanese-style room at the end.

Aose took a deep breath and looked around the social room. The cream-coloured walls were finished with a layer of plaster. According to the books he'd read, there used to be table tennis and billiard tables in here, but now it was empty. He looked up again at the naked light bulbs. There must have been between fifty and a hundred of them hanging from their bamboo pole fixtures. They were arranged in two separate rows, one on the left and one to the right, extending towards the adjacent drawing room. These lines were not straight; they were slightly wavy, and if you looked carefully, you could see that the length of each cord was slightly different. This must have been done on purpose. Perhaps they were meant to evoke ocean waves, but Aose felt he had been drawn in by some kind of clever trickery – the staging reminded him of a temple summer festival his father had taken him to in a village somewhere long ago.

He moved on to the 'western-style drawing room'. Immediately upon entering, to the left there was a sofa set, positioned to look out through wide glass doors on to the sea. However, Aose's eye was straight away drawn to the right. There were five steps leading up towards an elevated platform against the back wall of the room. The stairs took up the whole width of the room. Guidebooks to the house referred to it as the 'upper level of the drawing room'. Stepping up, Aose felt a sense of exuberance, reminiscent of climbing on to the stage at his school arts and crafts festival. Aose would have called the top of the space neither large nor small, but it was rather peculiar. The walls were covered with a dark red silk fabric, and the ceiling was fitted with a lighting fixture that resembled a skylight. He turned around to see the horizon of Sagami Bay visible through the French windows. The same view from the sofa on the lower level was slightly obstructed by a grove of trees, but here on the upper level you had a full view of the ocean.

From the point of view of an architect, it was clear that this small staircase to an upper level had been devised as a solution to the unfavourable conditions Taut had been faced with. Due to the sloping cliff, there was a difference in height of about one metre between the closed mountainside and the open ocean side of the house. In order to make it work as a single interior space, it had been necessary to find a way to bridge this difference in height. Taut had solved the problem by building a staircase structure that could also be called a giant piece of furniture. Or rather, you could say that he had turned a disadvantageous situation into an advantageous one. He had converted the space into a giant 'staircase chair' that could accommodate a large number of guests, allowing them to simultaneously enjoy a view of the sea.

The adjacent 'Japanese-style room' had a similar staircase structure. The upper level, about three tatami mats in size, was called the 'study' and also functioned as a special kind of seat with a view of Sagami Bay. The steps were a reddish-brown colour, and the columns and lintels painted to match. Aose recognized this shade from somewhere. His neck stiffened when it came to him – Taut's face. In his nightmares, the raging architect's face was always this exact hue.

'Aose-san?'

Aose spun around to see Ikezono with a stocky, middle-aged man beside him. The man offered Aose his business card, introducing himself as Kasahara, a reporter from the arts and sciences section of the local A— newspaper. He looked slightly disgruntled, as if he were always in a bad mood.

'How do you like it?' he asked Aose. 'Could you give me your candid impressions of what you've seen?'

Aose was a little annoyed to be asked such a blunt question by a man he had only just met. He was feeling a bit Taut-drunk – that would have been his candid impression – but in order to respond to blunt with blunt, he simply replied, 'It's quite tiring.'

In fact, Aose was exhausted. Nevertheless, Kasahara pressed on.

'Taut talks about his juxtaposition of the modern with traditional Japanese elements. How did you feel about that aspect?'

But Aose couldn't bring himself to respond. There was admiration in his heart, but he had no desire to attempt to put it into words right now for other people. He didn't feel as if Taut himself would have demanded an immediate reaction. Taut was saying, 'Take your time. Think about it.'

'Taut describes the three rooms in terms of composers, isn't that right?'

Ikezono had joined in the conversation.

'Beethoven for the first room – the social room; Mozart for the western drawing room; and then the Japanese room is Bach.'

'I think you are referring not so much to the composers themselves but rather to the metaphorical difference in their musicality?'

Kasahara said this with a perfectly serious expression.

'Yes, yes, of course that's what I meant,' said Ikezono casually.

Aose had thought that Ikezono had been offering him a helping hand, but apparently not. The journalist was clearly itching to get into a discussion about Taut. Even Kasahara seemed to have lost interest in Aose and his apparent apathy, turning not only his head but his whole body towards Ikezono.

'But Ike-chan, even that is open to misinterpretation. Taut didn't bring Beethoven's musicality into the social room, or construct a drawing room filled with the essence of Mozart.'

'I've read an article somewhere that claims he did.'

'And you believe it? No, it's not true. Taut was clearly misquoted. He merely said that he gave each room its own rhythm. I think the point he was trying to make is that he unified the three rooms in a single genre, in the same way that those composers are all creators of classical music, although with very different rhythms. That's the meaning of juxtaposition, isn't it? Although rather than juxtaposition, I prefer to term it as fusion.'

Until recently, Aose would have felt like a total outsider in this conversation, but after all the reading he'd done he could understand most of what the two were saying.

'I think you're making quite a dangerous leap there, Kasahara-san,' Ikezono said. 'Quite a lot of assumptions in your argument.'

'Huh? Assumptions? What's dangerous about it? That makes me cross. The whole attempt to modernize traditional Japanese style is precisely what fusion is. And that's exactly what's happening here in this villa. Taut has done it in each of these three rooms, and then in the three rooms as a whole. His obsession with bamboo can't be explained away simply by saying he fell in love with the charm of the material, can it?'

'Right, right. So, it's "nouveau Japan" then? This whole floor is.'

'Don't you think? Taut said he wanted to create something solemn and classical, incorporating the spirit of Zen.'

'Yes, I liked that story about Zen too. I feel it goes beyond his love for Japanese culture. I think it shows his gratitude to the Japanese people.'

'If you're going to put it like that, then maybe we need to show

gratitude to the Katsura Imperial Villa for making Taut a Japano-
phile. But, yes, I think that element of gratitude was there. Or
maybe it's just that I want to believe that it was.'

Aose held back his laughter. This reporter Kasahara had seemed
rather insensitive at first, but he might have been an okay type
after all.

I love Japanese culture.

Aose recalled the words carved into the stone monument at
Senshin-tei. Taut's blessing of Japanese culture. That culture had
been considered significant at the time, but after the Second
World War it had been forgotten. Traditional Japanese culture
had no longer been valued, drowned out by the loud chorus of
westernization and the prioritization of economic efficiency.
Still, the fact that it was once praised by the eyes of a great outsider, Bruno Taut, added weight to its relevance now, seventy
years later. It wasn't possible to overlook Taut. He had given the
art world the confidence to speak out in favour of the rediscovery
of traditional Japanese aesthetics. As someone who had passed
right by Taut without ever really taking any heed of him, this
was now Aose's opinion. He was well aware that it was the opinion of a man who had trained as an architect and, totally lacking
any self-awareness, repeatedly destroyed Japanese culture in his
own designs.

Aose looked up and took in the space that flowed from Japanese room to western-style drawing room to social room. The
coincidence of the reddish-brown colour matching Taut's face in
his nightmares was just that – a coincidence. He was certain
because these three spaces which became one single space had an
atmosphere of calm that had no connection to anger whatsoever.
It was Taut's legacy to Japan. In the autumn of 1936, less than a
month after completing the remodelling of this villa, Taut had
left Japan at the invitation of the government of Turkey. That
was where he'd spent the final years of his life.

It was two years later that Erica came to Daruma-ji temple to deliver the death mask. Had his soul really returned in death to somewhere he would have liked to stay when alive? Although he loved Japanese culture, Taut must have frowned at the political events in Japan at that time. Nineteen thirty-six was the year of the '26 February Incident', a failed military coup, and the subsequent rapid militarization of Japan. Taut, whose life and career had been completely derailed by the military dictatorship in his own country, could not have felt at ease. On 26 February of that year, Taut had written in his diary:

The snowy landscape of Mount Shorinzan is two colours; black and white. However, in Tokyo, red was added, making three colours: black, white and crimson.

The very restrained description that Taut had written suggested an attempt to observe events from a neutral position, but he was at the same time stating the truth. The diary entry concluded:

The war seems to be going full steam ahead under the guise of 'emergency situation'.

The invitation from the Turkish government had been the impetus for Taut's decision to leave Japan, starved as he was of employment in the field of architecture. But had that been the real reason? Aose suspected that in a corner of Taut's mind he'd felt he should flee Japan. At the time of his 're-defection', this time to Turkey, relations between that country and Germany hadn't been too bad. It was only Aose's supposition, but as Taut left Japan, the fear of a second failure or even a third must have run through his mind. The times could not have been calming to Taut in those last years of his life.

And yet in the space that stretched out before Aose there was not the slightest hint of fear or frustration. It was determination. The strong determination to leave something behind, to bequeath his work to Japan. And that was why this space had been carefully curated for over seventy years now.

Aose recalled how he had felt each time he drew up the plans for a new building. Each of those lines he drew would take shape somewhere there in the city. His heart always soared. There was nothing that compared with the sheer joy of dreaming up and creating a brand-new building. It had never occurred to him that these buildings would eventually disappear. But they did. In less than a decade, a number of commercial buildings designed by Aose had been demolished or remodelled, or had their walls painted in ridiculous colours. But he had to focus on creating. He couldn't imagine looking back at his old self.

'It's as if he was told to be sure to leave his legacy.'

Both Ikezono and Kasahara seemed very satisfied with Aose's reply to the last of Kasahara's many questions. Aose then slipped in one of his own.

'Kasahara-san, is there any progress with Atami City's project to preserve this place?'

'Yes, yes, it's all decided,' replied Kasahara cheerfully.

It was as if he'd had a complete personality change.

'A philanthropist from Tokyo – a woman, actually – has agreed to donate the money to Atami City to purchase the building, on condition that it is preserved.'

'I'm glad to hear that.'

'By the way, Aose-san . . .' said Ikezono, as if he had just happened to remember something.

Aose knew what he was going to ask.

'What happened about the chair?'

'I struck out,' Aose replied right away.

There were chairs everywhere. Just beyond the entrance hall, lined up against the wall in the social room, and on the upper level of the drawing room, but it hadn't even been necessary to take a close look. Anyone could see at a glance that they were different from the one at the Y Residence. Aose had wondered which of these Okajima could possibly have been talking about, but as he hadn't set out expecting to be able to solve the whole mystery right here at the Hyuga Villa, he wasn't too disappointed.

'Your colleague said that he had sat in a similar chair here in the house, didn't he?' said Ikezono.

'Yes, he did . . .'

'I wonder if it's in the storeroom?'

'Yes, if there's a custodian, I thought I'd ask him on the way out.'

'I see,' said Kasahara. 'I know you came here to check out the chairs in particular. Do you happen to have a photo? If you wouldn't mind letting me take a look . . .'

Aose nodded, and found it in his bag.

'Hah!'

The moment he set eyes on the photo, Kasahara let out a small cry.

'I know this chair! I'm sure it's the same one.'

'Really?' said Ikezono, excitedly looking around the villa. 'Where is it?'

'No, it's not here. It's at a soba restaurant in Kamitaga. Just a little way from here.'

'Oh, you mean that dining set you were talking about the other day?' said Ikezono.

'Yeah, that's it. The chairs look just like this one.'

Aose didn't let himself get excited. He was more puzzled than anything. First, here was talk of yet another soba restaurant, and second, even though Kasahara seemed like a decent type, with his sudden personality changes he didn't inspire much trust in Aose's mind.

29

Sagami Bay was shimmering in the sunlight as the three left the Hyuga Villa and took a taxi for Kamitaga. It was about a fifteen-minute drive.

'Actually, it's a story that was featured in another local newspaper about seven years ago,' Kasahara explained, scratching his head. 'The building that's now the soba restaurant used to belong to the Hyuga family. Well, technically, if you trace it back, it was in a different location and was a holiday home belonging to a completely different family. Hyuga bought it and in 1935 had it dismantled and moved to Kamitaga. He asked Taut to be present for that construction.'

Aose began to be drawn in by the story. It was full of specific, tangible details.

After receiving the request from Hyuga-san, Taut had rented a private house near the construction site, and he and Erica moved there from Takasaki. Taut designed the table and chairs for his new rental home himself and had them made by a local carpenter. After the relocation work was finished, Hyuga-san took over the furniture exactly as Taut had left it and placed it in his new, relocated villa. Since then, the building had changed hands several times, but the table and chairs remained, passing from one owner to the next.

'So now the relocated villa has become a soba restaurant?'

Kasahara nodded.

'Yes, the building's been a noodle restaurant for about

twenty-five years now. I remember, seven years ago, the owner's daughter, who was in junior high school at the time, did her summer research project on the topic. It was called "My House and Bruno Taut". I wrote an article about her for the newspaper.'

'Did you see the table and chairs at the time?'

'Yes, I did. I visited the family to do a follow-up article.'

'But you already knew about them long before that, didn't you, Kasahara-san?'

Ikezono sounded like a fan of Kasahara's, encouraging him to shine.

'Well, yes,' Kasahara admitted. 'Taut wrote in his diary that he was having a table and chairs made in Kamitaga. I had it in the back of my mind, but I hadn't got around to writing it.'

'So the daughter's school research scooped you then?'

'Ha ha. Yes. It felt exactly as if I'd been scooped. Her timing was perfect.'

Before Aose could ask any more questions, the taxi drove into the car park of the soba restaurant.

The restaurant was serving customers, but the owner recognized Kasahara and showed the three men through to a back room. The table and chairs were usually in the restaurant itself, but the kindly faced owner explained that he'd had a call from a relative asking to see the furniture and had moved it into the back.

'That was lucky,' Ikezono whispered to Aose, but there wasn't time to respond. The story was significantly different from the one he had heard from his boss, Okajima. The chairs had not been made for the Hyuga Villa. However, it turned out that this new story that had surfaced might just be the authentic one. Aose had the feeling that the implausible just might turn out to be true.

They were shown into a six-tatami Japanese-style room.

Aose gasped. His eye went immediately to the sturdy rectangular table and the six chairs arranged around it. He walked over and pulled one of the chairs away from the table. There was

214

no need to compare it with the photograph – his eyes recalled every detail exactly. It was the same shape and age as the chair at the Y Residence.

'Is that it?'

Aose answered Kasahara's question with a simple 'Yes'.

He was looking at the chair from the side. He turned it over to check under the seat. There was no Taut-Inoue stamp. Well, that was to be expected; this chair had never been for sale. It was a one-of-a-kind piece, designed by Taut for Erica and him to use in their daily lives.

He turned around to see the soba shop owner looking concerned.

'I'm so sorry.' Aose bowed and gently returned the chair to its original position.

'Would you mind if I tried sitting in it?'

'Go ahead.'

Aose lowered his body into the chair. It felt just right, as if there were something familiar about it. It was the exact same feeling he'd had sitting in the chair at the Y Residence. He closed his eyes and imagined he was there in that upstairs master bedroom. Even the blue sky that had filled his entire field of vision came back to him . . .

But no, that chair had to be different. Aose opened his eyes and counted the chairs again. Six, and the table was built to the exact dimension of those six chairs. This set wasn't missing a chair. In other words, the one in the Y Residence wasn't from here. The chair that Aose was sitting on right now in his memory had to be a copy of the original.

'Your chair isn't an original then, just an identical copy,' said Ikezono, sounding disappointed.

'But Ike-chan, it's not one of the chairs that was sold as merchandise that's been copied,' Kasahara cut in. 'Taut only used these in his home for a short time, and they've been here for the last seventy years. This dining set has never left the premises.'

'What of it?'

'You're not getting it. It means that whoever made the reproduction had to have come here and taken a really good look at the original.'

'Well, that's brilliant. But you know what, how are you going to check everyone who ever set foot in this building? It's been seventy years. The chair in Aose-san's photograph is certainly old, but there's no way to check if it was made fifty or even sixty years ago.'

'Or it could even be seventy years ago, couldn't it?' said Aose, getting to his feet.

He'd been listening to the conversation and had started to wonder if there hadn't been a seventh chair.

'What if the cabinetmaker who'd been hired to produce the chairs had secretly made one extra?' he continued. 'Perhaps to keep and use for himself? I'm finding it difficult to believe that the other one is a counterfeit. It's just too perfect.'

The two reporters nodded and spoke at the same moment.

'The cabinetmaker!'

'Well, he has to be dead by now. But perhaps we could find his descendants. His children, or maybe grandchildren? . . . Did Taut's diary happen to mention any cabinetmakers by name?'

The two men looked at each other hesitantly, and then Ikezono dared to make the first move.

'No, I don't think he ever wrote down a name.'

'No, he didn't,' Kasahara echoed him. 'There's a cabinetmaker called Sasaki-san who was connected to the villa reconstruction project, but the table and chairs in Taut's own home were made by an unknown craftsman.'

'Do you think you can find out who it was?'

Aose immediately regretted asking. As much as he would love to make use of the skills of these investigative reporters, he realized it would be a bad idea to let them dig any deeper into this case.

Ikezono pulled a face.

'When they moved the villa to this location, Taut was living in a house very nearby so it has to have been a local cabinetmaker. It's just that it was seventy years ago . . .'

He turned to the restaurant owner.

'Do you happen to know anything about it, sir?'

The owner looked blank.

'I'm sorry, they didn't really give me very many details about the furniture.'

'Of course. Well, we're just going to have to ask Kasahara-san, who has the home-turf advantage here, to amass all the man-power he can manage.'

Kasahara scowled and crossed his arms. He looked to be on the point of making some retort about lack of chivalry or the stub-bornness of a Taut specialist reporter.

Aose hurriedly intervened.

'I can't ask you to do that. It's not a serious matter at all. It's just a personal affair. I'm having a bit of trouble getting in touch with a friend, that's all.'

Kasahara immediately relaxed, but his expression still held traces of the irritation he felt at Ikezono.

Aose decided it was time to wind things up. He turned to the owner and asked the question that had been on his mind the whole time.

'Did a man by the name of Touta Yoshino ever come here and ask you about these chairs?'

'Ah, yes he did.'

For a moment, Aose was unable to react.

'He came?'

'A short man?'

'Yes, that's right.'

Aose's voice caught in his throat, so the restaurant owner con-tinued.

'I remember him well. The chairs were featured in the local

paper, and about two years later he came to visit and asked if I would show them to him.'

Aose was on tenterhooks.

'He said he had roots in Sendai. Is that the man you mean?'

'Y— yes, I think so.'

'He seemed really happy. Like you just now, he was examining and touching the chairs all over. He also sat in one. And then he said he had the blueprints for the chairs. I was really surprised.'

Things had taken a very unexpected turn. The word 'blueprints' shot through Aose's brain like an arrow.

30

On the shinkansen home, Aose had no choice but to sit with Ike-zono, even though he really wanted some time alone to think. The information he'd got from the Kamitaga soba restaurant was astonishing. Touta Yoshino had paid a visit to that shop, revealing that his roots were in Sendai in northern Japan and that he had the blueprints for Taut's chair. All of a sudden, details of the mystery were being filled in and there was a sense that he was finally getting results, but Aose's head was filled with the mystery of the family's disappearance, and Ikezono's was not. It was increasingly difficult for them to work together on a theory. He was already having trouble fielding Ikezono's questions.

'Aose-san, you didn't know that your friend Yoshino was from Sendai?'

'I thought he was from Nagano. Still, saying your roots are in a place doesn't necessarily mean that you were born there, does it?'

Was Yoshino from Sendai? Aose didn't recall ever asking. If a Tokyo resident doesn't mention where they're from, unless they're deliberately hiding their origins it means they're from Tokyo. Of course, Aose really didn't know Yoshino-san at all, and he couldn't help getting nervous at every one of Ikezono's questions. On the other hand, Ikezono, being such a Taut enthusiast, was flooding Aose with information on the chair mystery, which of course was linked directly to the disappearance of the family. In effect, it made Ikezono the best possible Watson to Aose's Holmes – just as long as he didn't step on any landmines.

'Pity. I wish we could have heard how this Yoshino-san came to have the blueprints for Taut's chair.'

The soba shop owner said he had asked, but unfortunately Yoshino had brushed off the question.

'It must have been about five years ago that Yoshino-san went to the restaurant. It was seven years ago that the article about the chairs appeared in the newspaper, so . . . yes, it was about two years after that.'

'Actually, I've worked out why it was two years later,' Ikezono said. 'About a year and a half to two years after that article in the local newspaper, an architecture magazine did a special feature on Taut and it mentioned the chairs in Kamitaga. Maybe Yoshino-san visited the restaurant after reading that article. You can't get local, Atami-based newspapers in Tokyo.'

Aose finally realized — a little late, but it had come to him. When he'd first seen the chair in the master bedroom of the Y Residence, he'd had a vague memory of reading an article somewhere about Taut's chairs. It hadn't been a newspaper — it had been in an architectural magazine that had caught his eye.

'But Sendai is a huge clue,' Ikezono continued. He looked at Aose with an excited expression. Aose knew what it meant.

'Taut was in Sendai for a while, wasn't he?'

'That's right. You're well informed. It was before he settled in the Senshin-tei house in Takasaki. The former Ministry of Commerce and Industry set up the National Research Institute of Industrial Arts in Sendai, and he was invited to be on the team there. It was created in response to the financial crisis in the early years of the Showa era. The country wanted to encourage and develop industrial crafts and promote exports. Taut happened to be there at the beginning of this period, which was really fortunate for the early days of the institute.'

'What did he do there?'

'Well, design, but the reason for inviting him was to help to change people's mindset. He proposed a bold business plan aimed at creating internationally competitive crafted products.'

'He didn't last long there, did he?'

Ikezono looked at him with curiosity.

'You seem to be becoming more familiar with Taut, Aose-san.'

'I've been reading a lot. You inspired me.'

'Inspired? Really?'

Ikezono laughed delightedly.

'So it seems you weren't able to evade Bruno Taut after all.'

'It wasn't that I was avoiding him or anything . . . Well, never mind. What happened next?'

'Oh, right. Well, Taut spent less than four months in Sendai. All of the staff at the institute were in favour of Taut's proposals, but somehow or other, in Taut's eyes, no one was doing anything about it, nor did they have any intention of doing anything. That made him frustrated.'

Ikezono looked as if he had been responsible himself.

'Did Taut make chairs up in Sendai?'

Brought back on topic, Ikezono nodded immediately.

'Along with desks and standard lamps, they were working on prototypes of chairs and door handles.'

'And Taut designed chairs himself?'

'Most probably. Just as in Kamitaga, he would have designed them and had the staff construct them.'

'Then it's possible that the chairs he designed in Sendai and the chairs at the soba restaurant were made from the same blueprints.'

Ikezono groaned a little.

'That would be too difficult to confirm. When we say "designed" in the case of things like chairs and industrial craft work, it's not like drawing up proper architectural plans. Often Taut just sketched something freehand and wrote the dimensions on it. But I hear what you're saying. It really gets the imagination going, doesn't it? For example, Taut might have proposed the design while he was in Sendai, but perhaps none of the institute's staff were able to build the chair to his specifications. Let's say when he got to Kamitaga he remembered the chair and got a skilled local cabinetmaker to construct it for him. Something like that.'

'Assuming that's the case, then that means the original blueprints must be at the National Research Institute of Industrial Arts office in Sendai?' said Aose hopefully, but Ikezono shook his head.

'The reason I said it was difficult to confirm is that the institute was dissolved back in the 1960s. The phrase they used means something like "dissolution in order to develop", but the brutal reality is that the Arts Institute was done away with completely.'

'Are there any documents remaining?'

'The Northern Japan branch of the National Institute of Advanced Industrial Science and Technology is located there currently. I can't say for sure until I've given it a try, but not much of Taut's contribution was saved, and I'm guessing a lot of the information has been lost.'

'Then how did Yoshino get hold of the blueprints for the chairs?'

'The most likely answer is that someone connected to the institute kept the blueprints for a long time and Yoshino-san somehow got hold of them.'

'Or perhaps Yoshino's father or grandfather worked at the institute,' Aose mused out loud, and was rewarded with an emphatic nod from Ikezono.

'Yes, yes . . . So, we're working with the theory that the blueprints were already there in Yoshino's home. Do we think that's the most likely one? As I think I've mentioned before, there are sometimes cases like this. Blueprints of Taut's work have turned up in the storerooms of houses where the family has worked in carpentry or cabinetmaking for generations. What's Yoshino-san's job? He doesn't happen to be a carpenter or cabinetmaker, does he? Ha ha.'

Aose paused for a moment before replying.

'He's a wholesaler of imported goods. Although he may have gone freelance lately.'

'How about his father or grandfather?'

'I don't know. Yoshino never spoke about his family.'

'Well then, it might be something in that kind of field. Maybe someone in his family was related to the Industrial Arts Institute . . . Oh, who's this?'

Ikezono looked at his vibrating phone, excused himself and headed out to the standing space between the train carriages.

Aose took a moment to breathe. The sounds and the shuddering of the train became more vivid all of a sudden.

He and Ikezono were on the same path, but with different destinations. Ikezono must be having his doubts by now. He must wonder who on earth this Yoshino might be, and what connection he had to Aose.

To be fair, he wanted to know the exact same thing himself: who was this Touta Yoshino, and what on earth was their relationship?

Had Yoshino grown up in a family of carpenters or cabinetmakers? He had no idea. At least, he'd never heard anything like that from him. All that Aose knew was that he had sold some imported furniture to the landlady of his rented house in Tabata.

Did he really have the blueprints for the chairs at the Kamitaga soba noodle restaurant?

And had the chair in the Y Residence been made according to those blueprints? If so, who made it? It wasn't Yoshino himself – he was neither carpenter nor cabinetmaker, and even if he were, he couldn't have made it because he wasn't an adult back when the originals were constructed. His father or grandfather must have made it. But when and where? It was probably safe to narrow it down to around when the originals were made. Maybe the 'where' was the Industrial Arts Institute? Perhaps Yoshino's father or grandfather had worked at the institute and was given the blueprints to make the chairs, and had then gone on to make the one at the Y Residence? Or perhaps after Taut had left the institute he'd noticed that the blueprints had been left behind and took them to build the chair? Perhaps the Yoshino family even owned the blueprints, and they were passed down to Touta Yoshino. It made sense that there would be multiple copies of any blueprints. Taut was a precise worker and a meticulous note-taker. He would have had a notebook into which he copied the design for the chair. He would have shown that notebook to the cabinetmaker in Kamitaga . . .

Aose watched the sun set from the train window.

In his recollections, Yoshino had always worn a broad smile, but these days when he pictured the man he was no longer smiling. His roots were in Sendai. There was something shady about that piece of information. It brought to mind the kind of professional scammers who deceive people on a regular basis. Aose had already stopped blaming or resenting Yoshino, had decided all he wanted was to see the smiling faces of the whole family. But now, despite Aose's change of heart, it seemed that Yoshino was continuing to deceive him. It didn't matter how far back Aose went in the history, there was always a lie. Yoshino had performed a classic vanishing act, and the Y Residence had been the cage he'd vanished from. Aose couldn't understand what Yoshino had to gain from this magic trick, but somehow he had pulled it off. Aose had been left to observe the empty cage and stare around, wondering how he'd done it.

'Aose-san?'

Aose opened his eyes to see the faces of both Ikezono and the train conductor. He got out his ticket and handed it over.

'Sorry about that,' he said to Ikezono.

'No, no. You seem really tired though.'

'Not exactly. I'm a little in-Taut-xicated.'

'Intautxicated?'

'Yes. I think it's the fault of the Hyuga Villa.'

224

'You got drunk on the Hyuga Villa and ended up in-Taut-xicated? Nice comment! Can I use it?'

'Knock yourself out,' said Aose, stretching his stiff neck.

'If it's all right with you, I could look into the Sendai connection for you,' Ikezono suggested, a little cautiously. 'I've got a contact at the M— newspaper there who knows quite a lot about the topic. Also, last time I was in Sendai I got to know a researcher specializing in Taut—'

'No,' said Aose, without elaborating.

'I'm sorry. Am I being too pushy?'

'No, not at all. On the contrary. As I told Kasahara-san back at the villa, I really don't want to put you to any more trouble.'

'But it's not any—'

'But could you introduce me to this Taut specialist?'

There was a momentary flash of disappointment in Ikezono's eyes, but he quickly recovered.

'Sure. I'll just go through my materials back at the office and I'll give you his details.'

'Thank you. I appreciate it.'

'But if you're going to Sendai, I'd like to go with you. It would make for an interesting article if we could find out the origin of that chair.'

Aose could only manage a vague nod.

The shinkansen's windows began to darken as it sped back towards Tokyo, but the Hyuga Villa was still looming in Aose's mind. Taut's semi-basement space couldn't seem to care less about all the fuss surrounding its maker's chair.

31

It was after 8 p.m. when Aose got back to Tokorozawa and stopped by the office. Mayumi was still there, and Takeuchi too, his back hunched over his desk. On the 'competition table' was a large pile of photos and documents.

'Welcome back.'

Mayumi was in great spirits.

'It's like having a second child,' she announced. Her first-born, Yuma, was in the care of her mother. Takeuchi had dark circles under his eyes. Ever since the firm had entered the competition, he'd been suffering from a constant low fever and been unable to sleep.

Okajima and Ishimaki were on a four-day inspection tour and would be staying the night in Kofu in Yamanashi prefecture. 'Domestic rep' Takeuchi had collected around a hundred items of information on museums and memorials, which the other four had sifted through and then Okajima had narrowed down to around a dozen. In order to avoid designing a museum that resembled a museum, they had first set out to visit the most museum-like museums. Before heading off, Aose had had a word in his boss's ear. He'd advised him to take the renderer, Nishikawa, along. Competitions were about the concept and the presentation but also about how well the perspective drawings were done. If Okajima wanted Nishikawa to draw something that would blow the jury's minds, it would be best to give him as much access to Okajima's thought processes as possible.

'Damn, I sure wish I could have gone with them.'

Even in the way he swore, Takeuchi still came across as a well-brought-up young man.

Aose patted his shoulder.

'Don't complain – you can come up with ideas here at the office too. Just keep churning them out. You too, Tsumura-san.'

'Me too? Are you sure?'

'Of course. You've seen buildings all over the world on your computer. Trust your mind, which has seen so many fine and beautiful buildings, and then picture what kind of memorial you would want to build. Even a fragment of a design is good. Then just put it into words or drawings to inspire the boss.

'I see. I see . . . I agree, it's good to have as many ideas as possible, never mind how off the wall they might be.'

Mayumi was more excited than ever, but Takeuchi remained glum.

'As much as I'd like to . . .'

He was flicking through a thick book as he spoke. *The History of S— City*. It was the homework Okajima had given him before he left. Takeuchi had been instructed to pick out any symbolic events that might give a hint as to how to 'win the hearts of the locals'. Mayumi had homework too. She'd been instructed to collect material on the working-class way of life in post-war Paris.

'Digging into S— city's history is a great idea. I'm sure the Tokyo offices would never think of that.'

'Yes, I think you're right. That's why I went to the library this morning, but I got called away for an emergency. A property in Fukaya got caught in a river.'

'You mean a boundary dispute?'

This was a common problem that came up when they were building properties close to rivers or streams. Local sewage departments would often quibble with them about the proper demarcation of boundaries.

'No, not this time. Yesterday a patrol from the Ministry of Land, Infrastructure and Transport came around to the house to tell them it was in a river zone.'

'The MLIT? Which house?'

'It's a Class A river, apparently. Protected. So they sent out the national team. It's not the house itself but some adjacent greenhouses. They were built alongside the home. Of course, the house itself was outside the river zone, but some of the greenhouses are within it, it seems. It was our oversight, but they were so over-bearing with our client, telling him to take them down immediately, that he was totally freaked out. So I ended up going to the MLIT sub-branch today to try to negotiate with them.'

Aose wasn't surprised to hear how far above and beyond Takeuchi had gone in trying to help the client. His dream was to provide low-cost housing for low-income families throughout Japan. He genuinely liked to help people and try to make the world a better place.

'Did you manage to sort it out?'

'I let them know that we planned to properly notify the authorities. But listen – the documents they want us to submit are laughable. There's one called a Plan for Demolition Form. Have you ever come across that one before?'

'No. A proper demolition plan for the house?'

'Right. We have to notify them in detail how many people, working how many hours, using what equipment, it will take to demolish the house, taking into account the fact that if the river exceeds a certain level at the upstream observation post we will be proceeding at our own risk. I added your name, Aose-san. When the time comes, I can get you to operate a power shovel or something.'

Aose laughed.

'I'm on the list too,' said Mayumi, handing him a cup of coffee.

'Mayumi possesses superhuman strength, so we've counted her as two people.'

'Takeuchi-kun, what a thing to say!'

Mayumi faked outrage, which of course made Takeuchi smile. It was a pleasant scene, but only served to gloss over what was not a laughing situation. Half a day had been wasted on the house demolition plan. Takeuchi was already overworked, without even taking into account the extra hours he was putting into the competition. He'd even been assisting Aose with some site supervision work while Ishimaki was out doing reconnaissance with Okajima.

Mayumi was also feeling the strain. Her computer screen was filled with an ancient map of Paris. On her desk was a pile of accounting books and bundles of unprocessed sales slips, as well as a number of unfinished room-interior presentation boards.

This is what happens when an office with a total of five people enters a grand-scale competition. *That's the ultimate select few, isn't it?* No matter how many times Aose had tried to get rid of it, the image of Hatoyama's face kept appearing in his head. At the far end of the competition table, Mayumi had placed a handmade tear-off calendar for counting down the days. It was titled 'Okajima Design Office's 90-day War!' and currently showed the number 79 in bright red lettering. Win or lose, would the office be able to endure this punishing work schedule for another seventy-nine days?

Underneath the title '90-day War!', barely visible even if you squinted, were the words 'Sorry, Yuma ♥' in Mayumi's rounded handwriting.

'So Aose-san, did you have any success today?'

The smile hadn't yet faded from Takeuchi's face.

'Success?'

'Didn't you go there today? Bruno Taut's villa in Atami?'

'Ah, yeah.'

'Well, how was it? Was there anything useful for the memorial?'

Okajima must have told the others that Aose was visiting to get ideas for the competition.

'To tell the truth, I'm not that interested in Taut,' Takeuchi continued. 'I feel as if he's a bit of a know-it-all. He only lived here a couple of years but talked about rediscovering the beauty of Japan.'

If Ikezono or Kasahara had been able to hear this there would have been steam coming out of their ears. Even Aose was quite offended.

'It scares me to think what would have happened if Taut hadn't come to Japan, though.'

At Aose's gentle rebuttal, Takeuchi acted with exaggerated surprise.

'Scares you? Eh? That's quite a compliment. If Taut hadn't come to Japan, would the history of Japanese architecture have been any different?'

'Can you say it wouldn't have changed?'

'Well, I can't say the effect was zero but . . .'

'Seventy years ago, maybe only a tiny amount, but Taut changed the way Japanese people see things. I'm sure of that.'

'You know, that doesn't sound like you at all, Aose-san.'

'Really?'

'Getting all passionate.'

Suddenly Takeuchi was in the mood for confessions.

'Mayumi-san and I talk about it all the time. How cool you always are. Like that manga assassin Golgo 13.'

'I never said that!' Mayumi interrupted him.

'Yes, you did. You also said he's just like Ken Takakura.'

'It's all lies,' said Mayumi. 'I don't even know these actors, Ken Takakura and Golgo 13 or whatever his name is. This is all stuff that Takeuchi said himself.'

Just as Aose and Takeuchi looked at each other and burst out laughing the office phone rang.

Presumably thinking it was a call from the boss, Mayumi hurriedly reverted to professional mode. She rushed over and picked up the phone. Right away, her expression changed and she tilted her head to one side quizzically.

Aose had also assumed it would be Okajima and had walked over. But now Mayumi was asking the caller to hold the line. Putting a hand over the mouthpiece, she turned to Aose.

'It's someone from a newspaper.'

'Ah, it's Ikezono,' thought Aose. He must have gone straight to his office to look up the Taut scholar in Sendai.

'I'll take it,' he said, grabbing the receiver from Mayumi.

'Oh, but—'

The reason for Mayumi's hesitation was immediately apparent.

'Is this Akihiko Okajima-san?'

The voice was slightly muffled. It wasn't unlike Ikezono's, but somehow shiftier.

'The president is currently on a business trip. Who's calling, please?'

'When will he be back?'

'Um, just a minute . . .'

Aose glanced at the whiteboard. Okajima and Ishimaki would be back by the evening of the next day, or the day after at the latest.

'We'll have him contact you. Could I have your name and number?'

There was an uncomfortable pause. And then the reason for it became clear.

'Are you sure you're not Okajima-san?'

Aose moved the receiver away from his ear. The caller thought he was Okajima? Immediately the suspicion in the caller's voice infected Aose's mood.

'No, I'm not Okajima. Excuse me, but what was your name again?'

'My name's Shigeta, from the *Toyo Shimbun*. Please tell me when Okajima-san will be back.'

The *Toyo Shimbun* was one of the two biggest newspapers in Japan.

'I'm really not completely sure. Can I be of some help?'

'Could you give me his mobile number?'

'I can't do that. Please tell me what it is you want.'

'If you were Okajima-san I'd tell you what I want.'

Aose was incensed by the man's arrogant behaviour.

'I can get in touch with Okajima, but I can't know what to tell him if you won't explain what it's about.'

Now the pause was clearly to give the man time to think. Possibly he was discussing with someone else what to do. Aose could hear the bustle of a newspaper office in the background. Had something happened to the Yoshino family? No, if that was the case, it would be the police calling.

Suddenly the voice was back.

'I'm calling to set up an interview.'

'What kind of interview?'

'It's better if I explain it to Okajima-san himself. It's a little complicated.'

He was still trying to find out if Okajima was in fact in the office. Aose was irritated, but at least the man had revealed his identity. Theirs was a legitimate company so a newspaper reporter was free to drop by at any time; insisting in this way that he talk to the boss wasn't going to get him anywhere.

'I'll let him know you called. The *Toyo Shimbun* . . .'

'Shigeta.'

'Which department do you belong to?'

The question rolled off his tongue, as he had just spent the whole day with two newspaper journalists.

'Local news division.'

The man's tone was filled with menace. Aose had had a hunch that it was something bad, but now it seemed he'd guessed right.

'When you say local news, does it mean this is in relation to a specific case?'

'I'll discuss that with Okajima-san.'

The door that had opened a crack was immediately slammed shut again.

'I see. Any other messages?'

'Just that I'd really like to meet with him. I'll call again tomorrow.'

'I'll let him know.'

Aose slammed down the phone.

'Aose-san?'

He turned to see two very worried faces.

'What's this case?' said Takeuchi, his voice subdued.

'I've no idea.'

Aose turned his back and dialled Okajima's mobile. After a few rings, he heard his boss's boomingly cheerful voice.

'Hey, Aose! You back already? How was it at the Hyuga place?'

It sounded as if Okajima had had a lot to drink.

'I'll tell you about it when you get back. Did you meet up with Nishikawa-san yet?'

'Yesterday. Do you have something you want to ask him?'

'No. Anyway, we just got a call at the office from a reporter by the name of Shigeta. Says he's from the *Toyo Shimbun* and wants to ask you something.'

He deliberately kept his tone light, but he heard Okajima's breath catch.

'A reporter asking for me?'

'Yeah, he said he's going to call back. He's from the local news division. Do you have any idea what he might want?'

'. . . No.'

Clearly, he did.

Aose also had an inkling of what it might be about but, conscious of the two staff members behind him, he purposely changed the subject.

'How's it going there?'

'What?'

233

'The memorial tour. Are you getting any inspiration from it?'

'Ah, yes . . . It's been very informative . . . This reporter – he didn't say what he wanted, did he?'

'He said he'd tell you when you met. Anyway, Okajima – more importantly, those chairs weren't at the Hyuga Villa at all. They were at a soba restaurant in nearby Kamitaga. And all six chairs in the set were there. Is it possible you remembered wrong?'

'Kamitaga? Maybe. Back then I was going around all the places that had some connection with Taut . . .'

Okajima was distracted.

'So when will you be back?'

'Tomorrow . . . tentatively.'

'Got it. Don't drink too much. And give my regards to Nishikawa-san.'

As soon as he hung up the phone, Mayumi was at his side, staring into his face.

'What did the boss say?'

She was frowning so hard it looked as if her left and right eyebrows were connected in the middle. But there was really no need for her to ask. She and Okajima were concentric plum blossoms. The fear felt by Mayumi here in Tokorozawa was also being felt by Okajima way up in Yamanashi prefecture.

32

He clearly remembered what Okajima had said: '*I bust a gut to get selected.*' Aose had smelt something fishy the moment he said it. He knew what must have happened – the reporter had also sniffed out something related to the memorial competition. Had Okajima done something reckless – and what?

Aose put his beer can down, turned off the TV and lay down on the sofa. They'd know tomorrow. When Okajima got back from the trip he'd ask him what happened, assess the situation and work out the best way to deal with it. It was all they could do. There was nothing to be done until then anyway.

He closed his eyes, but no matter how much he tried, he couldn't summon an image of the Hyuga Villa. But what he had was a sense of having been welcomed. The feeling of having been invited into a space and entertained lingered in his mind. Perhaps he felt that all the more because there hadn't been an exterior design to take in first. He hadn't seen the villa; he'd experienced it. Seventy years may have passed, but Aose had been one of its guests.

Should he go to Sendai? But the company was preparing for the competition, and now that there was the hint of some sort of cloud hanging over their entry, it wasn't a good time. If he dug too deeply around Touta Yoshino's roots, he risked learning more about the man's dishonesty. He reflected, too, on his over-reliance on Ikezono and other Taut-related specialists. Right now, Ikezono and Kasahara had the feel of museum curators about them, and they had nothing to do with the Yoshino case, but once they heard about the vanished family, would their attitude change? Ever since he'd got the call at the office from the reporter Shigeta, Aose had made up his mind to be more careful. He knew there were all sorts of reporters, but just because they were in different fields didn't mean their roots weren't basically the same. If the firm's entry into the memorial competition, for which Okajima had been working with more energy than he'd ever put into anything, were about to be derailed, and the mystery of the Y Residence were to simultaneously come to light, then Okajima Design Company would be in deep trouble.

Sendai could wait. There was no urgent need to extend the investigation to somewhere so far away. Anyway, Yoshino didn't want to be found. No matter how many times Aose had called the Y Residence or Yoshino's phone, the man had never once called back. He didn't want anyone to know where he was. In order to escape the red-faced man, Yoshino had gone missing of his own free will. And he had given no hint as to his whereabouts.

But what about the children? Sometimes Aose would think about them – the two girls in junior high school and the boy in first grade of primary. He'd met them twice – once at the ground-breaking ceremony in Shinano-Oiwake and once at the handover of the house. The eldest daughter had already been taller than her parents and had seemed mature for her age. However, she had given Aose no more than a shy smile, seemingly putting up a barrier. The second daughter had also been distant. When Aose had spoken to her she gave no more than polite answers, such as 'I'm looking forward to it' or 'Yes, I like it.' Nevertheless, both sisters had seemed happy. They had been glued to each other from beginning to end, giggling and whispering, stealing glances at Aose. On the day of the ground-breaking ceremony, the youngest child, the son, had stared at Aose sulkily from his mother's shadow. Nothing had changed by the day the house was handed over. The boy had returned to the car head down, playing his

Game Boy, and hadn't bothered to look at his room in the Y Residence.

Aose saw them now as a kind of paper-cut-out family. He imagined that the tall woman had been the cause of the Yoshinos' divorce or separation. The parents and their two daughters had done an impressive job of playing the role of a happy family finally getting their dream home, and only the son had given an honest reflection of the shattered family. The landlord had told Aose that Touta Yoshino had lived alone in the rented house in Tabata; Aose had believed that the Y Residence was intended as a symbol of hope – an attempt to reunite the family. But he knew nothing for certain and had no way of confirming or denying it. One thing he did know was that every aspect of the Yoshino family's situation couldn't be explained away simply by the appearance of the red-faced man.

Never mind for now about the parents. This course of events, their odd behaviour leading up to their disappearance, had to have had its starting point, its point of ignition, and it was a path they had finally chosen after many developments. But the three children had been left to deal with the fallout. What was waiting for them at the end of the road? Were they a family of five hiding in a small town somewhere? Was Touta Yoshino the only one on the run while Karie and the children were in hiding somewhere else? Or maybe the couple was together while the children had been left in someone else's care? Whatever the case, Aose could no longer picture those smiling faces. Where were they going to school? Did they have enough money to live on? He tried to find a ray of light in the possibility that they were living with their grandparents, but that might mean that the red-faced man was still a threat. How far did that fiendish hand with its three-finger cast extend?

Aose jumped up from the sofa. It was a frustrating habit of his, but the door to creativity always seemed to open when he was thinking about something other than architecture. Right now, he could see the eyes of the shoeshine boy and an easel with a portrait on it. Opposite was the small flight of steps to the upper level of the Hyuga Villa's drawing room . . . The first easel is not the only one there. There are seven or eight, perhaps more, lined up side by side, each one holding a brilliantly painted but rather terrifying portrait. He climbs one step of the staircase, and now there is another row of easels behind the first; climbs the second step and a further row appears. Three steps, four steps . . . ten steps – hundreds of paintings on hundreds of easels – and Sagami Bay is revealed in all its glory, as all the nameless people in the portraits simultaneously scream for their lives. That's right, in Haruko Fujimiya's body of work there was no such thing as an acknowledged masterpiece. Hers wasn't a conventional world in which any of her paintings were of higher or lower status than any other, or where the highest-ranked painting was given a room of its own. All of her portraits were both nameless and at the same time masterpieces. And that was why they deserved to be placed side by side, revealing the life of Haruko Fujimiya in a single picture. As you climb the stairs you hear her musings, her mutterings, witness her daily life, and finally, you touch the artist's very soul, the one that she sacrificed to depicting the collective souls of all these other individuals. But that's not all. It doesn't end there. Beneath the upper level of the drawing room, there's another, lower level. Branching off, halfway down the staircase, there is a second staircase structure that takes you down into a basement. There, you gradually sink down into Taut's chair from the Y Residence master bedroom. One step down, two steps, and the pictures disappear. Mount Asama disappears. Your vision is filled by a great blue sky. There is a massive picture window on the far wall through which all that can be seen is sky. You can go anywhere. Everywhere is connected by that blue sky. You can go as far as the Parisian sky that consumed Haruko Fujimiya's life . . .

Aose's home phone was ringing. He struck his knees three

times with both fists before getting up. But by the time he got there, the answer machine had already picked up the call.

'*Okajima here . . . I'm meeting that reporter tomorrow afternoon. I need you to be there with me.*'

He sounded dejected. Aose was on the point of picking up the receiver, but for some reason he stopped.

'*Please.*'

After a brief pause, Okajima hung up, and the red light of the answer machine began to blink.

It's a once-in-a-lifetime opportunity. I bust a gut to get selected. I want to win so badly . . .

I want to win so badly . . .

Still the blue sky didn't vanish. Almost like the enraged Taut from his nightmares, Aose remained in fierce pursuit of that flash of inspiration.

33

Again the following day there were no birds in the sky.

Aose left his apartment without eating breakfast. He drove the Citroën to City Hall to apply for a building permit, then headed to a restaurant in the area behind Marui Department Store.

Okajima was already there, arms folded, sitting at a table in the back. Even under the low lighting, Aose could see that his expression was uncharacteristically tense. However, when Okajima greeted Aose his voice sounded normal.

'What did you do with the others?' Aose asked, pulling out the chair opposite and sitting down.

'Ah, left them up in Kofu. I stood up the whole way back on the train, making phone calls.'

He already seemed to be inviting questions.

As soon as Aose had ordered the thousand-yen lunch, Okajima jumped in.

'The reporter will be here at one o'clock.'

'Where? Here?'

'Yes.'

Aose checked his watch. It was just after twelve.

'I got a call from Mayumi just now. She said the reporter had called again, so I rang the communications department and got them to send him here.'

'Communications department?'

'The *Toyo Shimbun*'s S— city communications department. That's who it was on the phone yesterday, right?'

'A reporter by the name of Shigeta?'

'That's the one.'

'He told me he was from the local news division.'

Okajima snorted in disgust.

'Scare tactics. He's one of those sorts of reporters, this Shigeta guy.'

Aose understood why Okajima seemed in slightly better spirits. Since the previous evening he'd been phoning around, and now he knew enough about his enemy to be able to refer to him as 'one of those sorts of reporters'.

Aose rested his elbows on the table, bringing himself closer to Okajima. They had about an hour before the reporter arrived.

'So, he's a nasty piece of work? How did you get mixed up with someone like that?'

Okajima didn't reply. He just stared into Aose's eyes.

'You're not going to quit the company, are you?'

Aose was taken by surprise.

'Quit? Me? Why?'

'As long as you're not planning to.'

Okajima looked away, but Aose kept his gaze on his boss's face.

'Talk to me. Did someone tell you I was planning to quit?'

'No, they didn't.'

'Then why would you think it?'

'Okay, okay, I get it.'

Okajima gestured to Aose to calm down.

'Take it easy. I'll tell you. Once – it must have been more than a year ago – a guy from a detective agency came, asking about you.'

Aose couldn't believe his ears.

'Did you say a detective agency . . .'

'Well, I guess he was a private investigator.'

'What did he want?'

'He said you'd got engaged.'

Aose physically recoiled.

'When was this?'

'Like I told you, over a year ago.'

'When exactly? Please try to remember more clearly.'

'Last year . . . in February. You know, when we had that heavy snow? It was still there on the roads.'

'So this detective—'

'There was no engagement, was there?' Okajima interrupted.

'No.'

Okajima gave a brief nod.

'Thought so. It smelt like a pretext for some other kind of investigation, so I did some digging myself. But I wasn't able to work out what he was really after. I thought maybe someone was headhunting you for another firm. That the new company might have been doing some sort of background check on you.'

'What are you talking about? That's crazy. If I was going to jump ship, then the detective was hardly likely to ask my current boss about me. If the contract had fallen through, then I wouldn't be able to stay on once you knew that I'd been sneaking around behind your back.'

'Right. A bird doesn't foul the nest it's about to leave. Basic rule of detective work.'

'What the hell are you talking about? Anyway, why are we talking about detectives when this reporter is about to turn up?'

'Hey, Aose?'

Once again, Okajima looked him straight in the eye.

'Can I trust you?'

A shiver ran down Aose's spine. Okajima, looking perfectly normal, but acting anything but, was sitting there opposite him. He couldn't believe it. He honestly couldn't believe what his boss and friend was asking him. It wasn't the story of the detective coming to see him that Okajima wanted to know about. He wanted to know whether it was Aose who tipped off the newspaper reporter.

'I'm grateful to you for everything. I've never once thought of quitting the company.'

He'd said what he needed to.

'Got it. I'm sorry.'

Okajima's demons seemed to have been appeased for the moment. But now they were replaced by the ones that had seized Aose's mind. Who had been investigating him, and why? The one-plate lunch arrived. The waitress's long hair was almost touching his pasta.

'What did that detective ask you?'

Aose had decided to go with this topic until he'd finished his lunch. Then they could talk about the competition.

'Lots of things. Where you're from, where you went to university, your family and your work.'

Aose knew that his eyes had turned hard.

'Did you tell him?'

'Just vaguely.'

'What is vaguely?'

'Well . . .'

Okajima's fork stopped moving.

'That your parents' job took you all over the country. That you dropped out of university. That you got divorced a while back, that you have one daughter. That you're a genius at your job . . . that's about it.'

'Did you tell him about Yukari and Hinako?'

'Well, I—'

Okajima dropped his fork loudly on to his plate.

'The detective talked to Yukari-san, too, you know. It didn't matter whether I told him about them or not.'

What the hell?

Aose scowled at Okajima.

'How do you know that?' he asked.

'Know what?'

'That he went to talk to Yukari too.'

'I got a phone call. From her. She told me a detective had come around asking about you. She wanted to know whether you were getting remarried.'

'Okajima . . .'

Aose also put down his fork.

'Are you in touch with Yukari?'

'That was the last time. Not since then.'

'So, before that?'

'Yes, but not very often.'

What the——!

'Two or three times a year. It's not that strange, you know. Back when you two were a couple, you know we all used to meet up and have a drink at parties and stuff.'

'When did this all start?'

'Six or seven years ago, I guess. We bumped into each other at a trade fair in Tokyo.'

They'd been divorced for less than a year at that point . . .

'Why didn't you tell me?'

'I wasn't hiding it from you. I just didn't know how to tell you.'

Whatever he asked, Okajima's replies were calm and without inflection.

'Have you been using me as a talking point?'

'Stop it.'

'You've been talking about me.'

'You're a mutual acquaintance. We just mention you in passing.'

'So this continued after I came to work for you?'

'She used to ask me how you were doing. Were you well? Nothing more than that.'

Aose was completely shaken. *How he was doing?*

He leaned slowly back in his chair. Three years earlier, when he'd been doing those soulless part-time jobs, he'd had a call from Okajima out of the blue asking him to work for him.

Or so the story went . . .

They both gave up on their pasta. Aose's appetite had vanished. Okajima hadn't touched his salad or yoghurt either, and he was chainsmoking, even though he was supposed to have given up.

'When did you start smoking again?' Aose asked.

'Yesterday.'

Frontier Lights. Aose didn't know the brand.

'They're light. Just one milligram of tar.'

'That's not the point.'

'That is the point.'

Aose looked at his watch. Only fifteen minutes before the reporter would arrive. He had no choice but to force a change of topic.

'Did this Shigeta tell you why he wants to interview you?'

'He said he'd tell me when he got here.'

'It's about the memorial, isn't it?'

'I suppose so, seeing as he had my name.'

Aose nodded. If the reporter had sniffed out something amiss at the Y Residence, he'd have been looking for that house's designer.

'Do you want me to stay with you?'

'Yes, please.'

Okajima's reply was brusque. He hadn't called Aose to join him because he was feeling weak.

'Then I'm not under suspicion after all?' said Aose.

'It could have been Mayumi who talked,' said Okajima, lowering his voice.

Again, he might look normal, but he wasn't acting normal at all.

'If she hears you say that about her, she'll cry.'

'I'm not so sure.'

'What happened to concentric plum blossoms?'

'She's weak. Just like me.'

Aose checked his watch again.

'Is he really such a nasty piece of work, this reporter?'

Okajima clicked his tongue in disgust.

'There are people who want to take down Mayor Shinozuka. Shigeta is a pawn in their plot.'

Aose was aghast.

'You mean it's about politics?'

'There's a prefectural assemblyman by the name of Katsumata. And Kusamichi is behind him. The mayor's a member of Inoguchi's faction so they're anxious to get him out before the next general election.'

Aose knew that Kusamichi and Inoguchi were well-known members of parliament, but it was difficult for him to picture all the different relationships in his head.

'And how is Shigeta connected?'

'Kusamichi used to be the chairman of the National Public Safety Commission. Until two years ago, Shigeta was the reporter covering the National Police Agency at *Toyo Shimbun* headquarters, so that's how they met. He screwed something up really badly on the job and got transferred to the communications department here in Saitama. So now he's trying to suck up to Kusamichi and get the backing of some influential types so he can get sent back to Tokyo. They're targeting the memorial because it's the city's flagship project. For them, it's the perfect weapon to attack the mayor.'

Naturally, it was somebody else's version of events, but it made Aose uncomfortable to witness Okajima spouting off about behind-the-scenes machinations so knowledgeably. It felt a little bit like a case of 'it takes one to know one'. Okajima's own backers were the same kind of people as the ones he had just painted as corrupt. They'd given him the lowdown on Shigeta, and he'd got instructions from them on crisis management. Maybe Okajima had been asked to confirm whether everyone in his office could be trusted.

He probably wasn't far off the mark. Okajima Design

Company appeared to be under the protection of the pro-mayor faction. That was why Okajima didn't seem particularly afraid of the press and why he was acting so normal. But he had to ask . . .

'Why is this journalist attacking us?'

'Because we're an easy target.'

'So, we've got mixed up in a political dispute? That's all, right?'

'That's it. That's all it is.'

'Your conscience is clean, then?'

It was the question he'd been dying to ask, and he'd finally found the right moment. But Okajima just stared into space. The hands of Aose's watch clicked over to one o'clock.

'Okajima?'

'Yes.'

If he claimed he was innocent, then Aose had no choice but to back him up. They were all in it together. Aose prepared himself.

'This is just part of the competition. We'll win.'

Okajima didn't reply. His gaze was fixed a short distance above Aose's shoulder, on the front door of the restaurant, which now opened with a loud jangle.

34

Shigeta had brought an associate. It was obvious at a glance which one of the two men was the reporter. A short, fat man in his mid-thirties, his eyes wary, but a thin smile on his lips. His companion looked young enough to be a university student. He seemed rather nervous and flushed and his movements were quite awkward.

Okajima held up a folded magazine in front of his face, which must have been some sort of signal, as the two spotted him right away and came over. Aose moved his seat around to be next to Okajima and the two approached and offered their business cards. Neither bowed in greeting.

Mitsuru Shigeta, Reporter
S— City Local News Department
Saitama Head Office, Toyo Shimbun

Shinya Fukano, Reporter
Saitama Head Office, Toyo Shimbun

With rather bad grace, Okajima fumbled inside his jacket pocket for his own business card.

'Are you Okajima-san?'

Shigeta took the card and checked it against Okajima's face. Then he looked at Aose.

'I'm Aose. I took your call yesterday at the office.'

'Oh, I see. I'm very sorry about that.'

Aose didn't offer his own business card. After hearing Okajima's story, his preconceptions of Shigeta were of a vulture or hyena-like creature.

Shigeta called the waitress over and ordered two coffees.

'And please put them on a separate bill,' he added.

'Let's keep the conversation brief,' said Okajima, folding his arms.

'Hm. I'm not sure how short I can keep it,' replied Shigeta.

He made a show of getting out a notebook and pen from his bag. The young Fukano did likewise, as if mimicking his senior.

'This one is currently employed at Saitama Prefectural Police Headquarters,' said Shigeta.

After this rather curious introduction, Fukano looked at Okajima and Aose in turn. The way the two of them were posturing was almost comical.

Okajima glared at Shigeta.

'Please get started. I know it may not seem like it, but I am rather busy.'

'With the Fujimiya *mémoire*?' Shigeta shot back with a rather sneering grin.

'Well, yes, that too. It's a big project for us.'

'It seems you went to a lot of trouble to get selected.'

'I'm sorry? Could you be a little clearer?'

At Okajima's retort, Shigeta pulled out a piece of paper from between the leaves of his notebook. Keeping his eyes firmly on the paper, he began to read.

'It seems you've been out drinking many times with Kadokura-san, director of the S— city Department of Construction. Let's see . . . China Paradise, a Korean Restaurant . . . Should I also mention the dates?'

'So what?' said Okajima, his expression unchanged.

Shigeta laughed.

'Dear me. Director Kadokura practically holds the authority

for deciding contractors. You treated him to dinners and drinks and, as a result, you became one of the selected contractors for the competition. In other words, you bribed him.'

'That's a shocking accusation! We split the cost of food and drink. There was absolutely no bribery.'

'Really? I see.'

Shigeta didn't look the least bit convinced.

'But ever since the competition was announced you've been drinking very frequently with Director Kadokura. And he's also one of the judges. Didn't it occur to you that it might cause misunderstandings?'

'Ah, just a coincidence. We never discussed the competition while we were socializing. Director Kadokura and I have a personal relationship.'

'Oh, what kind of relationship would that be?'

'Do I really need to talk to you about it?'

'Just for our reference. If it sounds reasonable to us then we will leave you in peace.'

Okajima lit a cigarette. He exhaled forcefully and then began to speak.

'I played soccer in junior high school and so did Kadokura, so we've known each other quite a while. There's a plan to revitalize the city by luring a J2 league soccer team to set up base in S— city. So we were drinking together and chatting about the possibilities.'

Aose listened with bated breath. This was the first he'd heard of any of this.

'I see. And, along with Mayor Shinozuka, the three of you went to a soccer game together.'

'What—?'

'You went to the National Stadium, didn't you?'

There was an uncomfortable pause. Okajima looked as if he was about to deny it, but finally he nodded.

'Yes . . . We went to see a match. It was the mayor who

originally came up with the idea of inviting a J2 league team to the city. We thought we'd go to a game, just to get an idea.'

'But it was the opening match of the J1 league season, not J2.'

'What's wrong with that? Going to a J1 game. Eventually S— city wants to attract J1 too.'

'I'm not saying there's anything wrong with it. Who bought the tickets?'

Shigeta was relentless.

'I did. I've already told you, we always split the bill. They reimbursed me.'

'And the transportation costs?'

'The same, naturally.'

'But the drinking parties weren't that way, were they?'

'Huh? What are you talking about?'

'Because when you had drinks with Director Kadokura, you paid his fare home, didn't you?'

'I have no memory of that.'

At Okajima's response, Shigeta's hand moved.

'Actually, today wasn't the first time I've seen your card, Okajima-san.'

His stubby fingers pulled a photocopy from between the pages of his notebook and spread it out on the table. It was an enlarged copy of Okajima's business card.

'This was in the possession of a driver from a certain taxi company in S— city. He was asked to drive Director Kadokura home and to bill the office named on this business card for the fare.'

Aose stole a quick sideways glance at Okajima's face. It was flushed. This had clearly taken him off guard. It was possible that this taxi driver had some connection with the mayor's political rivals.

'I have no memory of that.'

Okajima was adamant.

'Well, that does seem to be a problem. You don't recall, but I have your card, right here. How could you explain it?'

Shigeta continued his attack with obsequious politeness.

'If you paid for his ride home, it's natural to assume that you also took care of the food and drinks too, Okajima-san. I believe you also paid for the tickets for the director and the mayor to go to the J1 soccer match. Not to mention transportation to and from the game. Isn't that the truth?'

'No, it isn't.'

'But—'

Aose interrupted.

'It's pure speculation. On your part.'

His response was less like a counterattack than a coach supporting his boxer after he'd been hammered by a barrage of punches.

Shigeta looked at Aose as if he'd just remembered something.

'Certainly it's my own speculation. But it's not mere conjecture. I'm sure you can see that.'

'I think the president has answered enough of your questions.'

'Well, Mr, um . . .'

'The name's Aose.'

'Are you one of the five?'

'Sorry, what?'

'Don't you find it strange?'

'Find what strange?'

'That a design company of five people, with no experience beyond building public toilets and police boxes, could take part in a competition of this scale?'

'I'm under no obligation to answer such a disrespectful question. Anyway, we have a client meeting scheduled, so can we wrap this up now?'

Shigeta looked disappointed.

'Yes, let's leave it there. I believe I've understood your point of view. I'll try to schedule a further meeting with you. Anyway, I'm sure we will see each other again. I'll look forward to it.'

After this final throwaway comment, Shigeta glanced at

Fukano by his side. Fukano turned his gaze on both Okajima and Aose equally.

'I can assure you that the Second Investigative Division of the Prefectural Police is also taking a serious interest in this matter.'

As the two reporters walked away, it was as if the conversations on surrounding tables had been unmuted.

'Ha! Taking a serious interest in the matter! Shigeta made him say that.'

Okajima laughed out loud. However, from the expression on his face, it didn't seem that he found it amusing. He'd broken into a sweat and there was something sinister behind his expression.

'You see? Just like they warned me – full of empty threats.'

Aose just nodded. He didn't tend to read many articles about things like corruption and political disputes, so he couldn't gauge how much of a threat the just concluded interview would be to the company. He was shocked and felt rather betrayed by Okajima's secret manoeuvring, but back in his Akasaka office days, during the bubble economy, it would have been nothing more than one of those entertaining stories that businessmen exchanged in lieu of greetings. The only thing that Shigeta had confronted Okajima about with any certainty was the taxi fare. It was hard to imagine that this would immediately turn into the subject of a newspaper article or that the police would get involved.

Still, he couldn't understand why Okajima was in such a good mood. He hadn't even responded to Shigeta's attack. He'd made no counterattacks and hadn't even attempted to break down the reporter's argument. And now, he was making light-hearted remarks such as 'Looks like he showed all his cards,' as if the crisis were over. Did he think he had won the bout, or was he just happy to have got through it without being knocked out? Or did he believe that with the backers he had he could get away with anything?

Aose felt as if he had got mixed up in something bad. He had the urge to rehash Shigeta's questions and get a response from Okajima.

'What am I still doing here? I've got to get going, go and confer with a few people.'

With that, Okajima grabbed the bill and got up to leave.

'Thank you, Aose. Thanks to you, everything went well.'

Aose felt the rage bubble up inside at these words.

'Just a minute!'

'What?'

'Don't lie to me – or to Isso-kun!'

35

There was no further contact from Okajima, and he didn't turn up at the office for the rest of the day. Aose was of course bombarded with questions by Takeuchi and Mayumi. There was a call from Kofu, too, from Ishimaki and Nishikawa, who were both worried. Aose tried to brush off all the questions, telling them to ask the boss directly, but when that didn't do the trick he reassured them that there was no problem and surely no cause for concern, that some reporter had got the wrong end of the stick . . . But everybody had guessed from Aose's refusal to talk that it had something to do with the competition. In the uneasy silence in the office everyone was probably imagining how exactly Okajima had 'bust a gut' to get selected. They'd been vaguely aware for a while that something was going on with him.

It was gone 10 p.m. by the time Aose got back to his apartment building. He joined the elderly woman with the walking frame who was waiting for the elevator. He could tell she must live alone, as even that late at night she had a convenience store bag hanging from the handles of her frame.

Aose said good evening. Normally he would just nod to her, but tonight she looked particularly frail.

'They didn't have any plasters, so I got . . .' she mumbled, as if offering an apology.

'Did you injure yourself?' Aose asked her.

'It's just a scratch. Happens when you get old. Don't tell them.'

'Sorry?'

'The estate agents. Old people living alone – they won't renew the lease if I make any trouble.'

'Trouble?'

'My son's supposed to be living with me. But it looks as if they've found out he's not.'

The elevator door opened. Aose let the woman get on first.

'Tenth floor?' he asked.

The old woman smiled slightly.

'I shut up my house and moved here.'

'Ah, did you?'

'Keeping up the garden and the repairs on the roof all got too much.'

'I understand.'

'The weeds – you keep pulling them up and they just keep coming back. So I thought I'd just cut them, you know, with a lawnmower, but then after a few years there was nothing but weeds left in the garden.'

'Weeds are strong.'

'Yes, and the lawn was weak. I was against having one, but my husband planted it one summer.'

'I see.'

'It's easy here. I just need this.'

The woman showed him the key that she'd hung on a cord around her neck. The elevator door opened on the tenth floor.

'Goodnight,' Aose said, but the old woman rolled her walking frame away without a word.

He thought about the woman as he continued up to the twelfth floor and entered his flat. He still inevitably recoiled the moment he turned on the lights. Seeing the image of the silent room he'd left always felt to him like revisiting a scene from the past rather than living in the present.

In the kitchen he opened a can of beer. He put it up to his mouth, but then a thought occurred to him. He opened the door of his cabinet and got out an *Edo kiriko* faceted glass. It was a heavy, blue, patterned one that he hadn't used in a while. In fact, he'd forgotten he even had it. He'd treated himself to it back when he was still an intern architect at the Akasaka firm.

He sat on the living room sofa and poured the beer into the glass. He'd dreamed of drinking powdered juice from a real glass like the other children at school, and the dream had eventually come true. He'd forgotten that it had; here he was, sipping nonchalantly from his own glass. Just like the Hyuga Villa, his apartment had three rooms, but unfortunately that's all he had — literally nothing but room, lots of empty space. His senses felt numb. And yet he lived here. He was able to live here. And there were others who even loved this space. Even if Taut visited him again tonight in the darkness of his room, berating him for his distaste for his living space, he couldn't be angry at the old woman from the tenth floor who carried the key to her room like a cross around her neck.

Right now, today's interview had been relegated to a back corner of his mind. He was surprised to find he wasn't particularly bothered by it. Perhaps he believed in the power of Okajima's backers, or perhaps he had decided it was Okajima's problem alone. He found both feelings to be true. But in truth, it was a different problem that was niggling at him.

Who had sent the private detective to investigate him? Ever since he'd heard the story from Okajima he had been asking himself this question over and over. Who, and why? He didn't have a clue. The detective had even visited Yukari and fed her some story about Aose getting remarried in order to pry into his private affairs. It was unthinkable — the detective must have gone rogue. What could he have asked Yukari? About his character? Finances? His drinking? Womanizing? How must she have felt when the detective told her that her ex-husband was about to marry again, and then dredged up all their past life? She must have been so worried about Hinako, how upset she'd be when she heard, and so not being able to check the story with Aose directly, she'd called Okajima instead. He wondered what Okajima had told her. He'd probably told her that as far as he knew it wasn't true, but of course he couldn't have known for sure. This possibility that Aose was getting married again would have stuck with Yukari. She must have been trying to prepare herself for the news since last February, when the detective appeared. Aose was hit by a wave of emotion. It wasn't too late. He'd call Yukari and tell her from his own mouth that the remarriage story was total bullshit.

His eyes were fixed on his home phone, when suddenly it rang. Still in a belligerent mood, he marched over and picked it up. The voice on the other end was not one he had expected to hear.

'This is Tsumura. Have you heard from the boss?'

Mayumi's voice was strained. Aose looked at his watch. It was almost eleven o'clock.

'No. Where are you? At home?'

'Still at the office.'

'Where's Takeuchi?'

'He went out to get dinner.'

'You should go home. The boss said there was nothing to worry about.'

'But he's not answering his mobile, no matter how many times I call, and he's not at home either.'

Aose shivered.

'You called his home?'

'Yeah. His wife said he's not back yet.'

'Don't call again. You'll make her worried.'

'She didn't seem too worried.'

There was a chilling voice whispering somewhere in Aose's brain.

'No, I suppose not. Okajima always gets home late. Anyway, there's really no need to worry. He's just talking to the relevant parties.'

'By relevant parties, you mean to do with the competition?'

Aose hesitated before replying.

'Yes. He's been falsely accused by the *Toyo Shimbun*, so he's working on a strategy to respond to the accusations.'

'Who with?'

'I don't really know, but he has some allies.'

'What kind of accusations? Please tell me.'

'Like I've told you, you'll have to ask the boss himself. I can't just tell you the bits that I know—'

'But like I've told you, I can't get hold of him.'

Aose moved the receiver to the opposite ear.

'You really should go home. Yuma-kun is waiting for you.'

'He's already asleep.'

'You're his mother, right? Just go home. Shut the office up now and go home.'

He slammed the phone down and sat on the floor. He needed a moment for his pulse to stop racing. Then he called Okajima's mobile. It connected to voicemail. Without thinking, he blurted out the word 'dickhead!' He felt that Okajima had been playing him. Every single thing that man did or had ever done bugged the hell out of him.

He'd confessed that he'd kept in touch with Yukari. After Aose and Yukari had divorced. Three years earlier, Okajima had called him and told him not to sell himself short, said, 'Hey, why don't you come and work for me?' He'd known all about Aose's situation. Had heard the rumour that he was living a life of self-indulgence, selling his draughting skills for easy cash and then going out drinking it all away. Did the rumour float naturally to him on the breeze, or did someone blow it straight to him?

Anyone who was close to Yukari knew this about her: she could never abandon someone weak. Even when she got into an argument, if she felt the other person was suffering more damage than she was, she would try to bring her way of thinking towards theirs. Whenever she saw a little kid crying in a park or a supermarket, she would always run over to them and crouch down to comfort them. If there was a major natural disaster, it didn't matter whether it was in Japan or overseas, she would donate money that very day. She'd been obsessed with the story that Aose had told her about rescuing the long-tailed rose finch, from time to time wondering out loud whether 'Toshio-san' had managed to return it to the forest.

It may well have been Yukari who had asked Okajima to rescue him.

Even after that she had worried about Aose. Okajima had told him that she'd asked how he was doing, but now Aose no longer heard those words as Okajima had said them; in his mind they'd taken on Yukari's voice and worried intonation. She'd probably heard from Okajima that Aose was absorbed with the Y Residence project. That would be why she'd bought a copy of *Top 200 Homes* and asked him on the phone, 'Have you built any houses that really spoke to you lately?'

It had been her from the outset. The story of Aose's resurrection had begun long before Okajima hired him. His ears began to burn. It was humiliating, it was mortifying, and yet . . .

Ah! There was a flash of light . . . He'd seen an image in his mind . . . Something overlapping, superimposed . . . Those words had suggested something to him . . .

From the outset . . . Where it had all begun . . . point of ignition . . .

It wasn't to do with Okajima. Nor even Yukari. The thought had skipped somewhere else. It was to do with Yoshino. Yes, that was it. That was the key to solving the mystery of the family's vanishing act.

A phone was ringing. The phone in front of Aose was ringing. Without thinking, he picked up.

'I'm so sorry to call this late. This is Ikezono from J— newspaper. I just got some exciting news and I couldn't stop myself.'

Ikezono's voice was so bright and cheery that it made Aose dizzy.

'You're going to be amazed, but I found a man in Sendai who says he knows Yoshino-san.'

'Eh? What, there was somebody—'

'Yes. I think it was your friend Yoshino's father or grandfather. I was asking about Yoshino, about cabinetmakers, and the blueprints of the chair, and I was calling around people in the Sendai area who were scholars or experts in Taut's work, and I got a hit. A man called Kusao Yamashita. Where do you think he was working seventy years ago?'

Aose's head began to spin, but Ikezono didn't wait for him to reply.

'At the National Research Institute of Industrial Arts. He even worked under Taut while he was there! What's more, this Yamashita-san knew a carpenter by the name of Yoshino. Remembers him very well. Well, I haven't actually spoken to him in person yet; it seems it's a bit difficult for him to talk on the phone at his age.

'But—'

'Of course, it's possible that it's a different Yoshino,' continued Ikezono, anticipating Aose's question. 'It's a common surname, but I think it's going to be the right one. Definitely worth a trip to Sendai. If you go, you can hear what Yamashita-san has to say.'

Aose just came straight out with it:

'I won't be able to make it up there for a while.'

Before anything else, he needed to curb Ikezono's enthusiasm. It was certainly a major development, but he had to balance it against the other things going on in his life. On the opposite side of the scale were the competition, the reporter Shigeta, and one more unidentified heavy weight.

'Eh? . . . Are you busy?'

Ikezono's voice immediately turned quieter. Aose took that moment to recover his composure.

'Yes, unfortunately, I've got a lot going on right now. Work and other stuff. I really wish I could go, but the Yoshino case is not a priority.'

'I know it's a little indelicate to say it, Aose-san, but Yamashita-san is well over ninety . . . I once missed my chance to interview a survivor of the Maebashi air raid because I put it off and then he ended up passing away before I could reschedule.'

'I do understand, but—'

'Should I go to Sendai instead?'

'Ikezono-san?'

He just had to say it once and for all.

'To tell the truth, I'm regretting a little telling you about Yoshino-san that day at Daruma-ji temple. In fact, I don't really want to turn into a detective and search for him. I was just wondering where he'd moved to, that's all.'

He could feel Ikezono's disappointment in his reply:

'I'm so sorry. I wasn't trying to become a detective either. It's just that the story of Taut's chair was so fascinating to me. I thought I could help you with your search for Yoshino-san from the Taut end of things. I apologize if I've caused you any trouble.'

'No, not at all. I'm truly grateful to you for all you've done to help. I just wish it had been easier to find out about the chair and Yoshino's whereabouts. And the longer it went on, the more time I had to think about it. I began to wonder whether Yoshino really wanted me to look for him. It occurred to me that if he didn't tell me where he was moving to, then perhaps he didn't want me to find him after all.'

He'd wound his way through several lies but finally ended up with a truth.

'I understand how you feel.'

He imagined Ikezono nodding sincerely.

'Well, I guess we had better leave him alone for now. In the meantime, I'll email you Yamashita-san's contact details, and those of the other people involved, just in case.'

'Thank you.'

'If your feelings change at any point, please get in touch. Anytime. I'd love to go on another trip together, Aose-san. Also . . .'

It was Ikezono's turn to give Aose a glimpse of his true feelings.

'Please don't talk about the chair to any other member of the media. If the time comes to make the story public, I'd like to be the one to write it.'

After hanging up the phone, Aose let out a small chuckle. He felt that he had been saved by the small chink in his armour that Ikezono had revealed to him.

His throat felt parched so he returned to the living room and grabbed his glass of beer, but as he raised it to his mouth he felt his fingers slip and the lovely *Edo kiriko* glass shattered on the floor just beyond his toes. Amber liquid splattered all over the wooden floor. He stood stunned for a moment, then went to get a cloth from the kitchen. As he mopped up the beer he smiled wryly as he thought how his mother had been right all along, sticking to plasticware.

Aha!

This time he shouted.

This time the flash lit up everything.

He understood. The meaning of *from the outset* . . . and *where it had all begun* . . .

There was a chapter in the story of the construction of the Y Residence that Aose didn't know. A prequel, a preface . . .

The whole thing had been orchestrated from the outset. Someone had investigated Aose's affairs, checking that he had no plans to remarry or transfer jobs. That was in February of last year. A month later, the Yoshinos had shown up at his office. By then things had already begun.

They had come with those magic words. And a dream of a request. Aose hadn't made any effort to decipher its real meaning, letting himself be transported into the world of his dreams and cutting himself off from reality.

But the Yoshinos weren't just living a dream. They'd had some practical reason for commissioning Aose to do this job. He realized now that the mysterious disappearance of a whole family had begun with their investigation of Aose, their selection of him, and then their commissioning of him to design their home.

His toes tingled.

Better deal with this first.

Aose knelt on the floor and reached for the blue shards of glass. He restrained his mind, which was about to go on a rampage as he gathered up the geometrically faceted fragments.

36

Two days later Aose was sitting in the Tohoku shinkansen on his way to Sendai. He hadn't let Ikezono know he was going. Nor had he told the office more than that he'd be back that evening. Okajima hadn't put in an appearance at work since the day they'd met Shigeta. He'd called the previous evening, but according to Ishimaki, who answered the phone, he'd been deliberately evasive. His only question was 'Has Shigeta called again?' Aose had decided to go to Sendai anyway.

The Yoshino family's disappearance was no longer a case of a missing client but had turned into a theory that involved Aose. Yoshino had used a detective agency to investigate him. Aose had no solid proof that this was true, but he was pretty sure that he had guessed correctly. Those key phrases 'from the outset' and 'where it had all begun' had finally provided a logical frame of reference to his mind, which had begun to lose its grip on all the fragmented bits of information and the puzzling sequence of events.

From this brand-new perspective, the original reason the Yoshinos gave for commissioning Aose to build their house was pretty implausible. They'd said they'd fallen in love with the house in Ageo, but even back then Aose had been quite puzzled by that statement. The Ageo house had been built on a narrow, misshapen bit of land. No ordinary client would have entrusted their thirty million yen to an unknown architect based on that one house alone. In other words, they were *no ordinary clients*.

And yet, their way of thinking was like that of ordinary clients in some ways. They genuinely wanted to build a good-quality house. They'd even gone to the trouble of checking that Aose was a reputable architect. A house is the greatest investment of a person's life. There are people who spend a year, or even two, visiting architects to be sure of ending up with the perfect house. That said, going so far as to hire a private detective to investigate an architect was extreme. Yoshino had been given a private viewing of the Ageo house, and met with the homeowner, so he hadn't needed a detective for that. There was just one conclusion to be drawn – Yoshino had investigated Aose's background even before he knew about the house in Ageo. It was likely through the detective agency that he had learned of this house's existence, and he had used it as a pretext to get Aose to design him a house.

Unaware of all this, Aose had accepted the commission. The vague sense of unease that he'd harboured back then, which had never risen to the level of mistrust or serious concern, had become serious only after the house had been completed, with the unexpected disappearance of the whole family. If he were to believe what he'd heard from the landlord of the rental house in Tabata, by the time of his commission the Yoshinos had already been separated or divorced. And yet, to Aose they had seemed to be a close couple. In other words, the deception had begun from the very outset, and Aose had long believed that the key to solving the whole mystery was to go back to where it had all begun. Of course, he'd originally assumed that this beginning would be some incident related to the Yoshino family; he'd never dreamed that it could have anything to do with him.

But in fact, he'd been right there at the outset, where the mystery had begun. And he had been given a role. The very thought sent dread through his whole being. That role was the problem. What role had Yoshino assigned to Aose in this play he was directing?

He didn't know. He found it hard to believe there was any

malicious intent. There had been no indication of fraudulent words or conduct in the course of the building work, nor behind the scenes. No threats had been made against Aose personally or against his firm that might damage the reputation of either. Yoshino had commissioned the building of the house, and he had paid the design and construction fees in full. There was nothing that had affected Aose or Okajima Design Company negatively in any way. It had all been beneficial to both of them. The only remotely negative outcome had been his concern about the disappearance of the family, but if it hadn't been for the client from Urawa who had informed him that nobody seemed to be living there, he might never have learned of this development.

He looked out of the train window at the rural landscape that rolled by. It was so expansive and slow moving that he was almost unaware that he was on a speeding bullet train.

The previous night, he had been thinking about the past. He'd tried to trace the name 'Yoshino' back through his Akasaka company days, his student years and even those migratory schooldays, but his efforts had been fruitless. There may have been events or incidents that Aose had forgotten or that had passed him by entirely unnoticed. However, if their past connection was one that hadn't caused any bad feelings, then why would Yoshino not have revealed the truth behind his contacting Aose? Or did this mean that the bad feelings existed but the revenge was yet to fall on him?

Build a home you would want to live in.

There hadn't been a hint of malice in those words. However, it did sometimes feel like a great irony . . .

The PA system announced that the train would shortly be arriving in Sendai.

A family on the run, pursued by a red-faced man. That very simple version of events was alive and well in Aose's mind. It was still entirely possible that the disappearance had been nothing to

267

do with him at all. That it had been sudden and unexpected, caused by money troubles or by the tall woman.

He had to find Yoshino. If he couldn't find out the reason behind all this, he would be haunted by this mystery for the rest of his life. Why had he asked Aose to design his house? And why did it have to be him?

37

It was a little after midday. Aose got off the train at Sendai. He'd been imagining a small, deserted shinkansen station, as was usual in provincial cities, and was surprised to find it large and humming with life. However, there was no sense of hurry or bustle. It was as if the season had been turned backwards and was a whole month behind Tokyo.

Aose went out of the east exit and headed for the taxi rank. The old man who Ikezono had heard about through emails and had spoken to on the phone was Kusao Yamashita. He'd been employed at the National Research Institute of Industrial Arts, set up by the former Ministry of Commerce in the late 1920s. He'd been acquainted with Bruno Taut, who had been invited to the institute and had stayed there for three and a half months. It seems he had been taught directly by the architect. The previous day, Aose had got in touch with Yamashita's grandson, who worked at the town hall, who had told him that although his grandfather was over ninety and somewhat hard of hearing, his mind was still sharp and that he was happy to meet with Aose.

There were no passengers waiting for taxis. The driver of the cab at the front of the line was smoking a cigarette outside his car. He smiled amicably at Aose, reached in through the driver's side window and released the catch to open the automatic rear door. Aose slid into the back seat and checked his notebook.

'How far is Tsutsujigaoka Park?'

'No more than ten minutes away. It's one stop on the Senseki line . . . Could I take a look?'

'Sure. Thank you.'

The designated meeting place was in front of a junior high school by the park. There was supposed to be a monument dedicated to the former National Research Institute of Industrial Arts, so Aose imagined that Yamashita was looking to reminisce about his days there.

'Is there a junior high school by the park?'

'Yes, Miyagino Middle School. Shall I take you there?'

'Yes, please. Does that mean that the school is on the former site of the National Research Institute of Industrial Arts?'

'Industrial Arts . . . Oh yes, that place. There's a major road running through that area now, and apartment buildings and stuff all around, so I'm not sure where exactly the former site is.

'I heard there was a monument there.'

'Hmm, I haven't heard of that.'

Perhaps the driver was a little ashamed of his ignorance of the local geography but, once they'd arrived at the destination and Aose had paid the bill, he jumped out of the car and followed Aose, asking passers-by if they knew where the monument was. Aose looked towards Tsutsujigaoka Park and listened to the birds twittering in the leafy cherry trees.

Hiri hi hi hi hihiro hihiro hihiro.

He'd just about decided they must be narcissus flycatchers when the taxi driver called to him.

'Sir, this is it.'

A white-gloved index finger pointed through the wire fence of the school. In a shaded and inconspicuous corner of the school ground was a stone about three metres tall. Aose walked up to the fence and peered through. It was a bluish stone with a plaque inscribed 'Birthplace of the Industrial Arts' in exquisite calligraphy. At the base was a larger inscribed metal plate explaining the monument's significance.

'Excuse me?'

Aose turned around, expecting to see the driver, but it was a small-set middle-aged man. Behind him was an even smaller elderly man with a white wooden walking stick. These were Kusao Yamashita and his grandson, who didn't look far off fifty himself. Aose was surprised by their sudden appearance, but then he noticed a minivan parked at the side of the road.

'You must be Aose-san.'

'That's right.'

'I'm Yamashita's grandson. Actually, I took my wife's name.'

Aose knew from talking to him on the phone the day before that his name was Ozawa. The business card he held out said that he was a public employee, Head of the N— village General Affairs section. This village had not come up in conversation. And from the way the man had casually mentioned how he'd taken his wife's name, it was clear that it was an absolutely normal occurrence.

'Thank you for coming all this way.'

'No, thank you for being able to accommodate me at such short notice.'

Aose raised his hand in thanks to the taxi driver, who was just getting back into his car, with an air of a job well done. The man of the moment, the elder Yamashita-san, didn't address Aose; instead, he leaned on the wire fence and stared intently at the metal plaque at the foot of the memorial.

'The German architect Bruno Taut was invited . . . functional experiments . . . researching standard prototypes . . . pioneered the modern design movement . . . here was the birthplace of modern industrial crafts and design . . .'

When he'd finished reading, the old man turned and looked at Aose. There were deep wrinkles around his eyes.

'Taut was very conscientious about his work,' he said. 'He toured the workshops every day with a look on his face like this.'

He imitated a deep scowl, which had the desired effect of

making Aose laugh out loud. In fact, Aose was dealing with a whole mixture of emotions. Here was a man who had actually spent time with Taut and who still seemed as excited as he must have been seventy years ago. He must have many stories to tell. Aose realized it might be a while before he could get around to the subject of Yoshino.

'His wife, Erica, was a good person too,' Yamashita went on. 'And she was an excellent secretary. They were only with us for a little over three months, but I really wish they'd stayed longer, both of them.'

With small, tottering steps, Yamashita turned to face the street and held out both hands.

'It was a fine centre – a big place; the site was the property of the army. See, over there was a government office building and an annex; then there was the factory, a warehouse, living quarters and then a guardhouse.'

He seemed to have made up his mind to tell the whole story.

'We all really looked up to Taut-sensei. We were all determined to learn as much from him as we possibly could.'

The grandson, Ozawa, leaned in to whisper into Aose's ear.

'My grandfather wasn't a regular staff member. He was more of an errand boy, really.'

Aose pretended not to have heard him.

'When Taut was about to leave the institute, he told us something very important. In the hands of a skilled craftsman, a crafted object is as worthy as any piece of art. That's a great comment, don't you think? He also said that the quality of an object should be the same, no matter where it was created. And that when it came to adopting things from the West, whether it be houses, furniture, clothing or anything else, the Japanese were so uncritical that he wondered where their exceptional sensibility and taste had gone. He said that Japanese people would go into ecstasies over something just because it was popular in the West. He said that there was a lot of fake stuff coming out of Europe and the United States that was much worse quality than what was made here, and it was getting imported into Japan. But that it didn't matter what it was – if people here thought that it was to western tastes they would welcome it.'

Aose was surprised to hear that Taut was talking about this topic as long ago as seventy years previously.

'He told us there were four things to keep in mind in order to avoid producing low-quality goods: proper selection of materials; proper combination of materials; proper handling of materials; and finally, usability. If you didn't stick to those four principles, then you couldn't avoid producing low-grade products.'

Had Yamashita really picked this up from being around Taut? No, he must have read it in translation later. He probably read those words over and over again until he could hear the Taut in his head saying them in Japanese.

'But Taut also used to say it's not enough just to follow those four principles. You can't produce strong, quality goods without a strong foundation. He said he had often seen the children of craftsmen with a fine, established tradition fall into the dangerous trap of attempting to produce something completely new and different, and in the process abandoning long-held traditions. I think that's where Yoshino-kun lost sight of things. It was the same for me . . .'

Ah! Aose reacted to the mention of Yoshino, but the old man didn't stop there. He closed his eyes and began to recite, as if he'd committed it to memory, 'The desire to create something novel is already in contradiction with quality. Good technique is a long chain that should never be broken. Quality is preserved by this chain, which should be subject to no more than the very slightest of alterations in decoration or form . . . Nevertheless, whether it be in Japan or Europe, great technique can never simply be inherited from the work of one's predecessors. Japan occupies a special status among the peoples of the world—'

He broke off, his mouth still moving as if mumbling the words. His eyes remained closed and he looked to be in some state of meditation.

'Er . . .'

Just as Aose was about to prompt Yamashita, Ozawa interrupted.

'Aose-san?'

'Yes?'

'I'd just like to ask you one question: have you ever contacted our town hall by phone about this matter?'

Aose looked confused. He couldn't really understand the meaning of the question.

'I heard about you through Yamazaki-san and Okura-san,' Ozawa continued. 'They were contacted by a reporter who told them you were looking for someone. Of course, I have no reason to doubt the story.'

The two names were unfamiliar to Aose. Ikezono had tracked down Kusao Yamashita through his Taut connections.

'No, I never called the town hall. With the greatest respect, I only heard the name of N— village today for the first time.'

As soon as he'd replied, Aose realized he'd missed the important point.

'Are you saying that there were other people besides me calling to ask about Yoshino?' he said.

'That's right. Someone else took the call, but the caller was very insistent, mentioning the name Touta Yoshino and saying he'd heard that N— was his hometown. Asking if we knew where to find him. He was very pushy, according to my colleague.'

The red-faced man. He'd extended his search beyond the rented house in Tabata all the way here.

'Really?'

Aose feigned indifference. He worried that the frustration and guilt of not being able to explain the true situation might show on his face.

38

They decided to continue the conversation in the car. It really wasn't a great idea to stand by the side of the road talking, and Ozawa suggested they go to visit the grave of 'Yoshino-kun', about a thirty-minute drive to the north.

'I remember Yoshino-kun very well,' said the elderly Yamashita as soon as they were settled in the back seat. Aose hurried to open his notebook.

Ozawa had been telling the truth when he said his grandfather was still clear-headed, but only when he was talking at his own pace. His replies to questions were a little suspect.

'Was Yoshino-san a carpenter?'

'Yes, yes. Inherited the trade from his father. He was from the next village, so I didn't know him very well. My son moved to N— village, you see, after he got married.'

'Right.'

'Taut-san, he really liked Mount Taihaku, that triangle shape. He used to sketch it all the time.'

'Did Yoshino-san work at the Arts Institute too?'

'He didn't manage to become one, poor Yoshino-kun. He was so passionate about it too.'

'He didn't manage to . . . What does that mean?'

'Well, you see, he wanted to be an apprentice, but he was only fifteen.'

'I'll explain that for you,' said Ozawa from the driver's seat. 'Back then, the institute held training courses for young craftsmen about two or three times a year. Each course lasted about three months.'

'Right, right,' Yamashita agreed.

'Anyway, Yoshino didn't make the list, so he came to the institute to ask Taut-san directly if he would teach him. Taut-san had been walking from village to village in the area, and so Yoshino-kun had heard the rumour that a great German teacher was coming, and was determined to show him the chair he'd made.'

'A chair?'

'There's a connection there,' said Ozawa with a smile. 'But it's not clear whether Yoshino-san met Taut or not. My grandfather's recollection is a little vague.'

'I do remember. Taut-san saw Yoshino-kun's chair. And you know what? It was a classic case of the children of craftsmen with a fine, established tradition falling into the dangerous trap of attempting to produce something completely new and different, and in the process abandoning long-held traditions.'

Ozawa laughed.

'I'm not sure about that either. But when I heard that the Yoshino-san that you're looking for, Aose-san, has the blueprints for Taut's chair, it hit me. I'm sure Taut must have drawn up the blueprints and given them to this young Yoshino. Told him to try making something like that.'

Aose nodded deeply. Touta Yoshino was somehow connected to this young boy named Yoshino. He was sure of it.

'Do you know this Yoshino-kun's given name?'

Aose was addressing Ozawa, but it was Yamashita who replied.

'It was Isaku. He had an older sister, but she left home to work in a factory. As a weaver. It was like that back in those days.'

The car began to climb a gentle hill. The number of houses along the road was starting the thin out. Perhaps they were already in N— village.

'If his grave is here, does that mean that his home is still here too?'

'Long gone,' replied Yamashita abruptly. 'Stole rice and split up the family. Poor, poor Yoshino-kun.'

'Eh . . . Who stole rice?'

'Isaku-kun's father stole some rice from a neighbour's house.'

In the rear-view mirror, Aose could see Ozawa's expression darken.

'They say he was a really good craftsman but a heavy drinker. It's true that the family split up. In those days, if you stole rice, you were ostracized.'

'And because of that, Yoshino-kun was bullied by his friends. They called him "Kusai" – "stinky" – because that's what you get if you read his name, I-sa-ku, backwards.

'His father ran off somewhere and his mother got tuberculosis or something and was in a sanatorium in the mountains, but she died within a year. Nobody knew where the Yoshino boy went after that.'

Aose shut his notebook.

It was a heart-breaking story. His father had vanished, his mother had died, and Isaku Yoshino had left the village all alone, his dream of becoming an apprentice shattered. Where did he go? Yamashita had said that his older sister left home to become a weaver in a factory. Did he turn to his sister for help? Had she moved far away? Did Isaku ever make it there?

Aose had also left the dam workers' lodgings. In the summer of his last year of high school he had quit the migrant life and stayed with his sister. Eager to try the university entrance exams, he decided he was at a crossroads in his life and shook off all his father's objections. Now that he'd heard Isaku Yoshino's story, he realized that he'd been fortunate enough to fly his own nest in much happier circumstances.

Isaku Yoshino had been fifteen years old at the time. If he were still alive now, he would be over eighty. Touta Yoshino was forty. There seemed to be too many years between them for Touta to have been Isaku's son. If he was his grandson, then Isaku and his

277

own son must both have had children when they were around the age of twenty. The calculations didn't work otherwise. However, given the history of the times, and all the hardships that Isaku must have endured, it was probably safer to assume that he had married and had children late in life. In any case, the break-up of a family because of the previous generation's misdeeds must have cast a shadow over not only Isaku's but also Touta's upbringing. The break-up of a family. The disappearance of a family. It was distressing to think that this was part of a chain of events.

Aose turned to Yamashita.

'Whereabouts was the factory where Isaku Yoshino's sister worked?'

'Hm. I never knew. I heard that she was very beautiful, and very tiny. Yoshino-kun was also very small. He had a very young face too. Didn't even look fifteen. I wonder if that's why he couldn't become an apprentice.'

'Were there any areas famous for weaving that a girl from the village might have gone to?'

'I don't think so. In N— village and the village where I grew up the girls would all go to be maids at rich people's homes. Nobody ever became a weaver. That's why I remember it so well – because it was so rare. I feel really sorry for Yoshino-kun. All his father did was to steal rice, but Yoshino-kun built a chair. Taut-san didn't approve of it, but he gave him some blueprints or something. I guess that meant there was something there, that he had promise. I wonder if he became a cabinetmaker somewhere. Maybe he got his apprenticeship and became one after all.'

Maybe he did, Aose thought.

In fact, he was sure that he did. The chair in the Y Residence was indistinguishable from the original set, in terms of both age and workmanship. If Taut had drawn the blueprints, then it probably wouldn't have been long afterwards that Isaku had built the chair. If he had the skills at such a young age to build a chair like that one, then he could have found work anywhere in Japan.

That 'anywhere' was the problem when you were looking for someone. Turning it into a 'somewhere' was like trying to clutch at clouds.

Aose let out a silent sigh.

It had been worth making the trip up to Sendai just to learn about the life of Isaku Yoshino. Because now he could well imagine that in the heart of Touta Yoshino, the man who was presumably Isaku's son, there would be a core strength not easily crushed.

But Aose still couldn't see any connection with himself. After hearing the story from Yamashita, the only overlapping point that he could possibly see was the history of migration that they shared. He could imagine the young Touta Yoshino being taken by his father on a constantly nomadic journey. When Isaku had passed away, perhaps Touta had thought of settling down. Maybe he had heard somewhere about Aose's own history, had a detective check him out, then asked him to build a home he would want to live in.

'*Hold on just a minute!*' cried out another part of Aose's brain — the part that held all the information he had collected before today — but this latest theory was no doubt the most charitable of all that he had come up with. It was also the most consistent with the smile he had seen on the face of Touta Yoshino as he puffed on his pipe and looked up with emotion at the newly finished Y Residence. He recalled the look of deadly seriousness on Yoshino's face when he first came to Aose's office. What Yoshino had really been saying to him was 'You of all people should understand the kind of home I want to build.'

'Aose-san, is this your first time visiting Sendai?' said Ozawa, trying to lighten the mood.

'Yes.'

'Do you have any connections with the Tohoku region?'

'No . . . Well, I spent some time in Yamagata prefecture when I was a child.'

'Oh. Where in Yamagata?'

'In Zao. My father was involved in the construction of the dam there.'

'Dam construction? So you would have moved around a lot as a child?'

'Yes, we lived all over Japan.'

'Wow, I envy you. I've spent my whole life within a radius of three kilometres of where I was born. Since moving in with my wife's parents, the radius has become even smaller.'

Aose took the bait offered and laughed along with Ozawa.

There are all kinds of people in the world – some who yearn to travel, others who dream of settling down. Some long to put roots down in the ground, while others bid farewell to the ground and entrust their future to the higher floors.

'We'll be there any minute,' said Ozawa, and thirty seconds later, they came to a stop. From the spot all they could see was the sky, greenery and, way in the distance, a few scattered houses.

The plot of the Yoshino family grave stood alone in the corner of a hollow covered in mossy undergrowth. It was a little way outside the public cemetery. Was the crime of stealing rice really so heinous?

There was no gravestone engraved with the family name, just a simple stone, half buried in the ground. It looked like the kind of weighted stone used to make *tsukemono* pickles. At first glance, Aose thought the grave was abandoned, but as he approached his eyes grew wide.

Flowers had been placed in front of the headstone. They were no longer fresh – so wilted that he couldn't even tell what kind of flower they had been.

Who had— The moment he thought it, he got goosebumps.

It was Yoshino. He'd been here.

Aose froze. He felt the breeze on his cheek, and then a surge of wind that blew by his body like a train passing through a station without stopping. It ran across the fields and plains, sweeping through the grass and trees, and brought back memories of the swishing sound of the wind.

He took out one of his business cards and a pen, thought about it for a few moments, then wrote simply, 'Please get in touch'. Ozawa went back to the car to fetch a clear plastic file, into which Aose put the card, along with a clover leaf that he'd picked from among the moss. He placed the file in front of the headstone with rocks to weigh down the four corners.

He placed the palms of his hands together and closed his eyes.

He now believed he understood why Taut's chair had been placed in front of the picture window of the Y Residence's master bedroom. Yoshino had put it there for his father, Isaku, to sit in. Perhaps he had even placed his father's funeral urn on the chair. He'd showed him the sky. He was urging him to take his memories of Taut and return to the wide blue sky of this remote village.

From behind Aose came a sob.

'You've got somebody, Yoshino-kun, you've got somebody.'

39

Aose went back to Tokorozawa that day. He had to politely decline the elderly Yamashita's invitation to stay the night, because he'd got a call from Okajima.

'I really need to talk to you tonight. Call me as soon as you get home.'

He sounded desperate. That reporter, Shigeta, must have started the next wave of his attack. So, unlike the last time, Okajima had been outflanked.

Aose rang Okajima's mobile the moment he got back to his flat, as he had promised, but he only reached his voicemail. He'd bought a six-pack of beer for Okajima and himself, which he unpacked and put in the fridge. About fifteen minutes later he rang Okajima's phone once more, but again it went to voicemail. 'I'm back,' he said in a slightly irritated tone.

He'd been up really early that morning, so he'd dozed off on the shinkansen on the way back. Since coming up with the more charitable theory about Yoshino and his disappearance, Aose's feelings about him had softened. He couldn't trace Yoshino's steps any further than Sendai and N— village, but now he felt he was somehow closer to finding him. From the moment he'd seen the flowers that had been laid on his father's grave, he'd felt so close to Yoshino it was as if he were about to bump into him.

The first time they'd met at Aose's office, Yoshino had handed him a ticket. Next, Aose had stood with Yoshino on the same platform at the very beginning of the train line and they'd boarded the train together – a mystery train with an unknown destination. He didn't know when he'd arrive, but he did know there was a destination. He would get there eventually. The train would stop, the doors open, and then he'd know everything. No . . .

You already know. You already know the truth.

Aose was thrown into panic.

Did he understand? Did he know? Why did he believe he did?

Because he understood. Because he knew. The truth was right there on the other side of the sliding *fusuma* doors. All he needed to do was open them. But why didn't he?

It was after midnight when the doorbell rang. Aose's brain had shut down after running on full power without getting any results. Cursing the brain that had betrayed him by going off on its own rampage, leaving its owner behind, Aose had taken a painkiller for his headache and lain down on the sofa.

'Hey, it's me. Open up!'

Aose released the apartment building's downstairs auto lock, unlocked his flat door and waited. Okajima came right in. It was obvious at a glance that he'd been drinking heavily. He staggered into the living room, plopped himself down on the wooden floor and exhaled one ragged breath.

'You okay?' said Aose.

'Yeah.'

'Do you want some water?'

'I want a drink.'

'I've only got beer.'

'Give me one.'

Aose wasn't out of the room for more than thirty seconds, but when he came back there was a dramatic change in Okajima. His face had crumpled, his teeth were clenched, and both hands were in his lap, screwed up into tight balls.

Aose offered him the can of beer.

'What happened?'

Okajima didn't take the beer so he put it down on the table.

'Did Shigeta give you more shit?'

'. . . I'm finished.'

'Hey, hey, come on. Talk to me.'

Okajima stared up at the ceiling.

'There's going to be an article in today's *Toyo Shimbun*.'

Aose was more disbelieving than shocked.

'That's ridiculous. How could a story that insignificant become a newspaper article?'

'It can. It can. Like a conjuring trick.'

Okajima's head now hung so low it looked as if he were about to topple over.

'Shigeta tattled to the city council and got the liberal councillors to move. The anti-mayor faction of the conservative councillors got on board too. Today they're forming an Article 100 committee. The committee's going to investigate collusion between the mayor and contractors.'

'What the . . .'

'So that guy is just going to write some article about a subject he blew up himself?'

'That seems to be Shigeta's MO.'

Aose was infuriated. The police would never act on such trivial suspicions. And even if they did, it would take time to investigate. That's why Shigeta had gone to the city council and aggravated the situation. If the furore grew, then the police would have no choice but to act. Was that his scheme?

'Did Shigeta interview you again?'

'No.'

'No? I thought he said he was going to. He's going to write an article without another interview?'

'It's not Shigeta's idea. Kusamichi has been working through Katsumata.'

That was no doubt true. Katsumata was a prefectural assembly member. Kusamichi a member of parliament. There were forces at work trying to get the mayor replaced. But what had happened to Okajima's backers? Before coming to see Aose, he must have met with those people. Couldn't the Article 100 committee be quashed? Had they already lost the battle? They must already be discussing what to do once the article came out. Unimaginable, but that seemed to be what Okajima was telling him—

'They want me to be hospitalized,' Okajima mumbled.

'Hospitalized?'

No response.

'You?'

'. . . yeah.'

'Who told you?'

Again, no response.

Aose reached out and shook Okajima by the shoulders.

'Hey! Who told you to do that?'

Was it the mayor? Director Kadokura of S— City's Department of Construction, perhaps a city councillor or even a member of parliament?

Okajima's watery eyes flashed.

'I'm supposed to be hospitalized before I can be called before the Article 100 committee. I'm ill, so I'm withdrawing from the competition. It's all been decided.'

Decided?

Aose was speechless. Someone had decided. They'd decided to throw Okajima to the wolves. They were worse than Shigeta.

Then the disappointment hit. The competition was over. The dream of the Haruko Fujimiya *mémoire* had evaporated. The architectural structure that Okajima Design Company and Aki-hiko Okajima had worked hard to bequeath to the world would never be built.

'Aose?'

'What?'

'Look after the firm. Don't let it fall apart.'

As soon as he said that, Okajima put a hand over his mouth and bent double.

Aose led him to throw up in the toilet, rubbing his back for him as he did so. He was shocked by how skinny Okajima was – Aose could feel his spine against the palm of his hand.

Back in the living room, Okajima opened a can of beer as if he was about to start round two.

'Don't.'

'Leave me alone. When the sun rises in the east, I've only got a few hours left to live.'

'They've got nothing on you. Certainly not enough to take your life.'

'They will. I'm finished.'

'Okajima—'

'What did you find out in Sendai?'

He asked, but it was clear his heart wasn't in it.

'I'll tell you later. But more important—'

'About Sendai, please.'

Aose sighed.

'Touta Yoshino's roots were in Sendai. That's all.'

'How was the Hyuga Villa?'

'How do you mean?'

'Did you meet Taut?'

If he had really wanted to talk about that kind of thing, he'd already have invited Aose out for a drink. Okajima was frightened. He was trying to fill up the hours until the newspapers arrived on people's doorsteps.

'I think I met him. I've read all of the books you lent me. If you hadn't done that for me, I think he and I would have continued on our separate routes.'

'Why do you think Taut admired the Katsura Imperial Villa so much?'

The conversation had taken off. Aose decided to follow.

'He just liked it. You think there was any other reason?'

'You can't deny that the rise of modernism in the late 20s and early 30s played a role in Taut's opinion – well, that's what my professor said.'

'The architectural style wars?'

'Right. The Japanese modernists were trying to break the obsession with Greek and Gothic style, and the Katsura Imperial Villa was their pièce de résistance. So they turned to Taut. They took him to see the villa because they wanted the endorsement of a world-class master architect. It makes sense, doesn't it?'

'I don't think it can have been that simple. And Taut wouldn't have said something was good if he didn't think it was.'

'Of course not. Modernism is all about practicality and functionality. And beyond that, simple, functional beauty. But Taut was an expressionist, not a modernist. Well, by the time he came to Japan he may have had similar ideas, and he may have linked modernism to the simple, functional aesthetics of Japanese architecture, but it wasn't from the point of view of a pure modernist that he appreciated the Imperial Villa. Taut said it was beautiful, so beautiful that it made him want to cry.'

'Yes, he wrote that in his diary the day he saw it,'

'The long and short of it is, Taut personally loved the Katsura Imperial Villa, regardless of the intentions of the Japanese modernists. That complex, eccentric man appreciated the villa for its beauty, in other words in the simplest of terms. Perhaps he was mocking the style wars. Anything that is beautiful to the eye has value. No, beauty is the only true value. Isn't that what he wanted to say?'

'I don't think so,' said Aose. 'He was always harping on about the importance of practicality and functionality.'

'No, he wasn't. The most remarkable thing about Taut was that he believed in his own aesthetic sense and his self-confidence never wavered for a moment, throughout his whole career . . . But whatever – it doesn't matter.'

Startled, Aose looked into Okajima's eyes.

'It doesn't matter?'

Aose shuddered. Okajima's were the eyes of someone who had given up. Someone with a gaping wound in his heart. Aose didn't want the conversation to end on that note.

'You can't say it doesn't matter,' he said.

After a pause, Okajima opened his mouth again.

'Taut, Corbusier, Wright – I didn't care who it was. I just wanted to immerse myself in something. Something that would thrill me, intoxicate me. But getting to know them didn't mean anything. It kept feeling as if something had changed but then just seemed to wash off in the shower. I never seem to change. Once there was this girl sitting next to me who was so good at drawing that I got envious. I sneaked a peek at her work and copied it. That's my true nature, and it has stuck with me my whole life.'

Okajima got to his feet.

'Well, I'm going home. I want to see Isso's sleeping face.'

It sounded as if he'd snapped out of it, but his face still looked miserable.

Aose couldn't hold back.

'Don't go into hospital,' he said forcefully. 'If you're called before the Article 100 committee, just go. It's your chance to tell them what you did do, and categorically deny everything that you didn't do.'

Okajima didn't reply.

'Okajima, this is not over. Let's enter another competition.'

Okajima couldn't help laughing.

'Look who's talking – the man who's been avoiding things his whole life.'

40

The sky began to lighten. Aose ran down to the nearest convenience store and bought a copy of the *Toyo Shimbun*. Could it all
have been some bizarre delusion of grandeur on the part of Okajima? That glimmer of hope was extinguished the moment he
opened the newspaper. It was a major article with three separate
headlines.

Collusion between Mayor and Contractor?

Haruko Fujimiya Mémoire: Favouritism in Selection of Contractors

S— City Council to Set Up Article 100 Committee Today

The content of the article relied entirely on the claims of the
city councillors who had set out to pursue the allegations, and
was the exact scenario set out by *Toyo*'s reporter Shigeta and the
anti-mayor faction. Although it had withheld Okajima's name
and that of his company, the article included a so-called 'question
and answer session' conducted by the reporter.

*Both before and after the selection of the contractors, it seems you had
a number of meals and drinking sessions with Director Kadokura of
the Department of Construction . . .*

O-san: So what?

*Toyo Shimbun: Didn't it occur to you that it might cause misun-
derstandings?*

*O-san: We split the cost of food and drink. There was absolutely
no bribery.*

Toyo Shimbun: The return taxi was paid for by your company.

O-san: *I have no memory of that.*

Toyo Shimbun: You accompanied Mayor Shinozuka and Director Kadokura to see a soccer match in Tokyo.

O-san: That had nothing to do with the competition. The three of us happen to like soccer, and it was a completely private outing.

Toyo Shimbun: Your company paid for the tickets and the transportation.

O-san: That's not the case. We split the bill.

Aose felt feverish.

There had indeed been such an exchange between Shigeta and Okajima, but it hadn't gone quite the way Shigeta had reported it. He couldn't put his finger on what or how, but the interview had been presented in such a way as to give the reader the impression that Okajima was some kind of shady contractor, involved in illicit dealings. At the end of the article, for good measure, there was a comment from a city councillor:

Naturally, O-san will be called to speak to the Article 100 committee.

It brought back Okajima's words.

Look after the firm. Don't let it fall apart.

The industry would doubtless react strongly to an article like this one. There was a distinct possibility that the company would go under. As he got dressed for work, Aose prepared himself for the tough task ahead.

When he arrived at the office, all three staff members were already in, even though it wasn't yet 8 a.m. A copy of the Saitama edition of the *Toyo Shimbun* was lying on the desk. Ishimaki and Mayumi were both on the phone. Takeuchi looked totally flustered, and a look of relief came over him when he saw Aose.

'We've been getting non-stop calls from newspapers,' he said.

After reading the *Toyo Shimbun* article, all the other press agencies must have called immediately. The authenticity of the article probably didn't matter so much, but the establishment of an Article 100 committee was something that couldn't be ignored.

Ishimaki slammed down the phone receiver, and Mayumi, bright red in the face, followed suit.

'What are you saying to them?' asked Aose, looking from one to the other.

'The president is out sick, and I don't know anything – that's what I'm telling them,' said Mayumi, her tone still harsh from her phone conversation. 'He called my house early this morning. Said he was going to the hospital.'

Aose nodded. Okajima had decided to be hospitalized after all.

'I hope he's okay.'

Mayumi's face clouded over as she looked at Aose. In all the fuss, it seemed that the fact he yelled at her on the phone the other day had been forgotten.

'He's fine. He's not seriously ill.'

'I can't believe they'd write this shit!'

Takeuchi slammed the newspaper on to the desk.

'It's rubbish,' Mayumi agreed.

However, Ishimaki was staring into space, and after a few moments turned a sullen face in Aose's direction.

'Is this story bullshit?'

'Of course it is!' Mayumi's voice was shrill.

'I'm asking Aose-san.'

Ishimaki's deep voice dominated the room. Mayumi and Takeuchi also turned to look at Aose.

'Well, he is involved . . .' said Aose, without making eye contact with anyone in the room.

Ishimaki frowned.

'Involved? What does that mean?'

'There are people who are trying to oust Mayor Shinozuka from office. They used Okajima.'

'There are politicians involved?'

'Yes.'

'But . . .'

Ishimaki looked down at the newspaper.

'They do say there's no smoke without fire. Aside from the political fighting and all that, what's this about the boss taking the mayor and the construction department director out drinking before getting selected for the competition?'

'The president's not that kind of person,' said Mayumi, interrupting again.

Emotions were running high.

'Well, let me ask you something, Mayu-chan. Is it a lie that this taxi fare home after some drinking party or other was paid for from our company funds?'

'I can't answer that. I've calculated a lot of taxi fares.'

'You have to know that. He's a department director in S— city so he would have taken a taxi home somewhere in S— city. You could just go through your files and pull it out. That's what a reporter just asked me to do.'

'One of them asked me the same thing, so I looked into it. There were several invoices from S— city taxi companies. I think they were all trips made by the boss.'

Ishimaki recoiled.

'So there were receipts. I knew it!'

'They were the boss's taxi fares.'

'From S— city to another location within the city?'

'Yes, there were some like that.'

'Then it wasn't the boss.'

'Look, you two, let's not do this,' Takeuchi cut in. 'The boss could easily have used a taxi to get around S— city. And besides, just because the other guy works in S— city, it doesn't necessarily follow that he lives within the city limits.'

Takeuchi was trying to protect Mayumi rather than Okajima, but with a face that said she didn't need his protection, Mayumi continued to insist.

'It was definitely the boss.'

'What makes you so sure? I don't get why the taxi company would be billing the company anyway. It's weird. If I were the boss, I'd pay the fare when I got out of the taxi and then hand the receipts to you later.'

'From about two months ago, he started paying all the S—city taxi fares after the fact. He said it was because he was using so many.'

'The boss said that to you?'

'That's right.'

Mayumi stood her ground, but the conversation had only added to everyone's suspicion that Okajima had been involved in premeditated wining and dining for favours.

Ishimaki rubbed his beard and looked over at Aose.

'What about you, Aose-san? I'd like to hear your thoughts.'

His tone was accusatory. It was quite possible that Ishimaki thought he was complicit.

'I'm convinced that Okajima was doing the best he could.'

'I get that. He managed to land us a job that we otherwise would never have had the chance to get. I also believe that the boss was doing the best he could. But it's not acceptable if the firm paid for someone's taxi. I really want to know the truth. Did any of the things written here in this article actually happen?'

'They might have done. But unless Okajima himself tells us they did, we have no choice but to support him.'

This line didn't elicit a nod from either Ishimaki or Mayumi. Mayumi was about to speak, but she was cut off by the phone behind her starting to ring. She spun around to answer it.

'Yes, this is Okajima Design Company . . . Oh yes, thank you. Yes? . . . Yes, it is true that it was written about us, but I can assure you the content is rubbish. The newspaper just wrote it . . . No, there's nothing to worry about. Please continue with the construction schedule as planned.'

Ishimaki, who had been listening to the phone conversation, leaned over to Aose.

'So what happens now?'

'What do you mean?'

'The office. Now that this has happened, can we go on?'

Right now, Ishimaki wasn't an architect, he was a family man with a wife and four children.

'Have there been calls from any clients?' Aose asked.

'No. Well, not yet.'

Ishimaki made sure to emphasize the 'not yet'.

The newspaper had referred to 'O— Design Company in Tokorozawa City'. Okajima Design Company's participation in the competition for the Haruko Fujimiya memorial hadn't been officially announced yet, but it was only a matter of time before that information became public knowledge.

'What about the competition?' said Takeuchi. All of a sudden, his expression had turned anxious.

Aose let out a ragged breath. It was a direct question, so he felt obliged to answer. Mayumi had finished her phone call and was also looking at him.

'We'll have to withdraw.'

'No!'

Takeuchi's voice was close to a scream. And then the office fell into a deep silence. Ishimaki swivelled his chair around to look up at the posters on the wall. Mayumi stared at the competition table. The 'Okajima Design Office's 90-Day War!' calendar countdown was at 75.

The phone rang again. The atmosphere shifted once more as Mayumi reached out a hand to pick up. Ishimaki got up and went over to pat Takeuchi's slumped shoulder. Then he walked over to Aose.

'Dropping out of the competition means admitting guilt,' he said under his breath. 'I think this means even more trouble for the firm.'

'The reason for his withdrawal is that he's recuperating from illness.'

'That's not going to work. Everyone will believe that he

withdrew because of impropriety. After that he won't be able to work again.'

'Then why don't you look for a new job?' said Aose with an explosion of anger.

Ishimaki pursed his lips.

'That's not like you.'

'What are you talking about?'

'There was a time you were getting ready to quit.'

Had Okajima said something? Or had that private detective contacted Ishimaki as well?

'I'm not quitting.'

'And of course I'm not either.'

'Okajima told me he didn't want the company to fall apart.'

'But with a boss who does that kind of—'

'Ishimaki!'

Aose glared at his colleague.

'Have you forgotten? If Okajima hadn't taken you on, you'd still be slaving away for your father-in-law doing clerical work in a fertilizer factory right now. I was halfway to drinking myself to death when he picked me up. Who was it who took these miserable losers who were drowning in the pool of that burst bubble and gave them architects' business cards again? You and I are going to go down with the boss. You'd best brace yourself.'

Ishimaki went quiet and hung his head a little. Takeuchi's mouth hung open. Still gripping the telephone receiver, Mayumi chewed on her lip as she stared at Aose.

41

That afternoon Ishimaki and Takeuchi went out to supervise site construction, while Aose stayed in the office. The rate of phone calls coming in from newspaper companies and contractors had died down, but Aose didn't feel comfortable leaving Mayumi on her own.

He waited until 2 p.m., but when there was no word from Okajima he called the boss's mobile. Truthfully, he reckoned that if he was at the hospital he would have it turned off, but he was surprised when Okajima picked up.

'It's Aose.'

'Oh, Aose-san, thank you for calling.'

It was Okajima's wife, Yaeko. The reason Aose hadn't tried his home number was that he didn't know her very well. He'd only been to the house a couple of times, and on those occasions she had simply brought some tea and then left the men alone. They'd never really talked.

'How's Okajima?'

'He was just admitted to hospital.'

'I see.'

Perhaps because Aose seemed to take the news so casually, Yaeko's voice changed.

'He had a check-up and they found he had serious ulcers in his stomach and duodenum. That they were bleeding and it would be dangerous to leave things as they were.'

Aose was completely taken by surprise. Okajima wasn't faking his illness? Had the intense stress of the situation gnawed through the walls of his stomach and intestines in just a few days? No, it was more likely that he'd been pushing his body to extremes for so long in order to get selected for the competition. He thought of the resigned look on Okajima's face last night, and the feeling of his spine against the palm of his hand came back, more vividly than ever.

'Which hospital is he in?'

'Dai-ni Byoin. It's going to be a while. He's been bleeding a long time and his haemoglobin level has dropped to less than half of what it ought to be. It's not severe enough to need a blood transfusion, but they have to increase his blood levels while fixing the ulcers as well.'

Yaeko sounded bitter, and it made Aose feel guilty. He felt as if he were being told not to visit Okajima. Yaeko hung up without saying a word about the newspaper article or the management of the office.

'Did his wife pick up?'

Aose turned and saw Mayumi with a strange kind of light in her eyes. Aose had wondered before whether Yaeko's indifference to the running of the office and its staff might have something to do with Mayumi's presence.

'He's been hospitalized. They found he had severe ulcers.'

Mayumi turned pale.

'Oh no!'

'Yeah. He's going to be kept in for a while. So you'll have to keep that in mind when you're dealing with calls.'

'Does his wife seem worried?'

Aose wondered if she was trying to annoy him again. How could Okajima's wife not be worried? He was about to say it, but instead he let himself be pulled in by Mayumi's dark thoughts.

'Are you suggesting that she might not be worried? Why?'

'I don't trust her. She's done the worst thing that any woman could ever do.'

Aose's glare matched the ferocity of Mayumi's words. What was the worst thing that any woman could do? Had she found out that Yaeko was unfaithful? Mayumi had admitted in the past that her own husband's constant affairs were the reason for her divorce. Had that made Mayumi more sensitive to things of that nature? No, the concentric plum blossom story was surely just something that Okajima had made up, and it was straight-up jealousy that was motivating Mayumi. That was all he could think.

'I don't think it's any of your business, Tsumura-san.'

If it was her business, he wanted her to admit it now. Tell him that she and the boss were in a relationship.

'Yes, it is. I'm in exactly the same situation as you and Ishimaki-sensei. If the boss hadn't taken me on, I've no idea what would have become of Yuma and me. So, I would do anything for him. Anything at all.'

Aose flinched, but right then there was a knock at the door. It didn't open, so Mayumi called out:

'*Dozo* – come in!'

'Excuse me.'

An elderly man opened the door, bowing low as he entered.

'Can we help you?' said Aose.

The man bowed more deeply.

'The president, Okajima-san—' he began.

'I'm afraid he's been taken ill and was admitted to hospital today.'

'Hospital? Oh, really . . .'

The man looked dismayed.

'Then I'm afraid I'm disturbing you at a very difficult time. I'm a nephew of Haruko Fujimiya's. I met with Okajima-san the other day and was very impressed by his character. But when I saw the newspaper this morning, I felt I had to come over right away.'

Aose quickly offered the man a seat on the couch.

The nephew introduced himself as Koji Yanagiya, the son of Haruko Fujimiya's sister.

'Both my mother and I would like Okajima-san to design the memorial. That's why I was so disappointed, or rather worried, about this morning's article.'

'Well, it was a rather, shall we say, presumptuous article. And we don't believe it to be entirely truthful.'

Aose chose his words carefully, so they could be taken either way. However, Yanagiya's eyes immediately lit up.

'The article was fabricated?'

'I wouldn't go so far as to say that, but I can't say that it's true either.'

'Does that mean there's still a possibility that your company can design a memorial for us?'

'No, I really can't promise . . . Well, because Okajima is currently hospitalized.'

Aose was being evasive.

'I hope he can do it,' Yanagiya muttered to himself, and took out an envelope from his jacket pocket. He opened the flap and pulled out an old postcard. It was a sketch of the area around the Arc de Triomphe. On the back were several lines of scribbled text. There was no address or stamp. You could tell at a glance that this wasn't anything that had been sent by post.

'My mother was very worried too. She asked me to bring this to Okajima-san for luck.'

Aose read the faint pencilled lettering.

You try to fill it
To fill in what's missing
But no matter how much you try
That one space can never be filled

'Is this——?'

'I found it among her belongings. I think it's one of the postcards that my aunt used to sell on the streets.'

Aose nodded.

'That was the only thing she ever wrote in Japanese. When I showed it to Okajima-san, he was very moved. Filling in what's missing – he said that was what art was all about.'

Had it been a sales pitch? Or did he genuinely believe it?

'Then Okajima-san talked about how my aunt had hardly sold any of her paintings, that he thought she must have been painting them for a particular person. That was when I decided that we really wanted Okajima-san to design the memorial. In fact, my mother and Okajima-san had the exact same thought.'

'Which was what, exactly?'

'Have you ever heard of the Mugonkan, or Silent Museum?'

'Yes, I know it.'

It was an art museum in Ueda City, Nagano prefecture, built to exhibit works by art students who died in the Second World War. Okajima and Ishimaki had included it on their recent tour of museums and memorials.

'Two years before she died, my aunt made her only trip back to Japan. She insisted on visiting the Mugonkan.'

Aose was fascinated.

'Actually, my grandmother told me before she died that my aunt was greatly affected by her cousin's death in the war. He and my aunt had lived close to each other. He was an art student and a rather quiet type. When the war situation escalated, students were sent to the front, and he was deployed down south. On his way there, the ship he was on was sunk by the US military. My aunt was a little bit in love with this cousin. She was only fifteen or sixteen at the time but, according to my grandmother, he used to teach her about painting before he was taken by the war.'

'Are there any of his works in the Mugonkan museum?'

'No. They were all burned in an air raid, and none of them remain. I think that's why my aunt wanted to visit the museum. I think she wanted to appreciate the art of those students who had died young, like her cousin.'

Aose felt as if he'd been let into the heart of Haruko Fujimiya.

She'd been painting for her cousin. Young love, and the tragic death of a young man, had bequeathed over eight hundred paintings to the world.

Aose retraced the words on the postcard.

You try to fill it
To fill in what's missing
But no matter how much you try
That one space can never be filled

Okajima had understood. Creating for someone, bequeathing your work to them. He had understood the artist's burning passion.

'Please pass on my best wishes to Okajima-san. And tell him I would very much like him to design my aunt's memorial.'

After repeating his wishes, Yanagiya left the office. He left behind a pile of fresh materials relating to Haruko Fujimiya. Aose bowed deeply to him as he left, as he thought about how they were going to disappoint him.

But there was no time to get sentimental. Mayumi put Haruko Fujimiya's postcard into her bag and announced she was going to visit Okajima. Her eyes were wet. The tragic love story they'd heard from Yanagiya may have flipped some emotional switch in Mayumi.

'He's only just been admitted. Don't you think we should wait a bit?'

It was Aose's roundabout attempt to stop her, but Mayumi looked defiant.

'That's why I'm going right now. There'll be all kinds of things he needs. I'll need to go shopping.'

'Don't make me keep saying it – his wife will do all that for him.'

But instead of cold water, it was fuel to her fire.

'She doesn't deserve to be his wife. Leaving him to suffer until he gets a hole in his stomach!'

'No, that was because Okajima always did as he pleased.'

'You don't understand, Aose-sensei.'

'No, it's you who doesn't understand!'

Mayumi slung her bag over her shoulder and was about to leave, so Aose grabbed her arm. She immediately shook him off.

'Calm down a bit,' said Aose.

'I don't need to calm down. Do you know what state the boss must be in right now?'

'So don't upset him any more. If you go now, you'll just be in the way.'

'In the way?'

'Yes.'

'Do you know? No, you don't know, do you?'

'Know what?'

Mayumi's face contorted.

'Isso-kun is another man's son. The boss knows it, but he puts up with it without saying anything. He pretends not to know that his wife had another lover.'

Aose's vision froze. The only movement was Mayumi, who, as if in slow motion, crossed the room and exited the door.

He was still frozen to the spot. His mind hadn't caught up with his emotions.

'Bullshit!' he spat out.

There was nothing else to say.

42

The chaos at Okajima Design Company got worse with each passing day. There were constant phone calls from construction companies and subcontractors. Clients, too, called with all sorts of questions, and one couple in their thirties, both teachers, cancelled an order for an ecological house that Takeuchi had been planning. The clients in Osaka who had requested a copy of the Y Residence also called to ask what was going on. Aose had to offer them a sincere apology. Because of all the fuss, he hadn't managed to complete the plans for their house.

'When's your boss getting out of hospital?'

On the reception area couch sat a rough-looking man of about fifty by the name of Yaginuma. He'd called to say he had a question to ask, then within ten minutes turned up at the office. He claimed to be the S— city councillor who'd proposed the formation of the Article 100 committee, but then he'd thrust a business card against Aose's chest that described him as president of a waste collection company. Without waiting to be invited, he'd made himself comfortable on the couch and was now exuding an air of intimidation.

'I think it'll be a while yet,' Aose said. 'It's both his stomach and the duodenum.'

Yaginuma looked sceptical. It was obvious he thought Okajima was faking.

'He's been in there over a week now. You must be able to predict how much longer. One more week, ten days?'

'I'm sorry, I have no idea. It seems he needs to be treated to increase the amount of blood his body can produce.'

Yaginuma thrust his chin out in a challenging gesture. The old scar that ran diagonally across his jawline was uncomfortably conspicuous.

'As I'm sure you already know, I want to set a date to call him before the Article 100 committee as early as possible.'

'I'll let you know his prognosis shortly.'

'Is it that bad?'

'Yes, it's bad enough for him to be hospitalized.'

Aose let his frustration show but, truth be told, even he didn't know the full extent of Okajima's condition. The previous week he had visited the hospital twice. The first time Okajima had been undergoing tests, so he'd simply left him a gift and gone home again. He'd tried again the next day and had caught sight of Shigeta from the *Toyo Shimbun* hanging around the hospital corridors. Okajima was in an agitated state, having just managed to get himself a private room in order to avoid the reporter. His wife, Yaeko, was there, greeting everyone with a hostile expression. That of course included Aose, so he'd been unable to talk with Okajima in any kind of depth.

'I'm so sorry that we're unable to offer you tea,' Aose told the unpleasant character on the couch. 'I beg your understanding.'

Mayumi and Takeuchi were busy answering the phones. Yaginuma shot them a look, then clicked his tongue in contempt.

'Tell your boss there's no escape. It doesn't matter when he's discharged, he'll still have to come before the council.'

Threats and intimidation. Aose's brain overreacted.

'You know it's not necessarily going to go according to the scenario you've all got planned.'

'You've all . . .'

Yaginuma sat back down on the sofa and spread himself wide as if to intimidate Aose.

'What's that supposed to mean, huh? What's this scenario?'

Aose swallowed the excess saliva his nerves were producing.

'Political in-fighting may be your business, but can't you leave a tiny company like ours out of it?'

'Ha! The guilty have no shame. Don't try to talk big. You wine and dine government officials and sneak yourselves onto lists of nominees.'

'No one knows whether that happened or not.'

'He did it though – your boss. And you're all accomplices.'

'Hm. Bit of a case of the pot calling the kettle black, going after us.'

Yaginuma's complexion changed. Aose thought he was about to get punched, but the man simply rattled the table with his knees.

'Get in touch when you know his discharge date,' he spat, and marched out of the office, rolling his shoulders as if to shake off something unpleasant.

Aose made eye contact with Mayumi, who had just ended a phone call.

'What a gorilla,' he said, trying to lighten the atmosphere. However, Mayumi blew him off with a noncommittal 'yeah' as she reached for the phone again. Since the day she'd insisted on going to visit Okajima in the hospital, she had said very little. Possibly there had been some kind of encounter with Yaeko, Aose thought. His mind was full of so many unpleasant possibilities, but he just couldn't bring himself to dredge it all up again with Mayumi.

'I'm going to meet a client,' he announced, and escaped the office as fast as he could.

Outside, the sky was cloudy. He didn't know who he should blame for the bad feeling that he got from lying to Mayumi.

43

Aose drove his Citroën to Dai-Ni Hospital. It was nothing to do with the pressure Yaginuma had put on him; he had always planned to visit Okajima today.

As acting president, he needed to get a clear picture of Okajima's condition and discuss what he needed to do from here on. But above all, he wanted to see Okajima's face. There was no way of knowing whether what Mayumi had told him about his son, Isso, was true or not, so he wasn't going to bring that up, but he just wanted to meet Okajima and talk to him.

The atmosphere in the office seemed highly charged, but it was really a sense of futility. The competition had been taken from them, they'd lost sight of their goals, and nothing but empty noise and hassle remained, as if they were stuck fighting a lost battle or a throwaway match after the tournament had been decided. It was strange, though, how emotions refused to stay in the heart but continued to push their way outwards, outwards. These past few days, these past few weeks, Aose had let many years' worth of real emotions out to the surface. He was trying to relate to people. He'd awoken from the illusion of his own seclusion from the world, had thrown off his self-imposed resignation to his fate. It was because he had built the Y Residence. He had reclaimed the Y Residence into his heart.

Thus it was his hope that the reasons the Y Residence had come into the world were good ones and loving ones.

Build a home you would want to live in.

Aose eased off the accelerator as the lights ahead changed from yellow to red. Beyond were the white buildings of the Dai-Ni Hospital.

His brain tried to show him something completely different: Aose, standing alone on a beach at the edge of the ocean. Around his ankles the waves of truth ebb and flow.

He already knows. He knows the truth. All the elements are there. The *fusuma* sliding doors are about to open for the big reveal. All that's left is to—

His inside pocket began to vibrate.

He was already inside the hospital grounds. He pulled over to the left and stopped the car just before the entrance to the car park. His phone was still vibrating.

'This is Aose.'

'Hello. This is Kaneko. Thank you for all your suggestions.'

It was the president of Kaneko Engineering.

'I've got a report for you. I painted the rain gutters and all the outside light supports in burgundy to match the carpets, as you suggested, sensei. It looks amazing – like one of those stylish apartments you'd see around Shirokanedai. The owner was thrilled.'

'That's good to hear.'

'Sensei, please come and take a look sometime. The photos really don't do it justice.'

'Well, I'm a bit busy right now. Have you read the papers lately?'

'Ah . . . Yes, I read about what happened. It was obvious that it was just harassment to do with an election or something. I'm sick of all the pressure in this industry telling me who to support and who to shut out. Sensei, you should just ignore all that stuff and work as hard as you can. Work is all about people and relationships. I'm behind you, whatever happens.'

There was a prickle at the back of Aose's throat.

'Thank you. I look forward to working more with you too.'

At least as far as the young president was concerned, Aose's reputation was intact.

44

Evening visiting hours were until six o'clock. There was one hour left. Room 5 on the general ward. The corridor, lined with private rooms, was as drab-looking as a student dormitory. The name tag on the door of Room 5 had been removed. Aose glanced around then knocked on the door. When there was no response, he called out, 'It's Aose!' He put his ear to the door and could hear a faint reply. It was a man's voice.

There was no Yaeko in the extremely small and cramped room. Okajima was lying on the bed, trying to operate the switch on the bed to raise his upper body. There were two IV drip stands, but nothing was on them for the moment.

Aose swallowed. As the back of the bed rose up, the face that came into view was so emaciated it seemed to belong to a different person. Okajima's cheeks were sunken, his skin dry and chapped, and the dark circles under his eyes were so pronounced they could be mistaken for bruises.

'Well, you've lost all that fat.'

Okajima managed a weak laugh as he glanced at the IV stands.

'There's no such thing as a Chinese food or a barbecue drip, sadly.'

Aose tried to laugh, but his cheeks seemed to cramp up. Hiding his face from Okajima, he sat himself on the bedside chair.

'Don't worry, when you get out, you'll be able to stuff your face. Hey, don't try to get up!'

'How is it at the office?'

'All fine. Don't worry about it.'

'Any complaints or cancellations?'

'There've been a lot of enquiries. Even calls of support. Only one cancellation.'

'Are the other newspapers covering it?'

'Not much. Just something like a quick summary of what's going on.'

'How are Ishimaki and Takeuchi doing?'

'Takeuchi's handling the phone calls, along with Tsumura. Ishimaki is rushing around everywhere. I think he's in his element.'

Aose had noticed it the moment he came in – the postcard of the Arc de Triomphe on the bedside table. Mayumi had been here after all.

'Aose, stop looking so scared. The doctors say it's not as serious as it looks. But I can't sleep. Haven't been able to sleep at all, and now I look like this. Mind you, it has its uses.'

'Eh?'

'He just came to see me – Shigeta from the *Toyo Shimbun*.'

'Came here? Into your room?'

'Yeah, tracked me down. Came in without even knocking, camera in hand. But then he took one look at my face and got spooked. And right then Yaeko came back and yelled at him, so he got out as fast as he could. I wonder what he'll write this time? Maybe he'll have nothing to say. He'll just have to suck it up, I guess.'

Don't go into hospital. Aose's own line came back to haunt him.

'Look, hole up here for now until you get better. Leave the rest to me. Don't worry about anything.'

'Yes, I'm sorry. But it looks as if that's the only way.'

Okajima took a deep breath and, as if on the spur of the moment, he peeled back the top cover of his bed and swung his legs over the edge. He looked for his slippers.

'What is it? The toilet?'

'I need a smoke.'

Okajima stuck his hand under the pillow and pulled out a box of Frontier Lights and a cheap, hundred-yen lighter.

'You really shouldn't—'

But before Aose could stop him, Okajima walked over to the window. He looked frail and exposed in his blue pyjamas.

'This place looks a bit like Haruko Fujimiya's room,' Okajima remarked, as if to change the subject. He pulled open the sash window to waist height and, using his hands for support, lifted himself up a little so he could rest his buttocks on the windowsill. His hair stirred a little in the breeze. It looked a terribly dangerous manoeuvre for a sick person to perform.

'Please don't. We're on the third floor.'

Okajima lit his cigarette.

'The nurses will give you hell for this.'

'I'm careful not to get caught.'

Okajima took a very deep, deliberate drag on his cigarette, then turned his head, stuck it out of the window, and exhaled all the smoke outside.

'See?'

'Do that and the ulcers won't heal.'

'Aose?'

'What?'

'Taut said that when he saw the Katsura Imperial Villa it was so beautiful it made him want to cry.'

Aose studied Okajima's profile. Hadn't he said it didn't matter any more? He'd ended their previous discussion that way.

'I wonder if Taut knew? What the most beautiful thing in the world was. That there existed something either tangible or conceptual that could be called absolute beauty? Perhaps that's why he tried so hard to create something beautiful himself? Trying to fill his own heart. But no matter how much he tried, that space could never be filled?'

Aose glanced at the postcard on the bedside table. Okajima's gaze was there too.

'I heard that Yanagiya-san came to the office.'

'He did.'

Aose thought it would be too cruel to tell Okajima that Haruko Fujimiya's relatives hoped he would design the memorial, so he kept that to himself.

'When they showed me those original pieces at Yanagiya-san's house, it gave me the chills. Those filthy clothes, the wrinkles on the man's face that seemed to merge into the rubbish on the street, the knotty fingers clutching that stub of a cigarette . . . Yet every painting was beautiful. All my preconceptions of technique or realism, whether something has appeal or not, all of it was blown away. I was just overwhelmed by the beauty. The very word "beauty" seemed too cheap to use to describe them. And I wanted so badly to get ahead of you in the competition that I never said anything to you about it.'

'Brilliant, dark, scary . . . and also beautiful, eh?' said Aose.

Okajima took one last puff on his cigarette, then scrunched himself up to reach through the window and stub it out on the wall below. One or two sparks danced away on the breeze and vanished into the twilight.

'In her heart, Haruko Fujimiya had an unwavering ideal of beauty. You heard the story. A love that can't even be called love. An adolescent daydream of a memory. With the death of her cousin, that beauty had become timeless. For decades she fervently and single-mindedly painted beautiful pictures. She just kept on painting until she died, but she could never replicate the exquisite beauty that was in her heart. Could we have done it? Or was it impossible? Could we have won?'

Okajima was starting to get red in the face.

'Of course, it's impossible to match Haruko Fujimiya's talent, but I wanted to create something. I wanted to design a beautiful building that would be a worthy eternal resting place for her paintings. For a fleeting moment I felt as if we were in perfect sync, she and I.'

'Uh-huh.'

'But I didn't qualify to be by her side.'

Okajima had been hanging his head, but now he raised it to look at Aose.

'What Shigeta claimed is true. I paid the director's taxi fare. I bought him dinner once too, but I swear we split the cost of that opening match of the J League season, and the travel expenses. It was hard because the director and the mayor were both hardcore soccer fans and I didn't have any contacts in the soccer world. I mean, it's true that I played it in high school, but I was only a reserve and I quit partway through. So I took a couple of the soccer alumni from my school who were supporters of Mayor Shinozuka and a ticket tout or two out drinking. They weren't government officials so I didn't think it was a big deal. But this is what happens when you try to do something big. I'm truly sorry for getting everyone mixed up in this and ruining the competition.'

'Don't worry about it.'

None of this was a shock to Aose. In fact, he had imagined something much more extravagant.

'Before you do anything else, go back to bed and get yourself well.'

The door to the hospital room opened. Aose looked over to see the startled face of Okajima's wife, Yaeko. He automatically got to his feet, but Yaeko surprised him with a thoughtful 'Don't let me disturb you.' Before he could respond, she'd already closed the door and was gone.

'Are you sure?' he asked Okajima.

'It's fine.'

Okajima shut the window and sat on the bed.

'I think she caught me smoking,' he said with a laugh.

He crossed his legs and leaned towards Aose.

'You've got something you want to say, haven't you?' he asked.

'What? No. I've given you my report and I've got a pretty clear picture of your condition.'

'You came here because you wanted to talk to me. I can see it on your face.'

Aose hadn't given Okajima's son, Isso a thought since coming here. If Okajima's instincts were correct, he'd know that Aose was wondering about the connection between him and Aose's ex-wife, but he hadn't felt like talking about it today. He'd decided to wait until the company crisis had died down.

'Just spit it out. You've got me wondering. And too much wondering means a long night ahead.'

Aose didn't speak.

'Are you still bothered about that detective thing? That stuff about you being engaged? I'm sorry that I even mentioned it.'

Aose gave a sigh of resignation.

'Was it Yukari who asked you to hire me?'

'What?'

Okajima waved a hand in an emphatic no gesture.

'No, no. You misunderstood. I hired you because I needed to build up the business.'

'But you were in contact with Yukari even before I joined you.'

'I already told you that. We talked two or three times a year.'

'The two of you talked about how I was down on my luck. Knowing Yukari's personality, there was no way she'd have kept that to herself.'

'She was worried about you. But you can't ask to be hired, and nor can you ask someone to hire another person.'

Aose didn't nod.

'That was around the time that I started saying I didn't want to finish in the minor leagues. I knew what you could do, and that's why I hired you. Got it?'

'But I guess I wasn't the force that you were hoping me to be.'

'Huh? What?'

'Me. I was just a washed-up architect from the bubble-economy days.'

314

Look who's talking — the man who's been avoiding things his whole life.

'Hey! All this self-torture is pretty ironic, really. You built the Y Residence, didn't you?'

His heart agreed. And then, immediately, he was transported to another place. To a platform at the beginning of the train line, where he and Touta Yoshino were standing.

'Hey, Aose? What's up?'

'Can I ask you another question?'

'What? Oh yeah. Go on.'

'The detective agency thing. A private detective went to Yukari's place to ask about me. He said it was about me getting remarried, so Yukari was shocked and gave you a call?'

'That's right.'

'What did you tell her?'

'I said I didn't think you were. But that I couldn't swear to it, of course, because you never talked about your private life.'

Aose nodded.

'Did Yukari ever reach out to you again after that? Like, for example, what happened about the detective and the remarriage or anything?'

'No . . . No that was it.'

'But even besides that whole story, she still contacts you twice or three times a year?'

'Well, it's been over a year now that I haven't heard from her.'

'I understand.'

Aose really did understand clearly. A wave of emotion hit him.

'I think she was really worried about you,' said Okajima. 'But it was too hard to keep calling.'

'You may be right.'

'Is there no way you can fix things?'

The wording was vague, but Okajima's meaning was clear from the expression in his eyes.

'I think it's too late now.'

Aose's own words echoed emptily in his skull.

'These days, with a couple splitting up every two minutes, would it really be all that strange for one to get back together every twenty minutes, or even every couple of hours?'

It was possible that Okajima was serious.

Aose got up with a new-found determination.

'I'll drop by again.'

'Do you have to leave yet?'

Aose was surprised by the emotion in Okajima's voice. His face looked desperate. The angle at which he looked up at Aose made the dark circles under his eyes stand out even more. It struck Aose that there was something unstable about him. He seemed to be veering between self-confidence and extreme weakness. There was no regularity to his emotions.

Aose sat back down. He decided he'd stay with Okajima until the end of visiting hours.

Okajima flashed him a relieved smile.

'Ah, it reminds me of our university days, being here with you like this.'

'I was only there half the time, so I only miss it half as much.'

'I was a jerk back then, wasn't I?'

Aose grimaced.

'Yeah. When did you decide to change?'

'Haha. So, I'm a nice guy now, am I?'

'Better than Shigeta.'

'Pretty dark humour, but I guess that's what makes you Aose.'

'Am I really that dark?'

'Well, now that I think about it, you're more of a black box. I never have any idea what you're hiding there inside, what might suddenly come popping up. The Y Residence, for instance.'

'Was that a compliment?'

'I'm not sure. You're like Taut. So much of you that you don't even understand yourself.'

'Hold on. Is that some sort of backhanded compliment?'

'Hey, Aose, let me ask you something.'

'What?'

'What is the most beautiful thing in the world to you?'

Another change of direction. Aose was just about to say that he'd need time to think about it, but then the answer just materialized in his head. The one and only absolute beauty.

'North light.'

'I see . . . North light . . . So it wasn't all about the technology then, the Y Residence?'

'Might be my age. When I was working in Akasaka, I used to think it was all about appearances. I thought an attractive exterior equalled beauty.'

'I can see that.'

'What about you?'

'Huh?'

'What's the most beautiful thing to you?'

'What's the most beautiful thing . . .'

Perhaps he hadn't expected Aose to turn his question back on him. Okajima sat for a while, blinking thoughtfully. The pause lasted so long that the silence began to feel uncomfortable. Finally, he spoke.

'I think it's Yuma's smile.'

Aose couldn't believe what he had just heard. Was Yuma Okajima's son?

'Idiot. I'm joking. I'm joking!'

Okajima fell about laughing.

'You should see your face. Look, I don't even have the capability.'

It took a few moments for understanding to dawn on Aose.

The stage faded to blackout, and the next scene opened with Okajima naked under the lights.

'I want to talk to you seriously.'

The smile had faded from Okajima's face.

'I used to drop by Mayumi's apartment sometimes. I always felt comfortable there. And I got very fond of Yuma too. But I swear it's not like that with me and Mayumi. We're like brother and sister.'

'That has to be tough on her,' Aose commented.

The image of Mayumi distraught was burnt into his brain.

'I'm spoiled to have Mayumi. I admit that. We understand each other so well that I truly believe in the concentric plum blossom theory. It's always a bit awkward to talk about a friendship between a man and a woman, but I thought the plum blossom metaphor wasn't bad. And there are things that a man can't talk to another man about . . . That was a bad time, when I found out about Isso. You heard about Isso from Mayumi, didn't you?'

Aose nodded silently.

'The night I found out about Isso I got drunk out of my mind and vented to Mayumi. That was the worst thing I could have done. I dumped half of my hatred on her.'

Okajima's eyes gleamed with anger.

'Things had been bad between Yaeko and me for a long time. I mean, we had good times, and we had fun times, but Yaeko cared more about her insurance sales job than anything else. And I was a pretentious fully-fledged architect who spent his time going to parties and drinking. We just weren't on the same page. It was as if we were each looking down on the other. I used to mock the insurance business all the time, and Yaeko began to remark that I wasn't bringing in much income. Then five years ago I found out about Isso. A friend of mine who was a doctor said he was doing research into sperm count. He'd just treated me for a urethral problem and, just out of interest, I decided to take the test. I went crazy when I got my results – not about my infertility, but about Isso. But I didn't say a word to Yaeko. I slapped her one time, but I didn't tell her why. I didn't even ask her about it. I did think about killing her, but I never thought about divorce. You know why?'

Aose waited for him to continue.

'To avoid the disgrace. I was living that flamboyant-architect,

318

first-class lifestyle with all my artistic pretensions, but my wife had betrayed me, I'd been made a fool of, and I was raising another man's child. I didn't want anyone in the industry to find out. That's the kind of man I am . . . That's what I am.'

His lip was trembling, and he bit down on it.

'Isso is a good boy. He's clever and kind. I loved him so much that when I found out, I refused to believe that sleeping face wasn't the face of my own son. I thought, "Until yesterday, this was my son." It was just too much to take in. The world turned black, I cursed my misfortune. I even thought about setting the house on fire and reducing Isso, Yaeko and myself to ashes. I had nights like that . . . But . . .'

Okajima's expression softened.

'I loved him. Even though I knew he wasn't my child, I still loved Isso. Even though in my head I would wonder sometimes who on earth he was, where had he come from, my heart said something completely different. He was so cute, so adorable. It isn't about the blood that runs in our veins; it's that precious time we spend together, just Isso and me. He says he wants to be an architect. He wrote it in an essay for school. He wants to be an architect, just like his father.'

Okajima looked at Aose, who was nodding.

'I hated myself. I hated the conniving, bullying person I was. But I still loved Isso, even though I knew he wasn't my kid, so I knew I had something good in me. It made me cry, thinking I'd had a chance to reinvent myself. I had the chance to live for him, to leave him some kind of legacy. And that's when I really decided to focus on my work. That's how I came to hire you. I wanted to make my firm bigger and stronger, so I could hand it over to Isso. I'm still on frosty terms with Yaeko, I haven't forgiven her, but I'm able to live under the same roof. I can understand that she must have had her reasons. I think it's better that she hasn't told me and better I don't let her know what I know. That's how we've managed to get by. It's just become normal.'

The strength drained from Okajima's body. He rubbed his eyes, looking a little embarrassed, then clapped his hands together.

'And that concludes my talk. Thank you for your kind attention.'

'It's not over yet,' said Aose, trying not to let on he was about to cry. 'I'm looking forward to future chapters.'

There was the sound of activity beyond the door. It sounded as if the staff was coming around with dinner.

This time Okajima had a smile on his face as he watched Aose get to his feet.

'Next time let's hear your story,' he said, holding out his hand.

Aose was a little embarrassed and, instead of shaking it, just lightly slapped Okajima's hand.

'I'll come again soon,' he said, and left the room.

45

Aose went straight home to his apartment without stopping by the office. He lay down on the sofa with all the lights off, save the one in the entrance hall. He didn't get himself any dinner; he didn't even feel like opening a beer. He had a terrible headache, which he dealt with by popping one more painkiller than usual into his mouth. He didn't even bother getting a glass of water to take it with, forcing it down with nothing but his own saliva.

In his hand was the telephone receiver, which he alternately gripped strongly or more weakly, obedient to the waves of his emotions.

The image of Okajima was floating before his eyes. Maybe he had just heard so many stories from him that his emotions had crystallized; even his sympathy and empathy seemed frozen. That was Okajima's life . . .

Next time let's hear your story.

And that was what Aose was trying to do. He was trying to work out what his own story was, a story he should already know. Two hours had passed already since he had begun trying.

He sat up and squeezed both temples. The pain eased slightly. The wall clock read 8.25 p.m. He'd reached the time limit. If he didn't call now, he wouldn't be able to call at all today.

He dialled the number, wondering if the *Sazae-san* tune would play if he called from his home phone.

'Yes?'

Her voice sounded slightly nervous.

'It's Daddy,' he said quickly, wanting to reassure her.

'Huh? Daddy? What's up?'

He'd never called Hinako's mobile at this time before.

'Where are you now?' he asked.

'In my room.'

'Studying?'

'Ah, right now I'm checking to see if there are any countries in the world that don't have maths.'

She was funny.

'I see. Sorry I disturbed you. I just . . .'

Aose clammed up. He thought of the prism in Hinako's mind. This time, he'd expected a more adult-like reaction.

'What?'

Hinako's voice began to sound worried again.

'It's not a big thing.'

He tried his best to sound cheerful.

'Hey, remember when you said there used to be phone calls coming to the house? There were quite a lot but eventually they stopped?'

'Um, yeah . . .'

'Did you ever answer the phone yourself?'

There was silence on the line.

'It was a man called Yoshino, wasn't it?'

'Eh? Eh? How did you know?'

Aose closed his eyes.

'He's an acquaintance of Daddy's, so you don't need to be frightened. He's not a bad man, or a dangerous one, at all. Do you understand?'

'He's an acquaintance of yours?'

'Yes, I know him really well.'

'Oh, I didn't realize that. I thought he was a bit weird.'

Hinako sounded genuinely relieved.

'Let me guess,' Aose said. 'The first phone call was in February last year.'

'Hmm, let me think . . .'

'It was snowing a lot around that time, wasn't it?'

'Oh, yes. You're right. I think it was around the time it snowed. We kept getting calls. Mummy would get a weird look on her face and take the phone into her bedroom . . . Yes, then there were a few more after that.'

'When was the last one?'

'November. It should have a cross through it on the calendar. None since then.'

The dotted lines in Aose's head had almost completely joined up and turned solid.

There were three people standing on that train platform when this journey had begun. Yoshino, Aose, and one more. Yukari was there with them.

'But why did an acquaintance of yours call Mummy?'

'Because Mummy knows him too.'

'Oh, I see.'

'I'm sorry I scared you.'

'Oh, you don't scare me at all, Daddy.'

'I'm glad.'

He said it with his heart. Now it really was the end of it.

'Hey, Hinako, where should we meet next time?'

'Um . . . Café Horn?'

'Shall we go to the Y Residence?'

He hadn't been planning to say it, it had just occurred to him in the moment. He wanted to make Hinako happy.

'Really?'

He couldn't go yet. Not with the office in the mess it was.

'I might not be able to take you next time, or the time after that, or maybe even the one after that.'

'Let's go! I want to go! Promise me. Promise you'll take me.'

'The owner's away at the moment, so we'll have to take cleaning supplies with us.'

'Got it! I'll do anything.'

Suddenly her voice cut off.

'Hinako? Hello?'

Then he guessed. Hinako had raised her voice, so Yukari had come to see what was going on. As he thought, he heard her voice talking with Hinako. Then Hinako came back on the line.

'Mummy's here. Do you want to talk to her?'

Her voice was tinged with hope and excitement. For Hinako, it was an unexpected opportunity.

'No . . . I'm fine,' said Aose.

'Why not? Look, Daddy, I thought you wanted to ask about this Yoshino-san's phone calls. Mummy knows him too, right?'

Aose wasn't ready for that conversation. Yukari wouldn't be either, but because Hinako had just said the name Yoshino-san she was probably a little shaken.

'I'll call your mother later. Please tell her that for me.'

Hinako was about to say something, but Aose cut her off with a cheerful 'Good luck with the maths!' and hung up the phone.

He was dead tired. An exhaustion had come over him that he hadn't even felt during the bubble economy years when he regularly used to pull all-nighters. It was as if every cell in his body had been crushed by heavy rollers. The only cells that were still wide awake were those in his brain. He had finally solved the mystery by going back and reinvestigating from the point of origin.

Yoshino had had a detective agency investigate Aose. In the process he'd learned that Aose had an ex-wife. So next the detective went to Yukari. Surprised to hear the false information that Aose was planning to remarry, she had called Okajima to find out what was going on. This was the interruption to the smooth opening of those *fusuma* sliding doors that concealed the truth. Targeted by the detective, Yukari also became a victim of the same chain of events. But then there was a development. At some point, Yoshino had emerged from behind the detective agency cover he was using and tried to contact Yukari himself. They had spoken on the phone several times. Yukari had learned that the reason for the investigation wasn't Aose's remarriage after all, but in fact something else. She hadn't called Okajima again, because there was no need.

Yoshino didn't call him again either, because he had information that he'd got from Yukari. She'd probably told him about her ex-husband's current state of mind – how he had lost his passion for architecture and was stuck doing uninspiring work, drawing plans according to clients' specifications. So Yoshino went to Ageo to check out the house there, following up with a visit to Aose's office along with his wife, Karie, to ask Aose to design him a house.

Build a home you would want to live in.

Those had been Yukari's words. It had been a message from Yukari to Aose.

He had finally realized that they were words that only one person in the whole world could have said. It wasn't love; it was goodness. She just couldn't help herself – her goodness was innate and indiscriminate. She had cast a spell over Aose with those words. Aose didn't know whether to be happy or sad. It was as if a fairy tale created by some unknown person in a faraway land just happened to be playing out before his eyes. All he needed to do was watch, take a deep breath and surrender to the story. Many disparate pieces of information, relating to different characters in the tale, had been drawn together by the magnetism of Yukari's words. And now the story was whole.

Yoshino would have called Yukari from time to time to report on the construction progress of the Y Residence. The last call had been in November last year, when the Y Residence was completed. And the 'tall woman' from the soba restaurant in Naka-Karuizawa must have been Yukari herself. Yoshino must have invited her to visit the Y Residence. Or perhaps Yukari had asked if she could visit.

Was Yukari the director and Yoshino her player? No, it was

Yoshino who had sent the private detective to investigate Aose. And it was also Yoshino who had come up with thirty million yen – a huge sum of money. No, it was clearly Yoshino's initiative, and he had brought Yukari in. Before anything, there was his intent. He must have revealed to Yukari his reason for giving thirty million yen to a complete stranger. What's more, he had to have told her not to tell Aose the reason, and why the plan had to be completed without Aose ever knowing why.

Yukari had gone along with it. That's how those important words had been born. She wanted Aose to get back on his feet – in other words, she had managed to incorporate her own secret wish into Yoshino's plan.

Now he needed to know why Yoshino had come up with this plan, and also why he had felt the need to keep it secret from Aose.

He was expecting a phone call. He was sure that Yukari would call him tonight. So when his mobile rang, he answered right away.

'It's been a while.'

It was Takumi Nose's voice. It had to be ten years since they'd last spoken. He'd thought about this man a lot, wondering if he and Yukari might be the perfect couple.

'Where did you get my number?'

'I asked Nishikawa-san for it. I hope you don't mind.'

'No, that's fine. What is it?'

'I heard about what happened. It must have been tough.'

'Still a work in progress.'

'I hear you're retiring from the competition.'

'Uh-huh.'

'That's a pity. Just when we had a chance to go up against each other.'

'It'll happen again. There'll be a return match someday.'

'You think there'll be another chance?'

It was as if he had jabbed Aose right in the forehead.

'Get caught bribing someone and you're out,' he continued. 'They'll bring down your company.'

'Stay out of it! That's our business.'

'Come and work for me.'

There was a hollow silence.

'I don't mean right away. After you've dealt with the closing of the business and everything has settled down. Think about it.'

Aose closed his eyes.

'You want me to abandon a sinking ship?' he asked.

'No one but the captain is obliged to stay on board.'

'Akasaka was a sinking ship too.'

'Back then the whole industry was going down. Now I'm offering you a lifeboat. Hurry up and hop aboard.'

'Look. I'm really grateful for the offer, but it's not going to happen. I'm really indebted to my boss for all he's done for me.'

'Are you going to commit career suicide alongside him?'

'Don't be stupid. The two of us will build the firm up again from scratch. You worry about your own ship.'

The home phone rang. It must be Yukari.

'I'm hanging up. Please make a good *mémoire*.'

The same hand that had just set down his mobile now grabbed the receiver of the landline. But . . . Was that the sound of wind . . . Yoshino . . . No, it was a woman sobbing. It wasn't Yukari, though . . . It was Yaeko Okajima who was calling.

'My husband . . . The window in his room . . . He . . .'

He'd jumped.

Aose looked down at his empty palm. Only a few hours earlier this hand had touched Okajima's. As he stared, his fingertips began to tremble.

46

It was almost midnight when Aose arrived at the hospital. A police car was parked by the entrance, but otherwise there was nothing unusual and the ground floor was dark and silent. He felt a glimmer of hope; Yaeko said that he had jumped, but she hadn't said he was dead. Or at least that was what he told himself.

He wasn't sure where to go – should he go to Okajima's hospital room or not? He looked for the after-hours reception desk, but the only sound seemed to be the echo of his own footsteps. Turning a corner, he caught sight of Yaeko, who was talking on a payphone.

She took the receiver from her ear and hung it up, but then remained motionless, leaning against the wall. It was as if a flame had been blown out. The already dim corridor seemed even darker.

Aose approached her slowly, and she turned her reddened eyes on him. Perhaps it was the angle of her brows, but she looked more angry than sorrowful.

'Okajima-san . . .'

He couldn't get any more words out.

'He's down here,' said Yaeko in a faint voice, and moved away from her wall support. Okajima wasn't in his hospital room; he was in the basement mortuary.

On the staircase landing they passed a uniformed police officer coming up.

'I'd like to talk to you again later,' he said to Yaeko in a low voice as they passed. Yaeko bowed her head.

The mortuary door was slightly open and the faint smell of incense wafted into the corridor. Aose followed Yaeko into the room, staring at the nape of her neck. A human shape lay on the dais, covered by a white sheet . . .

Yaeko pulled the sheet back.

Somewhere in the back of his mind, Aose had been picturing Taut's death mask. He'd hoped Okajima's face would be like that. But it wasn't. There was a bandage wrapped around his forehead, ears, mouth and chin, and very little of his face was exposed. His cheeks and nose were unscathed, his eyelids serenely closed. It was a face free of pain or distress.

Aose had forgotten to perform the traditional gesture of placing his palms together. His body had lost all warmth – the source of heat in his chest seemed to have stopped working – and his feelings were numb. Logically, he knew what was before his eyes was real, but his brain had not yet got in sync with his feelings.

'He was still breathing, ever so slightly,' said Yaeko unexpectedly. She didn't blink. 'When I ran up to him, he was still—'

From her face, Aose could tell she was reliving the scene.

'Did he say anything?' he asked her.

'Nothing.'

'Was there a suicide note?'

'No, there wasn't.'

Yaeko covered her face with her hands.

Okajima had eaten most of the *okayu* rice porridge they'd served him for dinner. When Yaeko left, there didn't seem to be any change in his demeanour, and the nurses noticed nothing unusual either before or after the lights were turned out at 9 p.m.

It was 10 p.m. when a nurse on her rounds found the window of Room 5 open. Underneath that third-floor window was a row of azalea bushes. The lower half of Okajima's body had fallen on to those bushes, but his head and chest were on the asphalt. The doctors said that if it had been the other way around, he might

329

have survived. A number of police officers came, but the autopsy was a short one. It was an obvious suicide.

Yaeko placed the white cloth back on his face. It was as if her pale hand, with no wedding ring, had just brought down the curtain on the stage of Okajima's life.

'Isso-kun?'

It suddenly occurred to Aose. Yaeko looked at Aose with a hint of curiosity.

'He doesn't know yet. He was asleep so I asked my mother to come over.'

Yaeko didn't speak again until they had left the mortuary, climbed the stairs and were back on the ground floor. Then she stopped in the gloom and turned back to face Aose.

'You heard about it from my husband, didn't you?'

What?

'That I was the reason he killed himself.'

Oh.

It was because he'd asked about Isso that she'd realized. Aose hadn't given it a second thought, but Yaeko must have been thinking about it as they came back upstairs.

She looked at Aose's face.

'Poor man. Even you're not crying for him, Aose-san.'

Fresh tears welled up in Yaeko's eyes.

'My husband said you were his only friend. He said you'd always been close, that you were the person he got along with the best.'

Her mouth slackened.

Liar! You and I weren't that—

The heat source in his chest relit itself and the warmth came rushing back to his body. All the emotions that had been locked away broke out.

He was dead. Okajima had killed himself.

Just a few hours ago they'd been laughing together. They'd sat close together in his hospital room and talked so much.

Oh . . . That was it . . . He had been planning to die all along. He hadn't needed to write a suicide note because he'd already made Aose listen to his note. His long, long, suicide note. Every one of his stories, every single word, had been a last will and testament. Aose hadn't realized. He just hadn't realized.

His tear ducts had opened but now they suddenly seized up again.

Surely not?

Was that what had happened?

Okajima . . . the Okajima there with him in the hospital room . . . had he really wanted to die?

Aose bowed his head to Yaeko and began to walk away unsteadily. His steps gradually became firmer until he found himself hurrying. He followed the blue line drawn on the floor through a corridor that turned left and right and ended up in the main building. It was too frustrating to wait for the lift so he ran up the stairs instead. By the time he had reached the third floor he was out of breath. He passed by the nurses' station without stopping and opened the door to Okajima's private room. The electric-assisted bed was gone. He ran over to the window, undid the catch and pulled it open. Then he leaned out to look at the external wall below. It was dark, but he could see them – five . . . six . . . seven . . . no, eight. Eight marks from stubbed-out cigarettes. From the way Okajima had talked, that was not the only time he'd smoked cigarettes out of his hospital window. He'd smoked before then, and probably after Aose had left too.

It must have been an accident.

The memory was vivid. When Okajima had rested his buttocks on the edge of the waist-high windowsill, the toes of his slippers hadn't quite reached the floor. That was why Aose had warned him it was dangerous. And Okajima was in the habit of sticking his whole head out of the window to exhale, hoping to hide it from the nurses. He had held on to the frame with one hand, but what if he'd accidentally lost his balance? He could have fallen—

'What are you doing?'

The sharp voice came from the doorway of the room. He turned to see a young nurse watching him. He hurriedly closed the window and slid out past the nurse, muttering something about being in the wrong room. He was able to walk normally along the corridor – nobody seemed to be following him.

Whether it was by accident or suicide, it didn't change the fact that Okajima was dead. But for those left behind, especially Isso, who was still in sixth grade of primary school, the two were not the same thing. Even if those around him hid the truth, he'd still hear about it somewhere. His father had left him and fled to an easier place. The weight of his father's suffering had been greater than his love for his son. Isso would see that balance forever tilted away from himself. No, in fact, he might suffer even more pain. If the day ever came that he discovered he wasn't Okajima's son, he might end up feeling guilt about his death, blame himself for his own existence and finally despise his mother.

Aose suddenly thought of his own father. He'd fallen off a cliff to his death while searching for Kuro, the mynah bird who had escaped. He'd been looking for the lost bird because he thought Aose would be sad about losing it, even though he had just decided that by himself. Aose still carried the guilt that he had felt at the time – that his father had died for his sake, and that it was his fault. But the guilt hadn't tainted his memories of his father. Those memories still lived on, pleasant in his mind. That was because it was an accident. Because the manner of his death had had absolutely nothing to do with the way he had lived his life. If Aose had been told that his father had chosen to die that day, then his whole world would have changed; everything he had known about his father would be in question. His smiling face, his angry face, his kindness and his strictness, he would have taken the suicide as an end point and worked his way backwards, looking for different meanings hidden in everything he did.

There was no way that Okajima could have committed suicide. He had spoken about Isso with such love. In addition, his reflections on the competition, Taut, and Haruko Fujimiya's search for beauty – well, all of it – it had been preparation for, a prelude to, the future. It wasn't his last will and testament – it was an expression of his determination to start over, to get back on the path of architecture.

He took the lift down. As soon as the doors opened on the ground floor he leapt out and ran towards the after-hours exit. He'd had an idea; he knew how to prove that Okajima's death was from an accidental fall.

He ran to the car park and fetched his flashlight from the Citroën. Back at the main hospital building, he checked the outdoor signs until he got a general idea of where he needed to go. Making his way around to the back of the main building, he came out in a kind of courtyard. There was a lawn with a small hill in the centre and a path that ran around the outside. Azalea bushes had been planted along the edge of the path to create a low hedge. Aose walked around the courtyard, looking upwards. Rows of sash windows close together indicated that he'd found the private room area. But there was really no need to look up to find the spot. There was a large wet patch on the asphalt. It must be the remains of the water they'd used to wash away the blood.

Aose was spooked for a moment, but then he bent down and pointed his flashlight at the azaleas by the water stain. He moved the circle of light over the leaves, along the branches and down to the base of the bush. There it was – a cigarette butt, crumpled up because it had been smoked right down to the end and then extinguished against the wall of the building. There was practically nothing left but the filter. Aose brought the flashlight closer. He could read the lettering, 'Frontier Light' – the brand that Okajima smoked. However, what Aose was looking for was an undamaged cigarette. If Okajima had fallen while he was still smoking, then there must be one cigarette that had not been crushed out against the wall.

Two . . . three . . . four . . . there were so many cigarette butts lying there, but they were all crumpled. He ran over other possibilities – the cigarette could have continued to smoulder after it was dropped. Perhaps it had burnt an azalea leaf or two . . . or it could have continued burning on the ground, leaving behind just the intact filter.

Five . . . six . . . all of them crumpled cigarette butts. Aose had counted eight marks in total on the wall under the window. So there should be two more – plus one pristine one. Aose stuck his hand in among the branches of the azalea and pulled them apart. He widened his search area a little; scrutinized the path as well, but no luck. He couldn't find the other three cigarette butts anywhere.

Crap.

He followed the water stain and shone his flashlight on the opening of a drain. It was then that he heard footsteps. He looked up to see a man standing a short distance away under an outside lamp.

It was Shigeta from the *Toyo Shimbun*.

'What are you doing here?' asked Aose in a low voice that was just short of turning to fury.

Shigeta was unfazed. He had one hand behind his back, probably concealing his camera. He was there to take photos of the scene.

The bastard!

Aose approached Shigeta, a menacing look on his face. As he got close, he shone his flashlight directly in the reporter's face. Shigeta was too dazzled by the light to express any response.

Aose tossed the flashlight and grabbed Shigeta by both lapels.

'What do you think you're up to?'

'I heard from the police—'

'Get out of here!'

Aose shook Shigeta roughly, causing something to slip from his hand. It was flowers. A bunch of lilies wrapped in cellophane fell to the ground and were trodden underfoot as Shigeta staggered from Aose's assault.

Aose looked from the lilies to Shigeta's face. The reporter looked as if he were on the verge of tears. His collar pulled tightly around his neck, he gasped out some words. It sounded like 'so sorry'.

It was then that Aose's fury was truly unleashed.

'Don't be so arrogant!'

He tightened his grip on Shigeta's collar and shoved him backwards against the azalea hedge.

'He didn't die because of what you wrote. A pathetic article like that wasn't going to kill Okajima. This was an accident! Do your research, and for once write the truth!'

47

Beginning the next morning, it rained on and off.

Okajima's death wasn't reported in any of the newspapers. *'Suspect in bribery scandal commits suicide'* – Aose was prepared for that kind of headline, but perhaps a death occurring so late at night would not have made the deadline for the morning paper.

The staff were all in the office by 7 a.m. Aose had called them all in.

'Why didn't you inform us right away?' demanded Mayumi, and then she collapsed on the desk, sobbing loudly. Everyone else was silent.

The previous night, Aose had made the decision not to call Mayumi. He hadn't wanted to run the risk of her doing something dramatic, like clinging to Okajima's body in Yaeko's presence. That would have been a terrible scene.

'How could this have happened?' groaned Ishimaki. His eyes were bright red. 'When we went on the tour, he was so happy . . . He said we'd build a memorial that would amaze the whole world.'

Takeuchi had been looking utterly dejected, slumped in his chair, but at Ishimaki's words he sat up straight and looked over at Aose. His pupils, flooded with tears, flashed with rage.

'It's the newspaper's fault. If they hadn't published that shit, the boss would be alive right now.'

'And the city office people, the assemblymen and those city councillors,' added Ishimaki with resentment. 'I'm sure they're relieved the boss is dead. They drove him into the hospital and placed the blame for everything on him . . . Even if it turns out to have been an accident, it's all on them.'

Aose stayed out of it. He just sat there with his arms folded.

He'd put forward his theory that the fall was an accident, but nobody had looked convinced. It was as if they were letting Aose believe it because he needed to. It was understandable. Okajima's health had deteriorated after the newspapers wrote about his impropriety regarding the competition, and he had been hospitalized. These were a clear motive for suicide.

The police felt the same way. After leaving Shigeta in the courtyard, Aose had spent about half an hour talking to Yaeko, then had gone to the police station. He had met with a police detective who had attended the scene at the hospital, who took the opportunity to question him in one of their interview rooms. He had asked Aose a long series of questions about the competition, what kind of frame of mind Okajima had been in, how his behaviour had been, and whether he'd hinted that he was thinking of suicide. The final question had been the one he was most interested in.

Aose had managed to bring up the cigarettes. He'd showed the detective the six butts that he had wrapped up in a handkerchief, and pleaded with him to search the drains, as he was sure the rest would be there. The detective had found his story amusing. He'd explained that, normally, if it was a suicide by jumping, there would be marks from the soles of the dead man's shoes on the windowsill, and if there were no marks, then that would prove that Aose was right. But this was a hospital room, and any shoe prints on the windowsill were irrelevant, because Okajima had been wearing slippers, which wouldn't leave any marks. He had seemed very proud of this improvised reasoning. At the same time, he'd seemed very interested in why Aose was so insistent that it was an accident. He'd asked if Aose was worried that the insurance company might not pay out, to which Aose had replied

337

that unless he had just happened to sign up for insurance that day, they would probably still pay out even if it was suicide. The detective had smiled and said that yes, he was sure the insurance company would pay up either way. He had then added, with a hint of insinuation, that Okajima's wife was a seasoned insurance saleswoman and should already have known all this, and observed Aose's reaction. Even convinced that it was suicide, maybe the mind of a detective would always come up with an alternative theory that involved the wife of the deceased and her lover getting rid of an inconvenient husband. In any case, Aose had left feeling that Yaeko's questioning was now going to take longer than normal, and at the same time praying that the police would not find out the circumstances of Isso's birth.

'What's going to become of the company?' asked Ishimaki, bitterness in his voice. He looked as if he expected the worst.

'His wife asked me to shut it down.'

Ishimaki nodded and looked down at his feet. Takeuchi let out a long breath, and looked around the office, an expression of resignation on his face. Mayumi turned her head to look at Aose. The teary eyes suddenly became focused.

'But the boss wanted us to carry on.'

'That's what he said to me – that we should carry on. But this is the way it has to be now.'

'So his wife—'

'Don't!' thundered Aose.

He turned to Ishimaki and Takeuchi.

'We'll continue the projects we're working on; bring them to completion. Then we'll talk about how best to dissolve the company.'

The room fell silent. Aose was no longer keeping Mayumi in his sightline.

'Is there going to be a wake, or a funeral?' asked Ishimaki.

Aose had already wondered what was normally done when everyone believed it was suicide.

'Yes.'

Before going to the police station last night, Aose had asked Yaeko her plans. Although she shook her head and said she couldn't bring herself to do it, he had strongly recommended that she hold a funeral. He had told her about the cigarettes, that he thought it had been an accident. Said that, in his opinion, she should just give him a regular funeral. But no matter how much he reasoned with her, he couldn't seem to get through to her. All she did was cry. For Isso-kun's sake, he'd wanted to say, but he couldn't. When he had finally got home, at three that morning, he hadn't been able to sleep, deeply disturbed that he couldn't give Okajima what any person would reasonably deserve. Just before 6 a.m. Yaeko had called and said that they'd held a family meeting and decided that there would be a private wake, followed by a funeral at a funeral hall. His great-uncle had made the decision. It seemed that, secretly, Okajima's family had believed the bribery story.

'I told her that this office would take charge of the reception desk at the funeral. So that'll be me, and I need one other.'

Ishimaki and Takeuchi raised their hands at the same time.

'Okay,' said Aose, without picking either of them. His throat was dry so he ducked behind the dividing partition to grab a glass of water. He filled a glass from the sink and drank it down in one.

'Sensei?'

He turned to Mayumi, who was standing behind him, her body shaking. Her face was so contorted with crying that she was practically unrecognizable.

'What?'

'Is it okay for me to go too? To help?'

He couldn't tell her not to come. But if she was going to be there, he really had to ask her a question first.

'Tsumura-san, the day that Okajima went into hospital, did anything happen between you and his wife?'

Mayumi's watery eyes sharpened.

339

'Nothing at all.'

'I know you went to his hospital room. I saw the postcard.'

'I went. But the boss told me to go away.'

She was about to start crying again.

'Why did he tell you to go away?'

'He said that if I was in his room, I would fall under suspicion too.'

He must have been talking about the taxi receipts.

'I told him I didn't mind, but he told me, please, he was begging me, to go home. He looked really sad . . .'

'So you left. And you didn't see his wife?'

'I did see her.'

'You talked to her?'

'We crossed paths in the corridor. But she didn't seem to recognize me . . . Well, it's possible that she just ignored me, afraid of what I might say to her.'

'I see.'

He thought he'd better tell her. He moved his face closer to hers and lowered his voice.

'Okajima regretted telling you. He said he'd dumped half of his hatred on to you.'

'Why?' Mayumi glared at Aose. 'Why are you telling me this?'

Aose put a finger to his lips. He checked beyond the partition.

'Because you're so hung up on it.'

'That woman never even apologized to him.'

'Sometimes apologies don't help.'

'The boss is dead. I just can't believe he had to die without ever hearing the truth from her.'

Mayumi was getting more worked up.

'The competition was just the trigger,' she went on. 'His wife's the one who caused his death.'

'It was an accident.'

'The boss had been suffering for years, wondering whose child Isso was—'

Aose reached out as fast as he could and covered Mayumi's mouth. He put all the strength he could into his fingers to stop the words from coming out.

'Never talk of that secret again. You've already told me. I know I'll end up telling somebody else. And that somebody will tell another person. And then one day the story will reach Isso-kun. Do you understand?'

Mayumi's whole body trembled, but Aose didn't take his hand away.

'You are holding the grudge instead of Okajima. Okajima told me he could get along with his wife. He told me he was living for Isso-kun's sake. You can't go with him, because you have Yuma-kun, you have to go and live your own life . . . We all die alone. Okajima was no different . . . But he didn't die instantly. He was still breathing for a while . . . You know, he didn't call your name. He didn't need your help.'

Mayumi closed her eyes. A fat tear splashed on to Aose's hand. He jumped a little and let go of her face. Immediately, Mayumi began to choke. She put her hand to her throat and gasped for breath, as if hyperventilating. Aose hurried to rub her back, and at that point Takeuchi appeared to ask if she was all right. Aose asked him to get her some water, and Mayumi's breathing eventually began to calm.

'I'm sorry,' said Aose, his voice hoarse.

Mayumi put both hands over her face, turned her thin frame to the side and leaned against the wall. She looked just like Yaeko had the previous night.

'I really am sorry,' Aose repeated, and then walked away. He saw Takeuchi's worried expression as he stared helplessly at Mayumi's back.

Aose slipped past Takeuchi. He wanted to believe that this young man, neither calculating nor pushy, but reliable and good-natured, would eventually be able to turn Mayumi's heart.

48

The day of the funeral brought a soft light. The funeral home on the outskirts of the city had four ceremony halls and Okajima's final farewell was held in the smallest. That didn't mean that there were only a few mourners. In fact, a long queue of people in mourning clothes formed in front of the company-manned reception desk. Many were dabbing at their eyes, and everyone was silent. Two days earlier, a series of newspaper articles had appeared. Almost all of them stated that the contractor in the bribery scandal had committed suicide, but the article in the *Toyo Shimbun* said that it was being investigated both as a possible suicide or an accident.

Aose and Takeuchi stood behind the reception desk while Ishimaki sat in a chair and checked the *koden bukuro* envelopes of money offered by the guests. Mayumi was nowhere to be seen. She had called in sick from work for the past two days. The second day, Aose had taken the call. When he asked her how she was, she said she was still feeling faint but that she wanted to help out at the funeral. She sounded calm and told Aose not to worry about her, but now, as Aose was handing out tickets for the mourners to exchange for thank-you gifts, he was constantly checking for Mayumi.

He was also looking out for another woman. Aose was prepared for the strong possibility that Yukari would turn up. Representatives of the bank, the credit union, then the wife of the renderer, Nishikawa, who appeared with an expression of deep gratitude on her face. 'My husband was shocked at the news . . . He hasn't been able to eat . . . I'm so sorry for his absence . . . please forgive him . . .'

The familiar faces of construction company presidents and interior decorators followed. The young president of Kaneko Engineering arrived, accompanied by his elderly predecessor, leaning on a walking stick. Kaneko's eyes and nose were bright red. When it was his turn at the reception desk, his face crumpled and he grasped Aose's hand tightly, unable to utter a single word of condolence. Ishimaki and Takeuchi had similar experiences. They all realized that Okajima Design Company had made a difference in people's lives.

'Aose-san!' Ishimaki whispered in his ear, and Aose hurriedly handed over the ticket he was holding to the guest in front of him. His concentration had been broken when he'd spotted Yukari. She was right at the back of the queue, but it was impossible to miss her tall, slender figure, dressed in western mourning clothes. Aose also immediately noticed that she had a companion with her. *Of course*, he thought, *him again*. Takumi Nose was dressed in a black suit that was instantly recognizable as a famous brand label. When he reached the reception desk he stepped forward with Yukari by his side and pulled out a plain white *koden-bukuro* envelope. Ishimaki instantly reacted to the name 'Nose' on the envelope, giving the man a good look up and down.

'My condolences,' said Nose.

The formalities completed, he looked at Aose.

'We happened to meet in the car park.'

Just behind his shoulder, Yukari nodded her confirmation.

'I never imagined it would come to this,' Nose continued. Then in a whisper: 'Please think over what we talked about on the phone.'

Nose stepped away and Yukari came forward. She kept her eyes down as she opened the purple silk wrapping cloth that contained her money envelope. There was no shiny ring on her slender fingers.

'Could we talk later?' said Aose, handing her the voucher.

Yukari looked up and straight into Aose's eyes. Her eyes were wet, but behind her pupils there was a kind of resolve, or perhaps resignation. It looked as if she, too, had come with the intention of speaking to Aose, even before he had asked.

'Yes, maybe for a few minutes.'

Yukari moved aside to let the mourners behind her reach the desk, and then she was gone from Aose's view. But her image remained in his mind for a long while. It had been seven years since they'd met. Hinako had been starting primary school and the school had asked to meet with her parents. This subsequent meeting had been over in a matter of seconds.

'I'm going to take a look inside,' said Takeuchi after the queue of mourners had gone through. He had clearly been restless; Ishimaki watched him go then turned to Aose.

'Was that Nose-san?'

'Yes, President of Nose Architects.'

Ishimaki just nodded. Aose's possible career move must surely have occurred to him.

As soon as the chanting of the sutras began, Mayumi appeared. She didn't slip in from the side or the back but marched straight up to the reception and laid a *koden-bukuro* envelope marked 'Tsumura' on the desk. Then she walked around behind the desk and began to organize the pile of envelopes in the box. His job appropriated, Ishimaki was rather put out.

Her face was swollen from crying, but she was being brave now.

'Thank you,' said Aose.

Mayumi didn't look up, nor did her hand pause for a second.

'I skived off work – sorry,' she said.

'Eh? Really?'

'I was having some quality time with Yuma. He was getting mad with me for coming home late all the time.'

'Yeah.'

344

'He said to me, "Mama, you love copitition, don't you?"'

Mayumi tried to laugh, but failed, bit her lip to stop herself crying, but then gave a determined toss of her head like a model in a shampoo commercial. She looked at Aose.

'I'm sorry that I worried you.'

'Oh' came a voice from behind them. It was Takeuchi, back from the ceremony hall. The grin on his face when he saw Mayumi was rather inappropriate for a funeral.

'How are things in there?' Aose asked him.

Takeuchi's face suddenly clouded over. He told them that he'd checked all the floral tributes and wreaths.

'There wasn't a single one from either the mayor's office or the director of the construction department.'

Ishimaki's eyes turned angry. Takeuchi and Mayumi looked down at the ground.

'No problem. That's fine. We'll give him a proper send-off. Okay, let's take turns to do the incense offering.'

Aose set off towards the ceremony hall. Ishimaki followed in silence.

It was unexpectedly bright inside the hall. The queue of mourners waiting to offer incense had earlier spilled out into the reception area, but now it was short. As the line moved forward, Yaeko's face was visible at the front of the room. Her face was half hidden by a handkerchief. She bowed to the guests who had finished offering incense. Isso was by her side. His mouth was pressed shut and he was staring intensely at every one of the guests who passed in front of him. He was half a step in front of Yaeko, giving the impression that he was trying to protect his mother from the line of black-clothed mourners.

Next year he would be in junior high school. His face was just beginning to lose its childlike feel. Aose remembered how Okajima had always wanted to show him photos of all his excursions with Isso, wanting to remember every moment of the process of

345

him growing up. Right now, the scene of Isso standing there in the funeral hall looked like the latest snapshot.

It isn't about the blood that runs in our veins; it's that precious time we spend together, just Isso and me.

Aose was in front of the incense burner. The smile on Okajima's face in the portrait over the coffin was dazzling. He didn't know who had taken it, or when the picture had been taken, but he had never seen such an utterly lovestruck, unguarded smile.

I was a jerk back then, wasn't I?

Before Aose got to the 'yeah', it was too late. He started to cry, and couldn't stop. He didn't even want to stop any more.

49

Taxis were lining up in front of the funeral home, hopeful that they might pick up mourners heading home. Yukari was waiting for Aose right outside the building and stared at his face as he approached. He reflected that she'd probably never seen him cry.

He would have preferred to talk somewhere more comfortable, but he still had to help clear up after the funeral so this would have to do. He led her towards the lawn, and they sat down together on a wooden bench. Aose turned his body so that he was facing her; Yukari sat on the edge of the seat, her legs outstretched, and stared down at the toes of her shoes. Looking at the profile of her face, it was as if no time had passed.

'. . . So soon . . . he was the same age as you, wasn't he?'

'Yes.'

'His poor wife . . . And their son . . . Is he still in primary school?'

'Just started sixth grade.'

'There can't be a god, can there?'

'Maybe this happened because there is.'

'How do you mean?'

'I mean perhaps it was pre-ordained.'

'I heard some rumours. Weren't they true?'

'No, it was an accident. He accidentally fell out of a hospital window.'

'I see . . .'

Yukari sighed. It was a reaction to either possible version of events. The time spent grieving Okajima meant a slowing of the river that separated them. If they'd met anywhere else, it would certainly have been more difficult to talk about their feelings. As it was, it seemed that they could communicate with ease. When it came to Yoshino, it felt to Aose as if they'd be able to discuss him, and the best way would be to jump right in, leaving out the minor details. That would minimize the number of questions he'd have to ask Yukari.

'I'm looking for Yoshino-san,' he began.

Yukari looked at him.

'Looking for him?'

She didn't ask who Yoshino was. The abbreviation of details had worked for her.

'Yoshino-san is gone. He should be living in the Y Residence with his family, but they never moved in. I can't find out what happened to them after they moved out of their rented house in Tabata.'

Yukari seemed very surprised by this information. She clearly hadn't known that the Yoshinos had disappeared.

'Really?'

'Yes, really.'

'I thought they were just away . . .'

'I couldn't tell Hinako that the whole family had vanished.'

Yukari nodded.

'How long have they been gone?'

'Since November last year. We handed the house over to them in early November and they vanished without ever moving in.'

Yukari looked as if she were trying to recall something.

'Do you have any idea?'

'No . . . nothing.'

'You met with Yoshino-san, though, didn't you? In late November.'

The atmosphere turned strained for a moment, but Yukari quickly replied. 'Yes.'

'At that time, did he say anything? Something that hinted they might disappear?'

'He didn't say anything. I didn't sense anything either.'

'Did he seem at all preoccupied? Was there anything odd about his behaviour?'

'He was totally normal. He showed me around the Y Residence and treated me to soba. He seemed happy the whole time. Told me he'd be moving in shortly.'

The Y Residence . . . soba. . . it felt as if Yukari had offered him a rough sketch. Now he just needed to borrow her brush to fill in the details.

'As you know, Yoshino-san and his wife came to our office last March. They requested me specifically and asked me to design a house for them. I believe the story behind that and the reason for their disappearance are connected.'

He waited a few seconds, but Yukari remained silent.

'There may not be a connection, but I need to know,' he pressed her.

Yukari looked troubled.

'Tell me, please. Tell me how Yoshino-san came to commission me to design his house.'

'I can't. Yoshino-san asked me not to tell you.'

'I see.'

Aose conceded with grace. He had expected her not to be able to tell him anything, and she didn't have to if she didn't want to. He had come to this meeting determined never to exchange sharp words with Yukari ever again, and he wasn't going to now. He would have to ask Yoshino himself. He really wanted to ask Yoshino . . .

He changed his line of questioning.

'After you visited the Y Residence with him, did Yoshino ever call you again?'

'No, he didn't.'

'Not even once?'

'He hasn't called me, and I didn't call him either. Shall I call him for you?'

Aose was a little taken aback, but he quickly replied, 'Yes, please.' If Yukari called, it was possible that Yoshino would pick up the phone. Yukari took her phone out of her bag.

'Do you have his number? He always used to call me at home, so it's not in my mobile.'

As Aose read out Yoshino's number to Yukari, she entered it then put the phone to her ear. He could hear it ringing, and then it connected to voicemail. They exchanged glances. 'Until now he's had his phone turned off the whole time,' said Aose quickly, before the beep. Yukari nodded at him, swallowed once, then spoke:

'This is . . . Aose speaking. Could you give me a call? Minoru Aose is concerned about you.'

They released their breath in unison.

'I wonder if he'll call back.'

'That's the first time that his answering service picked up. It might be a good sign.'

'I hope so.'

'I really want to meet him and talk. It's not only that I want to know why he asked me to design his house, I genuinely want to find him. I'm a bit worried about his wife and children.'

Yukari gave a deep nod of agreement.

'There's also a suspicious man hanging around. He's been searching all over for Yoshino-san.'

'A bad guy?'

'I'm not sure. But I get the feeling that Yoshino-san is being hunted by that man and that he's on the run.'

Yukari put her hand over her mouth.

'Have you told the police?'

'I haven't. I'm just guessing, really.'

'And you have absolutely no idea of Yoshino-san's where-abouts?'

'I know that he went to Sendai at least once. His family grave is there in a nearby village.'

'There's a grave in Sendai?'

Yukari seemed puzzled.

'Isn't Yoshino-san's hometown Kiryu?'

Aose's thoughts immediately jumped to another time. Kiryu . . .

His complexion changed as Yukari's face seemed to freeze.

'Did Yoshino-san tell you that?' he asked her.

'Er . . . yes.'

'Kiryu in Gunma prefecture?'

'Yes, I think so.'

Aose was speechless.

'Is there something about Kiryu?' said Yukari.

'It's where my father died.'

'Oh . . .'

Aose started to say, 'When we were living at Kiryu dam,' but suddenly other associations popped into his head. Kiryu Textiles. That was it. Kiryu was a town that had long been known for its textile industry. If Isaku Yoshino's sister had become a factory worker there in Kiryu, then suddenly the dots were connected. After his family had split up, Isaku must have gone from Sendai to Kiryu to live with his sister. He'd settled there, married, and then Touta was born.

That must be it. Kiryu was where the story had begun. Something must have happened there. Aose hadn't stayed on in Kiryu because he'd been studying for his university entrance exams. Yoshino was five years younger than Aose, so he'd have been in junior high at the time. He'd narrowed it down. It was safe to assume that the connection was buried somewhere in whatever linked these three people: the junior high school boy Touta Yoshino; his father, Isaku; and Aose's own father.

'All right. I'll tell you.'

The sound of Yukari's voice dragged him back to the present.

Tell him what?

'We're beyond the stage where I have to keep promises. The story Yoshino-san told me might be a clue to finding him, so I've decided to tell you.'

Yukari looked flushed.

'I wasn't told the whole story either. Honestly, I don't even know if it's true or not.'

Aose's expression urged her to continue.

Yukari put a hand to her breast, as if to calm herself.

'Yoshino-san came to me saying that he owed you — owed Minoru Aose — a huge debt. Such a massive debt that, no matter how much he repaid it and repaid it, he would still owe you.'

Aose was stunned. A huge debt? Him?

'Do you understand?'

'No, I don't. Not at all.'

'I'll tell you from the beginning.'

Yukari told the story as rapidly as she could. She and Yoshino had exchanged business cards before this had all begun. Yoshino had been the supplier of an exclusive brand of Scandinavian wood furniture for a restaurant that Yukari was decorating. Yoshino had wondered about the relatively rare surname 'Aose' on her business card. By this point, he had already been looking for Minoru Aose for some time. He had a private detective check her out and found that Yukari was Aose's ex-wife and they'd been separated for seven years.

'The detective paid me a visit, and then Yoshino-san himself called me. I'd forgotten all about him, but then he reminded me about the Scandinavian furniture, and just as I was thinking, "Ah, that guy," he told me he wanted to talk to me about Minoru Aose. I got quite freaked out because of the whole private detective thing, so I hung up on him right away. I told him that you and I had split up and I had nothing to do with you any more. Ah—'

'Don't worry about it. And then?'

'It was the second or third time he called when he finally confessed that he was the one who had hired the private detective, and I was shocked and very angry. I demanded he explain why he'd done it. And that's when he said it was because he owed Minoru Aose a massive debt. He said he wanted to repay it, and that he'd like my advice.'

Yukari took a moment. Aose didn't interrupt with any questions. Apart from the bit about repaying a debt, the story was going more or less as Aose had imagined.

'He said he wanted to repay the debt without you knowing. That he would like to find a way of doing it without you realizing that it was the repayment of a debt, but that he hadn't been able to think of any way to do it.'

A way of repaying a debt without him knowing?

'It's an odd story, isn't it? But he said he couldn't explain the situation to me. I asked him many times, but he simply said, "Forgive me, but I can't." It's such a bizarre story, but Yoshino-san was utterly determined, completely serious. That's how I was drawn in. Then Yoshino-san told me he had a sum of money – thirty million yen, to be exact. He asked if there was any way he could get it to you. I told him that was totally unreasonable, and to stop. I told him you weren't the kind of person to go around accepting outrageous sums of money from strangers. I said not to interfere in your life. But Yoshino-san was desperate. He said that since he wasn't in a position to be able to reveal the full circumstances, the only way he could prove his intentions were sincere was with money. I was completely flummoxed by the whole thing. And that's when I—'

Yukari didn't finish the sentence. And Aose didn't ask. At that moment, Yoshino ceased to exist in that space. There were only Aose and Yukari.

Build a home you would want to live in.

Aose could see Mayumi in the distance. She was looking for him.

'I have to go.'

Yukari understood. She sat up straight and looked at Aose. She bowed to him.

'I'm truly sorry,' she said. 'I was his accomplice. I ended up helping him deceive you.'

Aose couldn't answer right away. He walked side by side with Yukari as far as the taxi stand. No longer was he thinking about Yoshino-san; he was thinking about the woman walking next to him. There was something he needed to say, but he didn't know how to say it.

In a few more steps the automatic door of the taxi would open. Aose stopped walking.

'The Y Residence saved me.'

Yukari stopped too.

'I didn't do it for you,' she said. 'I did it for me.'

'For you?'

'Yes. That's all. Um . . . what was it called? That sundial house – the one that marked the passage of time?'

'Eh?'

'I made a mistake. I should have let you build any house you wanted. It never mattered what kind of material you used – wood, concrete, brick, or even clay. I could have lived in any house.'

'Yukari.'

Aose said her name aloud for the first time in eight years. Her slender frame was already close to the taxi. Then, just as the door opened . . .

Kee kee.

Yukari looked up at the sky.

'That was—'

'What was that?' Aose wondered.

'A heron. It was definitely a blue heron.'

A victorious smile on her face, Yukari disappeared in slow motion into the back seat of the taxi.

50

That night he dreamed of Taut.

Taut was in his Senshin-tei home at Daruma-ji temple again and once more he was raging. Unlike before, this time Aose could see the other side of the *shoji* doors. There was no one there. Taut was yelling into an empty space.

Aose woke up once, realized it was a dream, and closed his eyes again. He was sleepy, so sleepy. So sleepy he couldn't bear it . . .

For a moment, Okajima's face floated before his eyes.

Where was Okajima's soul right now? Had he been able to make it home safely? . . . Oh no, he'd forgotten to ask: what was the most beautiful thing in the world to Okajima? . . . He really should have shaken his hand. In the hospital room, when he was leaving to go home, the hand that Okajima had held out to him, he really should have grasped it and given him a firm handshake . . .

Then he heard some snatches of Yukari's voice.

I could have lived in any house . . . I made a mistake . . . There can't be a god . . .

Visiting the Y Residence, enveloped by the scent of cedar wood and the north light . . . What had Yukari thought?

Then it was Yoshino's turn to cut in.

He placed a Taut chair, made by his own father, just one, in pride of place in the Y Residence . . . There was a connection between his father, Isaku, and Aose's father. The massive debt that Yoshino was talking about, could it be somehow related to his father's death . . .

355

51

About ten days after the funeral, Aose got a phone call from Oka-jima's widow, Yaeko, in response to which he immediately left the office and set out for Okajima's house in Iruma city. He had an idea that Yaeko wanted to talk to him about the liquidation of the company. Aose also had something he wanted to talk to Yaeko about. He was still wondering how to bring up the subject as he rang the retro Showa era doorbell.

Yaeko showed him into a Japanese-style sitting room. He'd correctly predicted the topic of Yaeko's conversation, but it turned out to be a far from amicable discussion.

'You will each be paid a commensurate severance package. And we will add extra to it for the inconvenience you have all suffered. And then please let that be the end of it. Forget about us.'

Yaeko's face was white, and her voice cold and without inflection.

Aose sat there blinking, unable to respond or even nod. The end of it? Forget about us? Who was this 'us'? Yaeko and Isso?

'I was eavesdropping outside the hospital room.'

She had been looking down, but now she raised her gaze to Aose's face.

'Please keep the truth about Isso a secret. Promise me here and now that you will never speak about it to anyone. Tsumura-san, too . . . Please tell her that my husband's firm wish was for her not to tell anyone. Please make her swear not to. I beg you.'

'Of course. I would never—'

'I wasn't constantly cheating on him. I didn't fall in love with someone else, or date other people. It was nothing like that. I used to visit many different firms in connection with my insurance sales job and there was a manager at one company who used to assist me in getting his new employees signed up with me every year. He kept asking me out for a drink, no matter how many times I turned him down . . . I really should have talked to my husband about it . . . And then I just found I couldn't . . . My husband never asked me anything, and he was so fond of Isso. But if I'd brought it up, he would have asked me who, and why, and so many questions. I didn't think he'd be able to take it, and everything would just blow up, and then it would all be over. I was afraid.'

'I understand. I—'

'But I should have told him. Told him and then got divorced. Someone else would have been there for him instead of me. And when that awful thing happened to him with his work. If someone else had been by his side, he wouldn't be dead now.'

She needed to stop for a while to cry.

Aose was now even more sure about what he'd gone there to say. It wasn't suicide; it was accidental death. He had come here to be sure that it would be engraved on Yaeko's heart.

The day before, he'd paid another visit to the police station and spent another thirty minutes talking to the detective who'd been on duty the night of Okajima's death. It seemed they had checked the drains after all but hadn't come across any cigarette butts. The detective, in an extremely patronizing tone, had told Aose that in order to take his accidental death theory into account, they had also had a forensic team check the windowsill. They hadn't found any fibres from the soles of his slippers but, unlike dirt from the sole of a shoe, it wouldn't have adhered to the sill anyway, and if someone had sat on the windowsill, smoked a cigarette and then killed himself, the slippers he had been wearing would have

357

flown through the air and out of the window without ever touching the windowsill. At this point, Aose had thrown out some new questions. First of all, who would jump to their death with slippers on? The detective had responded vaguely that it wasn't impossible. Eventually he had changed course and admitted that people tended to take off their shoes before committing suicide, but that he wasn't sure in the case of slippers, because there were so few instances of slippers in suicide cases. But he had finished by insisting that people who impulsively commit suicide and don't leave behind a note can't be bothered to think about things like shoes or slippers.

One thing the detective was right about is that you can't truly know another person. Aose couldn't entirely rule out an impulsive suicide. It was true that the Okajima he had seen in the hospital room was emotionally unstable, and Aose couldn't erase from his mind the way he had begged him not to go quite yet when he had got up to leave. Aose sometimes imagined that the more driven he was by the idea of living for Isso, the closer he could have been driven to despair by having to face his precious child while embroiled in a shameful scandal. So yes, it was possible that it was suicide. But that didn't mean that the possibility of an accident should be dismissed. There wasn't a suicide note, and there was the whole question of the slippers, but Aose had seen with his own eyes the precarious balancing act Okajima had performed when he exhaled the smoke out of the window.

'I'm sorry, I didn't even offer you tea.'

Yaeko stopped wiping her eyes and started to get up from the tatami floor.

'I'm fine. Please don't bother.'

Yaeko sat back down. Her expression had softened somewhat. Tears had the power to wash away all kinds of things.

Aose sat up straighter.

'I understand your story very well. I'll keep your secret, and I will take responsibility for making sure others keep it too. Please rest assured.'

'Thank you.'

'However, there is one more thing concerning Isso-kun. Okajima didn't commit suicide. It was an accident.'

'We've already talked about—'

'This is important, so please hear me out. Isso-kun will hear it at school. At first it will be behind his back, but then eventually someone will tell him that his father did a bad thing at work. No matter how much you or his extended family try to hide it from him, Isso-kun will hear gossip that his father committed suicide. And one day, Isso-kun will come to you and ask about it. And that could be tomorrow, or even today.'

Yaeko put her hand over her mouth.

Aose reached into his pocket, pulled out a sheet of paper folded in four, and placed it on the table. It was a newspaper article.

'Whenever that time comes, please show this to Isso-kun.'

'. . . *being investigated both as a possible suicide or an accident.*'

'This is the only article with the word "accident" in it. All the others say that it appeared to be a suicide. So please show this article to Isso-kun and tell him that in the end the police investigation found it was an accident.'

'But . . . I can't—'

'You aren't going to lie to him. It really was an accident. But if you don't believe it, then it's meaningless. If you don't believe it, then neither will Isso-kun.'

Yaeko looked distressed.

'That night, he was still breathing, wasn't he?' said Aose. 'But he didn't say anything. He didn't say anybody's name, right?'

'. . . No, he didn't.'

'Because he was trying to live.'

'What?'

'He didn't fall from that window intending to die. And consequently, he refused to believe he was about to die. He thought

359

he'd survive another five minutes, another hour, or even years more, so it hadn't even occurred to him to leave any final words. He must have been thinking, "Are you kidding? I'm not going to die like this. I'm going to live." He wasn't about to waste his strength speaking.'

Yaeko's head dropped and a couple of tears splashed on to the newspaper clipping.

'Please don't cry any more. You didn't cause his death. It was nobody's fault. It was an accident.'

Yaeko gave a faint nod. Her fingertips traced the tear blots on the newspaper article as if trying to wipe them away.

'Okajima-san, please let me continue to run Okajima Design Company,' said Aose. 'Please let me keep on as manager until Isso-kun comes of age. I will build it up, make it a strong company, and then hand it over to him. That's what Okajima wanted, and I want the same thing.'

Yaeko neither nodded nor shook her head. She just looked straight at Aose. Then, all of a sudden, she stood up.

'Please wait a minute,' she said, disappearing into the corridor, then reappearing with a B4-sized sketchbook in her hand.

Aose accepted it from her with both hands. The sketchbook was very thin. Apart from the thicker front and back covers, there seemed to be only about ten sheets left inside. The wire binder was filled with shreds of paper where pages had been torn out.

Aose opened the front cover and came across a drawing of a building, seen from a distance. It was a building with a gently arching roof like a grassy mound or a hill. At the very peak something round was protruding, but it was hard to make out. The shape was simple, but you might call it daringly simple. It was neither a copied sketch nor a reproduction. Aose's architect's eye could see that it was the artist's own design.

Preliminary sketch (esquisse) of the Haruko Fujimiya mémoire.

Aose's heart turned a little somersault when he realized what it was, although he had already suspected before opening the sketchbook.

'He was drawing it in his hospital bed.'

At Yaeko's voice, Aose looked up.

'In hospital?'

'Yes. A nurse found it slipped down between his bedside table and the wall. I just got it back from the police today.'

The police had probably seized it, guessing it might contain Okajima's suicide note. Perhaps with this in mind, Aose looked again at the sketch and noticed that a crude black circular object had been drawn on the side of the building. He turned to the next page, and there was another view of the building a little closer. The black circle had been stretched out and become an oval. On the third page of the sketchbook, the view was closer still, and it had become a rectangle. Now Aose knew what it was.

It was Haruko Fujimiya's apartment window, drawn from the photo of the exterior of her apartment in Paris. The lines were crudely drawn, but Okajima had also included the bricks and the peeling mortar surrounding the window. Aose immediately grasped the concept. The top of the memorial was a stunningly white building with a curved roof. The lower half of the building incorporated a tiny apartment window, the exact size of the original.

He turned to pages four, five, six, stared at them in wonder, then turned back to the first page. There was a story. Okajima had drawn a path approaching the building, straight towards that tiny apartment window. Visitors to the gallery would walk along the path towards the chalky-looking walls and wonder what that was in front of them. It would be too far away to tell that it was a window initially. At first it would look like a blotch on a discoloured wall. *What on earth is that?* They would walk forward, trying to make it out. Eventually they would see that it was a window in a brick wall. As they got even closer, they would find themselves face to face with a little-known version of Paris, one that is old, impoverished and grim. And then they would realize that this gaping black window is where the soul of a solitary painter dwells. At this point, they are so close to the window they are tempted to peer in. But the path curves to the left and descends a gentle slope, and the wall with its window disappears from view. Here, as it runs along the side of the building, the path is partially underground, with walls rising up on both sides. But these are not simple walls. They are covered with tiles from top to bottom. It's a lively walkway, a gallery of tiles. Streets, people, signs, singing, drinking, dancing, all depicted in the style of a picture scroll taking you on a journey through the past and present 18th arrondissement of Paris. This is the world in which Haruko Fujimiya lived. Oh, thinks the visitor. That beautiful curved line of the building's roof – that was the hill of Montmartre. The round projection on the top, the dome of the Sacré-Cœur. Nodding, they continue along the path, which now slopes back up to ground level. And there stands the simple, austere entrance to the Haruko Fujimiya *mémoire*.

Aose sighed with admiration.

It was an exquisite plan. And at the same time it narrated a whole story. Okajima hadn't set out to design a building to house the work of Haruko Fujimiya; he had made a place to display her whole life.

What about the interior?

There were only two pages with anything drawn on them, and the rest were blank. Aose tilted his head to one side to try to take in the first of the two pages. There were five straight lines, drawn horizontally, an equal distance apart. That was it. Here and there, in between the lines, daubed as if with a soft-lead pencil . . . what looked like clouds . . . Were they really clouds? If so, then you'd be looking up at the ceiling from below . . . The 3D function switched on in Aose's brain, and the answer came to him immediately. A saw-tooth roof – a style of roof that had been used in factories for many years to shield the workers from direct sunlight and glazed to allow gentle north light in – the advantage being uniform illumination.

Aose was speechless with surprise. He turned to the second page, which was covered in small sketches, drawn in perspective, including figures, but there were many crossings- and scribblings-out, reflecting the designer's trial-and-error thought process. Apparently, Okajima had been trying to decide how best to display the paintings. There was one rather eccentric proposal. There was a painting embedded in the floor under a panel of transparent glass or acrylic. A figure was bending to look down at the painting, and a smaller figure, perhaps a young child, was lying on the floor peering over the edge of the panel. The north light from the saw-tooth windowpane shone down on the two figures.

Perhaps he had come up with the novel idea of displaying the paintings on the floor first, and then had decided to incorporate the north light as a means of minimizing the reflection of light on the glass panels. Logic said that was it, but Aose's feeling told him differently. Okajima had embraced the beauty of Aose's design and brought it into his own plan. In other words, he was trying to break out of his narcissistic shell and to act in the proper manner of the president of Okajima Design Company.

'Aose-san?'

Finally, Yaeko brought him back to the present. It seemed that she had been observing him for a while.

'Yes?'

'I need to know the truth. As a fellow architect, you can understand that . . . Tell me, is that his suicide note?'

Yaeko's shoulders were tensed up, but her eyes said that she really wanted to hear that it wasn't.

'No, it isn't,' he said with gentleness.

But Yaeko wasn't convinced. She needed more.

'He was out of the competition and was drawing things he had no hope of building. Even then?'

'Yes, even then. Look how thin this sketchbook is. He must have torn up every single sketch he made on that reconnaissance tour he went on. Then, in his hospital room, he began to formulate his own ideas. He must have been secretly dancing with joy when he came up with this exterior plan that would make visitors gasp, but then he must have been stamping his feet with irritation when he got stuck on the interior plan. I can see it clear as day. I know because I'm an architect too. Okajima had no intention of ending things there in that hospital room.'

All the tension flowed from Yaeko's shoulders, along with the worry lines in her brow. She let out a long sigh that seemed charged with positive particles. It felt like a turning point.

'Do you think Isso could be an architect?' she asked.

Aose smiled and nodded.

'Back in primary school, I wrote an essay about it. About how I was going to be an architect.'

52

Aose went straight back to the office. The moment he opened the door, three faces turned his way. The air in the room felt stagnant. Ever since they had decided to shut down, they'd been unable to take on any new work, and since there were hardly any projects on the go anyway, motivation was tapering off too. Lively conversation was a thing of the past. Ishimaki had spent the past few days worrying about what the police were up to. Because the president was dead, or perhaps specifically because he was dead, Ishimaki was concerned that the company would come under greater scrutiny. Every time the office door opened, he would tense up. He seemed to be imagining a scene unfolding on the TV news in which police investigators carrying cardboard boxes would come swarming through the doors.

His fears were most probably groundless. Rumour had it that S— city's Article 100 committee had stalled. It had all been going in the anti-mayor city councillors' favour until Okajima's hospitalization. Up until that point they had been practically foaming at the mouth in anticipation of bringing down the mayor and his supporters, but their political circus had lost its appeal when Okajima died, not to mention that there was no proof that he had paid anything other than a few taxi fares. The whole affair had begun to fizzle out, and the conservative members of the anti-mayor faction had completely lost interest. Only very few of the liberal council members were even bothering to raise their voices.

Aose looked at the posters on the office wall. Haruko Fujimiya – the name that had started it all. He turned his attention to the competition table. Nobody could bear to touch it. The daily countdown calendar had fallen on the floor, its red number 75 staring up at the ceiling like a losing wrestler in a child's game of paper sumo wrestling.

'Sensei – here.'

Mayumi handed him a cup of coffee.

'Thank you.'

'Oh yes, I forgot to mention that your wife is a very beautiful woman.'

'My ex.'

'What a pity.'

Who knew what she was like when she was alone, but Mayumi no longer showed her gloomy face in public. However, Takeuchi was now straying into dangerous territory. He would burst into tears in the middle of a phone call with a contractor, he was forgetting or deliberately skipping appointments, not responding when spoken to, staring out of the window in a kind of daze . . . It may have been the uncertainty about his future, or the prospect of missing Mayumi, but of course it was mainly Okajima's death and the accompanying feeling of loss that were soaking deeper into his soul day by day.

Because of the age difference between the boss and the young newcomer, Okajima's death felt to Takeuchi like the loss of a father. In addition, he seemed to be feeling some degree of guilt about it, convinced as he was that it was a suicide. And this latter feeling was the same for both Ishimaki and Mayumi.

We're going to continue operating as before . . .

The atmosphere would change completely if he were to tell them now. Mayumi would be emotional, Ishimaki would pull himself together, Takeuchi's heart would lighten again, and the office would regain the strength and resilience it had had just a short month ago.

However, before then, there were things that needed to be done. It was no longer enough to continue to operate as a random architectural practice. In order to fulfil his promise to Yaeko, they had to continue as 'Okajima Design Company'. There was a burning knot of heat in his chest. It had not cooled down in the slightest since he had left Okajima's house.

He reached down and picked up the fallen countdown calendar. Calculating in his head, he began to tear off the pages until it showed 53. Then he placed it in the centre of the competition table.

'Sensei, what are you doing?' said Mayumi, rushing over.

'Continuing.'

'Continuing? Huh? With the competition?'

'Come over here, please,' said Aose to the other two, his unusually cheery tone immediately alerting them that something was up. He took a paper bag from his briefcase and spread its contents out on the competition table. There was Okajima's sketchbook, photos of Haruko Fujimiya's Paris apartment and various other material that Okajima had been given by the artist's nephew, Koji Yanagiya.

The two men dragged themselves over to the table, faces the picture of puzzlement.

Aose looked at each of them in turn.

'We're continuing in the competition,' he announced. 'We have a project to complete.'

'But that's . . .' said Takeuchi weakly. 'I mean, we've—'

Ishimaki chimed in.

'Aose-san, what's going on? Why are you bringing this up now?'

There was sorrow in his voice.

'Please stop. You're just making it harder.'

'Just take a look at this and see if you still feel the same way.'

Aose opened the sketchbook.

'Takeuchi, stand up straight and take a look! This is a

memorial design inspired by the hill of Montmartre. Look, you can see the dome of the Sacré-Cœur there on top. There's a window right here. That's from this photo. The walls and window of the Paris apartment where for forty years Haruko Fujimiya lived and painted will be kept alive at the foot of this hill, in the walls of this memorial museum. And look at this one. These tiled paintings that line this semi-underground walkway. They capture the neighbourhood and the period she lived in. Now, that's a memorial. These are the memories that should be preserved, these are the images that should be passed on.'

Mayumi looked at Aose.

'This is . . .?'

'It's Okajima's work. He drew it when he was in hospital.'

Ishimaki and Takeuchi now also looked at Aose. Then straight back at the sketchbook. Ishimaki reached out and turned a page. Takeuchi also reached out a hand, to trace the lines of the buildings. His expression became serious. There was no need for any explanation – the sketchbook was neither a suicide note nor a last will. It was the snapshot of the brain of an architect working at full power.

Eventually, Ishimaki let out a small moan. Takeuchi too. Mayumi pressed her fingers over her eyes.

'Ishimaki?'

'Y— yes?'

'Draw up the blueprints.'

'Eh?'

'We're going into battle with Okajima's plan.'

'Battle? No, of course, I understand. I want to do this too. I want to build it. But the competition is already—'

'Start drawing now. And don't forget that the saw-toothed roof is hidden behind the line of Montmartre.'

'It's impossible! These sketches aren't enough.'

'You can do it. I know you can. Use all your knowledge and

imagination to fill in the blanks. You know that, if you put your mind to it, neither Okajima nor I could hold a candle to you.'

Aose grabbed Ishimaki by the shoulders.

'Forget what happened after the collapse of the bubble economy. Defeat is neither crime nor shame. Believe in your own abilities and draw those lines.'

'Aose-san—'

'Look, I'll draw the exhibition hall. Columns and staircases, whatever – I'll leave it all up to you to decide. I'll match my design to whatever you come up with. If I come up with an idea first, we'll discuss it. And then, Takeuchi . . .'

'Yes?'

'Select the materials carefully. Keep the price per square metre under half a million.'

'Whaa—'

'There's no time to be shocked. Use all your low-cost-housing expertise.'

'But the original estimate was over 600,000 yen.'

'We can't beat them with that.'

'"Can't beat them"? Beat who?'

'Hatoyama of Nose Architects.'

Ishimaki's reaction was even more extreme than Takeuchi's.

'What are you talking about?'

'I'm talking about taking it to Nose Architects and holding a little preliminary-round competition with Hatoyama's proposal.'

'A pre-competition? And you think we'll win?'

'I do. The Okajima plan will outperform the Hatoyama plan. Both in substance and in cost. The rest will be up to that director of the construction department in S— city.'

'Oh, wow.'

'That's why we're in a huge hurry. If we bring it to them at the last minute, they'll send us packing.'

Aose grabbed the countdown calendar and ripped off even more pages. There it was: 21.

'We'll finish it in three weeks and take it to them. Got it?'

There were no more shouts of protest. Ishimaki was cracking his knuckles, and Takeuchi's eyes were shining.

'It's an avenging battle!'

'It's not vengeance. That said, Okajima will be devastated if we lose to old scraggly 'tache, after he disrespected us. And then—'

Aose clenched his fists tightly.

'Okajima's work will be there forever in that spot in S— city. Long after the mayor, the director of the construction department and all those politicians are dead, Akihiko Okajima's creation will live on.'

There was a moment of silence and then the war cries began: 'Yay!' 'Let's do it!' 'We'll show them!'

Mayumi's tears were those of joy.

'There's no time to cry, Tsumura-san. You're flying to Paris.'

'Eh? What?'

'You've still got your passport, right? I'll get the renderer, Nishikawa-san, to go with you. Do whatever you can to get on the earliest flight possible – get on the standby list at the airport if you need to.'

'B— but . . .'

'Ask your mother to watch Yuma. I'll call her too, and explain the situation.'

'No, that's not the problem. I want to know why me?'

'Because there are things you can't tell from photographs. I want you to go and take a good look at Haruko Fujimiya's apartment. And the neighbourhood. That painted tile walkway is one of the showpieces of our plan. I want to draw up these blueprints from real life.'

'But surely Nishikawa-san can—'

Aose pulled a face.

'I believe that Okajima wanted to see it with his own eyes. You go there instead of him. I want you to observe it, feel it, put your feelings into words and breathe life into the perspective drawings that Nishikawa-san's going to do for us.'

Mayumi turned her back and made her way slowly beyond the dividing partition. Then, suddenly, she rushed back.

'You don't mind if we book separate rooms, do you?'

Aose laughed.

'Watch out for that Nishikawa – they used to call him the Beast of Akasaka back in the day.'

There was a reaction from Takeuchi. An anxious look crossed his face and he stole a glance at Mayumi, who was enjoying the banter. Ishimaki looked up from the sketchbook and began to trace invisible lines in the air with his fingers. But when Aose suggested they order some takeaway food, he immediately reached for the menu.

'Oh yes . . . I forgot to mention one thing,' added Aose.

He genuinely had forgotten.

'Okajima Design Company will continue to operate as usual. When this competition is over, please go ahead and drum up new work.'

The place exploded.

Aose turned his back and took his seat. He closed his eyes and his ears and opened the doors of his mind to inspiration.

53

For the next three days and nights the lights stayed on at Okajima Design Company. Ishimaki lumbered around the office like a caged bear between the competition table with its sketchbook and materials, the computer desk with its CAD software open and the draughting board, as if the triangle between these three points marked the borders of his habitat. In the middle of the area was a table for eating, littered with empty bowls from ramen and soba restaurants. At the far end of the office Takeuchi sat calling tile manufacturers, patiently explaining how many of which type of tile they needed and doggedly requesting discounts on all of them. Mayumi and Nishikawa had left for Paris the previous evening and had probably just landed.

The right side of Aose's brain was occupied with the main exhibition hall. He'd originally come up with three plans but had just managed to narrow them down to one. His method had been to line up the three drawings on the table, close his eyes and make his choice. The important thing was that when he closed his eyes the image didn't disappear, instead remaining vivid and exciting in his mind's eye. He wanted his objective opinion to affirm his subjective one. It was the first step towards achieving universality.

He wasn't surprised by the one that remained freshest in his mind. The plan had been inspired by the upper level of the drawing room at the Hyuga Villa: rows and rows of easels filled with paintings, lined up across each step of a wide staircase. There's a third row, a fourth row, a fifth, then the last becomes one huge painting – the viewer is face to face with Haruko Fujimiya, the artist herself.

But he was just getting started. He was still resting on the giant shoulders of Bruno Taut. Time to take off. Expand without limit the world of images and fly towards it. Close his eyes and project on to the back of his eyelids the image of a glamorous Takarazuka revue performer descending a grand staircase that spans the whole width of a stage. Then zoom in close on to the ranks of the stern-faced terracotta army of China, the image of overlapping faces one after another, each peering out from behind the last. Then swoop upwards for a bird's-eye view over the desert and its ever-shifting patterns traced by the wind into the sand. The camera descends into the arena of Rome's Colosseum to observe the crowd stamping on the floor and pumping fists, hungry for blood. It's the viewpoint of the armour-clad gladiators, looking upwards and outwards over the tiers that expand around them in every direction, and then—

Aose pulled out pencil and paper, hurriedly sketching the image that had popped into his head. He gave the staircase to the upper level a curved shape, almost circular, like the Colosseum. He cut four openings at equal intervals to make connecting passageways and made the central space wider. Now the rows of paintings formed a pyramid shape. Interesting . . . and with those four cut-out spaces, the flow of visitors could be controlled even when the hall was crowded. He remained in this semi-dreamlike state throughout the working day, muttering to himself and giving only the briefest of mumbled responses as his colleagues chatted away about the project.

'Wow, Aose-san, the main hall is going to be circular?' Takeuchi asked him.

I'm still considering it.

'But that's going to make the shape of the saw-tooth roof a problem,' Ishimaki pointed out.

No, it isn't.

'It's impossible with those three saw ridges. The light won't reach the whole of the interior.'

It will if there are four or five ridges.

'Ishimaki-san, could you quickly calculate the length of the tiled walkway?' called Takeuchi from by the phone.

'Just a minute. I'm in the middle of something.'

'Negotiations are stalled because we can't decide on the number of tiles we need.'

'Look, we can't answer that yet because the design of the building is still in flux . . . Hey, Aose-san, if you make a five-ridge roof, the construction will get complicated, and reinforcement and leak-proofing are going to get expensive.'

'What? No! Please don't do that to me!' moaned Takeuchi.

This region doesn't get heavy snowfalls. Don't be nervous.

'No, I'm saying that a saw-tooth roof design and a circular hall aren't compatible in the first place,' Ishimaki persisted. 'Daylight will only enter from one direction – north – so it's impossible to have the whole circle covered.'

It can be reflected. With a giant structure like a ship's sail painted with reflective paint.

'No! We don't have the budget for all the extra work involved,' Takeuchi cut in. 'Maybe it doesn't all have to be natural light. We can supplement it with artificial lighting.'

'Just make the hall rectangular and everything's solved,' said Ishimaki, adding, 'Please reconsider.'

Go with a circular shape. Easels radiate out from the centre and spread throughout the hall. It would be a spectacular sight, viewed from above. Oh, that's interesting too . . .

Aose's hand moves. In the central space he draws a cylindrical, clear glass elevator.

'Wh— what are you doing, Aose-san? You're completely ignoring the structural calculations.'

Ishimaki sounded worried. Takeuchi felt the same way.

'Aagh! Have you any idea how much a fancy elevator like that would cost?'

'Hello? We're from Rairaiken. We've come to pick up your empty bowls.'

'Thank you. Could we put in an order for the evening now, too?'

'Of course.'

'Right, I'll have the ankake fried rice. Extra large.'

'On it. I'll have the regular size. What about you, Aose-san?'

The crab one.

'Oh, oh, I'll have that too.'

'So that's two Tenshin rice?'

'Make it three. Tenshin rice for me too, large.'

It's true. It doesn't make sense. Going up in an elevator doesn't help your appreciation of the art.

Aose scrubbed at the sketch with an eraser, causing the sheet of tracing paper to flutter off the edge of his desk and stick to the floor. The marbled pattern of the flooring was faintly visible through the paper. He recalled Okajima's quirky idea of setting the paintings horizontally into the floor.

What on earth was he thinking? A large number of Haruko Fujimiya's paintings feature a figure sitting on the ground. Her perspective was always to let the viewer experience the gaze of the artist, her own viewpoint. No, that wasn't it. That may have been part of it, but that hadn't been Okajima's real purpose.

'So what was it?' he said out loud.

'Yes? What?' said Takeuchi, but getting no reply from Aose, he came over to look at what he was drawing.

'Oh, the elevator's gone. Hey, Ishimaki-san, look.'

'Phew! You saved my life. I felt a close call with death.'

'Hmm, perhaps . . .'

'What is it?'

Takeuchi was still responding to Aose's every word.

Silence.

'He's back, Aose-san's Golgo 13 personality,' Ishimaki remarked. 'Even though he's been unusually chatty lately.'

'But in the early days, Golgo talked quite a bit,' Takeuchi pointed out.

'Really?'

'I can lend you a copy. I have the whole set of manga at home.'

All right, all right, Okajima, I've got it now. I should interpret it not as 'on the floor' but 'all the way down to the floor'. You wanted to use the floor in order to increase the number of paintings exhibited. Right? Haruko Fujimiya's works had been lying dormant for decades, unseen by anyone. Even once the memorial is completed, the majority of her eight hundred paintings would continue to languish in the storerooms. You tried to minimize that number. Was that it? You were looking for ways to increase the number of paintings in the permanent collection. Right, then I'll let it stay. Why don't we add a little elevation? Then the paintings will be easier to see. No, maybe not. If there are steps, the visitors might trip on them. No, a ramp instead. That's it. We could build a ramp that starts from outside the hall and winds its way up to the second floor. With handrails on the left and right and the paintings placed right through the middle. Place them just below floor level and cover them with transparent acrylic panels. How's that? All the paintings would automatically be given an angle of elevation. We could do the same on the entrance ramp. That would incorporate quite a few of the paintings into the permanent exhibit. And additionally, it would scale down the storage requirements.

'Yes? Aose-san?'

Reduce the number of storage containers. We only need half that number — enough for about a hundred paintings.

'Ah, yes . . . Ishimaki-san! Did you hear that?'

'I heard, but that's against the rules. If we change the specifications arbitrarily, then we'll be disqualified.'

'Oh, is that right? Ah, but . . .'

'What?'

'I can use that.'

'Use it? What does that mean?'

Takeuchi looked excited.

'Storage for one hundred built to a high standard, but the second hundred of a lower standard that we'll call utility space.'

'You're using it to cut costs?'

'That's right.'

'You're so cheap!'

'You're calling me cheap? Then tell me how else to do it. How else to reduce the unit price to 500,000 yen per square metre?'

'Yes, all right. I get it. No need to yell. My bad.'

I was forgetting – what are we going to do about the inside of the window? Yes, that's right – the inside. Is the window made of papier-mâché? That's not very exciting, is it? You want something beyond it, don't you? Yep, we definitely need something inside. Let's build something on the other side of that window, inside the memorial building. Let's recreate the interior of her apartment. We could even turn it into a separate gallery. Those piles of paintings can be replicas, but the top one on each pile should be an original for the visitors to admire. We'll do other rooms besides the one from the photograph, if space permits. Don't worry, Tsumura-san will take a good look at the apartment. For the preliminary design I'll do a rough sketch for now, and then after hearing what she has to say I can work up a more detailed design. How does that sound?

'Hey, Takeuchi, do you have a minute?'

'What's this? Oh, the south-side elevation diagram?'

'Just for this one, I'm including a drawing of the front facade.'

'Right. The contest's going to be won or lost right here.'

'What do you think?'

'Looks a little narrower than the boss's design.'

'Yeah. When it's actually built you can't stretch it to that width and still have elegant lines.'

'Hmm. I think it's still graceful enough. The line of the hill of Montmartre is still clearly defined. Are you not feeling it?'

'I'm worried that the whole building might just look like the Sacré-Cœur? As if the hill part has been completely taken over by the dome of the chapel.'

'Well, now that you mention it . . . It does a bit . . . it's that dome – once you've seen it in a photo or something, the image is just seared into your memory.'

'It's true. This design on the top looks too much like the tower or an ornament on top of the dome, so that the whole hill now just looks like the Sacré-Cœur itself. And now I've drawn it narrower, all the more.'

There'll be canvases that haven't even been framed – tons of them.

'Huh?'

'Never mind him,' said Ishimaki. 'He wasn't talking to you anyway. So, you're saying this dome part is too big? How about if we make it this size?'

'Hm. Now you're losing it completely.'

'Yeah . . .'

Now that's not good at all. I'll get in trouble with the curator if I do that to a painting . . .

'Why don't you try shifting it off centre? Like, to the right a bit?'

'Of course . . . About here . . . Like this?'

'Whoa.'

'Whoa.'

'That's good. The hill and the dome, they exist separately. The perspective is perfect.'

'Yeah, this really works. Thanks, Takeuchi!'

On the fifth day, Aose headed for the draughting board. He began with the ground layout. He found as he drew that the radiating lines were beautiful, like a kaleidoscope. It was a joy to work on. He believed utterly that the plan would work. On the sixth day, Ishimaki also began work on the draughting, using the CAD. The crucial part, the elevation diagram, was done in no time. In contrast, he struggled with the east face, which was where the entrance was located. His habit of stroking his beard evolved into one of pulling at it. Takeuchi was still almost constantly on the phone; whenever he hung up, he'd be punching numbers on his calculator as if taking revenge on it. His spreadsheet was getting more complicated by the day.

After ten days, they could no longer distinguish between day and night. It was like being back in the heyday of the bubble economy where offices were like the cities that never slept. They spent the night on the sofa or the floor. Aose had made it back home twice; Ishimaki and Takeuchi only once each, and then they hadn't even stayed the night, simply showering and packing as many changes of clothes as they could squeeze into their bags before rushing back to the office. The interior elevation plan was eating up their time. There were discrepancies between Ishimaki's diagrams and Aose's own, so they constantly had to throw them out and redraught. Aose kicked his chair across the room, Ishimaki knocked over his computer, Takeuchi smashed his calculator and howled like a coyote. But nobody hoped it would end. Aose was enmeshed in a comfortable cocoon, intoxicated by the kind of elation he hadn't felt since working on the plans for the Y Residence. Okajima was right next to him. The two of them worked together to draw lines then, together, they'd tear their drawings into little pieces. The two of them were searching for something so beautiful it would bring tears to their eyes.

'*Bonjour!*'

On the thirteenth day, Mayumi called them from Paris to tell them that the rendering of the tiled walkway was complete.

'In the end, we only needed the one hotel room. We stayed up all night together drawing.'

'Don't tell Takeuchi that. Send it asap.'

Aose waited in front of computer #1. Ishimaki, who had begun to resemble a lion, and Takeuchi, whose eyes had not yet fully opened that morning, leaned on the desk in anticipation.

The first perspective to arrive was the window of Haruko Fujimiya's apartment. They were stunned. Over the upper-right-hand corner of the window hung a semicircular plant pot overflowing with white flowers, possibly marguerite daisies. It couldn't have been Nishikawa's embellishment. It might have been just out of the frame of the photograph given to them by her relatives, or perhaps a neighbour had hung it there after the artist's death. The dark, forlorn window seemed to have taken on fresh life. It looked to Aose as if in death the gods had finally blessed Haruko Fujimaki, who had been driven to paint her whole life away.

'Let's go with that,' said Takeuchi, peering at it with his one open eye.

Okajima would have readily agreed. To the idea of offering flowers to her.

Aose was just thinking that this rendering alone was worth sending Mayumi and Nishikawa to Paris for when the second perspective drawing arrived. It was titled 'Painted Tile Walkway (left side)'.

As soon as he saw this vivid rendering Aose knew that with his team of three he could create something truly spectacular.

Giant leather shoes and high heels walking down the street. A colourful projection of a fashionable cityscape, reminiscent of the film *Amélie*, everything viewed from a low perspective. Distorted street signs and traffic lights, graffiti dancing along the walls. As you moved further along, the sun set and neon signs appeared, along with young people laughing together, an old couple snuggling together on a bench, dogs and cats, all suspended in time and the glow of a merry-go-round. Beyond, a lipstick with legs approaching the winking scarlet windmill of the Moulin Rouge.

Takeuchi had both eyes open now.

'Nishikawa has scary talent,' said Ishimaki.

Aose made a small discovery. In one of the carriages on the merry-go-round there was a woman with a paintbrush in her hand. It had probably been Mayumi's idea to include Haruko Fujimiya in the scene.

Amid all the excitement, 'Painted Tile Walkway (right side)' arrived. In terms of leaving them dumbstruck, this one was even better.

By contrast, this side of the walkway was almost colourless. An old run-down apartment building, cobblestones, gas lamps – it felt as if you had somehow lost your way and wandered off the vivid, bustling streets into a back alley. But it wasn't deserted – there were children running through the narrow alleyways. Seven or eight of them, mischievous grins on their faces, lined up about to play a game, or maybe start a three-legged race. Others ran this way and that, up one alley, down another, utterly care-free.

Grown-ups stuck their heads out of apartment or factory windows. Everyone was smiling. A woman with a laundry basket shouting encouragement. An old man with a cigarette stuck in the empty space where a tooth should have been enthusiastically clapping his hands. It looked like today was some kind of neighbourhood sports day . . . And then twilight falls on these paintings too. In the light of a window, a family sits around a table. A father pats his child on the head for having done so well. Another child is dozing off over dinner, perhaps exhausted from too much running.

Takeuchi was looking solemn. Ishimaki had the same smile on his face as the children in the drawing. Aose was still looking at the picture. There was one single window without a group of people behind it. Silhouetted against the light behind him, a young man was looking out, alone. He was holding up one hand in a greeting. There was no need to compare it to the left-side painting. Aose already knew that directly opposite would be the image of Haruko Fujimiya riding a merry-go-round. It was a scene frequently seen at fairs and amusement parks – the young man was waving to her as she passed by.

That was it. When Yanagiya had come to the office to talk about his aunt, Mayumi had been in the room. A cousin who died in the war . . . young love. The idea of yearning for a past love would have been painful for Mayumi. Perhaps she'd been given the courage by Haruko Fujimiya's history. Was it fair to see it that way?

The phone rang. Aose made sure he got there before Takeuchi.

'Hey, Ao-chan! What did you think?'

It was Nishikawa, calling from Paris.

'No words.'

'No good?'

'No, the opposite. The three of us were blown away by the sheer brilliance of everything.'

'Right? You know, I think this is my masterpiece. Because . . .'

His voice trailed off. Aose assumed it was because it was an international call, but that wasn't it.

'Ao-chan, I'm sorry. So sorry about the funeral. Your boss did so much for me and I . . . Well, I meant to go. I really did mean to . . .'

'Don't beat yourself up about it. I know it's because it hit you so hard. I'm sure Okajima is thrilled with your work too.'

'Thank you. I was so ungrateful, and now you've let me come to Paris. Mayumi-chan was so good to me too. She really helped with the work too. Thank you so much, really.'

'You're very welcome. Could I speak to Mayumi?'

'Oh, I'm sorry. She fell asleep.'

'What? But just now—'

'As soon as she hung up she just conked out. She must have been exhausted. Walking around the city day after day, night after night, with me. Should I wake her?'

'No, that's okay. Let her sleep.'

'Got it. I'd better put a blanket over her or she'll catch cold.'

'Don't do anything naughty.'

'What are you talking about? I'm as gentle as a lamb. In fact, they call me Mr Sheep.'

'Well, if you're going to put it that way, I'd say more Monsieur

Loup. Anyway, please pass a message on to Tsumura. Tell her, *bon travail*.'

'Hey, Ao, I didn't know you were fluent in French too.'

'Ha ha. Anyway, Nishikawa-san, please try to get some rest. And thank you for those incredible renderings. We'll do our best this end too.'

He hung up and looked over at Takeuchi and, as he'd expected, his back was turned. He was tapping away with intense concentration at a calculator he'd borrowed from Mayumi's desk.

It was late evening, six days later, that Aose finished the drawings for the main exhibition hall and the two smaller galleries. He was completely satisfied with the result. His sense of accomplishment was considerable, but it also came with a tinge of sadness. As the project neared completion, a thought was building in his mind — one that he really didn't want to contemplate. It was finally time to say goodbye. He was going to have to let go of Okajima.

Even though the basic plans were complete, it was too early to celebrate. Ishimaki was still putting on the finishing touches with the CAD. And the same went for Takeuchi. One hand on his calculator, he was grappling with a whole bundle of calculations. Mayumi had flown back to Japan two days earlier but was at home recovering with a high fever. Placed on top of a growing pile of materials on the competition table, the countdown calendar now read 3.

Aose looked at his finished drawings, nodded once, peeled off the tape, and removed them from the draughting board. After rolling them up, he placed them into a carrying tube.

The burning knot of heat in his chest melted away, utterly and completely. And his body, having lost its heat source, was suddenly drained of energy. When he announced that he was going home to bed, Ishimaki and Takeuchi both stopped working and got to their feet.

'Fantastic work. Leave the rest to us,' said Ishimaki.

He looked like Chewbacca, it was so long since he'd taken the time to shave. But he had become even more reliable than before. This would be the man to pass the helm over to Okajima's son, Isso, when the time came.

'I hope you can get some rest,' said Takeuchi. 'Thank you so much for getting us into that pre-competition.'

Tonight, again, only one eye was open. Mayumi was bound to tease him about how much weight he'd put on too. All he or anyone else had been eating were takeaways.

'Just get it done.'

Aose hurried out of the office, turning his face away to hide the tears. His knees were stiff, and he had trouble going down the stairs. He was a little nervous as he drove home – it had been six days since he had been back to his apartment.

His letter box was full and there were several advertising flyers sticking out of the slot. He opened his briefcase and stuffed everything into it. Then he took the elevator up to his apartment and opened a can of beer. He grabbed two glasses as a toast to Okajima, but he fell asleep before he'd finished even half a glass.

That's how another half a day went by before he read it.

In the bottom of his briefcase, mixed up with all the flyers and circulars, was a white envelope. The senders' names were written on the back: Touta Yoshino and Karie Kitagawa.

54

The sky was overcast as Aose travelled north on the Kan-Etsu expressway and joined the Kita Kanto expressway at the Taka-saki junction. He exited at the Isezaki interchange and headed for Kiryu city.

At Aose's suggestion, they had agreed on the Kiryu River dam as their rendezvous point. It was the place where his father had died. And it was also the place where Touta Yoshino had been born and raised.

> . . . I'm sure you must have found our behaviour very
> suspicious, abandoning the Shinano-Oiwake house that you
> took the trouble to build for us, and disappearing as we did.
> But more than anything else, we are deeply sorry that we
> asked you to build us a house without disclosing the truth of
> the situation . . .

It was a long letter. On the day of Okajima's funeral, Yukari had left a message on Yoshino's voicemail. After listening to it, Yoshino had decided that he could no longer hide the truth from Aose, and he'd written immediately. A confession and an apology. That was the content of the letter.

First of all, there was no Mr and Mrs Yoshino. Touta Yoshino was Isaku Yoshino's son, and Karie was his daughter. The pair, who Aose had once thought had grown to resemble one another after many years of marriage, were in fact brother and sister. The three children were all Karie's, from her marriage to a man called Kitagawa. Yoshino also had a wife and two children, but he was, at the time he had visited Aose's office, going through divorce proceedings, and she had returned to her parents' home in Nagano city.

It was a letter brimming over with surprise after surprise.

After his mother's death Isaku Yoshino, at the age of sixteen, had travelled all the way from Sendai to live with his older sister, who was working at a textile factory in Kiryu. The factory owner had taken pity on the boy and allowed him to live in the tiny three-tatami-mat room with his sister. An aspiring wood-worker, Isaku had taught himself a cabinetmaker's skills while working as an odd-jobs boy in the textile factory. By the age of twenty he had got himself a job in a factory that manufactured furniture. In his mid-thirties he had started his own business, and had married late in life, after turning forty. Eventually he would become father to one son and two daughters. He had set up his workshop in the northern part of Kiryu city, in an area called Umeda. It was a mountainous region and would later be the location of the Kiryu River dam.

> We were poor. From a very young age, Karie and I had to
> collect firewood and fetch water from the river. Our father was
> a true craftsman who never compromised in his work. He
> always put a huge amount of time and effort into each piece,
> but because he didn't have a famous name, none of the chairs
> and tables he made sold for a high price.

The Citroën crossed a bridge over the Watarase River. Beyond lay the urban area of Kiryu.

> When our mother died of pancreatic cancer, my father began
> drinking more heavily. I think he regretted that he couldn't
> afford better care for her. When I was in junior high school, I

386

rebelled against my father, who believed that it was only
natural that I should take over his cabinetmaking business
after him. But I wanted to go on to high school. I'm a little
ashamed to write this now, but I wanted to be a doctor. My
littlest sister was rather sickly, and would get pneumonia every
time she caught a cold. I was always terrified that she'd die
suddenly, like my mother had. It was the same that day. My
sister was lying on the floor one evening with a high fever
when my father came in from the garden carrying a black bird.
It was a mynah bird, which seemed to be very used to people
and liked to talk a lot. My sister was delighted. And of course,
Karie and I were too. The next morning, unbelievably, our
sister's fever was gone. Our father promised to make her a
birdcage for our new pet. My sister was so excited that she
started dancing around the house, and the whole place was
filled with laughter. It was the first time since our mother had
died that anything like this had happened. But—

Three nights later, Aose's father had turned up. Saying to himself, 'Minoru will be heartbroken,' he'd walked around and
around, searching for Kuro.

As soon as the man in the work overalls spotted the mynah
bird through the window, he yelled out, 'There he is! I've
found him!' and he came into the house. He was really
overjoyed. He took out a 5,000 yen note from his wallet,
which I remember was stuffed full of money, and offered it to
our father, saying, 'Thank you so much for finding him. Let
me give you a small token of my gratitude.' It was an
incredible sum of money to us at the time, but my father
wouldn't accept it. All he said was 'Just go ahead and take the
bird!' As I said before, he used to drink a lot and, whenever he
did, he used to get less and less communicative. But as soon as
the man left the house with the mynah bird under his jacket,

387

*our little sister began to wail as if someone had set her on fire.
It was closer to screaming. Coo-chan, Coo-chan! She had
already given the bird a name. Even Karie started to cry. My
father mustn't have been able to stand it because he got
unsteadily to his feet and told my little sister to stop crying.
That made me really sad. My father wasn't able to do
anything about it and he looked so pathetic to me that he was
almost invisible, and my sister wouldn't stop crying. So my
father looked around the house, took a deep breath and, saying
he would get the man to exchange the bird for a chair, he went
out of the house. I think he came up with the idea of
exchanging it for a chair because the man had admired the
chair in the entranceway to the house. That chair was my
father's pride and joy and, whenever he had some spare time,
he used to polish it. He told us that when he lived in Sendai,
he'd got the blueprints from Bruno Taut and he had built the
chair based on those. Ordinarily, it was not something he
would exchange for money, but at the time there was nothing
else in the house that would be worth 5,000 yen.*

Aose set off when the traffic light changed to green. He was
already in downtown Kiryu city. From the corner of his eye, he
caught sight of a saw-roofed building, and it gave him a start.
Even here, the gentle north light was illuminating craftsmen's
hands, silently supporting Kiryu's delicate textiles. Okajima's
drawing of the saw-tooth roof popped into his mind. He couldn't
help feeling that everything was mysteriously connected.

*My father returned an hour or so later without the mynah
bird. He was breathing heavily, and right away turned his
back on us and started drinking again. I asked him, 'Where's
the bird?' Normally, I wouldn't have said anything, because I
had a bad habit of giving up on things too easily. But that time
I did ask because when my father said he was going to*

388

exchange the chair for the bird, I'd been amazed, but more than that, really happy. I was happy that my father was willing to give up that chair for my sister's sake, the chair that he treasured like a precious jewel. But when that didn't happen I was really, really disappointed, and frustrated. 'Where's the bird?' I asked again, but my father didn't answer. I yelled it over and over again: 'The bird! The bird!' I even shook him, I was crying and shaking him, but my father never spoke a word. He just kept his eyes tightly shut and left us kids to our own devices. My youngest sister carried on wailing, Karie held her tight and stroked her head. Back then we didn't get a newspaper delivered to the house and our TV barely worked, so Karie and I were adults before we knew that a man had died that night.

The car left the city centre, and from there it was a straight road to the Kiryu River dam. There were very few houses along the road. There was a mountain up ahead covered in lush, bright greenery, and the road began to climb a gentle slope.

Our little sister died without ever making it past primary school. The episode of the mynah bird became no more than a sad story, and neither Karie nor I ever spoke of it again, as if we had erased it from our minds. It was three years ago that I discovered the truth. Our father suffered a stroke and was bedridden in hospital. His health was deteriorating fast, so he called Karie and me to his bedside, telling us he had something important he needed to say.

Isaku Yoshino had caught up with Aose's father on the mountain road and asked him to trade the mynah bird for the chair. Aose's father had refused, saying that the bird was his son's prized possession. When Isaku begged him to reconsider, he'd opened his wallet again and pulled out a 10,000 yen note this time, telling Isaku to use it to buy another mynah bird. Maybe it was the alcohol, but this had infuriated Isaku. He told Aose's father that he didn't want his money. Inside his head, he was thinking, 'Bloody dam worker! I'm a skilled craftsman. I'm not going to stoop so low as to accept money from a dam worker.' Then he raised his voice and said, 'If you have so much money, why don't you just go and buy your son a new bird?' Aose's father looked puzzled, and said if money was the issue, why didn't he just buy the chair from Isaku for 10,000 yen? But that just added fuel to the fire. 'That chair is too good for the likes of you to sit in,' Isaku had retorted. The proud concrete-form setter was enraged, and the two men got into a shouting match. And then they started to grapple with each other. Going simply by physique, one would have thought that Isaku would have been the one to go over the edge of the cliff, but as they struggled Kuro flew out from under Aose's father's jacket and he had on reflex reached up to catch the bird as it flew over his head. And that was the last thing that Isaku Yoshino saw before Aose's father disappeared from sight.

This is what my father said: 'I didn't deliberately push him over, but my hand was gripping his collar and I was shoving him.'

Isaku immediately ran home. He was afraid that he would be thought of as a criminal. Nightmares of his own father stealing rice and the family being split up came back to him. If he was put in prison, what would become of his children?

'And so I ran away,' our father told us through his tears. 'And I didn't help that man or call for help from anyone else. What on earth had I done? That man had a son too. If I had called for help, that man might not have died.'

Then Isaku Yoshino had taken Touta and Karie's hands and

begged them to find that man's son and make amends. He said he knew the son's name because the mynah bird had repeated it over and over.

'*Hey, Minoru Aose-kun!*'

Yoshino and Karie had been at a loss. How difficult was it going to be to find a man who had worked temporarily at a dam construction site a quarter of a century ago, let alone his son? Even if they did find him, they had no idea how to make amends. But above all, they didn't know how they would find the courage. Even though it had been a long time ago, every time they imagined telling someone, 'Our father was responsible for the death of your father,' they lost their nerve. The Kitagawa family, which Karie had married into, kept her great-aunt's psychiatric problems under wraps out of fear of public opinion. Having first-hand experience of this tendency to sweep things under the tatami, Karie also had fears that her husband and parents-in-law would find out about Isaku's confession. Touta Yoshino's own relationship with his wife was fast deteriorating, and he could never be completely at ease. Just like anyone else, the present was more important to them than the past.

But every time they went to visit him, Isaku would beg them to please, please, find Minoru Aose. It got so painful to listen to that they began to lie to him. 'Yes, we're actively searching for him. We've hired a detective. I'm sure he'll find him soon.' And while this went on, Isaku got steadily weaker and weaker. After being moved to a care home, his mind began to deteriorate too, and then, after six months, he became unable to speak. The brother and sister told themselves that this was okay. That they would be able to send their father off in peace.

Isaku lived for a little over a year after that. When Touta and Karie heard that his condition was critical they rushed to the care home, where he was lingering on the edge of life. The siblings sat by his side, and then—

*In his last moment he drew in one rough breath and then
exhaled with the words, 'I'm sorry.' I was so surprised. I
thought it was possible I had just imagined it, but Karie heard
it too. The doctor said that it was what was known as
automatic speech — a kind of involuntary utterance. That
sometimes patients who have lost their ability to speak, due to
a stroke for example, sometimes utter simple words right before
death. The doctor said that the words tend to be something
that they often used to say when they were still healthy, or
something that had been on their mind for a long time. When
we heard this, it was no longer enough just to grieve my
father. Lying in that bed for over a year, right up until the
very moment that he left this world, he had 'I'm sorry' in his
heart. That was how much my father had been agonizing and
repenting. Karie cried as hard as she had when our little sister
died. And we hadn't done anything to ease that pain. We
should have done it properly, as he had asked us to. That
night, we made up our minds to search for you — for this
Minoru Aose-kun. That was on 30 January last year.*

The letter detailed how Yoshino had hired a private detective
and had made contact several times with Yukari. The siblings
decided that, instead of explaining that they were atoning for
their father's crime, they would call it repayment of a debt, and
would do their best to proceed without Aose being aware of what
was happening. That was the only thing they could do.

*We were wrong. We should have told you the story our father
told us, apologize for what he did, and make that the starting
point. But even though we'd made the decision to act, I was
afraid. I had no idea what kind of a person this Minoru Aose
would turn out to be, and what kind of reaction he would have
to hearing the truth. I was a coward. In the end I came up
with what was a truly irresponsible plan that would neither*

392

affect our lives nor damage our father's good name, while at the same time having some positive benefits on your life, Aose-san. We had to pile on lie after lie to attempt to come up with a plausible story that would successfully deceive you.

What Yoshino seemed to regret the most was having convinced Aose to believe in his fictitious family. He apologized for that aspect repeatedly. He said he had done it only to be sure that Aose didn't see through the ruse. They had told Karie's two daughters that they were in a kind of play that had been written to help people, and made them believe they were performing some of the scenes. But they hadn't said anything to her youngest, the boy, telling him only never to leave his mother's side during the ground-breaking ceremony or the handover of the house.

I was completely self-absorbed at the time, and did something unforgivable. Not only towards you, Aose-san, but also towards Karie's children.

It was only Aose who had ever witnessed the mysterious disappearance of this 'family'. In fact, Karie and her three children were at home, living a normal life as the Kitagawas. Yoshino was the only one who had vanished. The reason was unrelated to the pseudo-Yoshino family, but was in fact real troubles related to his own family.

I couldn't return any of your calls. When you asked me why we hadn't moved into the Y Residence and where all five members of my family had disappeared to, I couldn't reply. If I were to explain, then I'd have had to tell you all about my fake family and my real one. When I called the Y Residence to check on things, I felt that my heart had been crushed when you picked up and told me how worried you were about us.

But I couldn't speak. I was becoming more and more sorry,
but it was becoming increasingly likely that we would never
meet again.

Yoshino also felt bad for Aose's two older sisters. He'd found out about them through the detective agency's investigations, but he couldn't offer them anything, only feeling able to contemplate fulfilling his father's dying wish of making amends to 'Minoru Aose-kun'.

The car was travelling through green countryside. In front and to the left and right were low hills covered in natural woodland. Mindful of the Citroën's overly soft suspension, Aose rounded a gentle curve in the road, and the dam came into view. He was almost there. Time to meet Yoshino again.

Aose examined his feelings . . .

His father had not been pushed off a cliff. It had been an accident. His father had died in an accident. In his final moments, he had tried to catch Kuro. For Aose's sake, he had done all he could not to let Kuro escape. Aose was glad to know this. Glad to hear about the last moments of the father who he'd loved so much.

He parked in the dam management office's car park, but as he'd arrived early, he got out of his car and decided to take a walk along the road that ran along the very top of the dam.

The wind was strong. To his left was the reservoir, and he could see another bridge in the distance. In between, on the surface of the water was a long string of orange-coloured floats crossing from one bank of the reservoir to the opposite side. It was what was known as a log boom, set up to prevent any dead trees that fell into the water from getting caught up in the water discharge facility. His father had taught him about all kinds of stuff.

Aose felt the pull of the dam. If he didn't keep resisting, his heart would always be drawn to dams.

Minoru Aose-kun.

Aose had the sense that he was being called. He turned around to see Touta Yoshino standing very stiff and upright. Beside him, Karie Kitagawa. Her head was bent so deep in a bow that he could see the back of her collar.

55

Karie looked pale, as if she had reached her physical limit before even meeting Aose. As soon as she saw his face, she collapsed to her knees and began to weep. Each time she tried to stop to apologize her throat filled up and she was shaken by violent sobs. Aose and Yoshino got her to her feet together and supported her over to Yoshino's car. Yoshino reclined the passenger seat and they lay her down to rest. Aose leaned over and spoke to her.

'Don't worry, I'm not the least bit angry. In fact, I'm grateful to you.'

Yoshino heard it too; he meant for Yoshino to hear. However, the tension in Yoshino's body didn't relax in the least bit. He stood back up, straight, and addressed Aose.

'Aose-san, I am truly sorry for everything that has happened. My sister and I were shallow, cowardly and dishonest. We caused you a great deal of trouble. I know it's too late to apologize for trampling all over your feelings, but please allow me to try. I am truly sorry, from the bottom of my heart. That is the truth.'

He bowed deeply.

Aose let out a silent breath and waited a beat.

'Please — there's no need to keep bowing to me. I accept your apology and I don't need any more from you. Let's leave it at that.'

'Yes . . . yes.'

Aose looked at Karie in the car. She was still sobbing, but she seemed to have calmed down a little. He turned back to Yoshino.

'Do you want to take a walk?'

Yoshino and Aose walked side by side along the footpath on the crest of the dam. The wind was growing stronger. Whether by wind or by rain, nature always had a way of giving people a push to express their feelings in words.

'What did you plan to do with the Y Residence after it was built?'

It was the first thing Aose wanted to know. He was curious to know if compensation was the only reason for building it.

Yoshino seemed to catch on right away.

'I didn't ask you to make that house only as a means of making amends for my father. I had my own reasons too. Perhaps it was a bit of a dream, perhaps I was taking a bit of a gamble, but I was hoping to make a fresh start with my family.'

'To start over?'

'Yes, exactly. At the time I hired you, my wife and I were in the middle of divorce proceedings. It was my wife who asked for the divorce, and I was pretty shaken up. I'd been so busy at work that I'd forgotten things like picking up the kids from nursery school, birthdays and anniversaries, and all the little things had just built up for her until it was a mountain she couldn't see the top of. Then, around that time, I closed our fixed-term savings account . . . well, there was a reason for that, but nevertheless, my wife was furious. She took the kids to Nagano to her parents' place. I went to meet them there many times, but I don't get on at all with my wife's brother, who lives with them. Well, anyway, my brother-in-law wouldn't let me see my wife and insisted that I needed to sign divorce papers . . . Sorry for telling you such a sad story.'

'No, please go on.'

'Yes . . . well, in hindsight, I really didn't need to work like crazy . . . You know, after the economic bubble burst, it was a complete gamble whether I'd succeed or fail.'

Aose looked at Yoshino's profile. *After the economic bubble burst . . .*

'Suddenly nothing would sell any more. Shops selling imported goods were the first to come crashing down. So I bought. I closed our fixed-term savings account, borrowed more money on top of that, and bought up all kinds of cheap goods. I bought furniture and tableware, sports equipment, anything cheap and imported. I planned to start my own business. Of course, I kept it secret from the company I worked for because I was essentially doing two jobs . . . but . . . well, I also completely forgot about my family . . .'

Yoshino stopped and stared into the distance.

'The land in Shinano-Oiwake was purchased a long time ago. My wife wanted it too, so we bought it jointly. Now they live in Nagano city, but until around the time my wife graduated from junior high school, her parents used to be caretakers of a recreation facility belonging to some big corporation near that piece of land. My wife loved growing up in Shinano-Oiwake. So there was a time when we used to talk of building a house and raising our children there.'

Yoshino turned to Aose.

'That's why I commissioned the Y Residence. I was always planning to build a house on that land, and then go to see my wife. I was going to ask her if she would start over again with me in that house, give me one more chance. But yes, I was making amends to you by trying to realize my own unfulfilled dreams. I am really sorry about that.'

'We've made a deal – no more apologies.'

'Oh, I'm sor— Ah.'

Aose chuckled. Caught out, Yoshino's expression softened.

'But anyway, my plan didn't work out. By the time my brother-in-law was finally away from home so I could meet my wife, it was December. Unfortunately, what I told her about the Y Residence wasn't enough to convince her. She just couldn't forgive me for withdrawing the money from our joint savings account without asking her first. I'd always been the one in charge of the household money, and so it was ten years before she noticed that the savings had gone. From my wife's point of view, I'd been deceiving her for ten years. I did what I did for my family's future. I'd even managed to triple my regular income by selling off all the furniture and miscellaneous goods I'd bought. But to my wife, the result was not important. She accused me of gambling with the future of our family, told me that she'd always known that deep down I was that kind of person. It's true, I suppose, that I did catch the fever. I said it was for my family, but I wanted to test my business acumen. I wanted to do something big.'

It was a bittersweet story. The irony was that the result had been the same for winners and the losers alike after the burst of the bubble economy.

'Talking to my wife, I realized that the savings account thing had just been a trigger. She had fallen out of love with me, and I came to terms with the fact that it was the end of the road for us. She passed over the divorce papers for me to sign and I thought I had no choice but to do it. But right at the last minute I begged her to just go and take a look at the house in Shinano-Oiwake. At that moment, my brother-in-law returned and began to threaten me. He shoved me hard in the chest and, because he used to be on the sumo team at university . . . well, I was no match for him.'

When Yoshino fell in the entrance way, his brother-in-law had picked up a metal baseball bat that had been propped up next to the shoe cupboard. In a panic, Yoshino had pulled open the sliding door and rolled his body out without stopping to put his shoes on. When he had sensed that his brother-in-law was coming after him, he slammed the sliding door shut as hard as he could. There was a terrible scream. Three fingers had been caught in the door — a sturdy door made of stainless steel. Yoshino had fled in his socks.

Believing his brother-in-law was going to kill him, Yoshino had done a vanishing act. Moreover, the brother-in-law had reported the incident with the door to the police. Yoshino had talked to his wife about the Y Residence, so he wasn't able to hide there. In the end, he fled to Ome city, where he had a rented warehouse to store his furniture and other goods. He'd also taken his belongings there from his rented home in Tabata. He'd already moved out of that house in case Aose showed up looking for him. Up until the incident with his brother-in-law, he'd been living in the warehouse, and from there had been visiting his wife's parents' home when he had any free time from work. However, after the incident, he had resigned from his company job to focus on his online shopping business. His brother-in-law had gone to Tabata looking for him, no doubt carrying the unsigned divorce papers.

'About a month ago, I signed them. I didn't want to get mixed up with my brother-in-law again so I gave my personal seal to a lawyer to complete the formalities for me, and then turned myself in at the police station. They interviewed me for about half a day and I was told they would probably send the case to the prosecutor. The only thing that saved me was that my brother-in-law — well, he isn't my brother-in-law any more — he didn't seem to be very well regarded by the police.'

Eventually the divorce was settled and Yoshino had felt safe enough to start turning on his mobile phone. And this was where the saga of Aose and Yoshino's miscommunications had finally come to an end.

Aose rested his elbows on the parapet. Yoshino did the same. The wind rippled the surface of the lake.

'What are you going to do about the Y Residence?'

It was the continuation of his first question. He was anxious about both the Y Residence's past and its future.

Yoshino just looked perplexed, so Aose carried on.

'I think, in this situation, you're going to have to sell.'

'Yes . . . but . . .'

Yoshino looked into Aose's eyes.

'I know it's a little late, but I'd like to give it to you, Aose-san.'
Aose shook his head.

'Sell it to me. I'll get a loan.'

'You want to buy it?'

'Yes. I made my mind up before I came to meet you.'

'But my father . . . My father will be furious with me.'

Now Aose was finally able to say it. He'd been waiting for the right moment.

'Your father had a hard life. He suffered for a very long time.'

'Aose-san—'

There was a long pause, during which Yoshino blinked his eyes several times.

'It was around there.'

Yoshino wiped his eyes, then pointed to the far end of the log boom.

'There used to be a lumber shed over there that my father had built. He used it as a workshop too. They told him that it was going to have to be flooded when the dam was built, so he got compensation. We were so poor that he really should have used some of the money, but he didn't spend a single yen of it. It was left to Karie and me in full. I used that money to pay for the Y Residence. Karie officially relinquished her share and gave it to me, saying that our father had wanted to make amends so badly that he'd be happy if we spent it all. That's why I can't sell it to you. I can't take the money.'

'Have you forgotten?' said Aose, more conviction in his tone. 'I built a house I would want to live in. That is enough for me. Your father's wishes were carried out properly. Please tell Karie-san that.'

Yoshino stared at Aose for a few moments, then pulled himself upright and bowed his head.

'Let's get back,' Aose said. He was worried about Karie.

As they started walking, Yoshino came up shoulder to shoulder with Aose.

'That day, I was remembering when you handed us the keys to the house,' he said.

It was an abrupt start. What day was he talking about?

'Karie and I were very emotional because we'd kept our promise to our father. But it's also true that I was captivated by the Y Residence. And then, that day, I was reminded of all my feelings about the house.'

'By "that day", you mean . . .?'

'Yukari-san spent three hours there.'

Aose stopped walking. Yoshino continued talking without looking at him.

'I'm talking about the day I went with her to the Y Residence. She looked at it from the outside for a while and then she began to walk backwards away from the house until she was so far away that she was just a small, distant figure, and then she stood there, looking at it again a while. When she came inside the house she just kept looking up. That gentle light just seemed to frame her face, and she was – how can I put it? – just so beautiful. She rested her hand on that circular built-in table. She stood there like that for so long that I began to feel as if I was intruding, so I went outside. Then she was in there for another two hours after that. I don't know what Yukari-san was doing in there. I dozed off in the car, waiting for her, then she was there, tapping on the car window. She said, "Thank you very much. Let's go home." But then she turned around again and looked at the house for a while longer.'

Aose could see the scene vividly in his mind. It was as if he'd been there too.

It's a good thing we didn't build that house.

Aose and Yukari stood together, surrounded by those words. They had never managed to walk away. They were still standing there.

Aose began walking again.

'It didn't work out for me,' said Yoshino. 'But how about you, Aose-san?'

Yoshino sounded genuinely hopeful on Aose's behalf.

'What are you going to do about Taut's chair?' said Aose, changing the subject.

'Eh?'

'You put it there so you could report back to your father, didn't you?'

'Yes, that's right. I showed the Y Residence to my father. Said, "Look, I've kept my promise."'

'Do you want to take it to your Ome city warehouse? I'm worried about burglars at the Y Residence.'

'Yes. Let's move it. If I abandon it there, my father and Taut-san will never forgive me.'

'Oh, that reminds me!'

Aose clapped his hands.

'When I saw both your names written on the envelope of the letter you sent me, it suddenly hit me! You were named after Taut, and Ka-ri-e is E-ri-ca backwards.'

Yoshino grinned.

'Ah, you spotted it. I'm a little embarrassed about it.'

'Your father used to be teased as a kid by having his name read backwards, didn't he?'

'Yes, I-sa-ku – ku-sa-i – stinky! That's why he did it.'

'It seems that your father's encounter with Taut in Sendai really made an impression on him.'

'I suppose it's because Taut gave him the blueprints for that chair. Whenever he made a table or a chair that he was particularly pleased with, he used to announce that he was a true apprentice of Taut-san. He always seemed so happy that it made us all happy too. He would also talk about Erica-san, how she used to give him *kompeito* rock candy. He said she would put three on the palm of his hand and then make him squeeze his fingers tightly around them. He said the candy was so sweet . . .'

Yoshino's face glowed.

'My father was an excellent cabinetmaker. He didn't really

know Taut well, or even work under him – it was only a brief encounter, really – but afterwards he continued to make furniture for the rest of his life. I believe he wanted to get better and earn Taut's praise and recognition, so he dedicated himself to the craft.'

'Yes, I'm sure you're right about that.'

Seventy years earlier, a master architect had been forced to take a vacation from architecture, and it had worked this small miracle. Taut had become the demon of the Senshin-tei, railing at himself, needing to burn up his inner rage so it would not ruin this, his vacation. He must have needed to believe that people like Isaku Yoshino would carry on his work.

In the distance, Aose could see Karie. She had stepped out of the car and was bowing her head again. But it looked like she was feeling better now. The words that Aose had said softly in her ear seemed to have run through her veins like the contents of an IV drip.

'Yoshino-san, I know it's a little early to be saying this, and I'm sure you're going to laugh at me, but I really hope you and Karie-san will come and visit me at the Y Residence someday.'

Aose held out his hand, and Yoshino took it with both of his hands and squeezed it.

'Thank you so much. I hope that we can be friends now. I'm truly sorry to have caused you so much trouble.'

Aose nodded and looked up at the sky and the clouds speeding by.

He'd have to give Ikezono at J— newspaper a call. Tell him that it was thanks to him that he'd found Yoshino. But that, unfortunately, Yoshino had told Aose nothing about Taut's chair before vanishing again, like a bird in the wind.

56

Please be sunny all day! When was the last time he had seriously wished that?

Early that morning, Aose had been driving round and round Akasaka in the Citroën, trying to find a parking spot. Even after parking, he had taken a wrong turn and it had been a while before he found the office he was looking for.

'Hey, who do you think you are, getting me out of bed at the crack of dawn on my day off, and then turning up late?'

Takumi Nose seemed genuinely annoyed.

The office was so spacious that Aose couldn't help staring. Draughting boards take up a lot of space, so it could be said that the size of an office is an indication of its success. However, these days a lot was done on computers, so at a glance it was difficult to tell the purpose of all the space.

'And all that stuff you said on the phone – just a big joke, was it?'

'Save all your complaints and sarcasm until you've seen it.'

'That's some confidence.'

'If I wasn't confident, I wouldn't be here.'

Aose took out the blueprints and the perspective drawings from the poster tube. First was the elevation diagram of the memorial. Next, the painted tile walkway—

'Let me see.'

'Wait while I lay them out.'

Three, four, five . . . Aose propped the blueprints up at the best angle against the computer monitors.

'Hey, be careful!'

Aose ignored Nose and continued to lay them out. Eight, nine and ten were the floor plans of the main exhibition hall.

The voice behind him stopped with its complaints. Nose must have known at a glance that Aose wasn't full of shit or drunk. After a moment, there was a presence by his side. Nose's shoulders leaned in further than Aose's . . . then his neck . . . then his whole head.

Nose slowly moved sideways, taking his time to examine each piece of paper. Immersed in them, no longer conscious of who had brought them here or where they had come from. Drawings and perspectives – Nose's mind was filled with nothing else.

He examined them for fifteen minutes. 'No!' That single reaction did not pass Aose by. Nose went and sat back down on the sofa and gestured to Aose to join him. His fingers were laced awkwardly together.

'What's the price per square metre?' he asked.

'499,000 yen.'

'What the—?'

'Check it.'

Aose stuck his hand into his briefcase and pulled out a hefty bundle of spreadsheets, as thick as *Top 200 Homes of the Heisei Era*.

Their eyes met. The light that shone into the office grew a little brighter.

The long silence was broken by Nose.

'I'm sorry, but you'll have to take them back with you.'

'Nose!'

'This whole thing is a ridiculous idea. How can I tell Hatoyama?'

'Then hire me.'

'What?'

'You already told me you want to hire me. Take me on as a temporary member of staff. Then Hatoyama and I will be on the same side.'

'Aose, you—'

'I haven't come here alone. Look at these again. Can you really let these drawings and perspectives lose by default?'

This time the silence went on even longer. Finally, Nose expelled a deep breath.

'It'll be your responsibility if Hatoyama decides to quit,' he said, his face perfectly straight.

Aose answered with an equally straight face.

'Let him go. People who quit their jobs for reasons that are nothing to do with architecture just aren't worth it. You've known guys like that in the past.'

Nose laughed scornfully.

'This'll be fun. I'm going to test Hatoyama's mettle. And what are your terms for giving us this plan?'

'No terms,' said Aose. 'It's free of charge. No credits, no mention of cooperation. We just have one favour to ask.'

'A favour? Now I'm worried. What is it?'

'If we win this preliminary round, if we pass the final competition and we get this memorial built on that field—'

'No need to get ahead yourself, but anyway . . . come out with it.'

'Allow me to tell Okajima's son that this was built by his father.'

Nose didn't respond. He sat for a while, thinking about this request, clearly dealing with some emotions. Perhaps he was recalling the image of Isso that day at the funeral.

He looked at Aose and gave a minuscule nod. Agreement . . .

Aose's phone vibrated in his pocket. Excusing himself, he went over to the window and pressed the button.

'Hey, Daddy, I only need to bring cloths, right?'

'Yeah. I've got the brooms and the mop.'

'I'm really looking forward to seeing the Y Residence!'

'You'll have plenty of time to sweep the floors.'

He'd been up there by himself the previous evening and had wiped the burglars' footprints off the flooring.

'Mummy says she can't go today. She's got a work meeting.'

For a moment, Aose was flustered. Had Hinako really invited Yukari?

'Hey, you know today is supposed to be—'

'She says she's got work so she can't go *today*.'

I see. Not today.

'See you later! Hurry and pick me up.'

Hinako hung up.

Hinako was in full matchmaking mode. Taking advantage of the situation to put her little scheme into practice.

Aose smiled and shook his head. Well, okay. That was just fine. He wanted nothing more than to be duped by Hinako's scheme.

He put his phone away and turned around. Nose was standing in front of the drawings again. Aose looked at the ageing profile of his former colleague and, in his mind, he nodded his thanks, then he turned and left the office without another word.

The Akasaka neighbourhood was still sleeping. Aose walked briskly back to the car park. He had one phone call to make before picking up Hinako. It was to his clients in Osaka, the young couple. He wanted to tell them that he would build a house just for them. Ask them to tell him more of their stories.

He heard a chirping sound and looked up at the clear blue sky.

A swallow flew overhead, carrying in its beak materials to build its nest.